LUMEN FATES SAGA

IGNITE

CHARIS CROWE

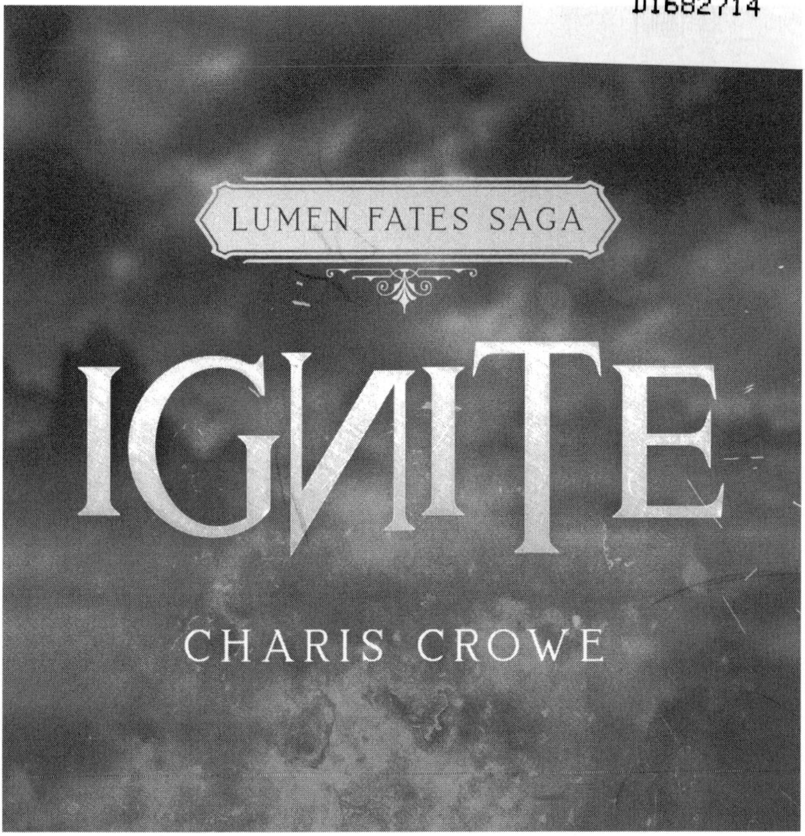

A Young Adult Urban Fantasy Novel

Published by

www.splickety.com

Ignite
The Lumen Fates Saga - Book One

Published by
Splickety Publishing Group, Inc.
www.splickety.com

Edited and formatted by Ben Wolf
www.benwolf.com

Cover design by Hannah Sternjakob
https://www.hannah-sternjakob-design.com

Print ISBN: 978-1-942462-30-9
Copyright © 2019 by Charis Crowe. All rights reserved.

Contact Charis Crowe directly for signed copies
and to schedule author appearances and speaking events.

All rights reserved. Non-commercial interests may reproduce portions of this book without the express written permission of the author, provided the text does not exceed 500 words. For longer quotations or commercial concerns, please contact the author.

Commercial interests: No part of this publication may be reproduced in any form, stored in a retrieval system, or transmitted in any form by any means—electronic, photocopy, recording, or otherwise—without prior written permission of the author, except as provided by the United States of America copyright law.

This is a work of fiction. Names, characters, and incidents are all products of the author's imagination and are used for fictional purposes. Any mentioned brand names, places, and trademarks remain the property of their respective owners, bear no association with the author or the publisher, and are used for fictional purposes only. Any similarities to individuals living or dead is purely coincidental.

Printed in the United States of America.

*For my 2nd grade teacher,
who snatched my first story out of the trash
and demanded to know who had been wasting paper.*

It was me.

Clearly, I have a problem.

EPISODE ONE

CHAPTER 1

Steven Parson had two things on his mind: getting out of the oppressive Kansas heat and abducting the last two names on his list.

He saw Jace before his sister arrived. Sixteen, tall, muscular, dark-haired, and sporting a farmer's tan, the teen looked like he played football or at least carried his own weight on the family farm.

Someone who knew his way around a farm would be useful.

Steven surveyed the park. He hoped to see Nora marching toward him, striding up the gravel road and cursing the humid weather. But there was still no sign of her.

Cottonwood Falls was a perfectly acceptable place for anyone that enjoyed living where there were no stoplights. The most exciting in-town attractions were a bank, a bridge, and a courthouse.

But Steven understood the appeal of living in a small community. That's what Lumen was, technically. And like any small community, they needed to induct new members in order to thrive. But Jace didn't know that yet.

Steven pulled out his phone, a relic of cellular technology. The screen was illuminated by blue backlight, but he didn't need anything complicated.

His fingers hesitated above the rubbery buttons, and he held off on sending a panicked message. She could be here any second, after all. Literally.

He tried to brush away his feelings of annoyance. It had been a long day. They were on pickup fifteen of sixteen.

Just two more left.

He held his distance and watched Jace.

Their eyes met. Jace broke their eye contact, his gaze lingering on Steven's old phone. The teen smiled before turning away, pacing in lazy circles around the decommissioned war tank near the park's memorial. He tapped rapidly on his own touchscreen.

Steven considered what the average Cottonwood Falls citizen could expect to get out of life. Some small towns were doomed to wither and die, the population moving away for better employment. Others seemed to trap their residents in a hereditary cycle of mediocre achievement with most people never leaving the community. Both lacked good leadership, a quality Steven prided himself on.

The last census he'd found listed the population of Cottonwood Falls at 869.

But today, quietly, and with no one to bear witness to it, the population would drop to 868.

With a tiny *pop*, Nora appeared at his side.

She met her brother's scathing look with a bored one of her own. "You know I can't resist Paris in the summer."

NAILEEN SHARP WAS DETERMINED TO TAME THE LEGENDARY dragon Valnax.

He was crucial to the team she had been building and was the rarest dragon in all of *Vortex Beyond*, attainable only after hours of grinding and difficult group quests. Getting him would send a message to every other player: *I'm serious, and I can wreck you.*

But as she relaxed on her best friend's bed, impatient and fiddling idly on her phone, she had to admit things had been weird in her online group. As each member faced off against the overpowered Valnax that day, they had gone silent. There wasn't a single message in the group chat from *8Ecraskrell*, *KeepingScoreMore*, or *EgoManiac1*.

Now only two of them remained—her and Len, their group leader.

Twenty-seven minutes prior, Len had sent her a message.

IGNITE

Lenneon0608: I'm moving forward with our plan. Will update once I'm out!

The fight had a thirty-minute timer.

Nail lay on Finley's bed, drenched in the warm Maine sunlight shining through the window. Posters of bands, quotes, graffiti decals, and Banksy knockoffs covered the walls of her best friend's bedroom. Finley's mouse clicked intermittently, and she sighed with frustration often.

As Nail waited for another notification, she studied Len's profile avatar for the millionth time. He was good-looking with dark hair, tanned skin, and a determined expression. He fit everything Nail liked in a guy.

Her own avatar, with a thin face, freckled nose, and flowing auburn hair, winked up at her. *Vortex Beyond* had converted her facial scan into a cartoon caricature, but it was definitely her.

Despite Len being their leader, his team was the weakest in the group. She knew he lived in a tiny town, somewhere between Wichita and Topeka. He never gave specifics.

Nail had helped him craft a strategy for beating Valnax, alternating dragons with high health and then high attack. But nearly the full half-hour had passed, and there was still no word from him. The timer kept ticking down, slow and resolute.

She compulsively swiped down on her phone to refresh the screen. The clock ticked away next to his name. Still nothing.

"Nail, you're not getting any work done over there," Finley chided sarcastically.

She looked up.

Finley sat at her desk, facing the wall that displayed an impressive array of track medals. Under Finley's racerback tank top, her lean back muscles flexed and relaxed as she tapped her keyboard more aggressively. Although her hair was naturally black, she'd bleached and dyed some sections green and purple.

Over Finley's shoulder, Nail saw a battle raging on Finley's laptop. Some sort of mashup of the old-school game RISK and ice zombies. An MMORPG—that was all Nail knew about it.

Nail looked at the social studies textbook lying next to her. She'd opened it but hadn't touched it since. It wasn't even turned to the right chapter.

"Freezing the tropics won't get our paper done any faster, either," Nail

3

replied as an avalanche crashed down upon Finley's online enemies, smothering everything from Mumbai to Hong Kong in snow.

Finley shrugged. "It's July. We've got another six weeks. And junior year is barely less of a joke than sophomore."

Nail's phone buzzed. She looked down. The timer next to Len's name turned into a gold star.

An invitation popped up on the app. She had an hour to reach the memorial fountain at Veteran's Park. It was only a twenty-minute walk.

Excitement surged through her, right down to her fingertips. She accepted the invite and tapped over to the group chat.

Len's strategy was a bastardized version of her own. She needed to know if there were any kinks to work out. She hoped Len wouldn't go silent like everyone else.

The Valnax fight was still in beta testing. Maybe beating it would force some sort of update that prevented communication with anyone who *hadn't* beat Valnax.

That might be it. Or it might not.

The silence from the group unnerved her.

But surely nothing awful could have happened to each of the other members in their group. They all lived in different parts of the country, different time zones. For a moment, Nail considered checking the news to make sure some apocalypse hadn't engulfed every other part of the nation except the east coast.

No. That was insane. She cleared her throat to distract herself from the building anxiety in her stomach. She was overreacting. If there was no update glitch, she would ream them all out later.

She tapped Len's avatar, and a message screen popped up. The keyboard clicked as she typed.

NailnNess: Just got my invite!
NailnNess: How did it go? Did the health/attack build work out?

Nail heard the quiet squeak of metal as Finley twisted something. An earthy, skunky scent filled the room.

"I love my parents being out of town," Finley said. "Don't have to hide this when they're gone."

Nail laughed. "Your parents are total hippies. Don't they know you smoke?"

Finley looked back at her. Her ice zombie game was on some sort of wait-screen with its own ticking clock. She nodded. "But they insist that I try to hide it from them. Something about the 'normal teenage experience' or whatever."

"What's the point of that?" Nail asked. "If they know you do it, why make you sneak around?"

Finley shrugged.

A thought occurred to Nail. "I bet it makes them feel better about hiding stuff from you."

Finley raised an eyebrow. "Parents are insane." She unscrewed the grinder and pinched little bits of green dust into a ball. "But at least they love their business trips."

"That's what they call them anyway," Nail said, a sing-song lilt in her voice. And even though no one else was home, she lowered her tone to barely above a whisper. "I think they're swingers."

"Gross!" Finley shouted. But curiosity got the best of her. "Why?"

"They have way too many friends," Nail said. "My dad doesn't have a tenth of the friends your parents do. Not like coworkers or friends from some hobby, but people they meet at grocery stores and stuff. And they're *adamant* that's how they met them. Like the organic produce aisle is *the* gathering place for aging couples."

"People can make friends while buying a tomato."

"Or an eggplant."

Finley threw a pen at her.

Nail laughed. "You never noticed that they *always* explain how they meet people? Plus, they take these trips out of town all the time, especially over weekends. And they're always whispering to each other about stuff. Every time I walk into a room where it's just them, I feel like I'm intruding on some secret."

Finley recoiled. "That's horrific. RIP to my emotional health." She loaded a glass bowl with the sizeable pinched green ball. "Does your Dad ever date? I mean, it's been like, what, thirteen years?"

Nail shook her head. "He's a content widower."

"What ever happened with you and Krista, anyway?" Finley asked. "The short blonde in Chemistry?"

Nail shrugged. "She thought my interest in cryptozoology was pointless. She kept asking me questions about that Bigfoot show, which I don't watch." *Lie.* "Besides, Bigfoot is the lamest undiscovered creature."

Finley shot a pointed expression at Nail's Area 51 t-shirt and rolled her eyes. "You're obsessed."

Nail looked down at the keychain on her backpack. It was the silhouette of a Plesiosaur, formed by the word BELIEVE. "Anyone who doesn't support my love of cryptids isn't worth romantic investment."

"Being straight is easier," Finley said. "But I guess you have twice as many options as I do."

Nail refreshed her phone. Nothing. "More like twice the rejection." She curled her legs to the side. "Your timer's about to go off."

Finley swiveled back, abandoning the bowl on top of her desk with a clatter.

Nail looked back at her phone. Still no reply from Len. Now it was definitely weird. He always gave her a summary of his fights before she went into hers.

She tapped over to their group chat. A gold star hung like an asterisk next to four of the names. All except hers.

Her Valnax fight would start in 50 minutes. And if she beat it, her own little gold star would appear too. Every member of the group would receive a Valnax in their inbox. Scaled down for individual use, but still the best dragon in the game.

She typed a message to the group.

NailnNess: Got my invite. 50mins to Valnax!
NailnNess: Any advice?

But no reply came. Definitely odd, especially for how excited everyone had been to be included in the beta testing. She tapped back to her conversation with Len.

NailnNess: Dude, u alive? Where r u?

She waited, refreshing the screen. Finally, the icon showed he was typing.

Lenneon0608: All good
Lenneon0608: GL

Nail sat there. He was never this silent after a raid. She started to type but deleted the message. She refused to come across as desperate in real life, and she wouldn't do it as NailnNess either. He'd reply when he got around to it. That was fine.

But there definitely wasn't a glitch. Even though Len had replied, it didn't explain why no one else in the group had responded. How could they all be offline at the biggest moment of the game?

She jumped back to the group chat. Still no messages.

The in-game timer gave her forty-two minutes until the start of the fight. Nail looked up.

Finley was deep into her MMORPG. Shoulders hunched, she clicked wildly and cursed in undertone hisses as snowy landscapes retreated north.

Nail closed up the book and slipped it into her bag. She grabbed the Nessie keychain and tugged. The sound of her backpack zippering caught Finley's attention.

"Dude, you're leaving?" Finley asked but didn't turn around. Her imaginary war between the living and the ever-frozen raged on.

"Yeah," Nail said. "There's a thing I gotta go do in my game." Nail wished Finley had lasted longer than three weeks in *Vortex Beyond*.

"That game is creepy," Finley said.

"What? How so?" She refreshed the chat screen with Len again. Nothing.

"It needs to scan your face and know your location in order to play? Freaking conspiracy, if you ask me."

Nail sighed. "No way. The facial scans prevent creepy catfishing." She considered the location feature. "But if we all start disappearing, you'll know where to look."

"Like I'd come chasing after you," Finley retorted.

"Hey, there's no competition." She refreshed the chat with Len one last time. *Not desperate.* "Like, zero."

Finley just shrugged and nodded toward the packed bowl. "I'm not doing that solo. You coming back?"

Nail already had her backpack over one shoulder. She stood there, pondering for a moment, then dropped it back onto the floor next to the bed.

Her dad would be working until the early evening, and he was always on call. People who locked themselves out of their cars or houses after 5pm always paid a higher rate. She would have plenty of time to come back.

"Yeah," she said. "Yeah, I'll be back in like… an hour and a half."

"'Kay." Finley's head angled toward the clock on the wall. "Bye, loser."

Nail smiled from the doorway. "Kill 'em all."

Finley chanced removing her hand from the mouse for a second and waved Nail away. "Go already."

Nail left the house, jogging down the back-porch steps and into the back yard. The scent of freshly cut grass swirled through the air, and warm sunshine beamed down onto her skin.

Her phone buzzed, and a message flashed across her home screen.

8Ecraskrell: has your fight started yet???

Nail kept walking and unlocked her phone, tapping the message to open the screen, relieved to hear from someone in the group. Although Skrell was her last choice.

NailnNess: No. I've got about 30 minutes.

Skrell was useful in a group, but he was endlessly annoying.

8Ecraskrell: DONT GO
NailnNess: What? Why?

She walked around from the back of the house and started down the sidewalk. The in-game GPS would have shown her the route, but she didn't need it. Veteran's Park was south of Finley's house, just east of the town's sad excuse for a downtown strip.

The park was a constant stop for her. In-game, something was always going on there. And although it wasn't big, it was worth the detour between her house and Finley's. She let her muscle memory lead the way.

8Ecraskrell: Something weird is going on. I've been messaging people since my fight but no one is replying.
8Ecraskrell: You hear from anyone after their Val fight?
NailnNess: Yeah. Len messaged me.
8Ecraskrell: He hasn't uploaded his screen record video.
NailnNess: He just messaged me a minute ago. Said it was all good.
8Ecraskrell: No one has uploaded their screen record.

Nail rolled her eyes and rounded a corner, her feet turning towards the town.

NailnNess: People have lives, Skrell.
8Ecraskrell: They're not answering messages either. Did you get the ones I sent this morning?
NailnNess: No, but I think there's an error. It's probably because of the beta-testing.
8Ecraskrell: I don't think you should go to the fight.
8Ecraskrell: I think something is going on.
NailnNess: I'll upload my screen record. Promise.

She slipped her phone into the back pocket of her jeans and kept walking.

The residential area quickly changed into businesses—fabric shops, seafood restaurants, mom-and-pop art shops, and a few cafes. A small billboard advertised a car repair shop and a psychic phone line. Another listed a local cover band with appearance dates and locations.

Nail turned east on the main road. Three and a half blocks later, she was two doors down from a popular café.

A group of six teens—her classmates—sat on the metal patio furniture. Two girls were using a lip-sync app. She saw a couple of the guys ribbing each other, laughing and calling each other names.

Nail groaned. She wished she'd noticed them sooner. She would've crossed the street. *Too late.* Crossing halfway down the block would only draw more attention to herself.

She stared at the sidewalk, hoping they were too self-absorbed to notice her.

"Hey! Hey, it's Sharp-as-a-Nail!" one of the guys called.

Nail walked in front of the café. She ignored the comment.

"You on your way to meet up with your *Mama?*" said another. The whole group whooped and *ohhhh*'d to the insult.

Nail froze. She turned to face the small, meaningless, destined-for-early-pattern-baldness-and-lower-middle-management douche who'd said it.

Todd. Of course, it was Todd.

Nail looked at one of the girls in the group, determined to keep her voice cool and calm. They wanted a reaction. They were gonna get burned. "You're dating a real winner, Kim."

Kim looked up with cold gray eyes. She pursed her lips and shrugged, returning to her phone.

"Yeah," Nail said. "I'm glad we don't hang out anymore either."

One of the guys nudged Kim. "You used to hang with Nail Polish?"

Kim shrugged the guy off. "Whatever. It was elementary school," Kim said with an airy tone.

Nail assessed the rest of the group. A heavyset guy named Wallace, who'd been unpopular until he'd gotten ahold of a fake ID, wheezed next to Todd, ready to have his new buddy's back in an argument.

"You think you're funny?" she asked.

He looked her up and down. Nail stood taller than most girls, but Todd towered above her. Easily 6'3" or 6'4".

"I *know* I'm funny," he replied.

"Because you crack jokes about someone's dead mother?" Nail said. "You find dead people to be funny now, too? I thought you just had disgusting fetishes."

Wallace coughed out a wet laugh, along with an oversized vape cloud from his mouth and nostrils.

Nail looked him up and down, from neckbeard to toe fungus. "Wallace, stop breathing so hard. You're stealing air from the rest of society."

He frowned, his stringy mustache hair sticking to his sweaty lips. He tried to stutter a reply, but either his vape hit him wrong or he was too stupid to think of one.

She looked back to Todd. "You know, you're not the dumbest guy in the world. But you'd better hope that guy doesn't die."

Todd and his friends fell silent.

She smirked and turned away, feeling more confident than before.

Todd called after her. "Well, no one likes you!"

Without looking back, Nail slow-clapped, hands raised high above her head. "Good comeback. You definitely saved face on that one."

She'd probably pay for that later online. But it didn't really matter. In two years, she and Finley would be off to college as roommates, or renting a studio apartment in a big city, or taking a gap year in Europe. It didn't really matter what they did because they'd be doing together.

She strode toward the park. A new bounce accented her steps. She sighed and loosened her shoulders, letting the tension roll off her.

The park was only five minutes away. Nail could see the landscaped trees and statues. She pulled out her phone. The front of the park had a couple check-in points for *Vortex Beyond*.

She loaded it up and swiped. Taming crystals, healing potions, and experience points popped out of the digital representation of the park's front sign. She looked around.

Couples walked their dogs or pushed kids in strollers. A dozen college co-eds ran around an open field playing ultimate frisbee. A lot of the guys were shirtless, and some of the women opted for shorts and sports bras. All of them were athletic. Nail admired the view.

She marched on through the park, enjoying the shade provided by the trees that lined the walkway. She took the long way to the fountain, stopping at in-memory-of benches and memorial sculptures that were points of interest in the game.

She used some taming crystals on a few trash-mob dragons. They were too weak for fighting, but she could use them for mass transformations and bulk gains in experience points to level up her character.

At the fountain, she settled on a bench. The fountain itself was a tall, abstract sculpture. A plaque on the stone rim dedicated its construction to fallen heroes.

Jets of water burst out at different intervals, changing their heights. At night, LED lights would shift with the water. It made for an impressive show. Dense trees surrounded the fountain's plaza, giving a sense of seclusion to the space.

Nail checked the countdown timer until her fight began. A little under nine minutes remained.

She reclined against the back support of the bench. Gazing over her shoulder, she couldn't see much of anything through the thick of the trees. The college co-eds were, unfortunately, out of sight. Somewhere, an ice cream truck played its siren song.

But she wasn't entirely alone. A man and a woman loitered around the fountain. The woman caught her attention first.

She was overdressed for the park, wearing black cigarette pants and a white-and-green-striped top. She had shoulder-length brunette hair, cut and straightened to a precise edge. She looked like she'd just stepped off the streets of France and accidentally landed in Maine.

Nail tapped over to her message box in *Vortex Beyond*. Still nothing new. Len had been offline since he last messaged her.

Maybe something *had* happened to him. She wanted to tell him about what Todd had said. Len knew her mother had passed when she was little. He'd understand.

The fountain was never this quiet during summer. On a day so warm, kids usually splashed each other in the shallows.

The man stood on her right, and the woman on her left. They both looked intently at their phones.

At first glance, it was innocuous, until Nail realized both of their phones were old, bulky, rectangular things. They looked like models that had come out ten years ago. There was no way *Vortex Beyond* would work on them. They probably didn't even have an Internet connection.

Nail's phone buzzed with a five-minute warning. She confirmed her lineup—fiddling a moment with the order—and healed up her team. Her messages were still empty. She switched over to her screen recording app and got it running. She could edit the video later.

She heard footsteps and casually glanced over her shoulder. *Vortex Beyond* chimed another alert.

Three minutes to go.

She clicked on the game's digital rendering of the fountain. It displayed as a castle tower.

Her phone buzzed. A text from her father. Naileen didn't open it. The preview read, *"I'm so proud of you. See you soon. KICK ASS!"*

Huh?

The approaching footsteps grew louder, but she didn't look up.

She cocked her head to one side and reread the preview. *Odd.* She didn't remember telling her dad about the Valnax fight.

"Naileen Sharp?" said a voice.

The man who'd been texting on the old phone stood in front of her.

He seemed normal otherwise. He had dark hair, green eyes, an average build, and average height. He wore a blue button-up shirt and the same jeans every man in his forties bought in bulk. He reminded her of a reality TV show host, the one where the cast is abandoned on an island for a month.

He smirked at her.

It should have set her on edge. But there was something warm and comforting about his eyes.

"Yes?" She wondered if he was a substitute at her high school. The thirty-second warning buzzed in her palm.

The man's smirk grew into a smile of straight, white teeth.

Nail realized that the woman stood just as close.

"I'm terribly sorry about this," he said.

The woman placed a hand on Nail's shoulder. Before she could move or react, everything went dark.

CHAPTER 2

What happened?
       Nail awoke. Her eyes barely opened to a slit. She tried to orient herself, tried to move, but every voluntary muscle in her body was paralyzed.
Where the hell am I?
She felt dizzy and nauseated. Confused. Her stomach hurt.
She inhaled, and the sharp scent of wood and stone caught her by surprise. She heard breathing all around her.
There was no wind. She was sitting up.
Nail tried again to open her eyes and was met with half success. Her arms rested, unrestrained but heavy, on the wooden arms of a chair. She still wore the same clothes she'd worn at the park.
What's going on?
She was in a room… something like an old church or maybe a large house? She wasn't sure.
Glancing left and right, unable to move her head or neck, she saw other teens in chairs on either side of her. She didn't recognize either of them.
The guy on her left was rail-thin and blonde. The girl on her right wore sunglasses.
Nail ran through a list of scenarios in her head. She was certain she'd been kidnapped. She didn't feel injured, but everything was hazy.
She remembered leaving Finley's house. She remembered the café and

Todd's awful words. But the park was a blur. Had there been a talk show host? No, a reality show host. That was it. He and a woman had been at the fountain right before...

No. Valnax! She tried to move her arms and look for her phone—maybe call for help—but her arms wouldn't budge. Her right index finger twitched, but that was all.

She swore and found that she had use of her voice, but only at a whisper. She'd never entered the fight! Wherever she was now, that window had closed. She hadn't participated. She'd be the only one in her group without a Valnax.

The group. Had any of them seen that she hadn't entered the fight? Skrell would've noticed by now, surely. He'd be worried.

Yes. Skrell! He'd be out of his mind with anxiety. She wondered how long he would wait before calling the police. Relief flooded her.

Except he has no idea where I live.
This can't be real. This can't be happening.

She struggled against the chair to no avail and thought back to Finley's house. Finley was no stranger to molly and mushrooms, but she wouldn't have laced the weed with stuff like that. Not without telling Nail, anyway.

But, no. They hadn't smoked. This wasn't a hallucination.

Nail's eyes were fully open. She cleared her throat and found that her head could turn a bit. She looked around the room.

It wasn't just three of them. There were over a dozen. Guys and girls, they all looked roughly the same age as Nail.

She saw a pair of twin girls dressed in rock band tee shirts. A jock-looking guy with Polynesian tattoos on his arm. A gorgeous blonde who held her nose up like this entire thing was beneath her dignity. An Indian kid with overly gelled hair.

One other guy, frowning in confusion, looked incredibly familiar, but Nail couldn't place him.

The room looked like something out of an English castle: a high ceiling with stone walls and floors. Decorative torches and sconces lined the walls. Built-in shelves, recessed into the walls, held books and antique figurines. Ornate paintings of regal families hung in groups.

Some of the other teens had found their voices, too. The room swirled with low, anxious whispers.

Nail faced three stained-glass windows. The left panel showed a Chinese dragon swimming in a lake. The right panel showed a woman, in an angular straw hat, fishing. The center image depicted the dragon and woman swirling together. It reminded her of the yin-yang symbol.

There were two doors set into the same wall, each in opposing corners.

Two ways out.

Nail tried to stand. Her legs didn't even quiver. She sighed, immobile and defeated.

Behind her at the back of the room, someone cleared their throat.

Nail turned her head to look.

It was him.

The man she'd seen at the park strode confidently forward, hands clasped behind him. There was no sign of his partner, the younger woman.

He'd changed out of his dad jeans. He wore a loose, lavender-colored tunic made of woven cotton that came down to his knees with a matching pair of cotton pants. He walked barefoot.

Fear and hatred rose up in her at once. Nail and everyone else in the room tried to cry out. But all their objections came out as strained whispers, a chorus of disgruntled murmurs.

The man reached the front of the room and turned to greet them. He was way too tan to be from her town. He smiled, and a warm, unwelcomed calm trickled over her.

Nail didn't want to be calmed. The unexpected emotion was revolting. She wanted to level him with one good punch and run as far away as possible.

But the smile's effect was undeniable. Her breathing shifted—deep and even—and her thoughts of escape washed away.

"My name is Steven Parson. You may refer to me as Steve, Master Parson, Steven, or any combination thereof. I am the leader of the Lumen Society," he gestured around the room, "which is where you all are now.

"I would like to apologize for the abrupt departure in your normal routine. Although you don't remember how you got here, I can personally promise that no harm came to any of you in the process."

Does he expect a thank-you?

He stood there, smiling, his hands visible and at his sides. Nail knew he was trying to send non-threating nonverbal cues.

She still wanted to punch him.

"You may be expecting an apology for bringing you here in the first place. I cannot offer that. After much trial and error, we have found this to be the best way to welcome new members into the society. I do apologize for the confusion, but soon enough, I think, you will understand why we use such methods."

"You mean kidnapping." Nail's voice barely reached above a whisper.

He smiled serenely, and again the calm feeling she fought to reject nipped at her anxiety.

"I would like to make three things very clear." He held up his right hand, middle, ring, and pinky fingers extended. "One, none of you are a prisoner here. If after these first few hours you want to return home to your normal lives, we will be happy to help you do that.

"Secondly, everything you see here is very, very real. No one is playing a joke on you. This is not some hidden-camera reality show. And third, you are welcome to stay on Lumen Island for as long as you wish."

"Island?" Nail's voice returned in full. She couldn't shout the word like she had wanted, but everyone could clearly hear her. "What do you mean, 'island?'" Had he taken them to a boat, holing them up somewhere off the coast of Maine?

"Yes, a small patch of land surrounded by ocean," Steven explained.

"Where the *hell* are we?" Nail demanded.

A few others grumbled in agreement.

Steven replied in an even tone, "This island is east of Hawaii and west of Mexico. It is uncharted on all maps, apps, and globes. Except ours."

How long have I been out? Nail shut her eyes hard enough to see spots, wanting to will herself out of the room and back home. *That must've taken at least ten hours on a plane, assuming he's telling the truth.*

Steven looked around the room, slowly making eye contact with everyone.

Nail looked around too. The girl wearing sunglasses smiled. Everyone else seemed somewhere between pacified or confused. The room's medieval décor wasn't helping anything.

"In good time, you will all be bonded with a partner," Steven said. "The society will help prepare you for your bonding, and we will provide guidance during and after hatching."

"Hatching?" asked the guy with Polynesian tattoos. He sat with his arms folded over his chest. "We gonna raise chickens?"

Steven chuckled. "Certainly not. And I won't tell them you said that."

Everyone waited for a more detailed explanation.

Steven clapped his hands together. "I'm getting ahead of myself. It will be easier—and more convincing—to simply show you. I think you'll all find that you have full control your bodies once again. Please follow me outside. Everything will be made clear."

Nail shifted her feet and found that her paralysis had lifted. Everyone stood, and Steven turned and headed to the door at the left side of the room.

A few of the others shrugged and followed Steven. Trepidation tugged at their footsteps, unsure what held more danger—following or staying put. Quick, hushed words went through the group. Herd mentality took over as everyone else gathered and followed them toward the door.

Nail ended up in line behind the twins. They spoke in low, hurried whispers. It seemed they were the only ones who knew each other.

If Nail had doubted they were on an island, or in the Pacific, her disbelief evaporated the moment she stepped outside.

The warm, golden glow of late afternoon sunlight overwhelmed her. She stepped over the stone threshold and onto soft, spongy grass.

The land in front of her was lush with greenery. Exotic flowers of every color blossomed on bushes. Palm trees swayed overhead, casting long shadows onto the short grass. Fruit-bearing shrubs dotted the landscape. The air was fresh and laden with sweet pollen. Somewhere, a songbird hummed a tune.

Looking side to side, Nail saw they were deep in a valley. Jagged, red rocks jutted up on either side and behind them. Far down the valley, she could make out a white sand beach and the vivid cyan of ocean shallows.

A river cut down the left side of the valley. It deposited into a wide, round pond—complete with a small isle at the center—and flowed out again toward the beach.

Nail heard rushing water, the patter of it hitting rocks. Her gaze followed the river upstream. A waterfall, easily 200 feet tall, crested over the mountain behind her and cascaded into a pool at the head of the river.

She turned around. The building she had just left was built into the side of the rocky cliff.

The line dissipated as everyone fanned out, jaws dropping and eyes looking everywhere.

The beautiful blonde clapped. "I'm gonna 'gram the *hell* outta this place!" She searched her pockets. When she found them empty, her eyes went wide. "Wait... where's my purse? Where's my *phone?*"

Steven walked closer to her but addressed the entire group. "Cell phones have no use on the island. There is no reception or Internet. And pictures are against our rules." He chuckled to himself. "For obvious reasons."

The collective group groaned and gave too many protests for any single voice to stand out.

Steven held up his hands to silence them. "I'm certain you'll find that the tradeoff is more than fair. And as I said before, if you want to leave, we will be more than happy to help you do so."

With no phone, and no one she knew, Nail could only follow Steven's lead.

He led them down the riverbank. Everyone moved faster than they had when leaving the building. The grass grew almost into the water, with only a thin line of rocks and pebbles outlining its flow.

Nail estimated the valley to be at least the size of ten football fields put together. Little groves of trees and towering bushes grew everywhere. Some of the trees had initials carved into them or other strange blemishes.

She saw scorch marks that crawled up entire trunks, burnt bark, and snapped tree limbs. An avocado tree looked like it had taken a beating. Long, smooth cuts penetrated deep beneath the bark and revealed the wood within. Nail touched the wood, examining the unusual cuts.

They continued until they reached the lake. The river's flow sent ripples across the otherwise calm water. A few fruit trees stood on the lake's sparse, rocky isle. Their bark looked worn down, and some of the lower branches had been broken off, discarded on the shore.

Steven sat next to the water's edge. Everyone else found sizable rocks to settle on. Nail wasn't sure what to expect, but she took a seat anyway.

He looked around at the group of teens that gathered on either side of him. "Everyone comfortable? You may want to brace yourselves. We don't want any concussions the first night."

Nail casually placed a hand on the rock behind her. She tried to look relaxed, like she would've done that anyway. Just chilling.

That feeling of unnatural calm swept over her again. This time, she didn't try as hard to resist it. The scenery was beautiful, and the setting promised an unforgettable sunset.

Nail sighed.

Not knowing what came next didn't seem as important anymore. Steven leaned forward and dipped his hand into the water. He left it there for a moment.

A few yards away, something beneath the surface moved.

Nail's heart skipped a beat.

A long, massive shadow circled the lake isle beneath the gentle waves. Steven withdrew his hand from the water and wiped it on his tunic.

The shadow flashed by again. Heart racing, Nail leaned forward, peering into the depths, trying to discern what lurked below. The shadow raced by a third time. Ripples became waves that crashed onto the rocks at their feet, splashing their shoes.

Could it...?

She held her breath.

For a moment, it seemed as though the water itself had defied the laws of physics and burst up from the lake. At the far side of the lake isle and perfectly in view, a massive shape arose, spraying mist everywhere. But the shape had two eyes, a face of blue scales, and an undeniable silhouette.

Nail had seen it in art and video games. Every culture in the world had produced the same basic picture.

Fierce.

Battle-hardened.

Sometimes evil, sometimes benevolent.

Knights had claimed victory over them, and ancient civilizations had worshipped them as deities.

A dragon. A real *dragon*.

It moved over four powerful legs, its body curling around like a snake. Ten feet wide, at least sixty feet long, the massive Chinese dragon settled on the lake isle. It raised its head, exhaling mist from its huge nostrils. Water dripped from the dragon's crested mane of long yellow tendrils.

Nail heard a voice in her head—melodic, seemingly feminine, echoing. Somehow it transcended the very ideas of time or scientific limits.

"Welcome to Lumen Island, little humans," the dragon's voice said. *"I hope most of you survive."*

CHAPTER 3

Adrenaline surged through Nail. She felt it pulsing between the skips in her heart, jolting her fingers and quaking through her legs.

A dragon. A real, *actual* dragon. She should have been afraid. Every basic instinct in her mind should have set off warning bells: *Predator! Danger!*

But they didn't.

She grinned. Tears ran down her face. She didn't care how she looked.

Dragons are real.

It was insane. It was impossible. It was everything Nail could have ever dreamed of and more.

She'd never solidified what she wanted her post-high school life to look like. Her father had never insisted on it. She knew she'd figure it out at some point, possibly before graduating, possibly after.

But as she sat on the bank of the pond, staring up at a real dragon, she knew. This was her purpose in life. No question about it.

A piece of her had always been missing. She'd felt it for as long as she could remember. It was why she obsessed over Nessie and could get lost in the fantasy section of bookstores. Finally, at long last, that piece wasn't some childish wish or the disappointing result of an overactive imagination.

Dragons are real.

All at once, so many things made sense. Dragon myths existed worldwide. It wasn't some subconscious, leftover, pre-evolution fear of large predators. It wasn't the result of crocodiles or whalebones or dinosaur fossils or drunken sailors.

They were real. They had always been real.

It didn't matter what Steven or anyone else had done to get her there. Whatever it would take to stay on Lumen Island, she was all in.

The dragon looked both terrifying and regal. Piercing green eyes stared down at them. Its double set of horns twisted and curved like the helmet of an ancient warrior. Its brow and neck sprouted a mane of golden, wavering tendrils light enough to move in the slightest breeze. And its brilliant blue scales shone in the midday sun like flawless steel.

The only noise to break the silence came from a girl to Nail's right. She sat curled up into herself, hiding her face under an unruly mop of brunette ringlets, choking with sobs.

The dragon shifted its body, and its scales moved and settled in a hypnotic wave.

Again, Nail heard the voice of the dragon in her mind. She noticed this time that its mouth stayed closed.

"*My name is Oracle,*" said the dragon. "*I am the oldest resident of this island.*"

Nail couldn't contain herself. "There are more, then? More than just you?"

Everyone stared at her—she could feel it.

"Not that you're *not* the most magnificent creature I've ever seen," Nail backtracked. "You are. Truly. But..." She couldn't hide the excitement in her voice. "There are more?"

Oracle stared down at her. The sheer size of her eyes should have made it impossible to tell where Oracle was looking, but Nail could feel her gaze. It was more than simple eye contact. It was as though Oracle was looking into her, singling out Nail's energy or soul or... *something.*

It should have felt like scorn. It should have been terrifying. But Nail was exhilarated.

This time when Oracle spoke, her voice did not echo. "*There are more, Nail. Now, hold your silence.*" Oracle's tongue flicked out, forked like a snake's.

Nail looked around. If anyone else had heard Oracle's words, they gave no indication of it. Still, they all stared at her as though she had dared to break some great, unspoken rule.

The crying brunette girl rocked back and forth, mumbling indistinctly.

Oracle continued and the echo returned to her voice. *"It was I who saw into your lives and hearts. I have seen that each of you has a place here."*

"Should you wish to claim it," Steven interjected.

Oracle exhaled, sending a warm breeze down upon the group. *"With that place comes the privilege and responsibility of one of the oldest pacts this world has ever known. It is a truce of peace and trust between dragons and humans.*

"We have built the Lumen Society upon this agreement. It is paramount that you understand this. That trust and care must be maintained, or your privileged place among us may be revoked."

"Who does the revoking?"

Nail turned. The girl wearing sunglasses had spoken up. Magenta, lime green, and electric blue streaked through her naturally dark hair.

Oracle bared a smile revealing long, pointed white teeth. *"I do."*

The great dragon shifted again and glanced down the row of humans.

"You are our newest class. Each of you was born during the year of the Metal Dragon, sometime between February 5th, 2000 and January 23rd, 2001. For many of you, belonging to this society has passed down through generations. For others, you are the first in your ancestry to be invited."

Oracle shivered. Her head lowered and hung above the water. She stared at them all, and when she spoke, there was a threat in her voice.

"Your ancestry does not make you better or worse than anyone else, and it will gain you no special privilege. This is a place of tolerance and acceptance. All gifts and abilities are strengths. Mistreatment of anyone will not be tolerated by the society. Is this clear to everyone?"

Some gave a loud "yes" and others murmured in the affirmative. The distressed brunette didn't respond at all.

Oracle looked satisfied. A softness formed at the corner of her eyes. *"I look forward to the days to come, and each of you knowing your selves more."*

She looked in Steven's direction, hesitating for a moment. Then, in a manner less spectacular than how she had entered, Oracle crawled back into the lake. The water rippled, and waves splashed the rocks. The dragon was gone.

Steven stood and faced them all. "She knows how to make an entrance, doesn't she? I think you'll all find that you're sufficiently hungry. Please head back the way we came for dinner." He added in a softer voice, "Tally, would you please stay behind with me?"

The girl finally raised her head. Her face flushed deep red, and tears streaked her cheeks and neck, staining the collar of her t-shirt. She heaved deep, rapid breaths.

Nail had expected to see her crying, but her ragged and shallow breathing suggested a panic attack.

Everyone stood. Nail pretended to stretch, letting most of the group go on ahead. She wanted to hang back and catch what Steven would say to Tally. She wondered if he would use that calming smile on her, maybe force her to stay.

She didn't fully believe Steven's posturing about them being free to leave—especially after what they'd just seen. If he allowed people to leave, wouldn't that put the entire island at risk?

Maybe not.

An uncharted island inhabited by dragons? Who would believe it? No one sane.

Nail had run out of stretches to feign. The only other person left was neon-haired sunglasses girl.

Steven looked at them both. "Muari, Nail, please go on ahead. We'll be along."

Nail shrugged away her disappointment and fell into step with Muari.

When they were a couple yards away, Muari leaned in and whispered, "Don't worry. I have excellent hearing. I'll tell you what they're saying."

Nail smiled. Making friends was normally not an effortless endeavor for her. But there was something about this girl. Perhaps it was the dyed hair. She reminded Nail of Finley.

Finley. Nail hadn't even considered Finley. Or her own father! Nail was in the Pacific, and the sun was beginning to set. How much time had passed? Surely Finley and her father would have realized that Nail was missing by now.

She remembered what Oracle said about ancestry. She wondered, had her father been here? It would explain a lot of his personality, now that she considered it. He was a locksmith, but his only hobby was studying medieval history. And he'd seen every movie and TV show ever created that had a dragon in it...

If he had been here, why hasn't he ever told me?

"Wait until you're seventeen to figure out what you want to do in life," he'd always said. "You can't know all your options until then. Fretting about it beforehand is unnecessary."

Nail stumbled. *He knew! He totally knew!*

"You okay?" Muari asked. "You tripped."

"Yeah," Nail replied. "I was just... considering implications back home."

Nail heard soft, musical tones coming from what looked like an old-school Walkman clipped to the pocket of Muari's jeans.

"I'm the first in my family," Muari said. "They came to my house, told my family there was an opening in a special school. Someplace for 'gifted' individuals with unique abilities. My parents ate it all up. They showed some pretty convincing paperwork for it, too. Or so they told me." Muari smiled wide.

Nail liked her smile. It was genuine, the kind of smile that follows an honest compliment.

"So," Muari gestured behind them, "you want to know what they're talking about?"

"Definitely," Nail replied with a wicked grin.

They parted ways around the trunk of a mango tree. When they had fallen into step again, Muari leaned in. "Tally is having a total panic attack. Steven is asking if she'd like to increase her anxiety meds. Tally is insisting that wouldn't do any good, and there's no way she can handle being here."

"Whoa." Nail looked behind her. Steven and Tally stood at least ten yards behind them. "You can really hear that?"

"Tally is saying that she can barely cope with her anxiety at home. Even before dragons entered the picture, this place was way too much for her to handle. Steven is explaining that Oracle chose her to be here for a reason. That..." Muari's mouth was a hard line. "That perhaps there is some healing for her here if she stays."

Muari paused, listening while they walked. She frowned and quickly tried to hide it. "He's naming some of the things he's seen 'healed' here. She's hyperventilating again."

Nail wondered exactly what kind of "healing" the society offered. Emotional counseling, maybe?

"Steven wants her to stay through dinner. He's saying if she still wants to leave, then he will make that happen. But he sounds... disappointed. No, worse." Muari tilted her head. "There's despair in his voice."

"That's kind of weird," Nail said.

They followed as the group veered left. Nail could smell the food before they saw it.

An expansive wooden pergola stood shrouded in greenery. Green and red vines snaked over most of the structure. Trees of pink leaves and yellow flowers blossomed and filled the air with fragrance.

Nail heard a din of voices beyond the entrance. Most of the class was already inside. Someone, somewhere, hummed *The Lion Sleeps Tonight*. They stepped onto the terrace. Metal chairs and tables were set up. Some of them had two seats, others had four, six, or eight. A thriving koi pond took up the center of the space, and budding vines cascaded down like chandeliers.

"This has a lovely feel," Muari said.

Nail looked up. Tree limbs grew overhead, giving shade and casting color onto the packed earth below. A breeze snuck through the branches. Nail caught a glimpse of a butterfly's wings before it disappeared through twisted veins of ivy.

All around them, the new class had found tables in random groups. Conversations had begun to pop up, with people exchanging names and where they were from.

"Let's find a table for two," Muari suggested.

Nail looked around. She pointed to one about ten feet away. "Will that one work?"

"Lead the way," Muari said.

Most of the others were seated and soaking in the setting with awed expressions. Nail had to admit, the place was beautiful. Every inch of the island looked like desktop wallpaper or the background of an annoying inspirational poster.

Nail took the farthest chair at the little table.

Muari reached out and pulled her own chair. She steadied herself against the table and sat. "Overwhelming, isn't it?"

Nail nodded. She faced the entrance and watched as Steven and Tally crossed the threshold. He pointed to several tables with other students and empty chairs.

Tally ignored him and chose an empty two-person table. She dragged the chair through the packed dirt and sat facing away from the group.

Nail felt pity for her. How could anyone encounter a real dragon and not instantly feel complete?

Nail thought back to Oracle. She'd certainly been intimidating, but not terrifying. It hadn't reduced Nail to a puddle of anxiety. Muari hadn't reacted that way either.

A man in a robe similar to Steven's appeared at their table with two plates. He set them before Nail and Muari.

"What's on the menu tonight?" Muari asked.

"Fresh-caught salmon filet, sautéed kale grown on our farm, and a bruschetta with goat cheese and tomato," he replied.

"Thank you, Thomas," Muari said with a smile.

Nail searched him for a nametag before the man disappeared. She didn't see one. "How did you know his name?"

Muari had already picked up her fork and began prodding at her salmon. "Steven brought me here three days ago, ahead of everyone else, so I could get my bearings."

Nail tilted her head, ready to ask why, but Steven cleared his throat. He stood next to the koi pond and spun in all directions to address everyone.

"Could I have everyone's attention, please?" Steven looked toward the back of the room.

For the first time, Nail noticed the archway leading to another pergola.

Over a dozen people in robes or tunics poured through. Their ages varied. The youngest looked to be in her mid-twenties. The oldest man looked close to eighty.

They all smiled at the new group. They must've each had some role on the island, but thanks to their homogenous outfits, Nail couldn't tell anyone's specific job.

Steven held the attention of the entire room, except for Tally. She sat with her head in her hands, her plate completely untouched.

"I just wanted to take a few moments to welcome our newest members, the Class of Metal Dragons!"

The people under the archway clapped. A few of them whooped in approval.

"Oracle has given her words of caution and made her grand entrance." He looked over to the rest of the staff. Many of them chuckled. "I would like to welcome a few more of our partners to the meal."

Nail heard the beat of tremendous wings overhead, pounding like a drum before the march of an approaching army. Wind rushed through her hair. She looked up. A brown and gold dragon swept above them mid-flight. The gold of the dragon's wings cast an ethereal light into the room, basking everything in a heavenly glow.

Three butterflies flitted through the air as if on cue. Only, Nail realized, they weren't butterflies at all. Their wingspan was a foot wide, but their little bodies had fore and back legs. Slender necks arched as the tiny dragons whirled through the air as gracefully as ballerinas.

Two more dragons, each with four legs and no wings, entered the dining space through the same door the class had come through. They were both the size of large dogs, their reptilian heads just level with the tabletops. One was pewter gray with brilliant green eyes. The other bore ombré white and purple scales and a crested mane like Oracle's. The gray dragon lowered its maw into the koi pond, snatching out a fish and carrying it off.

Four more dragons, walking on two rear legs and with foreclaws set into their wings, lumbered around outside the terrace. The smallest of them was Nail's size. The largest could have dwarfed a Clydesdale. They bore large teeth and heaved hot, heavy breath through the wood and vines.

Nail's jaw hung open. It wasn't just the sight of them. There was an aura around them that struck goose bumps down her arms and spine. The air had shifted, like fickle winds sending in a summer thunderstorm. She felt it crackle with every inhale.

"I've died," Nail said to Muari. "I've died, and every dream I've ever had has come true."

A rapturous smile had overtaken Muari's face. "Same."

The dragons mulled about, nodding at the new students. The ombré dragon nipped at someone's salmon. The guy laughed and told the dragon to take it.

Nail stared at his face again. She'd recognized him when they'd woken up. Where had she seen him before? Was he a YouTube star or something? Had she watched his videos once and forgotten him?

No matter where she recognized him from, he was undeniably hot. Muscled, tan, dark hair. She could see the joy in his face, heard his easy laugh.

One of the small dragons tore her attention away. It landed on their table.

Nail admired the dragon's body. It flapped its translucent wings. More beautiful than any butterfly's, the little dragon's wings swirled with a palette of pastel shades. They reminded Nail of the stained-glass windows she'd seen when she'd first awakened on the island.

The dragon spun, tiny claws clicking on the metal, showing off and clearly reveling in its own beauty. Nail picked off a small piece of her salmon and offered it.

A voice like a chorus of tiny bells popped into her mind. *"Oh, you're a kind one, aren't you?"*

Muari grinned down at the dragon. "You have a lovely voice, little fae. What's your name?"

The dragon turned toward Muari. It spread its wings as far as they could go and lowered itself into a bow. *"I am Aenu."*

Then Aenu flapped its wings rapidly and took off, flitting around the room and settling on other tables.

"Short attention span," Muari said.

Nail watched as the other dragons made their way to the back room where the staff had eaten.

"There's a courtyard out there for all of them," Muari said.

Nail nodded. "Obviously they can't all fit in here." She dug into her mostly ignored dinner. Between mouthfuls, she asked, "What did you call Aenu? A 'fae?'"

"Faery dragons," Muari said.

Nail gasped. "Are fairies real, too?"

Muari cocked her head. "I don't know. It could just be a name. But then again, after all of this, it seems like anything is possible, doesn't it?"

"It certainly does."

Nail watched the fae dragons flit from one table to another, mooching food from anyone polite enough to offer it. A teal fae dragon landed at the table where the familiar guy sat.

Nail made eye contact with him. He smiled and raised a hand to her. She waved back.

She was certain she knew him from somewhere. If only she could place it.

After the meal concluded, all of the staff members left together. They passed the tables, smiling at the teens.

Steven returned to their section of the dining hall. "It's time, everyone. Follow me."

CHAPTER 4

Everyone looked around. Nail wasn't sure what it was time for, but so long as it included more dragons, she couldn't complain.

Steven led them to the pool under the waterfall. Large rocks covered in green vines and moss created walls around the water. Several people stood waiting at the shore, including the woman Nail had seen in the park.

Lounging on the large rocks, several dragons groomed their scales, some watched the approaching group, and others merely snoozed in the waning sunlight. Ripples of whispers went through the crowd. Nail couldn't stop staring. Just watching them breathe was mesmerizing.

Steven indicated for everyone to fan out and held up a hand for silence. "Before you see more, you need to understand something. The offer to join the Lumen Society is open to all of you—and I will show you exactly what you'll gain.

"Joining Lumen is not a decision to make lightly. Once you join, there can be no going back. I guarantee that through Lumen you will become a different person. I can guarantee you a dragon partner, and I can guarantee you magic."

Nail could barely hold still. At the mention of the word "magic," the entire group had redoubled their attention.

"Do you think we'll get wands?" Muari whispered in her ear.

Nail shrugged.

Steven waited for the group to settle. "We can offer you something you won't find anywhere else in the world. But it comes at a price. You can never tell your friends about this place. You will be separated from your families. You might wish to never return home.

"The journey ahead of you is dangerous. I cannot guarantee your safety. There will be injuries. Some of you may not live to fully realize your new selves. I don't want anyone entering into this thinking it's all a tropical vacation." He paused and stared across the crowd of teens. "If you join, you can never go back to who you once were."

Nail looked around. She didn't need to go back to who she was. A chance to live with dragons? She was all in.

Most of the others looked determined, too. Tally hung at the back of the crowd, looking pointedly at the ground. Nail surveyed the rest of her class again. They were a decent-looking bunch overall.

"You will be the class of Metal Dragons," Steven said, "should you wish to join."

Steven gestured to the short-haired woman behind him. She joined him. "This is my sister, Prioress Nora. Some of you might recognize her."

There was a shift in the group, a ripple of distrust. A fae dragon coiled around Prioress Nora's bicep. She smiled at everyone. "This is my partner, Aenu. Some of you may have fed ver at dinner. Aenu is a bit of a mooch."

The fae dragon leaped from her arm with an arched jump and fluttered away to a sunny rock.

"Lumen offers you not just dragons, but magic as well," Steven said. "Every Lumen member—each dragon and each human—has one magical gift."

"After Aenu hatched, we began to bond," Prioress Nora said. "As our bond strengthened, our unique magical abilities awakened. Aenu can cause temporary paralysis, as you all experienced earlier. I have a different gift."

Prioress Nora shut her eyes. Everyone leaned closer, not sure what to expect.

There was a small popping noise, like the distant sound of a champagne bottle. She disappeared.

Nail and the rest of the class gasped.

Prioress Nora's voice sounded from behind the group. "Which is quite useful if you want to have breakfast in L.A. and lunch in Tokyo."

Everyone swiveled. She stood a few yards away from the back of the group. With another pop, she reappeared next to Steven.

Teleportation. Nail blinked rapidly, not quite believing her eyes. *Well, that explains how we all got to this island.*

Prioress Nora did something between a bow and a curtsey and wandered into the crowd.

Steven gestured toward an older man behind him. He looked wizened, with short, precisely cut salt-and-pepper hair that reminded Nail of a veteran Marine. Crow's feet accented the corners of his eyes, and deep laugh lines were forever carved on his stoic face.

"My name is Prior Adams," he spoke with a deep, almost monotone voice. Turning his torso, he gestured to the gray, wingless dragon of the group. "And that is my partner, Rankor."

Prior Adams stood a little taller. "After becoming a part of the Lumen Society, I served in the United States Army for parts of the Vietnam war, the Gulf war, the war in Afghanistan, and other tours in various countries."

One of the guys behind Nail called out, "Thank you for your service!"

Prior Adams gave a small nod, a smile nearly invading one corner of his mouth. He continued, "Lumen gave me a unique gift—the ability to repel metal. Master Parson will assist me in demonstrating."

Prior Adams reached into the back of his waistband, pulling out a revolver. He popped the cylinder out of place, checking that it was loaded, and it clicked back into place smoothly. Holding onto the barrel, he offered the gun grip first to Steven.

The two men stood five yards apart. Steven raised the weapon to Prior Adams, leveling it to his chest.

Nail glanced anxiously between them, wanting to believe Prior Adams's claim, but unable to fathom it.

"Ready?" Steven called.

Prior Adams nodded.

There was a loud bang, and a few students cried out in surprise. A wisp of smoke hung in the air around Steven's still-outstretched arm.

Prior Adams remained unmoving for a moment. There were no holes in his shirt, no bleeding wound. He bent down toward the grass, and pulled out something small and silvery, holding it up for the crowd to see.

It had been a bullet, but it was crunched and flattened like it had been fired into a steel wall. The crowd gasped in wonder.

"My magical gift can be turned off at will," he said. "I don't send forks and knives flying away like a negative magnet at dinner. But in battle, my gift has saved countless lives—including my own—and prevented many serious wounds."

Steven handed him back the gun. Prior Adams opened the cylinder again, this time emptying all the bullets into his palm. He dropped them into a pants pocket and stored the unloaded revolver in his waistband once more. Then he walked with purpose over to the dragon called Rankor.

Steven remained in front of the crowd. "Not all magical gifts are as visually stunning as Prior Adams and Prioress Nora have demonstrated. For example, our society survives financially because one of our members is gifted with supernatural knowledge of which stocks will return exceptional profits. Another of our members is a world-renowned surgeon, able to visualize, predict, and heal nearly any physical trauma."

Steven winked, beaming at all of them. Nail could tell he loved this —exposing the group to Lumen's secrets and abilities.

"A long while ago," he continued, "we had a member who could teach beetles to sing. So if you ever hear two lines of a song being endlessly repeated, you can be sure you're sitting next to a hummingbug.

"Your dragons will receive one magical gift as well, although, on the whole, Lumen dragons are hesitant to display these gifts until you've been fully welcomed into the Lumen Society." He smiled at the group. "And I think it's time we do just that."

Steven parted the group down the middle and led them south alongside the stream. Tally dragged behind the others. The scent of salt drifted in the air, blown in from the surf of the beach.

Nail's head was reeling. There wouldn't be any wand-waving or incantations, it seemed. The magical gifts were more like one single superpower. Even if they weren't all stunning or impressive, any magical gift was a cherry on an already irresistible sundae to her.

Nail heard a hummingbug buzzing the chorus to *Gangsta's Paradise*. Other hummingbugs filled out the bass and beat.

They continued on, and before they reached the sandy divide, Steven took a hard right turn. The group shuffled into a single-file line and followed.

They were close to the beach. To Nail's right, she could see a pavilion with a fire pit and outdoor furniture. Steven navigated their route past palm trees and shrubs.

A narrow set of steps, carved into the western side of the valley rock, led to the top of the ridge. The group climbed, barely murmuring to each other as they went. The stairs snaked higher and higher, turning and twisting.

Halfway up, Nail looked around and down. She had lost sight of Muari, who she'd been certain was right behind her. But there was no sign of her telltale hair.

The valley was breathtaking. Little groves of fruit trees and flowering bushes dotted the landscape. Two dragons ran along the grounds, chasing each other for an unknown reason.

She grinned. It was paradise.

Nail again paused at the top as the rest of the group made the last leg of the journey. The ridge formed a U around the valley. Atop the ridge across the way, a few white wind turbines spun in the ocean breeze.

What had been a gentle zephyr below escalated to a strong gale, tossing and tangling Nail's auburn hair. The scent of salt and dirt drifted through the air. She spotted Muari up ahead, waiting a short distance away from the group with Prioress Nora.

Steven looked over the group like a sheepdog and beckoned everyone onward. They continued south across the ridge, moving closer to the edge of the oceanside cliff.

The entire staff had gathered on opposing sides of a round, stone dais carved with an image of a compass. Poised in an aggressive crouch, a crimson wyvern, roughly the size of a Great Dane, waited behind the dais. The image of a dragon encircled the cardinal directions.

Steven stood on the ground, below the step of the dais. He raised his hands in a messianic gesture.

"You've met Oracle," he said. "You've seen what we offer here. Now the time has come to choose your path. If you proceed, you will be magically bound to the Draconian and Anthro Treaty. You will be paired with a dragon and receive magical gifts. In return, you cannot leave until your gifts and your paired dragon are mature."

He shifted his weight from one foot to another and continued, "Let me be clear. If you step onto this dais, there is no turning back. Joining the Lumen Society has never been the safe choice in life. Your life is no longer your own, but it will be more than you could have ever dreamed."

Prior Adams stepped forward, handing Steven a rolled-up piece of parchment. Steven held it aloft, leaving it rolled up, and recited from memory.

"You shall not harm a Lumen dragon through malicious intent or negligence. No Lumen dragon will lay claw, breath, blood, or any other malady upon you. You shall respect the bond between yourself, your dragon, and all other members of this treaty. You shall live and die by these words in full knowledge that you relinquish your old life and take up the yoke of your new fate."

His gaze turned steely as he assessed the group. "Consider carefully."

Everyone looked around at each other. Steven walked around to the rear of the dais, next to the red dragon, clearing the way for the rest of the group. He laid the treaty upon the stone.

Nail gently pushed through the crowd and was the first to step onto the dais. The cute, familiar guy went next, smiling coyly as he took his place next to Nail.

The rest of the group followed quickly, reminding Nail of a crowd during a Black Friday doorbuster. Muari was the last to step up.

Except for Tally.

She stood rooted to the ground, and looking sideways to the horizon, ignoring the group.

Steven frowned.

Tally turned away from everyone and shuffled back toward the staircase.

"You've all made your decision," Steven said. "You will now be bound."

The wyvern rose, walking on its hind legs and the claws at the center joint of its wings. Placing its muzzle along the spine of the carved dragon, the wyvern circled the group. Red light glowed from the carving as it moved. The treaty smoldered red with magic.

After the wyvern's second lap, the light began to reach out, wrapping around the ankles of everyone on the dais. Red magic snaked around their legs, climbed up their torsos, and enveloped their arms. By the wyvern's third lap, the light domed over their heads.

Nail looked around. Everyone was covered. Something buzzed in her fingertips, growing into a hum that vibrated down to her bones. Every cell in her body seemed to be curving, changing, accepting a new evolutionary rule.

The light started warm and grew progressively hotter. What had begun as a pleasant sensation changed to a dangerous heat. Nail was sure her sweating skin would soon blister. Her whole body tremored in the heat like a forgotten pot of boiling water.

Then the light changed, suddenly shifting to blue. Icy chills engulfed her, and she gasped for air. The buzzing sensation ended just as abruptly, changing to an inability to move. She couldn't even blink.

In a rush of white light, her temperature returned to normal. The magic popped like a water balloon. Light flooded the feet of the nearby staff harmlessly.

Steven stood in front of the group again. "Congratulations," he said with a broad smile. "You are now a part of the Lumen Society."

DOWN IN THE VALLEY AGAIN, ALL OF THE TEENS GATHERED NEAR the base of the staircase. Staff members slowly trickled down the stone steps behind them, talking excitedly in poorly hushed whispers.

Steven stood a small distance away, addressing the new crowd. "Ladies, Prioress Julia will show you to your dorms. Gentleman, Prior Adams will show you to yours."

Prioress Julia had a severe, heart-shaped face and graying blonde hair tied up in a perfect orb of a bun. Her lips were pursed, and she eyed the group of girls suspiciously.

Tally shuffled her feet, standing away from the newly inducted group. Steven went to her, placing a hand on her shoulder. She shrugged out of the gesture, and he didn't attempt to repeat it.

Prioress Nora joined their conference. Together, the three of them headed back toward the main building. And for the first time all day, Tally walked with confidence, her spine straightened and head held high in defiance.

Prior Adams gathered the guys and led them north, directly parallel to the western edge of the valley. The setting sun cast long shadows from the trees. Nail hadn't noticed before, but farther down, she saw glass windows and balconies set into the natural rock.

Nail's attention shifted toward the guys again. The familiar one turned around. He pointed at her.

She *knew* she knew him. But where?

With an eyebrow up and his head cocked, he mouthed one word. *"Nail?"*

It hit her. It hit her just as hard as Oracle's grand entrance. That smile. His jawline. The quizzical, easygoing look.

She had seen him before, only she hadn't. She'd seen his avatar hundreds of times. Thousands. They'd shared jokes and competitive banter over countless conversations.

Her stomach dropped. It flipped. It jumped into her throat and dropped again.

"LENNEON?!" She hadn't meant to screech his name.

Nail felt a sudden urge to jump, or hug him, or run a marathon. How? How was he here there? What were the sheer odds of that?

His smiled widened. He nodded once, waved goodbye, and jogged to catch up with the rest of the group.

Nail stood dumbfounded, totally rooted to the spot. Excitement and joy raged through her all at once. Then Lenneon rounded a group of exotic ferns and disappeared beyond the brush.

Muari approached her. "Paradise, isn't it?"

Nail shook her head in disbelief. "You have no idea. I thought my mind couldn't possibly be blown more than it was already."

Muari adjusted her sunglasses. "You were wrong."

"I was totally and completely wrong. Oh, my God. So many questions. Dragons? Magic? And then…" She fruitlessly looked in Len's direction. "And then *that?*"

"And a part of you doesn't even care about the answers, does it?"

Nail turned toward her. "You get me. That's really rare."

"I figured." Muari said. "Pick up your jaw if you have to. The rest of the group is probably staring at you."

Nail looked over. Half a dozen girls gawked at her. The beautiful blonde wore a wicked smirk with pink matte lip stain.

It had been disdain-at-first-sight for Nail. Being silently jeered and judged reminded her of being back at school. She thought of her interaction with Kim earlier that day.

Nail shook her head. That seemed like a lifetime ago. And really, it had been only hours.

The blonde smirked again and flipped her hair over her shoulder.

"Go fix your eyeliner," Nail snapped.

The girl raised one perfectly penciled eyebrow at her and turned away. But her hand rose to the corner of her eye all the same.

It was Nail's turn to smirk.

"Ladies, follow me, please," called Prioress Julia.

For a while, they headed north like Prior Adams had done. Nail harbored hopes that their dorms might be close to the guys', but Prioress Julia took a right turn, back toward Oracle's lake. Nail realized the guys' dorms were on the west side of the valley, and the girls on the east.

Her head still spun from seeing Len. She realized that wasn't his name. And he likely didn't realize Nail *was* her name.

The girls around her chatted. In the din, she *uh-huhed* to Muari, who hadn't actually said anything. Nail contemplated how things would be with Len. Would their online chemistry translate to the real world? Would they get along just like they had before?

And what if they didn't? She couldn't imagine how painfully disappointing that would be. And when you know someone that well, how do you introduce yourself to them?

She vaguely registered the sound of their footsteps echoing on a wooden bridge as they crossed over the stream.

Nail internally kicked herself for acting like a total idiot. And for looking so shocked. And most of all, for not placing his familiar face before he recognized hers.

"Careful," Muari said. "You might start steaming from the ears if you think much harder."

"Sorry," Nail replied. "I know that guy and yet I don't. You know?"

"Not at all," Muari said genuinely.

The group came to a stop. Prioress Julia faced them all. Behind her loomed a stone arch with words carved in Mandarin, Greek symbols, and Gaelic script. There was no door.

"Your dorm entrance," she said. "Roommates have been preassigned."

Nail raised her hand. Did no one else have a desire to ask questions? "Based on what?"

"Based on who Oracle thinks will be your best-suited matches."

The twin sisters turned to each other, grinning.

The stone archway led to a huge corridor that stretched left and right, decorated in a similar style to the room she'd woken up in. Couches, easy chairs, and tables adorned the space.

The center area of the room was mostly empty. Two kitchenettes capped both ends of the room. A pool table stood invitingly, balls racked and ready. Above them, chandeliers forged to look like dragon skulls illuminated the space. Huge floor-to-ceiling windows of tinted glass overlooked the valley and, in the distance, Oracle's lake.

Prioress Julia led them to a staircase opposite the entryway, the stairs carved and finished from the rock that comprised the mountain. They curved around in a giant U.

The landing opened into a giant hallway lined with half a dozen rooms, all with open wooden doors.

Prioress Julia pointed left and right. "There are bathrooms at the ends of each hallway." "There is no strict time for lights out." She frowned. "But try to keep the noise level low and be considerate of others.

"Breakfast will be at 9 tomorrow in the garden terrace. There are alarm clocks in your rooms. The island is not entirely safe, and especially not at night. Please don't break a leg or fall off a cliff."

Everyone glanced around, silently questioning if she was serious.

Prioress Julia's mouth remained a straight, serious line. "Let's start down here and work our way back."

When they reached the door numbered 6, Prioress Julia pulled out a folded sticky note and read. "Vienna?"

The beautiful blonde bounded forward.

"You'll be with Kerris."

A girl with caramel skin, brunette hair, and apparently a bubbly personality rushed forward to meet her new roommate. They hugged, giggling throughout the embrace.

Nail rolled her eyes, immediately relieved that she hadn't been paired with either of them.

"Excuse me," Vienna flashed a whitened smile, "is it okay if we tag along with the rest of the group? So we know where everyone is staying?"

Prioress Julia gave her a bored expression. "If you like."

"Thank you," she said brightly.

They walked back the way they had come.

In front of door 5, Prioress Julia consulted her sticky note. "Hazel?"

Both of the twins stepped forward. They were nearly identical—both tan with a Latin-Asian influence to their faces. Fortunately, they had different hairstyles. One of them had shorter hair that barely kissed her collarbone. The other's cascaded to the middle of her back.

"I called only for Hazel," the Prioress said with a scowl.

The twin with longer hair took a hesitant step backward.

"Hazel, you will be with Josephine."

A lithe, dark-skinned girl stepped forward. A judicious, observant look shone in her eyes. She smiled and shook Hazel's hand, introducing herself as Jo. Hazel looked back to her twin and mouthed an apology.

The long-haired twin looked confused. Jo remained with the group, and Hazel went to speak to her sister in furious whispers.

Prioress Julia stopped at room 4. "This one is empty. We've prepared it as a study space. I would ask that anyone in this room treat it as though it were a library." She sighed, nearly smiling but not quite getting there. "Respectful silence."

They moved on to door 3.

"Elsie?" said Prioress Julia.

Elsie, the smallest of the group, shuffled forward. She couldn't have been more than five feet tall, and she was painfully thin and pale. A stringy curtain of clumped blonde hair covered her face.

"You'll be paired with Maeve in room 3."

The other twin stepped forward, casting dark looks back at her sister. Maeve forced a half-smile at Elsie, who squeaked out a quiet, "Hi."

Nail glanced down the hall. "Roommates?" She smiled at Muari.

Muari frowned. "I'm not sure."

They progressed down to room 2. "Naileen, I had you paired with Tally. But as she has decided to leave the island, I suppose…" Prioress Julia looked over the group.

The twins had returned to whispering incessantly, their voices occasionally raising at each other. Hazel seemed to accept their rooming situation. Long haired Maeve did not.

"Adamuaris, I know we had slated to give you a room alone, to make your studying easier. In the interest of fairness to the others, would you be okay rooming with Naileen?"

Muari smiled. "Of course!"

"Grand. Naileen, your possessions are in Room 2. You can move them over at your convenience." Prioress Julia looked them all over. "I meant what I said. Keep. The noise. Down. The staff are over in the main building should you need anything. But some of us like to sleep with our windows open. And sound reverberates through the valley."

Everyone muttered agreement.

"Additionally, if you hear small children screaming, don't be alarmed. It's just the boars. They're nocturnal." Prioress Julia gave them a slight nod. "I bid you good night."

The group had already begun to disperse. Vienna and Kerris practically skipped back down the hallway, arm-in-arm. Jo and Elsie had returned to their rooms, but Hazel and Maeve remained in the hallway, arguing too far away for Nail to properly hear.

In the quiet, melodic tones hummed from Muari's Walkman again.

"C'mon," Muari said. "Let's go."

Nail followed her inside and shut the door behind them.

The room was unlike any dorm Nail had ever seen. It was easily quadruple in square footage, and the left and right sides were mirror images of each other.

Each had a queen size bed with a fluffy white comforter and matching pillows, a double-wide dresser, and a carved oak wardrobe. A privacy partition, complete with a full-length mirror, stood between the two wardrobes. At the far end of the room, a pair of sleek desks and chairs sat opposite each other next to a lounge area complete with two couches and a single-serve coffeemaker.

Nail stepped through, inspecting the space. The far wall had a floor-to-ceiling window on the right corner. The left side had... a garage door? It was massive and could have easily fit an entire truck if it hadn't been on the second floor. The sun had set, but Nail could still see the sizable balcony that lay beyond the door.

"For... dragons?" Nail asked.

Muari sat on the farthest bed. "Hm? What is?"

"The giant garage door?" Nail asked.

"Oh, yes. Dragon sizes are quite unpredictable, and we'll have partners before long. Not all of them will fit up the steps, I imagine."

"That makes sense." Nail idly studied the room, wondering what her dragon would look like. Excitement surged through her. "Did you see that gold-bronze one that flew over us?"

Muari scoffed. "Well, obviously not."

"What do you mean? Where were you looking?" Nail fidgeted, afraid she had missed something even more impressive.

Muari sat up straighter. "Wait, are you being serious?"

"Yeah. Did I miss something?"

"Oh, my God," Muari said. "You're *clueless*."

"I am not clueless!" Nail fired back.

But Muari had erupted into laughter. "I gathered you weren't very observant. But that is just... It's too *funny* to be insensitive." She dissolved into giggles again.

Heat rose to Nails cheeks. "What's so funny? I am *not* unobservant."

She laughed harder. "You're so lucky I have a good sense of humor."

Nail heard paper on stone and looked toward the door. Someone had slipped a note under it. "Just tell me, then!"

Muari had to force her laughter to stop. She tapped the frame of her sunglasses with a fingernail. "I didn't see anything, Nail. I've *never* seen anything. Ever. I'm blind."

CHAPTER 5

Muari couldn't hold her laughter in any longer. She rolled onto the bed, laying on her side and laughing so hard that she began to cough and sob from it.

More heat hit Nail's cheeks. She turned away so Muari couldn't see her embarrassment. Then she realized how utterly stupid that was.

She crouched and picked the note up from the floor, just to give her a chance to pause and run the entire evening through her head. She couldn't recall if she had already made more insensitive remarks.

Nail didn't excel at social rules. She didn't expect this to be any different.

She stood again, note in-hand. Muari still lay on the bed, but her laughter had calmed down.

"I'm sorry," Nail said stiffly. She didn't appreciate Muari's amusement at her mistake. "I didn't mean to… to be an ass."

"You weren't an ass," Muari insisted. "Being blind is usually the first thing that sighted people notice about me. You spent all evening with me and you didn't have a clue."

"Yeah," said Nail. "Because I'm an ass."

"No, you're not," Muari said. "Look, just keep treating me like I'm your friend. Like I'm anybody else. I can get around just fine."

Nail looked at her face. How could she have not realized the purpose of the sunglasses? She still wasn't convinced of her own not-an-ass status.

"You *are* my friend. I'll try to not be insensitive. Will you tell me if I am? Or if I just... do something I didn't know I wasn't supposed to do?"

"Of course I will," Muari said. "Now open the note and read it."

Nail looked at her with open suspicion. "How can you know about that?"

"I told you. I have excellent hearing. And what else could it be? A power bill?"

Nail looked down at the pink paper in her hands. It was folded into an origami heart and addressed to "Naileen & Adamuaris" in perfect cursive with gold ink. Nail flipped it over. It read:

You are cordially invited
to a
Meet & Greet
in Room #4
at 8:45pm
hosted by Vienna and Kerris

Nail read the note aloud. Muari double-tapped her watch. A computerized female voice read out the time.

"8:32pm," it said.

"A meet and greet?" Nail whined. "We've met. We've greeted. What more does she want? This sounds like torture."

"No." Muari sat up in her bed. "It'll be fun. We can get to know everyone."

Nail grumbled but didn't argue it further. "Fine. But I won't have fun."

NAIL AND MUARI SAT ON THE BALCONY OF ROOM 4 WITH THE SIX other girls. Vienna, the preppy, perky blonde, wore a different dress than she had at dinner. It reminded Nail to check room 2 for her own belongings—whatever that meant. It wasn't like she had packed a suitcase.

Despite Prioress Julia having left only an hour prior, Vienna and Kerris had set up chairs, string lights, tables, crepe streamers with helium balloons, and somehow, hors d'oeuvres with drinks, all on the balcony. Pitchers of passion fruit juice and water sat atop a table along with an assortment of fruits, crackers, cheeses, and thinly sliced meats.

Maybe it had all been in the kitchenettes in the main area? Nail didn't know. And she wasn't hungry.

Vienna stood, and the already quiet conversation died down.

"I just wanted to say thank you to everyone for coming on short notice. And, of course, a huge thank you to Kerris for helping me put this little gathering together. I'm sure we'll all get to know each other incredibly well. I'd like to think we've just been invited to the most exclusive sorority in the world. Congratulations to everyone!"

She beamed down at them all. A couple of the girls clapped feebly. Nail ground her teeth while restraining her desire to roll her eyes.

For once, Vienna's smile faded. "I would also like to take a moment to respect Tally. I think we all knew that she was really struggling to cope with this change. I'd like to ask that we have a moment of silence in her memory, and send good vibes to her for a speedy recovery."

Vienna bowed her head as though praying and opened her palms toward the stars. Nail looked around. Everyone except Kerris—who was the perfect shadow of Vienna's posturing—exchanged glances. Someone shrugged, and the shrug rippled through the group. Most of them at least closed their eyes.

Nail lowered her chin slightly but kept her eyes open.

She couldn't understand Tally's total aversion to the island. Would she calm down in a day or a week and regret her decision to leave? Was it possible to return? How could anyone *know* dragons existed and live happily apart from them?

You couldn't drag me away from the island. Not for anything.

Vienna cleared her throat with a polite *ah-hem.* "Now then, should we start out with how—"

A chorus of loud, deep shouting resounded through the valley, followed by laughter and howling.

"Ladies!"

"Hey, ladies!"

"C'mon out, girls!"

They all turned west. Flashlight beams moved through the trees.

"The boys!" said Hazel and Maeve in perfect unison.

Elsie somehow curled farther into herself.

"Oh," said Vienna. "Well, we're not going to invite them up here, are we?" She looked over to a visibly uncomfortable Elsie. "This is a girls-only space. They have us separated by sex for a *reason*, after all."

Elsie relaxed her arms, but only a little.

Nail looked at her. *If we lose another one, it'll be Elsie next.*

Jo shrugged. "I didn't hear any rules against it."

Kerris tugged on Vienna's dress. "Let's go down to them."

Vienna glanced at her well-prepared party and frowned. "Well, I suppose. If that's what the group wants to do?"

Nail rolled her eyes. It was a group of teenage girls. Of course that's what they wanted to do.

Plus, Len would be down there.

Double-plus, it got Nail away from this "sorority" setting.

Triple-plus, it would ruin Vienna's plans.

"Yeah, I think it is," Nail said with feigned concern.

Jo smirked at her. "Well, we all know who *you* want to see."

The girls giggled, except for Vienna.

Heat rose to Nail's cheeks. She was glad the sun had set.

Vienna sat and leaned over her knees, revealing ample cleavage down the front of her dress. Nail already despised her, but she still found Vienna's posture distracting.

Vienna sighed in defeat. "Okay, but before we go, we've all been dying to know what that was about, Naileen."

"It's Nail," she said. "Naileen is an obnoxious name."

Vienna smiled and nodded. "Of course. Nail. Please, give us a little gossip?"

The boys continued shouting from down in the valley. "Meet us at the fire pit!"

"C'mon, we're waiting!"

Nail cleared her throat, and her hands fidgeted in her lap. She locked eyes with the person across from her, Jo.

"Let her keep her secrets," Jo said as she stood, waving her hand to brush away Vienna's question. "This was a meet and greet, not an inquisition. Or was my invitation wrong?" She looked pointedly at Vienna.

Vienna noticeably bristled and pouted, but for only a flash of a second. She relented with a smile that was still obnoxious at night.

"Of course. We're all friends here." Vienna held up a finger. "But we need to be smart about this. We don't really know any of those guys. Everyone should have flashlights in their rooms. And I think it would be best if we employ a buddy system. Roomies, stick with each other. It's our first night. Like Prioress Julia said, we don't want anyone to wander off and get lost—or *worse*."

Jo scoffed. "Wild boars." The guys continued to holler, too far away for any single word to be picked out from the echoing noise. "That was probably a metaphor."

Nail hated how painfully practical Vienna was. But she also agreed with her.

"Let's all meet down in the common room in five minutes, yeah?" said Kerris.

The group split up. Nail waited for Muari in their room.

"I can't find any flashlights in here," Nail said as Muari entered.

Muari laughed. "Duh. You weren't supposed to be in here. All your stuff is in room 2. And obviously I don't need one."

"Oh. Right. Sorry."

"I find your self-absorption to be somewhat endearing and entirely entertaining."

"Yeah, right." Nail paused and watched Muari tuck neon hair behind her ear. She admired her unconventional highlights. "Okay, I have to ask about your hair. I mean, you can't see it, so what's the point?"

Muari tilted her head. "I've never seen color, obviously. But I know that some colors have meanings. Associations and stuff."

"Sure," Nail said.

"I like the idea of teal. Everyone describes it as calm and pleasing. Like the waters of a lake. Lime is sort of an electric thing. It's alive and vibrant. And fuchsia, it's a girl color. Feminine but with a kick."

She paused again.

"A lot of people—you not included, obviously—see my sunglasses and immediately put me into this helpless, deformed, deprived category in their heads. I'm *the blind girl*. For people who are sighted, you're all speaking this totally silent language all of the time. Body language and facial expressions and clothing style and talking with your hands. Well, I can't stop people from judging me. But with these, I get to speak a little bit of that language."

Nail considered this. She was certainly guilty of judging books by their covers. "So you're doing it for everybody else?"

"Hell no," Muari said. "I do it for me, to help everybody else realize you don't need sight to be awesome. And anyway, don't *you* need a flashlight?"

"Yeah. Are you ready?"

Muari opened her nightstand, retrieving a thick white stick, roughly the length of her forearm. She tucked it under her left arm and removed the toning box from the hip pocket of her jeans.

"I'm ready," she said.

As they headed over to room 2, Nail heard footsteps excitedly trotting down the stairs to the common room below.

Room 2 was almost identical to room 1, but there were a few more personal touches on the walls. A Nessie poster hung behind one of the beds. On the desk sat books on all kind of topics—everything from biochemistry to financial planning—and a few cryptozoology tomes as well. Some of them looked downright ancient.

She opened a desk drawer and found stickers from some of her favorite bands, as well her preferred brand of hair tie. Inside the dresser were socks and underwear of her size and even the same deodorant she used at home.

"Creepy," Nail muttered to herself.

New clothes—size tags still attached—filled the wardrobe. There were casual tops, some graphic tees, jeans, yoga pants, and two dresses. There was a pair of hiking boots and a pair of Converse shoes, custom-done in blue, purple, and pink.

That's a nice touch, Nail thought, continuing her search for a flashlight.

"Does night time just suck for you?" Muari asked, sitting on the bed beneath the Nessie poster. "I mean, personally. Do you find it frustrating?"

Nail finally found a flashlight on top of the desk. Their five minutes were up. She'd have to come back for the rest of her stuff later. "Frustrating in what way?"

"I mean, you basically lose one of your senses half of time and have to rely on stuff like flashlights to get around. Isn't that… annoying?"

"I dunno," Nail said, flicking the flashlight on and off to test it. "I never thought about it that way."

Down in the common room, all of the other girls were waiting. A few of them had changed clothes. Nail tugged at the corner of her Area 51 t-shirt, wondering if she should've changed while she had the chance.

Someone switched on a flashlight, and the rest followed suit. They headed out into the night.

Muari whipped out her stick, and it lengthened into a cane. "Mind if I take your arm?" she asked Nail in a low voice.

Nail nudged her right elbow into Muari's waiting left hand. "Not at all."

The guys had told them to meet at the fire pit. Nail vaguely remembered passing it on their way to dais, but the valley looked different at night. They all followed the noises, and Muari had no trouble pointing them in the fastest direction.

They moved west of the stream, crossing a different bridge than before. Muari turned them south of Oracle's lake. Orange light spilled out from behind a circular group of tall, fronded ferns. A stone-and-gravel path split the greenery, leading the way inside. Long shadows extended within the circle, moving in the light of a fire.

The girls paused before entering. Meeting the guys was inevitable, but it seemed no one wanted to be the first to enter.

Vienna stepped up with Kerris close behind. "Shall we, ladies?

She tossed back a curtain of hair and strode confidently into the glowing light. She was met with raucous cheers and her own greeting of a prolonged "Hey!"

Nail shrugged at Muari. "Here goes nothing."

They walked hand-in-elbow toward the path.

"How can you tell if a guy is hot?" Nail asked quietly.

"Easy," Muari replied. "I listen to the pitch of his voice, and how he talks to others, and then check him for arm hair. Thinking I'm deaf or treating me like I'm mentally stunted are immediate deal-breakers. Bonus points if he laughs at my blind jokes without hesitation. That's my definition of hot."

"Same," Nail said with a laugh.

The guys cheered when the girls entered the fire pit circle. Outdoor couches, some large enough for eight and others meant for only two, sat all around them, all facing the center. Leafy, red shrubs grew between some of the sections, giving the illusion of privacy.

There were about as many guys as there were girls.

Nail looked for the only one that mattered to her.

Lenneon stood on the opposite side, clutching a blue can of soda. He smiled, big and broad when he saw her. She returned it.

Muari leaned in. "Spotted him yet?"

"Yep."

"Oh, good. I'm gonna go shake hands and check for arm hair. Go meet your online boyfriend."

Nail turned to refute the comment, but Muari had already walked away, tapping her cane as she went. Sheepishly, Nail turned back to face Lenneon. He pointed to a couch for two, tilting his head to make it a question.

Her stomach flipped. Sweat coated her hands. She nodded twice.

She tried casually wiping the sweat onto her jeans. Partially effective. She walked over. With each step, she looked everywhere except at him.

When she finally arrived at her destination, she fought the impulse to run.

"So," he said. "No Valnax for us, huh?"

Ohhh, his voice was deep and smooth. She looked at him.

Len had thick, dark hair and arm muscles that looked naturally lean —not like those earned through hours spent in a gym. He wore dark shorts and a distressed t-shirt that stretched over his pecs and biceps. He sat with his right ankle resting over his left knee, left arm draped casually across the back of the couch.

Nail sank into the cushion next to him. She could feel other people looking at them. She really, really didn't care.

"Funny thing," she replied. "When you didn't reply, I got worried that you'd been kidnapped."

He laughed. It was a hearty, honest sound. He stretched out his right hand. "I'm Jace."

A much better name than Len. She quickly tried to re-wipe her palm before shaking his hand. "Nail."

"So that's a real name, huh? Interesting."

She nodded. "Lenneon isn't even similar to Jace. Where did that come from?"

He shifted to better face her and she did the same. "When I first downloaded the game, I was at a Mom and Pop bookstore."

He reads, she thought. *Oh, thank God. He reads.*

"They have records, too. And a neon John Lennon in the window. Hence, Lenneon."

She grinned at him. "That makes sense."

A lull lingered between them.

Nail had feared it would be like this. Some friendships blossomed in the delayed realm of online messaging, where words could be considered and edited for minutes. But in real life, those conversations had to happen at a normal, instant pace with silent, fluent body language.

For a moment, she feared Jace would find her much less intelligent now. Google was no longer one tap of the home screen away.

Nail looked around at the group. All of the girls milled about with the guys. Groups of four were the most common.

One lanky guy fit every stereotype of the word "nerd." The Indian kid with red-rimmed glasses and overly gelled hair talked to the Polynesian guy with tattoos around his big biceps. The twins were talking with a Hispanic guy and a thin, blonde guy with a wispy mustache.

Muari was engaged in conversation with a strawberry-haired guy who lacked noticeable arm hair but who was definitely making her laugh.

Nail struggled for something to say. "Did you get a good roommate?"

Jace pointed to the Polynesian guy. "Dax. He's talking with Jagdesh." He settled a little deeper into the cushions. "So, who's yours?"

Nail pointed. "The girl with the badass hair."

"The one with Rorik?"

Nail's smiled. Rorik was a good name.

Jace nodded in thought. "Badass, indeed. I like her."

Nail raised an eyebrow at him. "Like her? You don't even know her."

He shrugged. "Don't have to. Clearly you guys are friends. You were practically joined at the hip all evening." He leaned closer and lowered his voice to a mock whisper. "Does she know you kept pointing at things?"

"God, I hope not. But probably." Nail shot him a stern look and topped it with a mischievous smile. "Were you staring at me today?"

"A little."

"Creeper."

"Totally."

Nail loved his smile. It wasn't over-whitened like Vienna's. And despite his undeniable bulk, he seemed incredibly relaxed. Something about him reminded her of a giant dog that didn't realize it was too large to be a lap companion.

She cleared her throat. "So, obviously you figured it out before I did."

He nodded. "Yup."

"How quickly? What gave me away?"

"I knew it back in the initiation room. You kept talking, remember? I'm betting I got a good look at you before you got a good one at me."

"So it was my face, then?"

He half-shrugged and shook his head. "That didn't hurt. But I figured it out when you started interrupting with all those questions. Everyone else was too shocked to speak. But you've always leaped right into danger without looking. It used to drive Skrell insane."

Nail blushed at the compliment and hoped the light of the fire wasn't bright enough to reveal it. "You're welcome for all that help with the Valnax fight, by the way."

He huffed. "Yeah. Lot of good all that prep did, huh? But giving up virtual dragons for real ones? I'll take that trade any day."

Nail agreed. "Okay, so…" She turned toward him more, leaning in closer. "Skrell sent me a message when I was on my way to the fight. You guys hadn't been posting and so…"

"Yeah, yeah, yeah!" he agreed. "I was thinking the same way. They must have some sort of connection with that app. Used it to find some of us."

"But Skrell isn't here, is he?" She looked around the group and pointed to the lanky nerd who had somehow managed to trap Vienna in conversation. "I mean, if he is, that's gotta be him."

Jace laughed. "No, that's Quinn. I don't think Skrell is here. The rest of the group got picked up, though."

"Seriously?" She scanned everyone again, trying to identify the other two.

Jace pointed to a Hispanic guy who was using his hands as much as his mouth to talk to Jo. "That's Rodrigo, AKA Igo, AKA 'EgoManiac1.'"

"Seriously?" Nail said. "What about 'KeepingScoreMore?'"

Jace crossed his arms and raised one eyebrow. "You mean Tally?"

Nail opened her mouth to speak but found nothing to say.

"That was her," Jace said. "Remember all those times she would talk about how we were all her closest friends and that relationships in the 'real world' made her so uncomfortable?"

Nail nodded slowly. "She was always so resistant to do any fights that were too far from her house. I assumed she didn't live in a super safe neighborhood but… jeez. That makes so much sense."

Nail felt a new sense of pity for Tally. She hadn't just been some girl who couldn't handle the change. She'd been her friend.

Nail paused, feeling guilty. "She was supposed to be my roommate."

Jace stretched again, his arm still laying across the back of the couch. His hand didn't touch Nail, but she was painfully aware of its proximity. "Makes sense. I wonder if all of the roomies here have some sort of connection that they're not aware of yet."

Nail considered it. "The twins aren't rooming together."

"Really?" Jace said. "Well, go figure on that."

"At least Skrell and Tally will have each other, in a sense."

Before Jace could reply, Vienna flounced over to interrupt their conversation.

"Hi!" she said brightly, smiling down at Jace. "I'm Vienna. And you are…?" She reached out, her immaculately manicured nails gleaming.

He leaned forward politely and shook hands with Vienna. "Jace." She cocked her head to the side like it was the single most interesting word she had ever heard. "Oooh, such a strong name. It fits you." Vienna's gaze crawled up and down Jace's muscled arms. She turned her head toward Nail. "Muari was asking for you."

"Oh. Okay." She turned back to Jace. "I'll be back in a minute."

Nail hated to leave him. Even worse, she was leaving him with Vienna.

He winked at her, and her stomach fluttered up into her lungs. "Make sure you are."

Vienna's perfume assaulted the air as she practically floated down onto the sofa. Nail caught part of Vienna's question as she left for Muari. "So what's the story behind arms like…"

Annoyance boiled through every vein in Nail's body. *That girl.*

She might come off as a concerned do-gooder, party planning, sorority queen, but Nail knew better. She was a vanilla cupcake with a mercury-and-thumbtack filling.

Muari was still deep in conversation with strawberry-haired Rorik.

Nail placed a hand on her wrist, and Muari nearly jumped out of her skin.

"Relax," Nail said defensively. "It's just me."

Muari frowned. "Pro-tip: don't touch me unannounced. I can't tell who you are, especially with all this noise. Speak first, okay?"

Nail hated being ignorant. "Yeah, of course. Sorry. You wanted to talk to me?"

"Uh, no?" Muari said. "But since you're here, Nail, this is Rorik. Rorik, this is my roomie, Nail."

"You didn't?" Nail asked.

"Not especially," Muari said, confused.

Rorik extended Nail a greeting, but she wasn't listening.

Her gaze shot back to Jace.

Vienna had one hand on his thigh and the other on his bicep.

You sneaky little bitch.

CHAPTER 6

Nail sat on a four-person couch plotting painful ways to murder Vienna. Disengaged from Muari and Rorik's conversation, she watched as the action unfolded around her.

Most people were having a good time, just conversing. Hazel and Maeve sat in opposite corners. Passing the point of quiet arguments half an hour earlier, they each stood with their arms folded, determined to not be the one to cave in. Across the circle, Vienna still had Jace's attention all wrapped up and winding tighter around her glittery pinky finger.

This is war.

Two of the guys, Igo and the blonde guy with the wispy mustache, had been egging each other on all night, howling and laughing at the dares they came up with.

"That's Igo and Luca," Nail overheard Rorik saying.

Their current stunt was to see who could jump over the flames the most times without catching on fire.

A few of the others stopped to watch their show of impressive stupidity. The entire group rioted with laughter as the canvas on Luca's shoes began to smoke and burn. He ripped the burning shoe away from his foot and bolted toward the ocean.

Igo was practically rolling on the ground, laughing.

Maybe I could trip her into the fire pit.

"Hey," Luca called out from the beach. "Who's up for a midnight swim?"

The group turned to whomever they were currently paired up with, and most of them nodded in agreement.

Muari muttered to Nail. "I don't think I'm up for swimming."

Nail nodded. "Me neither."

Although drowning Vienna would look more like an accident....

As everyone rushed out to meet Luca down at the beach, only Elsie and Maeve remained behind. Jace had disappeared. Maybe he'd expected Nail would come down to the beach.

Or maybe he just didn't care.

It was a quiet walk back to their dorms.

Nail stopped into Room 2 to grab something to sleep in. When Nail got back, Muari was already tucked in for the night.

Nail slipped into her pajamas, procrastinating her shower until morning. The springs in her mattress squeaked quietly as she sank into the bed and programmed her alarm clock.

Through the open window, muffled voices carried from the beach. Noise really did echo up the valley. And though they weren't much louder than the wind, it was enough to keep Nail awake until the late hours of the night.

In the morning, her alarm went off at 8:00am. With a flailing gesture, Nail smacked the noise to a stop.

She stumbled out the door and found a notice taped to it. She brought it back into the room and read it aloud. "Breakfast is from 9 to 10. And there's some sort of orientation or tour happening afterward. We're supposed to wear hiking shoes."

Muari rolled over and grumbled an acknowledgment.

"Do you want help with anything?" Nail asked, hoping that the answer was no.

With her back to Nail, Muari raised an arm and flapped her hand to shoo Nail away. "You're not my dog."

From Room 2, Nail gathered all the stuff she would need to get ready.

The amalgamation of items perplexed her. She found her favorite body wash and jeans there, both brand new. But the makeup brand was more expensive than what she could have afforded, as were the sunglasses and yoga pants in the wardrobe.

A tablet sat charging on the desk next than island guidebook. Nail took the tablet with her. In the drawers, she found an assortment of cryptozoology t-shirts, tank tops, socks, and other necessities. They all fit perfectly with Nail's style. She wondered if Steven had gotten access to their online wish-lists.

Nail shifted her weight at the thought.

Something about Steven seemed just a bit... off. He wasn't the oldest of the staff that she'd seen. What had happened to make him the Lumen Society leader? And was kidnapping-recruitment his idea or a policy put into place before his leadership?

Nail showered and got ready. Her path crossed occasionally with Muari, Elsie, and Maeve. Elsie had freshly showered but didn't bother with makeup. Maeve took extra care to make sure her waist-length hair was pin-straight. Nail and Muari headed for breakfast shortly before 9:30.

The morning air still felt cool from the night before, but the breeze was beginning to warm up. The sunshine warmed her skin. Nail enjoyed the variety of fruit-bearing trees mixing their scents with endless flowers.

Somewhere, a hummingbug sang a few verses from *The Final Countdown* on repeat. Small, light-blue birds tweeted and darted through the branches, and several times Nail caught glimpses of green parrots hopping along in the grasses. Nail paused at a grove with colorful trunks. From a distance, she thought they had been painted. But up close she saw that it was actually the bark itself, peeling away in rainbow hues.

At breakfast, Nail saw Jace already there, sitting at a four-person table with Vienna and Kerris. He motioned for her to come over.

Nail frowned and stuck with Muari.

They sat at the end of a long table. On the opposite end, Igo and Luca were laughing and retelling the stories of everything that had happened out in the ocean. After a quick glance around, Nail was happy to see no one had drowned.

She heard Vienna and Kerris laughing.

Well, mostly happy that no one drowned.

A few of the dragons milled about through breakfast. They didn't make a grand entrance like they had the night before. But their presence stopped all conversation as everyone's attention turned toward them.

Some dragons seemed to revel in it, most especially the fae dragons. They flitted from table to table, happily conversing and accepting bits of everyone's breakfast.

Undeniable wonderment accompanied the dragons. Some staff members wandered in and out of their dining area, silently assessing the new class and ignoring the dragons. Nail wondered if she would ever become numb to the dragons' presence.

Nail propped up her left elbow on the table, her hand relaxed as she ate. Aenu landed on her index finger. The tiny dragon felt lighter than a lizard, all smooth scales and miniature claws.

Aenu's wings flapped, casting rainbows of light farther than what seemed possible.

She smiled. "Hello, you."

Aenu looked up at her and winked. But when a survey of Nail's breakfast did not prove satisfactory, the fae dragon flitted off to another table.

After breakfast, everyone filtered outside the terrace, hanging around in loose groups. Steven was nowhere to be seen. Nail decided to take her own exploratory walk.

She wandered closer to the main building. Veering west, she spotted a large stone door set into the natural rock. It was ornately carved but adorned with a language Nail didn't recognize. She ran her hands over the stone and found no handle, knob, or any other way to open it. She pushed on the cool stone, but it didn't budge.

"It takes magic to open it," said a voice behind her.

Nail turned to find Elsie there, her eyes wide, quite possibly shocked by her own voice.

"Oh," said Nail. "Well, I don't have any of that."

Nail reintroduced herself and extended a handshake. Elsie returned it, barely squeezing with her thin thumb and only two fingers.

"Not yet," Elsie said. "But we all will soon enough."

Nail cocked her head.

"You didn't read the guidebook yet?" asked Elsie.

"No."

"Oh. Well, I suppose they'll go over it all today anyway."

"That makes sense," Nail said, feigning confidence. "I bet you do a lot of reading. You don't seem like the social-butterfly-making-friends type."

Elsie blushed and looked down at the toes of her Mary Jane shoes. "Thanks for pointing that out."

But before Nail could correct the offense, Elsie rushed back toward the group.

Nail sighed. She'd meant that *she* wasn't the social-butterfly-making-friends type *either*.

She followed the same trail back toward the dining terrace, maintaining a good distance behind Elsie.

It looked like everyone had finished their breakfast. Prioress Nora stood with Muari under a tree with yellow blossoms. Jace still hung around with Vienna and Kerris, now joined by Igo and Luca.

Nail joined Muari.

Prioress Nora extended a hand to Nail.

Nail shook it. The prioress's handshake was firm but not dominating. "Nice to see you," her voice wavered slightly with uncertainty.

"You too," Nora said. "You guys will be going on a hike today. But since it will be a bit precarious for Muari to climb, I'll be giving her a hand with getting around the island."

A loud voice cleared his throat, pulling Nail's attention away.

Steven Parson stood at the terrace entry with Rankor at his side. The dragon's scales were much larger than most. Their size and color reminded Nail of a knight's armor. They bore a grainy texture, a stark contrast to the shimmering fae dragons.

Steven made brief eye contact with everyone. "Class of Metal Dragons, I would like to formally introduce you to Rankor. Rankor is one of the most distinguished and educated dragons on the island. Ve will be your educator on our hike today."

Nail stumbled over the odd word. Had Steven said "ve?"

Rankor surveyed the group, the dragon's intimidating gaze occasionally lingering slightly too long.

Nail tried not to shrink away from it.

Just like Oracle, Nail heard Rankor's voice in her mind. It resounded in a chorus of deep notes, like someone playing on a piano one octave too low to be melodious. A pleasant lilt lined the dragon's voice.

"We will start with the basics," Rankor said, *"because that is the most logical place to begin. The full history of everything we cover today is available on your tablets. Additional in-depth reading can be found in each of your rooms, both in the guidebook and in* The Draconic and Sapien Documentarium.

"There are eight stages. You have all passed the first stage by electing to stay and be bound to the magic of the Draconian and Anthro treaty." Rankor paused. *"You are currently in the second, general education. Thirdly, you will each be paired with a dragon egg."*

Rankor paced around the various small groups, weaving around students. *"Next, after self-reflection, the egg will hatch. The time it takes for the egg to hatch is different for every pairing. You and your new partner will bond.*

"Sometime during this bonding process, your unique magical abilities will manifest. You will then spend as much time as needed to master the full breadth of these gifts. And lastly, when you are ready, you will find your purpose."

Rankor paused, apparently waiting to see if anyone had questions. Nearly every group erupted into low whispering, speculating on what sort of dragon they'd pair with, and what their magical gift would be.

"Today, we will focus on your general knowledge of the physical traits of dragons. We are a diverse species with as many similarities as differences. One of the most important similarities we share is hermaphroditic reproduction. Meaning, we self-reproduce."

A murmur of chuckling softly rippled through the group of teens. Rankor ignored the interruption.

"We are all both male and female. Yet, the single label of one or the other is not appropriate. You will need to learn and practice gender-neutral pronouns. I am aware that to most of you, my voice and physical traits read as 'male.' But I am not. You will learn the ve/ver/vis pronouns. The draconian society has used these for millennia, and we won't be reversing that today."

Rankor ran through a list of examples with the pronouns.

> He/she flew high | Ve flew high
> Go talk to him/her | Go talk to ver
> His/her scales are blue | Vis scales are blue
> The prey is his/hers | The prey is vis
> He/she did it by himself/herself | Ve did it by verself

"Your first assignment is to write a 1,000-word essay on what you think would be your most ideal and least ideal dragon pairing as well as what you think your joined purpose could be. You must use each of the pronouns a minimum of five times in this essay. It is due by midnight tomorrow."

The class groaned collectively at the assignment.

"You can dislike it, but if you call a wyvern 'he,' you may very well find yourself missing crucial limbs." Rankor's eyes narrowed. *"Unlike creatures you've studied in lesser classes, dragons are completely unique in this reproduc-*

tive quality. Within all of us resides the ability to reproduce alone and diversely. We all contain the necessary genetic information to create nearly any classification of dragon."

Rankor straightened vis spine and vis pewter scales shifted in a ripple. *"I myself have laid three eggs. Although I am what you would call a drake—possessing four legs and no wings—my eggs could yield a wyvern, a hydra, an English dragon, or any other classification. The single exception is fae dragons. They are more like cousins than true kin, but they are dragons nonetheless."*

"Now for the fun part," Steven said with a smile. "A tour of the island, and introduction to other Lumen dragons!"

"Follow me," Rankor said.

"That's our cue," Prioress Nora said. She gently wrapped fingers around Muari's wrist.

Muari smiled, sunlight glaring off her glasses. "See ya!"

Prioress Nora shut her eyes. Her nose scrunched up in concentration. With a slight *pop*, they both disappeared. Nail staggered backward a step.

Rankor and Steven led the group out behind the dining terrace. Beyond a grove of fruit trees, they came to a hiking trail that wound up the north-western side of the ravine. Grass and bushes grew along the stamped-down red-and-brown rock. The smell of earth and moss permeated the air.

The trail was narrow, allowing them to walk only one or two people abreast. Nail paused halfway up the climb. The entire valley was visible, including the white sand beach and calm ocean beyond.

The winding climb took at least half an hour in an almost single-file line. At the top, Nail looked out over the rest of the island. They stood on a higher elevation than the dais. She followed the line of the ridge extending in its direction.

The valley splayed out to her left. To her right, a barn and crops were visible in the distance, and a shimmering stream sliced the farmland in half.

She turned around. Beyond the farm lay a densely green forest, its trees growing around the base of an old volcano. The high-pitched chatter of birds echoed up to them. Far to her right and beyond the valley loomed an even taller volcano. Steam and smoke rose from where the island met the sea. South of the active volcano and east of the valley were sprawling grasslands, sparsely dotted with tall, thin trees.

She spun slowly once, taking in the entire paradise. The island was much smaller than she'd imagined. It couldn't have been more than four or five miles wide.

Rankor and Steven continued north toward a rocky crag. Ten minutes later, they met Prioress Nora and Muari in front of a maze of rock and stone. Flowers and hardy vines adorned its natural pillars, some easily twenty feet tall. A dry wind had picked up and whipped against them.

Rankor turned vis back to the maze. Vis baritone voice filled her thoughts once more.

"The island has diverse habitats and inhabitants. Thanks to the dry wind and elevation, wyverns tend to prefer this area. Wyverns have one set of rear legs and a pair of wings with three to five claws at the second joint. These claws function well for hunting and have the dexterity of forelegs for walking."

The wind picked up. Nail fought to keep her hair tucked behind her ears but to no avail.

Rankor turned vis thick neck toward the maze. After a momentary pause, a vicious roar broke over them, echoing strangely through the rock.

A massive dragon burst out from within the maze. Ve quickly caught the wind and soared above them, spiraling through the air. Nail stared at the wyvern in awe. Gold flecks accented vis brown body, and marbled gold-and-bronze wings allowed for splotches of sunlight to pass through.

The dragon landed near Steven. Ve looked down at them, towering over even the tallest pillars. Spiked scales lined vis eyes and maw, and long pointed horns grew from vis brow like a crown.

The class watched ver in awed silence. The dragon shifted vis weight, sending refracted light off vis golden scales.

Rankor spoke again. *"This is Aurumis. Ve was laid by a hydra dragon. Aurumis has a very special gift."*

Aurumis nodded to Rankor and shut vis eyes. The smaller scales of vis brow furrowed in concentration.

The whipping wind halted. The air was calm, quiet. Then the wind rushed back in intentional bursts, like the beat of a song. It ceased once more for a long moment.

Aurumis smiled with long pointed teeth, and a silken, jazzy voice filled Nail's mind. *"Brace yourselves, small ones."*

With an undeniable force, wind crashed over them. Nail struggled to keep her feet from slipping over the stony ground, her entire body acting like a sail against the assault. It lasted for only a moment until Aurumis released vis control.

Aurumis nodded first to Steven then to Rankor. Ve contracted vis body like a cat about to pounce and launched high into the air. Vis massive wings outstretched, ve caught the wind, and Aurumis disappeared into the crag maze once more.

"Next, we head to the rainforest."

Rankor led the way back toward the trail they'd hiked up. Nail looked for Prioress Nora and Muari, but they had already disappeared. This time, Rankor and Steven turned right, heading down the opposite side of the slope. The teens followed.

The new trail resembled the first, but greenery grew more abundantly on that side of the ridge, and the heavy air hung sticky with humidity. The slick, overgrown path slowed their descent.

Nail found the uneven rock and dirt more difficult to traverse going down rather than up. Going up, there was little danger of overexerting herself and going too fast. Going down, there was a much greater risk of misstep. One false footfall could've sent her slipping down the path and careening over a cliff.

Several times, Nail watched as Vienna "slipped" into Jace, steadying herself against his shoulders. Nail gritted her teeth but kept her focus on navigating the slope.

The bottom of the trail emptied into a moderate rainforest, dense and wildly green. The trees grew so tall that from where they stood on the thick grass, the tip of the old volcano was no longer visible.

Steven and Rankor continued on. Mist collected on the leafy canopies above and fell like a passing rain shower as they walked. The sound of crunching leaves and darting forest creatures cracked and whispered all around them. Nail caught sight of the odd, hopping green birds she'd seen before breakfast.

"Those are kakapo," Elsie said to Jo.

Jo only tilted her head as a reply.

"They're flightless owl parrots," Elsie explained. "Native to New Zealand. It's in the guidebook. They help keep the insect population at bay and…" Elsie paused, fidgeting with her hands. "They're easy prey for young dragons."

Nail nodded along with the conversation, wishing that Muari was with her. Or that Jace wasn't so deeply ensnared by Vienna's acrylic grasp.

At last, they came to the bank of a creek. The waterway looked shallow, and it curved out of sight not far from where they stood. Tree limbs stretched over the divide, and vines dipped into the water.

Prioress Nora and Muari stood on the grass, away from the edge of the riverbank.

Nail approached her. "You're definitely getting this tour the easy way."

Muari scoffed. She'd worn new sunglasses that day. Encrusted with fake gems, they would've shimmered if it weren't for the dense canopy overhead. "More like the boring way. We get to where you're headed and then have to wait for you all to take the long way."

"You wouldn't want to do the hiking trails anyway," Nail said, looking down at her muddy boots, already caked with a layer of red dirt and mud. "*I don't want to do the hiking trails.*"

Muari smirked. "Sounds like a lot of work."

"And dirt," Nail added.

The sound of splashing water caught Nail's attention.

Rankor continued vis lesson. "*The rainforest is home to many, including a sizable population of nocturnal boar. Exploring the rainforest on your own is not advised. More than one new Lumen member has been gored to death in our history.*"

The splashing grew louder. The class collectively turned to look in the direction of the noise.

Lumbering down the creek on four powerful legs, a green-and-brown dragon appeared. At first, Nail thought it was another drake like Rankor. But as the dragon came closer, more than one serpentine neck and head came into view—four in total.

"*This is Ivisus,*" Rankor spoke. "*Ve is one of the oldest hydra dragons on the island.*"

Ivisus's long, thick tail dragged through the water as ve approached. The four heads swayed, looking over the class.

Fully drawn up, the dragon stood easily twelve feet tall. Snakelike tongues flicked out of vis mouths at random. The green of vis scales blended perfectly with the forest. Light streamed intermittently onto the water, and shimmers of brown reflected off vis hide.

Nail noticed an old wound, scarred over on its chest and near the base of the hydra's necks. It was round but not as wide as the rest of the necks.

Rankor turned to face the massive hydra. "*The newest Lumen class would like to see your gift, Ivisus.*"

Eight eyes of various colors squinted down at the group. All four of the hydra's heads nodded once. A chorus of noise filled Nail's mind. Four separate and clear voices spoke, together sounding like the keys of a grand piano, all working to build one chord.

But there was a note missing, lending a dissonant tone to the voice, as though the middle note had been struck from the song. *"That will be easy/Revel at our might/Our gift is perfection/ How entertaining for them."*

Nail found the effect of their voices dizzying. Clearly, sharing one body did not mean they shared one mind.

Four sets of eyes closed. Vis necks began to sway in rhythm, and Nail heard a low-pitched hum reverberate from the dragon's chest. It was more melodic than a growl, like the bass vibrations of a cello holding a single note, fluctuating from flat to sharp.

At first there were only a handful of splashes… then dozens.

Soon the entire surface teemed with fish, all leaping out of the water. They began to encircle Ivisus, jumping in arches around the dragon. It reminded Nail of a maestro, conducting a grand symphony, with every instrument subject to his whim and artistry.

Ivisus spoke again. *"Silly little fishes/They obey our command/Hunting is so simple/Our call is irresistible."*

All four heads bent down and snatched at jumping fish, catching them in long, pointed teeth. Once Ivisus had vis fill, ve stopped humming and the fish ceased their jumping.

Ivisus's heads looked back at Rankor. *"We're leaving/Are we done now?/Travel safely/We've shown the gift."*

Ivisus turned around slowly, thick tail dragging through the water. Then ve meandered back up the stream and was soon out of sight again.

"As you saw," Rankor said, *"Ivisus has a gift with freshwater fish. Ve keeps their population at sustainable levels while maintaining the health of our freshwater streams, which are crucial to our survival on the island.*

"Ivisus is a hydra dragon. Hydras always have a minimum of two heads. At a young age, the heads often do not get along. If one among them is too troublesome or sickly, the other heads may choose to kill it. You may have noticed the healed wound at the base of Ivisus's neck. Contrary to legend, they do not grow back." Rankor nodded solemnly.

Steven was the first to move, and Rankor kept stride with him. They led the class along the uneven path of the creek. Glancing around, Nail realized that again Muari and Prioress Nona were already gone.

The rest of the group went nearly silent. The twins, Hazel and

Maeve, walked on opposite sides of the group, arms folded. They glanced at each other occasionally, but neither ever caught the eye of the other.

Vienna and Kerris walked arm-in-arm behind Jace. Luca and Igo, laughing and shoving each other, wandered farther away from the group and deeper into the forest.

Rankor spoke as they walked. "*There are wyrm dragons who lack legs and wings. Lung dragons, like Oracle, have long, thin bodies similar to wyrms but move upon two pairs of short legs. Lung dragons are also notably more... elegant than wyrms. Drakes, such as myself, possess two sets of legs but no wings.*" Ve added with a laugh and a swell of pride, "*And we are wiser than all the rest.*"

Although Nail found the sound of vis voice pleasing, the tremor of the bass had a foreboding tone that sent shivers over her skin.

Somewhere in the forest, Nail heard a faint squealing sound.

The stream led them out of the rainforest. Dense brush grew to their left, but the rocky terrain of the bank had prevented overgrowth. Ahead, the tall hill sloped down to meet the creek, then it rose up again on the other side, forming a giant V for the stream to pass through.

The forest erupted in laughing, shouts, and high-pitched squealing. Luca and Igo barreled out from behind a thorny brush. In Lucas's hands, a small, brown piglet, screamed and writhed in protest.

For a moment, they were the only ones moving. The entire group stood frozen in horror as they stomped closer.

Rankor charged toward them.

Steven shouted, "What in five hells do you think you're doing?"

He rushed to catch up with Rankor, unable to match the drake's impressive speed. His head was on a swivel, his arms outstretched like a fence, putting himself between the group and the forest beyond.

"Everyone back up toward the water!" he roared.

Luca still held the pig, lowering it to waist height. They both looked dumb-struck, glancing at each other for reassurance.

"It was abandoned," Igo said. "We found it laying in some bushes."

Rankor had assumed a defensive crouch, vis head turning constantly, scanning the tree and brush line. Nail could hear branches moving but couldn't pinpoint where the noise came from.

"It *wasn't abandoned*," Steven hissed. "Put the damned thing down!"

Luca dropped the piglet, and it scampered into the bushes, squealing.

For a moment, everything went silent.

Then, like lightning, a boar burst from the trees.

CHAPTER 7

The boar charged straight for Luca—big, heavy, and hurtling with anger. Everyone screamed and darted away from its trajectory.

Before the boar could close half the distance, Rankor lunged in front of it, vis maw open in a guttural roar. Vis claws lashed across the boar's face, and it squealed and rolled onto its side in shock.

Rankor pressed the point, coming down hard, claws raking over the boar's ribs. Vis teeth closed around the boar's neck, blood dripping down matted brown fur.

The boar tried desperately to escape, kicking up mud in its feeble scramble. Rankor released vis grip, sending the wild pig running back into the forest after its terrified piglet.

But Rankor wasn't finished. Ve watched the forest line a few seconds longer and let loose another menacing roar.

Steven moved in vis path, his arms now blocking Igo and Luca from Rankor's rage.

Blood streaked down Rankor's maw and neck, running in rivers along the crevices of vis deep scales.

"You fools!" Rankor boomed, vis voice a thundering of deep notes.

"They're mine to deal with," Steven said.

"Someone could have died! Oracle should toss you both into the sea! I could gut you here and now!"

"They are mine," Steven said, emphasizing each word. "Harm them and you break the treaty."

Rankor snarled but turned away, growling with each pace.

"Nora!" Steven yelled, his voice carrying.

He had to wait for only a second. She appeared at his side. Prioress Nora scanned the group. Everyone stood trembling, or clutching their chests, or with fists clenched and jaws set. They stared at Igo and Luca.

Nora looked around. "What's happened?"

Steven pointed an accusatory finger at the pair of morons. "My office. Take them. *Now*."

Nora looked confused, but she didn't contradict him. With one swift motion, she laid hands on them both, and all three disappeared.

A minute later, she appeared back in front of them again. Her face was red and her breathing heavy. She and her brother shared a long look. Her jaw was tense, clenched tight.

"Whatever you decide is fitting," she said, "I will fully support it in *any* way I can."

Her meaning was clear. If Steven wanted them removed Lumen, she would be happy to do it.

Steven nodded. "Later." He marched back toward the front of the group, standing a ways off with Rankor in private conversation. Everyone waited around, unsure what to do or where to go.

When Steven returned to the group, the color in his face was returning to normal. "We'll continue the tour. But let me say this again: This island has dangers. This is not your playground. Even with a fully-grown dragon at your side, you are not always safe. What you just witnessed could have been fatal stupidity."

Without a word, he continued walking, determined to finish the day the way he had planned.

The group silently followed the stream to the V-shaped divide in the rocky ridge. A stony embankment lined both sides of the water that bridged the rainforest to whatever lay beyond.

Nail tried to admire the tall stone walls as they passed through the canyon, unable to force her mind to stop wondering what would happen to Igo and Luca. She thought back to the treaty. Did their behavior put them in violation of it? Nail wasn't sure.

She sighed, rolling her shoulders. She wanted to soak in the sights of the island, not worry about those two idiotic clowns.

Lines of red, black, and cream rock streaked through the ridge. While the island felt alive and youthful, the geological signs of age reminded Nail of how old the island—and the Lumen Society—must be.

Beyond the canyon, the air grew lighter and less humid. A few wooden buildings stood ahead of them. One looked like a large house, another was unmistakably a barn, but Nail couldn't place the third. Peeling paint revealed worn, gray wood on the third building—it hadn't been maintained like the others.

Horses, goats, and a herd of cattle grazed within separate fences, and the noise and smell of chickens tinged Nail's senses. The creek stretched onward, and channels siphoned off water into irrigation canals that flowed into fields of different crops.

Over the landscape, a pair of wyverns lay napping on a rocky outcrop, and Nail saw the purple ombré-patterned drake watching them at a distance by the barn door.

"This farm," Steven moved to the front of the group with a forced spring in his step, "has been in operation for several hundred years. It's crucial to our survival here. And as such, it needs a protector."

Steven looked to the sky and smiled. Nail looked up too.

The sky itself seemed to move. In the bright sun, it took her eyes a moment to adjust and understand what she saw.

A dragon—what Nail pictured when she heard the word "dragon"— flew overhead. Vis underbelly matched the exact same shade of blue as the sky, giving ver perfect camouflage from the ground. The thrumming beat of the dragon's wings kicked up a strong wind that tousled Nail's already knotted hair.

The dragon landed near Steven. Ve folded vis wings and approached him softly on four strong legs.

Crossing the ground, the blue of the dragon's underbelly shifted to a mottled green and brown. The coloring extended over vis back. Even the dragon's wings changed and became excellent camouflage.

"This is an example of an English dragon," Steven said.

Easily three times Steven's height, the dragon lowered vis face to Steven's and nuzzled his forehead with vis nose. The English dragon didn't have spiked scales, but two long, curved horns grew from vis temples. Ve exhaled through wide nostrils and Steven's hair ruffled.

"Class, meet Vigilus, my partner," Steven said.

Vigilus looked out over them all with piercing, bright-green eyes. A warm kindness radiated from them that Nail hadn't seen in the other dragons.

"Vigilus has a gift of guardianship. Vis vision can see with perfect clarity at night or during the heaviest rainstorm. Ve can even detect heat and see far beneath the surface of the ocean. Vigilus watches over our island." He smiled. "Mostly protecting the farm from boars and misbehaving new members. But more dangerous foes have been known to find their way to our sanctuary."

Vigilus bobbed vis head with pride, showing off vis long horns and rattling the pointed scales that cascaded down the back of vis neck like a mane.

Steven and Vigilus seemed caught in their own little word for a long moment. The group began to spread out, disorganized without an engaged leader and needing considerably less babysitting without Luca or Igo.

Steven elected to stay behind on the farm with Vigilus, and Rankor brought the class to the southwestern edge of the farmlands. A tunnel had been carved into the ridge, leading back into the valley.

The group stopped just short of where their trek had begun. Rankor stood under a blossoming tree unlike any other that Nail had ever seen.

Little alcoves pocked its trunk. Gnarled branches twisted out and upward. Rather than leaves, vines like a weeping willow dangled a few feet down, swaying in the breeze. The scent of honeysuckle, strawberries, and fresh cotton filled the air.

Buds grew and flowers bloomed from the vines. The buds resembled miniature acorns but pink and tiny. The blossoming flowers were spherical, like hydrangeas, and every imaginable shade of pastel.

This had to be the home of the fae dragons.

Rankor paused near the base of the tree. The rest of the group shuffled in closer. The sound of their feet over the grass and rocks disturbed some of the sleeping faes.

Tiny snouts poked out of the alcoves. Then at least a dozen little dragons leaped into the air, spreading their large, lovely wings. Some of them were the size of Aenu, similar to a lizard. A few of them were much larger, resembling colorful, lithe, and winged iguanas. Together, they reminded Nail of a butterfly sanctuary.

Rankor addressed the class. *"Fae dragons are almost always small, brightly colored, possessing two sets of legs and a pair of insect-like wings. They tend to be charming, sly, and adept mooches. Their gifts are... mischievous. So much so that none of them would volunteer to display them."* Ve glanced at them. *"Proceed with caution, or you could very well find your-*

self sleepwalking, or speaking in iambic pentameter, or convinced you can fly."

Vienna stepped forward in the group, finally breaking away from Jace. "What kind of tree is this?" Her voice was breathy, full of airy lightness, and the blue of her eyes lit up.

Rankor answered her to the group. *"This is a fae willow. It is the only one in this world."*

In the corner of Nail's vision, she saw Jace silently slip away from where Vienna had stood.

Rankor continued. *"Faes will only produce other faes, and they thrive best when roosting in this tree. There are groves of fae willows in their home world, but to ensure the civilizations of Earth didn't fall to their bewitchment, their natural habitat has been limited to this place."*

Everyone in the class glanced around. Rankor had said "home world" so casually, but ve clearly wasn't speaking about the world Nail knew. Were there other places? Did dragons come from another *world?*

"These classifications are practical for your own use," Rankor continued, *"but typically only fae dragons appreciate being simplified down to a species name."* Rankor paused and stared intently, vis gaze settled directly on Jo. *"Every human is unique. You are more than where your ancestors came from, be that Africa or Ireland or Mexico."*

Jo shuffled uncomfortably. Rankor hadn't looked away even once. Others had noticed it too and were now eyeing Rankor suspiciously.

"Asking a dragon what it is, *is simply no different than posing that question to a human. Tread carefully."* Rankor continued. *"I expect lunch is waiting for you. On a logistical note, appointment times for meeting with Steven will be posted in your dorms this evening. And remember your assignment."*

With that, Rankor dismissed the class and plodded off toward the main building, abandoning the students under the fae willow.

Nail looked around. Muari had yet again found herself in Rorik's presence.

A hand touched Nail's arm.

"That was fun, wasn't it?" Jace smiled down at her.

Nail shrugged him off with a smirk. "Eh, I dunno. Could've been more impressive."

Jace laughed. "Oh, yeah," he said with a sarcastic lilt. "I'm sure you've seen much cooler things than a dragon tour on a tropical island. I've never even been west of Colorado."

The group lazily made their way to the dining terrace for a late lunch. Nail and Jace walked together, chatting about the different areas and dragons on the island, hypothesizing over their own eventual pairings.

"I bet you get a wyrm," Jace quipped with a wink.

Nail crossed her arms in mock offense. "You *are* a worm."

He grinned down at her. "You're taller than I envisioned."

A dozen retorts sprinted through her mind, all of them terrible and embarrassing and far too on the nose. She stuttered, "You…walk slow."

"I walk slow?" He laughed.

She cringed internally, but it was too late. She was committed. "I mean, you're more laid back than I imagined." *Saved it.*

Jace's face darkened. "Things are slower here. Back on the family farm, I'm the oldest of six. Now I barely know what to do with my time."

"I'm sure you'll think of something," Nail said with a wry look.

They rounded a corner and crossed the entryway into the garden terrace. Everyone sat at a large table, discussing the tour.

Rorik seated himself at Muari's side. Nail sat with Muari on her left and Jace on her right. The meal was family-style, with dishes and bowls passed around. There was no sign of Luca or Igo.

"Who would've thought a remote Pacific island inhabited by dragons would come with a gender sensitivity lesson?" Jace said, dialing back their conversation.

Nail smiled at him. Had she pushed things too far? Her hand twitched as she reached for a napkin. "I suppose it makes sense."

Rorik called from down the table, "How long do you think we'll have to wait until we get our partners?"

Nail shrugged. "It hasn't happened yet, so I'd say too long."

Jace nodded in agreement.

The scrawny guy in glasses nudged Rorik to take a large bowl from him. What had Jace said his name was? Quinn, that's it.

Nail unfolded her napkin and laid it across her lap. "So how are Kerris and Vienna liking Lumen Island?"

Jace smiled and reached past Nail and Muari to Rorik, accepting the bowl from him. It contained raw tuna, cut into bite-sized cubes, marinated with dark sauce and green onions.

"Real pair of clingers, huh?" he said.

"Just a bit." Nail took the offered serving spoon and dished herself some of the fish. "To be fair, I think Kerris is clinging to Vienna more than she's clinging to you."

Jace glanced toward Vienna at the opposite end of the table. She tucked a blonde lock behind one ear, laying her other hand on Jo's wrist.

"Vienna means well. That's for sure." Jace passed the dish down the table. "I think she has genuine concern for everyone on the island."

She's very concerned about your biceps.

Nail's mouth puckered. "I really doubt that. It seems you're the only one she's concerned about."

Jace pointed down the table. Vienna and Kerris sat on either side of Jo, who looked to be trying very hard to not get upset. "I think it's genuine emotion. She's naturally like that."

Annoyance bubbled in Nail's gut. "Or she's trying to get herself crowned the new queen of popularity. I'm sure that's who she was back home. Her concern is as natural as her bleached teeth. And she seems like she's got two lonely brain cells rattling around in her head. They're miles apart and they don't cross paths often."

Jace frowned but didn't say anything for a long moment. A dish of rice passed wordlessly between them as he paused. "I understand if you're feeling jealous. But that doesn't make her a bad person."

"Jealous?" Revulsion filled Nail's throat. "Jealous of what?"

Jace's brow furrowed. "I think you're jealous that she's been hanging out with me. Am I wrong? Or are you lying?"

A sudden, unmistakable anger emerged behind his eyes. Something she'd said had hit a nerve. But if he wanted to get unnecessarily defensive then that was his problem.

"Definitely not." Nail's voice went flat. "I'm not lying. You're wrong."

His expression only grew grimmer. His upper lip curled for a flash of a second, and he rolled his shoulders. "I guess that's your answer, then."

"It is."

Muari knock on the table to get Nail's attention. "You're slowing down the line."

She looked. Five platters surrounded Rorik and Muari's plates. Nail reached for the closest one as Jace spoke.

"She uses an organic toothpaste, by the way," Jace said. "I asked. So, yes, her teeth are natural too."

Nail slowly lifted the first heavy platter as she pivoted away from Muari. She hadn't meant to snap at Jace. But she hadn't expected him to throw a fit over nothing.

When she turned back and opened her mouth to apologize, she found his plate empty and chair abandoned. Jace was gone.

CHAPTER 8

In the mid-afternoon of the next day, Nail waited outside Steven's office.
The main building branched out far beyond the initial room. As Nail explored it, she discovered that the first room was more of an atrium than anything else.

There were proper classrooms, a medical bay complete with an operating room and a very friendly nurse, several libraries, and an unattended supply warehouse. The empty desk in the supply warehouse was adorned with a nameplate that read "Hank" and a "Gone Fishing" sign.

It had taken her a little while to stuff down her curiosity and climb the stairs to the third floor, where the schedule had said Steven's office was located.

From her wingback chair, she tried to stifle a yawn. Between the essay, moving the remainder of her belongings into her room with Muari, and stressing over her conflict with Jace, she hadn't gotten enough sleep.

Jagdesh had the counseling session before hers, and his appointment had spilled over into her own.

She turned her attention to the small table next to her chair. A clean, glass ashtray sat atop the island's guidebook. Nail picked up the guidebook, leafing through the pages, but not really absorbing any of the information. She missed having a phone to pass the time.

The door opened at ten minutes past the hour, and Jagdesh smiled at her sheepishly. He wore red glasses that complimented his dark hair which was still styled with too much gel.

"Sorry about that," he said.

Nail rose. "No worries."

She closed the door to Steven's office behind her.

Bookshelves crammed with ancient texts filled his office. An old-fashioned globe stood in the corner. A banner hung on his wall, depicting a hand and five symbols on each fingertip.

The thumb's symbol looked like a dragon's claw, but she didn't know what the other four stood for. There was a burning feather on the index finger, a mountain on the middle finger, a snowflake on the ring finger and a crowned lion on the pinky.

A few plants on Steven's long desk complimented his landline phone, and an empty aquarium sat on a table in the corner. He slid a plain leather-bound brown journal to the center of the desk.

She tentatively took a seat opposite of him in a nail-head leather chair.

"So," Steven said, "how do you think you're adjusting?"

Nail leaned to one side in her seat and grinned. "Pretty well, considering I was kidnapped less than forty-eight hours ago."

He smiled back. "Everything going well with Muari?"

Nail nodded. "She's awesome."

"That's wonderful to hear." He leaned forward, resting his forearms atop the desk. "The point of these sessions is to give everyone a space where they can ask questions or receive guidance on anything that may be concerning them. I've found it to be common that what someone is willing to ask in front of their friends is different than what they'll ask in a private setting."

Nail nodded.

"And no topic is off-limits," he said. "So, fire away. What's on your mind, Nail?"

She knew he'd used her name to help her feel more comfortable. But at least that bizarre feeling of calm hadn't returned. She decided to start on something easy. "I haven't seen Luca or Igo since yesterday."

Steven's mouth immediately became a hard line. "They're around, likely hiding their faces in shame. As they should."

"Are they... going to be dropped into the sea?" She didn't really expect the answer to be yes.

"One of our faes has an odd little gift. Ve emits an aura that causes anyone to see a false vision of their worst shame. Since it was so recent, I assume they both saw a very similar vision of yesterday's events, but with a very different ending. I expect that will have sobered them up."

"Isn't that a bit... cruel?" she asked.

Steven shrugged. "But effective. And who knows. Their newfound caution may save a life someday. Hopefully we'll never have to know."

Nail silently agreed. She'd wondered if they hadn't been kicked out, sent back home. She felt a little braver. "What happened to Tally?"

Steven's face darkened. "That... that was a very sad event."

Nail raised an eyebrow. "If nothing is off-limits, then...."

He shook his head and raised a hand, palm facing her. "It's not off-limits. It's just very unfortunate." Steven stood and paced the room for a moment. "We returned her home, and I helped to influence her memories of that day. She won't recall ever being here."

"What do you mean, you 'helped influence her memories?'" Nail asked, concerned.

"My magical gift," Steven replied. "I give a command, and if it's something you already want to do, you'll do it."

Nail considered the ramifications of such a gift. Even with good intentions, it could have disastrous consequences. "That's horrifying."

"I agree," Steven said with a heavy sigh. He faced her again. "It took quite a bit of work to master it—to not accidentally overstep my bounds. I choose my words and inflection carefully."

"Could you demonstrate it?"

He frowned but followed it with a shrug. "I don't see why not." He stood squarely, looking straight at her, and gestured behind her. "Nail. Get up and spin the globe once."

She was already on her feet. Warm happiness flowed through her as she stepped around the chair and stood in front of the globe. She looked down at Europe, and with one wound-up swipe of her hand, she spun the globe. It whirred and knocked satisfyingly. She smiled at him.

He gestured back to the chair.

The warm feeling faded away as the globe slowed to a stop and she sat down again. "How'd you know I wanted to do that?"

He half-smirked. "Everyone enjoys spinning a globe."

"So that's what you did for Tally. She didn't want to remember this place. And now it'll be like it never happened at all?"

Steven nodded. "For her, yes. But... not for the dragon she should have paired with."

Nail shifted. "What happens to the dragon? It's not... destroyed, is it?"

Steven looked up at the hand with the symbols, letting the question hang in the air.

"We would never harm an egg. And we have no way of knowing which egg would have paired with her." He sighed. "It was her choice. The decision to stay can't be forced upon anyone. I do think she would have overcome her anxiety had she stayed but... but it was her choice to leave. As such, she'll never develop into the person she might've been, and that dragon will never hatch."

A shiver went through Nail. "Never? It's just doomed to wait?"

He nodded. "Doomed to wait for a pairing that will never come."

"What if she overcomes her anxiety? Can she ever be invited back?" Nail thought all conversations she'd had with Tally in *Vortex Beyond*. She didn't like her anxiety. She didn't *want* to be that way. But she couldn't just will it away either. "You'll keep an eye on her, won't you?"

Steven shook his head. "Oracle is not a babysitter. The purpose of that gift is not to constantly monitor people's lives. Tally's decision was final. She understood that."

Nail wasn't satisfied.

Steven continued, "We've put great care in determining when we bring in new members. Fourteen was always too young. Even at eighteen or twenty, too many candidates already had other plans that they wouldn't abandon. Sixteen—or nearly so—seems to be the best blend. Old enough to have all the basics of who you are as a person yet young enough to be willing to rearrange your entire life."

Steven looked out the window, down toward the valley below. "Tally won't able to remember the island. It will be a blank spot in her memory. You'd be surprised how well that works. We can rarely pinpoint the things that we can't remember forgetting."

Nail thought about Skrell. He would point out the blank spot to Tally. Nail wished she could do something about it. Making Tally realize that she couldn't remember something wouldn't help her anxiety.

She opened her mouth to warn Steven but reconsidered. After all, he'd just said that monitoring dropouts wasn't the society's role.

Silence fell between them for a long moment. Steven sat down at his desk once more. "There are two topics I would like to address with you, if you don't have anything further for now."

Nail shook her head.

Steven pushed the leather-bound journal toward her. "Everyone is being asked to keep a daily journal. We find it's useful to review the thoughts and experiences later on in the process, particularly if hatching or development of magical gifts proves difficult."

Nail took the journal. The top right corner of the cover displayed her name embossed in silver letters. It looked a bit like a Bible.

"Sure." She raised an eyebrow. "A dragon diary. Awesome."

He smiled kindly in spite of her sarcasm. "It really can help, and I think it may prove especially useful in your case."

"Why?"

"Well, that brings me to the other topic." He cleared his throat. "Oracle has taken an unusual interest in you."

Nail scanned his face, looking for any hint of emotion. "Is that a good or a bad thing?"

"Neither, really. She wanted me to give you some 'words of wisdom,' but I think they're meant as more of a warning."

"Which is?"

He looked over her shoulder, beyond her. "Your path will be alone."

Nail leaned back in her chair. She mulled over the words. Did it ring true for her?

No, she had Muari. And Jace would come around eventually. Hopefully. She didn't need a crowd of fans. But she wasn't *alone.*

Nail took the warning and threw it out of her head like a boomerang. Maybe it would come back. Maybe it wouldn't. Her father's words echoed in her mind, *"Fretting about it beforehand is unnecessary."*

"I appreciate the heads up for… whatever that means."

He shrugged apologetically. "Yes, Oracle… she can be infuriatingly vague. And her gift is less like watching a hidden camera and more like interpreting tea leaves."

He had slipped, and Nail caught it. "You said 'she.' Don't you mean 've?'"

His eyes gleamed. "No, I mean she. Oracle—"

Sounds of shouting came through Steven's windows. He quickly rose to look outside. Curious, Nail joined him.

Daredevil Luca and overly muscled, tattooed Dax were shoving each other out in the valley.

"I hate to cut our meeting short, but I need to go deal with this," Steven said.

Nail, journal in hand, followed him out of the office and down onto the grounds.

Exactly what had started the conflict, Nail couldn't say. But Luca had picked the wrong guy to piss off. Easily six-and-a-half feet tall, Dax's muscled frame gave him an easy hundred pounds over Luca.

"Bet you can't!" Luca shouted.

Dax got in his face, his chest the same height as Luca's chin. "Say. That. Again."

"Bet you won't!" Luca challenged back.

A crowd had formed around the pair. Igo began chanting, "Fight, fight, fight!"

Steven marched between the two guys and forced them apart. "Enough! Who started this?"

Luca pointed a finger at Dax. "He did."

Based on Dax's balled up fists and contorted face, Nail could tell Dax wasn't the instigator.

"You scrawny little *liar*. I didn't start anything! I don't need this." Dax turned to walk away, but he didn't make it even a full step when Luca shot back at him.

"You sure did. By being a giant f—"

Faster than Nail would have believed, before Luca could finish his sentence, Dax turned back around again and launched a full-powered punch around Steven and into Luca's left eye.

Luca went down hard.

"Dax!" Steven grabbed him by his arm. "In my office! Now!"

Dax stared from Luca to Steven and back at Luca again. His upper lip curled into a snarl, and he looked ready to lay Steven out too. With one deep breath, he woodenly turned away and marched off to Steven's office.

Igo leaned in front of Nail and whined to Jo, "Man, I bet him he couldn't get Dax to punch him. Now I owe him twenty bucks."

Jo and Nail gave Igo disgusted looks.

Steven helped Luca stand up. "Get your sorry face to the medical bay. And then get it to my office."

Luca walked off. Once Steven's back was turned, Igo chased after Luca.

"That was the dumbest thing I've ever seen," Jo said.

Nail agreed. "I have to wonder what criteria Oracle used to justify bringing Igo and Luca here."

Jo shook her head. "Well, they make the rest of us look a lot smarter by comparison."

AT DINNER, LUCA'S EYE WAS SO BRUISED AND SWOLLEN THAT HE couldn't open it. Dax kept shooting him dirty looks from down the table. Suspiciously, Muari and Rorik didn't turn up for dinner.

Nail spent the evening with Jo in the common area doing their pronoun reports, and they both got them submitted before the deadline.

She learned that Jo was from Philadelphia. Her mother owned a bakery, her father was an accountant, and her whole extended family got together to watch football games in the fall.

"Manning won it for Denver this year, but someday my Eagles are gonna win it all," Jo said with a grin on her face.

Nail nodded as enthusiastically as she could. She didn't really follow sports.

Her mind lingered on Jace. She didn't know if he had a favorite team.

She'd watched him at dinner. Sitting with Vienna and laughing with Kerris, he hadn't looked her way even once.

He sure wasn't on Team Nail.

"I hope Dax isn't in too much trouble," Jo said. "Luca had it coming."

Nail agreed. "First the boar, now this? I hope Steven sets him straight. Maybe he can get Luca to mellow out a bit."

"He's driving me crazy." Jo flipped through a record book on magical gifts.

Nail wondered, would Steven use his gift to make Luca more behaved? Was that... ethical? He was putting only himself in danger. Until, of course, one day when his pranks would backfire onto someone else.

She thought of Tally, half-heartedly regretting her silence toward Steven. She wasn't sure if it was her role to say something, but she was certain that Tally's memory blank spot wouldn't stay hidden for long.

Nail watched the sun setting over the western edge from through the common room's windows.

It'll be fine, she told herself. *She's only missing a few hours. How bad could it be?*

CHAPTER 9

The assignments following the pronoun essay got far more interesting, or at least Nail thought so. Some of it involved the history of the Draconic and Sapien bond, as well as theories surrounding pairing and magical gifts.

The teens were often split into groups for their projects, sent off to various parts of the island to interview different dragons or members of the society. Nail usually got paired with Dax, Hazel, and Quinn. She liked their company but missed Muari and hated seeing Jace traipsing behind Vienna for almost every assignment.

Muari got lucky. Rorik was in her group more than half the time.

The few times Nail and Jace ended up in the same group, he was friendly. Cordial, even. He didn't seem bitter, but his guard was up. His easy laughs and relaxed demeanor had been replaced with stiff head nods and single-syllable answers.

The groups switched up, but not perfectly. Ironically, Hazel and Maeve were never paired together. Within a week after arrival, the two seemed to have stopped speaking to one another.

Petite, mousy Elsie came out of her shell a little. She was always the first to answer questions in class, and she carried at least three books with her at all times.

Contrary to her appearance the first day, her hair was always washed. A few times she dared to trade out her baggy tee shirts for floral tank tops, and even a dress, once.

Nail never found out what other punishments Steven might have placed on Luca. But even he and Igo settled into a calmer routine with their chaotic antics decreasing daily.

The group became tighter knit. There were a few clique-like lines, but they weren't hard rules. Vienna seemed to have crowned herself as queen bee—as Nail knew she would—but not many others were interested in that game.

Over time, Kerris's bubbly personality seemed to wear thin. As they approached two weeks on the island, she became increasingly annoyed with the constant attention Vienna received from most of the guys.

She loudly interrupted a dragon interview to inform everyone that she had been junior homecoming queen, and while everyone else busied themselves with the properties of the fae willow, she boasted about raising money for the homeless by running a car wash.

"Try-hard," Jo had muttered to Nail when Kerris announced that *actually* she was a quarter of an inch taller than Vienna.

Nail had nodded in agreement. "Someone isn't used to second place."

Two weeks after their first lesson with Rankor, Steven made an announcement at the end of a group lesson on the island's ecosystem and meteorology patterns.

"I am very proud of everyone," he said. "You've built a solid foundation. And tonight, we will gather together and conduct the pairing ceremony."

A few cheers and nervous murmurs went through the group. Nail could hardly contain her excitement. She looked around. Everyone else wore broad smiles. Even Elsie looked excited.

Nail made eye contact with Jace. Her smile dampened a little, but his didn't. Maybe their rift had ended.

After that night, dragons wouldn't just be inhabitants of the island. They would be their partners, and a whole new journey would begin.

And despite the overwhelming joy Nail felt coursing through her, Oracle's boomerang warning came back.

Your path will be alone.

CHAPTER 10

No classes or counseling sessions were scheduled for the rest of that day. And it was a good thing, too. No one could have possibly maintained any focus.

Igo and Luca threw a massive party that afternoon. Thanks to items in the supply warehouse, they had managed to dress up a chicken in tacky Hawaiian accessories and a tiny sombrero. It squawked madly all afternoon as several of the dragons enjoyed a game of chase-the-poultry.

Jo shook her head. "Can't imagine why Hank keeps all this stuff."

Nail thought back. "The guy in charge of the supply room?"

Jo nodded. "Real nice. Not all there, if you know what I mean." She chuckled. "Funny guy, though."

By dinnertime, the jovial atmosphere of the afternoon had calmed and quieted into a somber, introspective silence. Most of the teens merely poked at their dinners, and what little conversations were still being had turned hushed and whispered.

When the staff finished eating, Steven gathered up the class of Metal Dragons from their mostly uneaten meals. He directed them outside.

"Single-file line, please. Don't be picky. The order won't matter."

They all jostled into place, with Igo and Luca bickering over who was first in line. Nail found herself roughly at the middle of the group, with Elsie in front of her and Jo behind.

Steven led them into the valley, and Nail realized they were headed toward the immovable door she'd encountered on her second day.

A procession of sorts formed for their walk. Every few yards, a human and a dragon stood on opposite sides of their path—sentries to their march.

When the procession ended, Steven stood them in a semi-circle several yards away from the door. They all had a clear view of the immovable stone entryway.

A woman approached. And yet she wasn't just a woman. She had pale, blue-tinged skin and long, golden hair. Easily over six feet tall, she walked the inside of their semicircle with lithe, bare footsteps. She surveyed the class.

At first, Nail thought the lines on her face were wrinkles. But they were too exact, and her skin didn't sag. She looked ageless.

For a moment, she considered if they could be tattoos. But as the woman got closer, Nail realized they were scales. Small, nearly flat lines of smooth scales the texture of human skin.

The way she walked wasn't human either. She moved with pride, but the thin silk of her dress revealed that her knee joints were different. They bent in reverse, more like the hind legs of a dragon.

When the woman stood before her, Nail finally realized it was Oracle—in a humanoid form. In all of her reading, through all the homework, she'd never come across anything that remotely resembled a human and dragon hybrid.

Nail wondered if this was a magical ability, a gift that somehow complemented the ability to see into the hearts of others, or if it was the result of something else entirely.

It explains why Steven said 'she.'

Oracle finished her appraisal, approached the door, and placed both hands upon the stone.

It moved.

As if weightless, the door floated, inching out toward them. Then it slid sideways and rested against the wall of the cliff. White light glowed from within the opening.

Oracle stepped forward, appraising the group one last time.

"There are many kinds of death," she said. "Your old self—your first self—died when you stood on the dais and swore yourselves to Lumen. You have waited in limbo since that death.

"When you emerge, you will again be changed. Consider this a fresh beginning. Leave all your old quarrels and bias out here. Drop them from your shoulders and stand taller. This is your rebirth."

The group was silent. Oracle moved aside and nodded deftly to Steven. He led the group—what had been the back of the line first—into the stone atrium.

Igo and Luca punched each other's arms. They entered last.

Inside the cave, the path sloped and spiraled down a giant stone staircase. Each step was wide and deep enough to hold the entire group. Fiery red light glowed in the hollow center far beneath them.

They all stood in the entryway landing, and the room grew darker. Nail turned to see a sliver of Oracle's silhouette and the door shutting behind them, sealing them in.

With the door shut, lights flashed on from every surface. Tiny recessed lamps glowed on the steps, on the inside handrail, on the walls.

And the walls… Nail's mouth hung open at the sight of the walls.

All the way down, built-in crevices pocked the walls like empty bookshelves. Some were rectangular, some ovals. And within the carved-out spaces sat eggs. More eggs than Nail could count.

Some sat alone, others were in groups—as many as eight. And no two were identical. Some were small, only a few inches in diameter, while others were the size of a small child.

They came in every color and pattern, scales and geometric designs. Some looked like they dripped wax, and others bore a resemblance to leather or bleached bone. Many of the shells were metallic or neon and glimmered in the light like lost pirate's treasure.

Nail couldn't yet tell how far down the cave wound. There could've been hundreds of dragon eggs. The group, which had been silent, spoke in hushed murmurs.

Muari leaned in close. "Can you feel that? I can feel ver!"

Nail could feel the enigmatic energy of the place.

Steven gathered them all closer. "What you're feeling is entirely unique to you. Somewhere in the incubation chamber is your partner. That partner will change you, define you, help you to become the person you're meant to be.

"We never teach you how to know when you've found the right one because it is not something that can be taught. It's a feeling, pulling you even now, tethered right down to your soul. Touch the egg that's waiting for you, and you will know. Touch an egg that *isn't* calling to you and… Nothing happens." He grinned at them.

Then he turned his attention to Luca and Igo, and his voice hardened. "Touch gently. This is not a game of football."

But for once, Igo and Luca weren't joking or behaving like morons. They stood rapt, no longer jostling for position or attention.

"There's no wrong or right time," Steven continued. "If you think you're feeling the bond, go ahead and reach."

They took the first step down. Everyone gazed at the recessed shelf and the eggs it contained. Shockingly, it was Elsie who stepped out first. Her fingers brushed against two eggs, but the third was right. She exclaimed with a soft, "Oh!" and looked back to Steven.

He nodded. "Go ahead. Pick it up."

The egg looked oceanic. Swirls of rough rock, a sandy texture, and blue ripples like water adorned its shell. Tip to tip, it was roughly the size of a spiral bound notebook.

Tears fell down her face without blinking as she lifted the egg. She said, "It's so light!"

Rorik leaned into Muari's ear, whispering a description of Elsie's egg.

Elsie hugged the egg close to her like a mother with a newborn baby. She moved to the back of the group, letting everyone else go before her.

The next two steps and their inset shelves didn't yield any pairings. But on the third step, Vienna moved away from the group.

Within the alcove sat four eggs that shone like gemstones, each smaller than a quail egg and brightly colored. They looked incredibly delicate, as though they were made from overlapping layers of insect wings or flower petals in alternating shades of purple, teal, fuchsia, green, yellow, and fiery orange.

Vienna moved to the egg sitting farthest back and gently plucked it from its resting place. "Yes. We're a pair."

The pastel egg fit easily into her hand, and she joined Elsie. Nail was certain Vienna had paired with a fae egg.

On the next step, gangly Quinn stepped toward an egg. Roughly eight inches tall, it looked to be made of overlapping pieces of black leather. He reached out, and they were paired.

Nail looked over to Muari, whose smile grew broader and broader. She'd worn round sunglasses that day and carried her cane. She looked like she belonged in the 70s and she pulled it off well. The entire group seemed giddy with euphoria; it was even rubbing off on Steven.

But as they continued to move down the cave, Nail's wonderment dwindled. She didn't feel a pull or a sense of complement with each step. What if there was no egg for her?

That, of course, couldn't be possible. Steven had reassured her that everyone on the island had an egg waiting to pair with them.

And yet, fear sent shivers over her skin.

Three more steps down, the twins both moved away from the group. Neither seemed to realize the other was moving until they both stood at the edge of the alcove. They smiled and hugged, as all their feuding and fighting seemed to finally fall away. They held hands and each reached toward their pairing.

Maeve touched her egg first. It was a deep, emerald green, with swirls and veins of tropical colors. Teals, pinks, yellows, and oranges of every shade wound over the egg like a tapestry of rivers.

Hazel was not so lucky. Her pairing looked diseased. Splotches of the egg looked like charred flesh. Angry boils welled up erratically, and slashes of red cracked the surface. Some patches looked like aged skin or soaked leather left to boil in the sun.

Compared to her sister's radiant egg, it seemed like a cruel joke.

But they both smiled, nodded, and moved to the back of the group.

Jagdesh was next. His egg was smaller than all the others' except for Vienna's. Perhaps only five inches tall, the surface of the egg looked white, but swirls of blue moved under its shell in a rhythmic motion.

Nearly half the group had been paired, and still, Nail's connection to the place waned. Perhaps her egg was back at the top. Perhaps she felt the connection less and less the farther they moved from it.

A lone egg, roughly the size of a volleyball, sat in the next alcove, by far the most stunning one yet. Its smooth surface shimmered. Beneath it, thousands of multicolored crystals gleamed and danced in the light.

Nail felt a strange sense of sorrow at the idea that a dragon would someday burst forth and destroy the magnificent shell. She hoped to feel something more for it, to feel pulled toward it.

Judging by Kerris's half-step forward, she felt the same envy.

But it was Dax who moved toward the egg.

His cheeks reddened. It was difficult to imagine overly jacked-up Dax pairing with such a beautiful egg. But he took it, nodding once to Steven, and shuffled to the back of the group.

On the next step, Kerris did move forward. Her egg was one of the largest. Its shimmering red scales danced black when the light hit them.

Luca and Igo were next. Igo reached out, and although his selection was vaguely egg-shaped, it was also geometric and angular. It reminded Nail of something that would've come from an early 3D printer.

Luca's was a simple, smooth, yellow ombré bleached white at the top.

They went down five more steps. The end of the cave was visible around the corner.

Nail's heart fluttered. There weren't many eggs left.

Rorik and Muari stepped out at the same time. He stepped aside and let her go first. Muari's egg was solid white with intricate swirls of textured pattern inlaid on the surface. She cradled the base of it between her palm and her chest.

Rorik paired to an egg with hundreds of interconnected silver circles, similar in size to Muari's egg. He held it gently in both hands.

Three steps from the bottom, Jo paired with an egg that looked as though it had been dipped in gold a hundred times. It looked molten, like it might slip between her fingers and dissolve into liquid on the floor. But she carried it gingerly and joined the group.

Only Jace and Nail remained. The next two steps, nothing happened.

Beyond them, ten yards down, a pond of lava surged, pumping heat up at them. Nail wiped her sleeve across her brow.

The alcove of the final step sheltered two eggs.

She was certain the last two eggs were meant for her and Jace. One of them looked to be made of twisted branches and leaves. They interwove into a complex pattern with all the beauty of a forest wrapped together and changed from fall to spring.

The final egg was slightly smaller, with raised waves and white dots that glimmered like pearls. The shell was beautiful and violent, reminding Nail of the way the wind would knife across the ocean's white tips, blowing mist and spray into the air.

They both stepped forward and shared a smile.

This was the moment that would bond them together again. Just like it had for Maeve and Hazel. They would pair with the final two eggs together, and it would mean something. It would mean everything.

Jace reached out to the flora egg. Nail touched the aquatic one.

He smiled immediately. He had felt the connection, the bond that the last two weeks were meant to prepare them for. His exhale turned into a laugh and erupted into a jubilant cry.

Nail did not.

She expected it to feel like the opposite poles of a magnet, immediately drawn together. Or like glue. She expected to be pulled, connected, tethered to the egg.

She expected to feel happy and fulfilled, overflowing with purpose.

Instead, she felt nothing.

CHAPTER 11

Nail looked to Steven in a panic.

She hadn't felt anything. Her fingers remained on the last egg for a moment, trying to will herself into feeling something. But all she felt was the warm, smooth surface the shell. It wasn't her egg.

Steven quietly congratulated Jace and pulled Nail aside.

Tears fell before she even realized how upset she had become. The stress and disappointment washed over her in an inescapable flood.

"It's okay," Steven said. "It's going to be okay. Did you feel anything in here?"

Nail took a few deep breaths to find her voice again. "I felt… I guess it was awe when we first came in."

Steven nodded. "Did you feel like you were being pulled? Called? Drawn to anything?" His voice was directed only at her.

The crowd of paired classmates watched with curious stares. They didn't back down when Nail made eye contact.

But Steven seemed oblivious to them. "This happens sometimes. It's normal if you were too shy to step out and reach."

Nail shook her head vigorously. She wished she could wipe away the entire awful moment. "I didn't feel anything like that." Sobs threatened to take her over. "Th-there's no egg for me, is there?"

Steven put his hands on her shoulders.

Her tears started. "I'll have to leave, and you'll have to wipe my memory like Tally. Everything will be gone, and I won't be here. I'll have to go back to my old life. This will all be a big, blank hole. Please, *please* don't make me go back. I can work here! Let me stay. Please? Please don't make me leave!" She clutched at his shirt, staining it with tears.

Steven let her get it all out of her system. Gently, he pulled away and placed his hands on her forearms, gliding them to her hands, squeezing her fingers in his own.

"You're strong. Don't let this break you," he said. It was a command.

His words centered her. She felt a warmth that wasn't coming from the lava, like she'd just drunk an entire mug of hot chocolate. There was comfort in knowing he was still there. She felt her doubts slip away. She breathed deeply.

"I won't make you leave. No one will. You have a place among us, Nail. We just haven't found it yet."

She shuddered and forced herself to stop crying.

"Here's what I'd like to do," he said in a soft tone. "I'm going to lead the group back up to the top. You take as much time as you need. Touch every egg on your way up. Just in case. And if nothing happens, it will be okay. There is still a pairing for you. I'm here to help." He held her gaze, gauging her reaction. "Can you do that?"

She nodded and watched as Steven addressed the group. Jo and Jace both tried to move past Steven toward her, but he held them back. She couldn't hear exactly what he said, but she caught the words "on her own."

And Oracle's warning came back to her again.

Your path will be alone.

She was certainly alone as Steven led the group away. Nail waited until they had climbed far enough that they couldn't see her.

She took a deep breath. Then two.

With a third inhale, she shook out her hands and steadied herself for a lonely climb.

She began with the aquatic egg again. Still nothing.

Each step brought new opportunities to pair, but she felt no response. She would know, wouldn't she? Everyone else had known. They had all paired without question. As her fingers traced every egg, each stair marked another defeat. Another dragon not meant for her.

She counted them as she went.

She stood back at the top, on the landing with the group. The number in her head was two hundred and forty-six.

None of them were for Nail.

Steven smiled at her, but the corners of his mouth turned down. He held up one finger and gestured toward the wall, suggesting she wait there.

Nail's mind was blank. She couldn't fathom what had happened—what *hadn't* happened—so she waited on her own.

He knocked on the stone door, and it began to slide open.

"Everyone, stand back against the wall, please. Out of sight. I will lead you out one at a time."

They all moved, and Nail shuffled to the corner farthest from the door.

Steven led Elsie outside. "Show them your pairing," he said, encouraging her into a rare streak of boldness.

When she disappeared from the incubation chamber, she was met with applause and the roars of dragons. Steven returned and took Vienna outside next. More applause and roaring.

It continued that way, each of them being led out in the same order that they had paired. Soon it was down to four of them. Then two.

Jace waited until Rorik had turned the corner to speak.

"I'm so sorry," he said. "What are they going to do?"

Nail shook her head. She didn't know.

"Whatever you need, whatever it takes, I'll be here to help you, okay?" He cradled his egg in one arm and took her hand. He brought it to his lips and kissed the back of her fingers. But his gallantry couldn't shake Nail out of the spiraling despair she felt.

"They'll make me leave," she repeated her fear, choking on the words.

Steven returned and waited for Jace. He said, "It's time."

Jace hesitated to move. But he had to.

Nail watched him leave. She stood with her hands against the cool rock behind her, breathing in a four-count, holding it for seven, and exhaling for eight. Would they laugh? Would she be scorned? Maybe Oracle could close the door again and come back for her when no one was looking. Did she have to face them?

She opened her eyes and Steven stood ready.

Nail approached him and they walked together. "What am I supposed to show them?"

"Your bare hands." He smiled genuinely, with no emotional trickery or influence. His grin carried a somber lilt. "Twenty-four years ago, that's what I did."

EPISODE TWO

CHAPTER 1

Finley had been annoyed when Nail was an hour late coming back to her house. The unsmoked bowl taunted her, so she texted Nail, went outside, and hit the bowl.

Another hour passed. No reply. After three hours, Finley actually called her. But her phone went straight to voicemail.

"This is Nail's phone. Not gonna listen to your voicemail. Just text me."

Fine, Finley thought. It wasn't totally out of Nail's character to flake on her. But it was unusual for her to not respond all night.

In the morning, Finley checked her phone. Lots of social media notifications—a couple news articles on the presidential election she was too young to vote in—but nothing from Nail. She got out of bed and tripped over a backpack on the floor.

Swearing, she caught herself on a dresser. The backpack wasn't hers. It was Nail's. Staring at it, she resolved to take it to Nail's house if she still hadn't heard from her by noon.

At 2:30, Finley begrudgingly slung it over her shoulder and locked her front door.

Anger and annoyance punctuated her steps as she made the walk to Nail's house. And, if she was really honest with herself, a little bit of worry. Nail had gone MIA before, usually down some sort of cryptozoology-conspiracy-theory hole, but never for this long.

She knocked at Nail's house, but no one answered. A peek into the garage revealed that their Volvo was gone. Finley waited on the porch for half an hour, grumbling over the time she was missing in her game. She thought she showed the patience of a true friend. But when no one showed up by 3:15, she left the pack on the front porch and went home.

When she got back to her room, she sat at her desk, drumming her fingers on the wood. She had an hour until the next major raid in her game. What better way to pass the time than by cyber-stalking Nail's accounts?

But in the last day, Nail hadn't been active once. No posts, tweets, reblogs, or pics. The only pic on any of her stories showed Nail sitting on Finley's bed the previous day.

She looked bored, and the top of a textbook was visible at the bottom of the frame. The caption read, "What lame teacher gives homework over summer?"

Finley checked her phone. Nothing on Nail's Snap story either. It stayed that way all day.

Nail didn't post any updates over the following days. None of her casual friends at school knew where she'd gone. She left voicemail's on Nail's home phone. But they weren't returned. By the end of the week, Finley was ready to go to the cops.

But the more she thought about, the more ridiculous she felt. It wasn't just Nail who was gone, her father was missing too. Finley felt certain they were together. And she knew Robert. There wasn't a single speck of him that was angry or violent.

She didn't know where Nail was. But she knew she wasn't in danger. She just wasn't *home*.

Finley lurked on cryptozoology forums. She looked into a way to bug Nail's phone and pinpoint her location. But without the device in her hand, she couldn't pull it off.

One week turned into ten days, and ten days became two-weeks. She spent sleepless nights in her game, raiding for hours, whatever it took to chase away the dark realization that she was slowly unable to ignore.

Nail hadn't just left. She'd abandoned her.

Even on days when there wasn't track practice, Finley found excuses to go on a run—always past Nail's house. But there was still no car. That backpack still sat on the front porch, untouched. Their lawn wasn't mowed. Their garden wilted at the side of the house.

Finally, three days past the two week mark, and three weeks away from the start of Junior year, Finley found the Sharps' silver Volvo sitting in the driveway. She felt a rush of relief that she hadn't done something drastic like go to the cops, but it was quickly replaced with an intense, raging anger.

Finley marched up to the front door and pounded. "Nail? NAIL! Where the HELL have you been?"

But it was Nail's father who opened the door.

"Oh." Finley took two steps back. "Hello, Mr. Sharp."

He looked down at her, all gray hair, laugh lines, and thin lips. He was tanner than she remembered, and his beard made her believe he hadn't shaved in a week.

"Finley," he smiled. "Would you like to come in?"

"Is Nail home?" Sweat dripped down her forehead and pooled in the back of her shirt.

He frowned. "Didn't she tell you?"

"Tell me what?"

He folded his arms. "Nail was accepted into a two-year foreign exchange program to Greece four months ago. She's staying with a family over there."

"She's in *Greece*? For *two years*?"

"I'm so sorry, Finley." His eyes wrinkled with concern. "She really didn't tell you?"

Greece. A hot knife stabbed through her, into her chest, severed her heart, and went straight out her back. Her stomach swelled and sank. *Two years!* The knife twisted, turned icy, and yanked back through her again. *How could she?*

"No, she..." Finley stammered out, her breathing heavy and labored from more than just the run. "She didn't. She never said anything."

Traitor.

"Oh. I'm so sorry. It'll be hard to get ahold of her. It's in a pretty remote area."

Finley nodded like she understood. Like she accepted it. Like Nail abandoning her best friend and leaving without a word was a totally normal thing to do.

"I could give you the post office address, and you could send her a letter?" he offered.

Finley waved him away. She wasn't really listening. She coughed, the shock turning the water in her stomach into acid.

When she turned to leave, she saw the backpack, still sitting there. "I hope she enjoys the rest of high school."

On her run home, she paused at an intersection and added a pic to her own story. Frowning at the camera, she flipped her middle finger, captioning the image, *Did anyone know that Naileen Sharp was going to GREECE for TWO YEARS?!?!*

She seethed as she stumbled home in shock, her mind spinning. *Greece? Two years? How could Nail not tell me?*

But the more she thought about it, the less sense it made.

By the time she got out of the shower, she was falling down a rabbit hole of conspiracy and questions—just like Nail would've done.

All summer, they'd made plans for junior year. They were going to try out for powder puff football. They made a pact that if either one of them didn't get a date for prom, they would go together.

They were partners for all their summer homework. Finley had been ignoring it, but Nail had even done some of it! Why bother doing homework she would never have to turn in?

There was just no way that Nail would leave for two years and say nothing. *Maybe she wouldn't tell anyone else, but she would've told me.*

She'd never even mentioned applying for an exchange program. Because, after all, they would have done that together, too.

She sunk into her bed, staring at the empty space on her floor where she'd tripped over Nail's backpack two weeks earlier. Because even if she disregarded everything else, there was still the question of the backpack. That damned backpack.

Why leave it? Why make Finley take it to her house and wait so long to find out where she'd gone?

No, Nail wasn't in an exchange program in Greece. Finley was sure.

Nail wouldn't have left her alone. She wouldn't have walked out to play a game and never come back.

Finley smacked herself on the forehead. It had been right in front of her the whole time.

Nail had said it herself, standing in the bedroom doorway. *"If we all start disappearing, you'll know where to look."*

Back at home, she got online and posted a new thread to r/MissingPersons. "My friend went missing playing VORTEX BEYOND."

She expected trolls and some sympathy comments. She expected her story to be dismissed as yet another teenage runaway. But maybe some other Redditor had the same thing happen to their friend.

And a private message from u/8Ecraskrell revealed more questions than answers.

CHAPTER 2

Nail sat alone in her shared room, waiting for literally anything to happen.
She had done what Steven said, holding up her empty palms to the crowd. She never could have predicted their reaction.

The entire society had gathered outside the incubation chamber—more dragons and humans than she'd ever seen on the island.

The automatic applause came first. Then the realization of her empty hands rolled over them.

Then the crowd did something bizarre.

Almost every human averted their gaze and bowed their heads. They lowered down to one knee. The dragons, though many shapes and sizes, spread whatever wings they had and sank into a low bow.

And Steven had stood next to her, his hand on her shoulder.

When her paired classmates had gone to meet the crowd, Nail lingered for only a moment, staring at her feet, the grass, absolutely anywhere other than the eyes of the gathered group. When their laughter and congratulatory noises became too much to bear, she ran back to the dorm.

Something is wrong with me.

She was the only one who hadn't paired. Why hadn't she paired?

A soft knock rapped at her door, snapping her out of her spiral. She folded her arms tighter.

"Naileen?" came a concerned voice.

Nail stood. She knew that voice. Her father's voice. Instinctively, she rushed toward the door. Hand on the knob, she paused.

Why should she open it for him? She was convinced he had known, that he had lived on Lumen Island many years ago. And he never said anything.

"Nail? Are you in there?"

She stormed away from the door, reaching the opposite end of the room with long, angry strides.

What is he doing here?

"Honey, I just want to talk."

I don't. He'd had sixteen years to explain everything, to even warn her. And he hadn't. He'd never said *anything.*

Tears boiled to the surface. She couldn't recall moving but she stood in the middle of the room.

"Please."

She needed to rage and sob. She hadn't paired with a dragon egg and it felt like it was her fault. It felt like it was everyone's fault. Her heart had never been broken so completely. She wanted to hate the world. She needed a shoulder to cry on.

And his was the best.

Nail went back over and opened the door. She couldn't look at his face. But she knew it was him by his worn out, brown slip-on shoes.

As her dad entered, Nail sulked back to her bed and sat. He sat beside her.

She wanted to explain everything before the tears overtook her again. "Dad, I—"

His arms wrapped around her in a hug. She unleashed an unholy sob into his chest. Disappointment and betrayal raged through her. Anger laced with jealousy vented out with each wet exhale as she mourned what she could have been, what she could have had. There was no dragon for her; she was sure of it.

He stroked her hair and held her. "It's going to be okay. I'm here. Everything will be okay."

She let grief course through her until she felt empty. Her father didn't try to fix it. He simply listened.

Finally, Nail pulled away and sat up straight. Mucus clouded her voice. "Sorry."

"You never have to apologize for crying with me." Her father had kind brown eyes and a careworn brow. He retrieved a box of tissues from her desk. "You can always be honest with me."

Nail blew her nose twice. She took a deep breath, then two. The best place to start was the beginning. "So, you've been here, right?"

"Yes. I'm Lumen."

She threw the damp tissues into her bedside trashcan. "Did you pair?"

"I did." He moved the tissues back into reach again. "But we did have a man in my class who didn't initially. Everyone pairs eventually, Nail. Your time will come."

She shook her head. "What if it doesn't? What if...." All the fear and anxiety she felt at the bottom of the incubation cave came flooding back. "What if there's no partner for me?"

Her father took a moment to answer. "It... It will be different for you. I spoke to Steven before I left the group."

"You were there?"

He nodded. "Lumen family members are always invited for the pairing presentation."

Nail picked at her cuticles, flicking dead skin onto the cold floor.

"Steven told me he would schedule a meeting with you first thing tomorrow," he said. "You can trust him. He knows what he's doing."

"How well do you know him?" Nail asked.

"He was in my class. We were the Fire Dragons. And...."

"And what?" She looked up at him.

His smile dampened. "And so was your mother. That's how I met Gillian."

Mom was Lumen too?

"Oh." Nail didn't have any memories of her mother. She'd only been two when her mother had passed. There were pictures of them together. She remembered those.

Over the years, she'd tried to convince herself that she did remember those happy moments. But the reality was, those memories were just trapped in 5x7 two-dimensional windows. Her mother, pregnant at a Y2K party. A toddler-aged Nail in the tub with her mother kneeling on the tile floor. A summer picnic in the park.

"So she had a dragon too. Is ve on the island? Is yours?"

"No, they're on Drasol."

Nail cocked her head quizzically. "Where?"

He grinned. "That's a lesson you haven't reached yet."

A realization hit her. "Wait, wait, wait." She pulled away from him, a smile unwittingly playing out on her face. "So you have a magical ability?"

Her father smiled sheepishly. "I do."

"Well," Nail led. "What is it?"

"It's pretty underwhelming." He rubbed the back of his neck. "I can talk to locks. And if they aren't too cranky, I can usually get them to open up."

"You... talk to locks?"

He laughed. "I know, it sounds weird. And it was a tough gift to figure out. They're very lonely, you know. Don't get a lot of attention. And when they do, it's usually pretty negative. My gift doesn't work on computer locks, though. They all speak binary and I'm not fluent."

They stared at each other.

He grinned awkwardly.

Nail broke into the kind of laughter that could only follow loss. Sure, she hadn't paired, and everything would be different. But at least her magical ability couldn't be more underwhelming than unlocking locks.

They both laughed and cried and laughed until there was nothing left.

She used her sleeve to wipe away a few amused tears. "I guess it doesn't really matter what my magical ability turns out to be, huh? Low bars are easy to surpass."

Her father grabbed a tissue to blow his nose. "I'd be insulted, but you're not wrong." He leaned over her and threw the tissue away. "You could never disappoint me. Well, you could. But I probably wouldn't admit it."

She hugged him. Having him there made everything easier. "Thanks, Dad."

He squeezed her back. "Just doing what a dad does."

He rooted around in his pocket and pulled out a small jewelry box. Navy and felted, he opened it.

A prismatic dragon scale, about the size of a quarter, was set onto a delicate silver chain necklace. The scale shimmered in pastel tones with glittering white flecks. It reminded her of an opal.

"This was your mother's," he said. "The scale came from her dragon, Liliganth. I kept it after we lost her. She wanted you to have it, if you became Lumen."

"Wow. I don't know what to say." She unclasped the chain and put it on. The scale felt cool against her skin. "Thank you."

"Lots of things are going to happen, Nail. You'll travel farther than you ever dreamed possible. This way, if you come across Liliganth, you might recognize ver."

"Thank you. I'm sure ve would have lots of stories about you guys that I'd love to hear."

Her father squirmed. "Yes, well—"

The door opened and Muari stood there, shoulders back and proudly holding her white egg in one hand, her cane in the other.

"Sorry," she said. "I didn't mean to barge in, but I've been out in that hall for five minutes. And I need to put this down so I can go to the bathroom."

"It's not a problem." Nail said. "Muari, this is my father, Robert. Dad, this is Muari, my roommate."

"It's wonderful to meet you," her father said. "Is Nail driving you crazy yet?"

Muari placed the egg on her bed, cradling it in pillows. "Not yet. But there's still time."

"Well, she's your headache now." He winked at Nail.

Muari paused before reaching the door. "Everyone is gathering at the beach tonight, Nail. You should join us."

Nail shifted uncomfortably and Muari left the room.

"And actually, I was just about to leave. Some of us are getting together tonight for a bit of a class reunion."

"Are you sure?" Nail stood and grabbed his hand. She wasn't ready for him to leave yet.

He brushed a lock of hair from her eyes. "You'll be okay. I'll be around for the next few days if you need me. But I'm sure Steven will be making plenty of time for you. And you'll want to spend time with your friends. Try to share in their joy, okay? Your time will come."

"Promise?" Nail asked.

"I promise," he said, but his words didn't ease her anxiety.

They said their goodbyes, and Nail was alone again.

She didn't feel a desire to share in anyone else's joy. Her gaze fell on Muari's egg, resting on the bed.

She wanted to believe that her time would come too. But in the silence, doubt crept up on her.

Without question, the gathering at the beach would turn into a full-blown party. Nail wasn't in the mood to celebrate something she didn't have.

When Muari returned, Nail made a watery excuse about having a headache. Muari, being emotionally oblivious for perhaps the first time since Nail had met her, accepted Nail's excuse and left as quickly as she'd arrived.

Nail couldn't blame her. If she'd paired, she'd have wanted to celebrate, too.

She closed the window in an effort to shut out the sounds of laughter and happiness rolling up from the valley.

A new depth of loneliness fell over her. Nail realized that this night was only the beginning. Pairing with an egg was the next step for everyone else. She had fallen behind. There were going to be a lot of things—parties probably the least of it—that she'd be excluded from.

IN THE MORNING, NAIL DRAGGED HERSELF DOWN TO STEVEN'S office. Out in the valley, she passed groups of parents happily swapping memories, basking in the tropical sunshine. She spotted the twins arm in arm and practically skipping to breakfast. She changed her path to avoid them.

Twice she passed green kakapos scuttling through the grasses on their awkward legs. As she neared the main building, a group of hummingbugs repeated the chorus of *Twist and Shout*.

Outside Steven's door, she could hear an angry voice from within. Judging by the man's accent, she guessed it was Dax's father.

Nail took a seat in the winged armchair opposite the door and waited.

The voices behind the door vacillated from near silence to angry screaming. She caught some of the phrases Dax's father used. Without ever seeing him, Nail had an instant dislike of the man.

After five minutes of waiting, Nail grew impatient. She knocked on the door.

"Not now!" roared Steven's angry reply.

Nail released her grip on the door handle. Staring as though her gaze could piece the wood and strike Steven, she huffed and turned around.

No point standing here and listening to this garbage.

She meandered through the main building, down halls and stairways she'd never explored before. Eventually, she found herself in a wide hallway. It ended at a gray stone archway closed by a red curtain on the opposite side.

Nail looked around for any signs that would discourage entry. She didn't see any. Pushing past the curtain, Nail realized that whatever she had assumed the room to be used for was wrong.

It looked like it had been cut out of a museum and transported to the island. Paintings and artifacts with little metal placards hung on the walls.

There were cave drawings, chiseled out from their original stone and rehoused, tile mosaics in sturdy frames, baroque paintings perfectly preserved, shelves with glass cases that housed ancient chipped clay vases and one vial containing golden wool. All of it depicted dragons and humans, sometimes at peace, and sometimes at war.

In the center of the room, under several spotlights, stood a raised glass podium containing a single piece of parchment. It reminded Nail of how the Constitution was preserved.

To Nail's surprise, Elsie stood beside the podium, her oceanic egg tucked safely in a pouch slung across her chest. She frowned at Nail and returned to examining the document.

Nail walked the perimeter of the room. The placard under the vial of wool claimed it was the last remaining threads of the Golden Fleece. The tile mosaic dated back to Mesopotamia. One of the baroque paintings—depicting a man with an obsidian dragon—was credited to Oracle.

She cautiously approached the glass case. The parchment it protected was aged and yellow, but its black ink looked as fresh as the day it was written. What language the letters came from or what the words said, Nail didn't know.

"It's the Draconian and Anthro Treaty," Elsie mumbled.

Nail bent over to examine it more closely. Its layout resembled the Constitution, even though she couldn't read it. "Is this what Steven laid on the dais on our first night?"

Elsie's reflection nodded in the glass, and she said, "It's crazy."

"What?"

"All the power of Lumen, the magic of the dragons, the gifts we receive... it all comes from this."

Nail kept staring at it. "Countries have been built on things like this. Wars have been ended. Just paper and ink."

Elsie gave her a sidelong glance.

Nail straightened up. "I'm sorry for what I said that day, in front of the chamber. I didn't mean to insult you."

Elsie snorted. "I'm used to it."

"You shouldn't be," Nail said. "I'm sorry I made things harder."

At that, Elsie actually laughed. "You have no idea how hard things are or aren't for me. No one does."

Nail looked at Elsie. Something dead and cold lingered behind her eyes. Elsie adjusted her stance, resting a protective hand upon her egg.

"At least you paired," Nail said.

Elsie's eyes narrowed. "At least your father showed up, or was allowed to show up. We're not all so lucky." She took one last look at the treaty and swept out of the room.

Elsie's footsteps grew quieter until silence followed. Nail waited a few minutes longer and then left the room, headed back for Steven's office.

The men were still arguing. She resumed her seat outside the office, but she didn't have to wait long.

Dax's father burst through the door. Nail had expected to see someone of Dax's height and build. Although he was covered in traditional tattoos, that was where the likeness ended. He stood least half a foot shorter than Dax and most of his mass was concentrated in his torso.

He scrutinized Nail then turned back to Steven. "I don't care what he thinks he wants. If you use your gift to turn my boy into a… a…"

Steven stood at the doorframe, gripping the wood with white knuckles. "That is not what I do. I have no ability to influence him into becoming anyone he's not. And neither do you. I've tolerated your spiteful existence in my office for long enough. Get out, and take your bullshit with you."

Dax's father shrank down like a cartoon bomb right before a comically large explosion.

Steven's voice changed from anger to commanding. "*Walk away.*"

The man let out a frustrated, unintelligible groan. But obediently, he turned and stomped down the hallway out of sight.

Steven sighed heavily, rubbing his temples. "The day after the pairing presentation is hell." He retreated into his office, waving her forward.

She shut the door behind them, choosing to sit in the same chair as before. Her gaze fell upon the odd hand banner again. She'd forgotten to look into what all the symbols meant.

"I'm sorry you had to endure that. I was going to send Prioress Julia to get you at breakfast before I was interrupted."

Nail fidgeted. "Well, I'm here now."

Steven smiled. In the two weeks she'd been there, Nail knew that smile well enough to tell when it was genuine or fake.

He sighed again. "What can I do for you?" Fake smile.

He asked casually, as though he had no idea why Nail was there, or what was concerning her.

Is he serious?

"My dad said you'd be making time for me."

"Ah, yes," he smacked his forehead. "Of course I will." Faker smile.

She stared at him waiting for him to say something.

He stared back.

"Shouldn't you be leading this conversation? You said the same thing that happened to me also happened to you. You didn't pair either."

"You're right. And I'm happy to hear any and all of your concerns."

She waited again. She didn't even know where to begin or what questions to ask.

Surely he had the answers. Why wasn't he forthright with them?

"Well," she cleared her throat. "What the hell happened in there? Am I staying? Do I get an egg? Am I still Lumen, still bound to the treaty?"

He sighed, but it seemed to come from a place of relief instead of stress. "Well, yes, you're still bound to the treaty. More bound than anyone else, really. No one can change that. There is no going back."

His face had turned gray.

Nail flooded with relief. *I won't have to leave Lumen.*

But she wasn't even close to satisfied yet. "So I'm definitely staying?"

He turned green, frowning. "You'll be with us for a very long time."

Nail didn't like the way he said "a very long time." It sounded less like an invitation and more like a prison sentence.

"And I'm getting an egg?"

He fidgeted in his seat, readjusting his weight. "The short answer is yes, though it may take quite a while. You have to understand, there's a lot of moving pieces, and things need to be put in place in the correct order. It's an ordeal, and—"

A knock sounded on the door.

"Come in," Steven called, a bead of sweat rolling down his forehead.

Nail bristled. Dax's father's tirade had been an uninterruptible meeting but hers wasn't?

Prioress Julia entered. Her hair was once again in a pinned-up, perfectly round bun, and she wore a severe expression. "Sorry to interrupt, Steven, but you're needed on the northwest side of the island. We're picking up substantial seismic activity. And I haven't been able to find Naileen—"

At the mention of seismic activity, Steven broke into a broad grin.

He's hiding something.

The Prioress noticed Nail sitting in front of the desk.

"Oh," she said. "*She* found *you*."

"Indeed, she did. Not to worry on the interruption, Prioress."

The Prioress nodded and quickly excused herself.

"Seismic activity?" Nail asked. "We're not getting a tsunami, are we?"

Steven shook his head, sighing. "No. It's probably just the volcano."

"Is it dangerous?"

"Impossible to say while sitting in my office," he answered. "If this is what I'm expecting, it's nothing to be concerned about today."

He rose, went to a coat rack, and pulled on a windbreaker in a hurry.

"It seems like the only parents who are here are the ones in Lumen," Nail said. "Why is that?"

He zipped his coat, looking around for a pair of shoes. "It's one thing to be told your child is going to a secret dragon society. It's quite another to be taken to it yourself. We don't exactly bring Vigilus along for visiting the non-Lumen parents. It's too risky."

He'd found a pair of hiking boots and laced them on. "All the parents are given paperwork for a student exchange program in Greece," he said. "It's convincing enough. And so long as the parents don't report their own children missing, any questions surrounding the disappearances quickly, well, disappear. There's just not enough of a trail to follow."

That was a solid answer. Which meant he wasn't acting odd because of the confrontation with Dax's father. He was dodging her questions because he didn't want to answer them.

She rose from her chair and rushed to stand in front of the door.

"You still haven't explained anything, not really. I don't understand what happened last night. Or *why*."

He looked down at her. "I wish I could explain further. But I have to consider the safety of the island first. Once I'm back, we'll talk more."

"When will you be back?"

"As soon as I can, and not a moment later." He smiled. "I promise."

Fake smile.

CHAPTER 3

Nail stood in the valley, watching her classmates leave breakfast. What was she supposed to do now?

Steven had left to go deal with the island's seismic issues, and everyone else was cooing and coddling their eggs. She folded her arms, not sure if she should socialize or go hide in her room.

The hummingbugs had changed their tune. Somber background music more fit for a funeral march now played around the sunny island.

Leaning up against a tree, Nail surveyed the valley. Classmates stood in groups, casually wandering in and out of the dining terrace, some of them with their parents. Jo's mother looked at her daughter, pride clearly beaming from her face.

To Nail's left, she saw Dax standing with his father. Shoulders hunched and his head hung low, he clutched his egg protectively against his chest.

His father began to shove him. Dax pulled his egg away, making no attempt to stop his father's aggression. When his father actually took a swing at him, Dax reflexively caught the fist, shoved it away, and stomped down toward the beach.

Nail's anger boiled at the man. It was hard for her to imagine any member of Lumen being so blatantly horrid to their own child.

"Hey," said a voice behind her.

Nail turned to see Jace. Her face faltered, trying to hide the emotion rising inside her. She glanced back over her shoulder to Dax. His father hadn't chased after him, but he stood watching his son leaving, flailing his arms wildly and shouting curses.

She turned back to Jace. He held his flora-embellished egg in one arm.

"Hey yourself," Nail said, trying to force a smile. Her father's words came back to her. *Share in their joy.* But she struggled to find the empathy. "So, any movement from that thing yet?"

Jace sat under a palm tree and invited her to join him. She did. "Not yet. Who knows how long it will take? We're supposed to have a 'bonding lesson' with Rankor and Prioress Nora pretty soon."

Nail leaned back, her hands dampened by the morning dew on the grass. "That sounds great. Like an old school health class."

He ran a hand through his hair. "How've you been?"

She shrugged. "Could be worse. I'm pretty sure they're not kicking me out. So there's that, at least."

"Have you talked with Steven yet?"

"Yes and no." Nail recapped the awkward, dodgy meeting for him.

"You really think he's hiding something from you?"

Nail was sure, but she shrugged anyway.

Jace tilted his head back. She noticed he hadn't shaved in a few days. Dark stubble appeared on his face and neck. She didn't mind it at all. "I wonder what that means, 'a very long time.'"

Nail stole a glance at his egg. "No idea."

"Well, it must mean you're going to get a pairing at some point."

"That's true," Nail said. "But I have no idea when. Or how."

He leaned toward her. "Maybe Rankor will lay an egg *just for you*."

They both laughed, but she thought the joke might have some merit. "Maybe that's what it is. My egg simply hasn't been... laid?"

The image of Rankor squatting and pushing out an egg came into her head.

"Ugh, can you imagine Rankor just, like...." Jace said.

Nail squeezed her eyes shut, failing to stop the mental picture. "Yes! Yes, and now that I've thought it, I can't unthink it, and it's awful."

"Thank goodness," a feminine voice said. "Here you are!"

Nail opened her eyes to find Vienna striding toward them, her little Fae egg wrapped in what looked like a macramé necklace.

Is there a craft this girl doesn't know?

Nail looked up at her, hoping her own expression read as inviting as an axe murder. "Looking for Jace?"

Vienna sat with them and touched Nail's knee. "No, I was looking for you. You weren't at breakfast this morning and after last night…" She looked to Jace. "Oh, we've just been so worried about you."

"We?" Nail shot a look to the hand on her knee and then to Jace.

"Well," Vienna started, "I'm sure everyone is. That was quite a reception, but you disappeared before anyone had a chance to talk to you. How are you holding up?"

Nail remembered that she still hadn't apologized to Jace for insulting Vienna. But as the girl stared at her, all perfect hair and symmetrical eyebrows, her will to make that apology disappeared. "I'm fine, thanks."

"Are you sure?" her grip on Nail's knee tightened. "Is there anything we can do?"

You can stop using the word we *so much.* "I'm fine. I talked to my dad last night."

Vienna frowned and nodded. She was the perfect image of empathetic sympathy. "Will you be leaving with him, then?"

Nail recoiled, and Vienna's hand finally left her leg.

Jace cut in. "Vienna, she's not—"

"Leaving? Of course not," Nail cut him off. "I have a place here, same as any of you."

She didn't truly feel it, but in front of Vienna she felt an intense fire to prove the claim.

"Oh," Vienna looked genuinely surprised. "I'm sorry. I just thought that—"

"Did you?" Nail rose to her feet. "Did you think at all?" She shot Vienna one scathing glance then steeled herself to look at Jace. She held up a pair of fingers. "Two cells. Two lonely cells and they're miles apart."

She stormed off down the valley, leaving Jace to figure out which of them he was going to stay loyal to. Nail knew there was absolutely no way she could ever—even for a moment—consider Vienna to be a friend. Vienna was clearly willing to do anything to get rid of her, just like she had the night of the bonfire.

If you want to be enemies, fine. Bring it on.

On her way to brood alone in her room, Nail crossed paths with Muari, carrying her engraved egg.

"Hey," Nail said casually without stopping.

"Nail?" Muari asked. "Where the hell have you been?"

Nail shrugged. *Silent language.* She stopped herself and replied. "Here and there, I guess."

"Well, where were you going now? We have class."

Nail rolled her eyes. "*You* have class. Everybody else has class. I don't have to do a damned thing."

Muari widened her stance. "Oh, so you're never going to get an egg then?"

"What? No. Steven says I will."

"Then you're coming to class," Muari declared. "Just because the teaching isn't helpful now doesn't mean it won't be later."

She was right. Nail hated it.

"And you're going to tell me everything that's bothering you while we walk there," Muari said. It wasn't a request. It was a command.

Nail sighed. "Fine. But I won't like it."

She and Muari made their way to a grassy clearing where class would be held. Nail told her about the meeting, recapping it in more detail than she had for Jace. She told her about Vienna's remarks.

"I do think she means well," Muari said.

Nail disagreed. "She's just so… irritatingly perfect. Does she realize she comes across as a know-it-all?"

Muari paused on that. "I don't think so. She does seem to care an awful lot about what people think about her. If she knew that's what people thought, I think she would change."

"Maybe I should tell her," Nail said. "Take her down a few notches."

"Maybe," Muari said, but her tone implied "no."

They passed several groups of parents—mostly couples—on their way to the clearing. As they rounded a grove of berry shrubs, Nail was surprised to see her father standing with some of the other parents, as well as Prior Adams and Prioress Julia.

"I don't think we want to be here," Muari said.

"No, my dad is ahead—"

"It's an awful thing to have happen, Robert, but it's certainly not unheard of," Prior Adams said, his voice carrying.

Nail stepped closer.

Her father nodded. "It was a shock. I thought I knew her. But…."

"It's not your fault," offered one of the women.

"Sometimes it just doesn't turn out like we hoped," offered another.

Nail looked on in horror. Were they discussing her? About how she was a disappointment because she hadn't paired? Heat flooded to her face.

Prioress Julia cleared her throat loudly, alerting her father to Nail's watchful gaze.

Her father looked apologetic and embarrassed. He looked like he'd been caught saying something he shouldn't have.

"Nail," he started.

"Let's go." She reached for Muari's arm.

Nail turned them both sharply in the opposite direction, and they fled. She fought back tears. Of all people, she thought her father would always be on her side.

I was wrong.

Sniffing, she wiped her face clean with her free hand.

They arrived at the clearing the long way. Most of the class was already gathered and spread out over the space in patchy groups, sitting with their knees folded. Each of them had brought their journals, though Nail hadn't thought to bring her own.

Rankor and Prioress Nora waited roughly at the center of the group. Nail was relieved for a moment to see Jace and Dax sitting together. Vienna had coupled with Kerris on the opposite side of the group.

She couldn't get her father's words out of her head. *"I thought I knew her."*

When everyone else had arrived, Rankor began the class. *"Welcome to your first day of the fourth stage—self-reflection."*

Everyone sat a little straighter.

"The timetable of a hatching is unpredictable and unique to each individual and egg. Some eggs require more self-reflection than others. There is no set amount of time that it will take for an egg to hatch. There is only a right time."

"One of the keys to hatching your egg is to be open to possibilities," Prioress Nora said from the center of the group. Her hair was pulled into an easy ponytail that bobbed enthusiastically. "Within each of your eggs exists a world of endless possibilities. You will need to consider as many as you can, and find peace with each of them, before your egg can hatch."

Nail thought of her father. She hadn't asked him anything about his dragon, or vis abilities.

"The other key," Rankor said, *"Is to be honest about yourself. Over the many centuries, dragon and human pairings have almost always incorporated*

some sort of balance to their relationship. We see this most often with complementary strengths."

Prioress Nora nodded. "For example, my ability to teleport and Aenu's gift of paralysis. In a sense, I have the gift of uncontrollable motion, and ve has a gift of stopping all motion. We balance each other out. Which is how you all arrived here."

Elsie raised a hand. "Why don't we remember anything after that, though? I mean, we all disappeared, and time passed, but none of us can remember how we got to that room."

Everyone shifted, intently interested in that answer.

Prioress smiled. "You have my brother to thank for that. Steven's gift is to, as he says, inspire. Your first teleportation can be quite a shock, especially when you don't know it's coming.

"That moment was a bit, well, jarring for each of you. The mind is being suddenly forced to accept a premise that it finds quite ridiculous. He inspired each of you to forget that moment so you could all start with a relatively clean slate, free of trauma."

Although Prioress Nora was framing it in a positive light, the thought of what Steven could do made Nail shiver. It sounded like mind control. She must not have been the only one thinking this, as the group—especially the girls—glanced around.

"Never fear," Prioress Nora said. "His ability can't *make* you do anything you don't want to do. You, and the rest of the world, are quite safe. You'll find that most magical gifts could be abused for something sinister. Part of what we do on this island is to help cultivate your gift and guide you in using it appropriately and morally."

Nail's father came to mind again. Had he not been a good person, the ability to unlock any door or window would have been terribly dangerous in the normal world. And his gift was relatively tame.

"*In addition,*" Rankor said, "*sometimes the shell of an egg can reveal something about its inhabitant. Please gather around and form a circle.*"

Nail helped Muari resettle and they sat again.

Rankor surveyed the circle and found it to be satisfactory. "*We'll each take turns going around. On your turn, everyone must give their thoughts on your egg. Please do not repeat anything previously said, and focus your thoughts on the egg alone. The idea of this exercise to help everyone expand their expectations and accelerate your acceptance of possibilities.*"

Nail wondered what they were going to do when it was her turn.

"Record these opinions in your journal," Prioress Nora said. "You will be writing a paper on them tonight."

The sound of rustling paper filled the group as everyone turned open their journals. Muari pulled out a voice recorder from her back pocket.

Nail watched Vienna whisper something to Kerris.

Kerris nodded and raised her hand. She didn't wait to be called on. "Is it really fair for Nail to be here? I mean, we're all criticizing each other's partners, essentially. But we can't give *her* a critique."

Everyone turned their attention to Nail. She felt heat rising to her cheeks and braced her palms on the grass, ready to rise up and to flee from the group.

Prioress Nora scowled at Kerris. "Nail is still a part of your class. No, her pairing hasn't happened yet, but it will follow this same process. I'd like to remind you of what Oracle said your first day. Treating anyone differently will not be tolerated."

Nail smirked. She liked the idea of Vienna and Kerris on the receiving end of Oracle's wrath.

Kerris shrunk down, stabbed an angry glare at Vienna, then stared intently at the grass.

They went one by one around the group. The suggestions for Jace's dragon focused on trees and plants, ranging from an ability to recreate extinct species to growing super-efficient crops. Everyone agreed that Elsie's egg would involve water. And the suggestions became more and more ridiculous with Luca's ambiguous yellow egg.

"Maybe ve can swallow the sun," Igo offered, basking in everyone's laughter—or eye-rolls.

Nail frowned, remembering that Igo had been part of their *Vortex Beyond* group. Maybe his personality was different online or maybe it was Luca's influence. She didn't like this version of him.

After Luca, the opinions became more and more outlandish. Nail noticed Muari getting stiffer and fidgeting as it came closer to her turn.

When it was her turn, she hesitantly clicked on her voice recorder. A bead of sweat rolled down her temple, under her sunglasses. Some people thought that the designs on her egg meant the dragon would be able to do something with patterns. Luca suggested crop circles. Quinn suggested an ability with mathematics or physics.

Everyone spoke carefully and kindly, as though their words alone might cause Muari's egg to crack and crumble.

Vienna was last. She offered the suggestion that everyone else had likely been thinking.

"Maybe it will restore your sight!" she offered brightly.

Muari sighed, like she had known the suggestion had been inevitable. She switched off the recorder. Nail was positive she'd just gained a new ally in her Vienna-vendetta.

"*Restoring* sight means that it would be returned to me, implying that I lost it, like misplaced car keys." Muari reflexively clutched her egg closer. "I've never had sight, so *that's* impossible. You mean to say that I would be *given* sight. And if accepting that possibility is what it takes to hatch my dragon, then this egg's gonna remain an egg."

Everyone stared somewhere, anywhere else—the sky, the trees, the person across from them—waiting for someone to break the silence.

"Well, if it's okay, I think we'll skip you, Nail," Prioress Nora offered.

Nail nodded. She leaned closer to Muari. "You okay?"

Muari frowned. "Let's talk later."

The group continued giving opinions, but everyone hesitated with Hazel, who had the gray, diseased egg. No one wanted to state the obvious idea—that the dragon in her egg would bring about the next black plague.

When they finished, the class journaled their first reactions to the suggestions. Nail didn't have anything to write, and Muari would audibly review her suggestions later and in private. They sat quietly. Muari's hands shook as her fingertips traced the patterns on her egg, waiting for the class to end.

Prioress Nora called back everyone's attention. "Steven has canceled all personal appointments today. Something has come up on the north side of the island, and he will be away addressing that issue for the remainder of the day. Please prepare three thousand words on the suggestions your classmates made and have them turned in by noon tomorrow. Class is dismissed."

Nail and Muari immediately stood and headed back to their room. Muari tremored with rage. Afraid she might emotionally explode, Nail waited until they were alone before asking about it.

Nail shut their door. "So… Vienna, huh?"

Muari sank to her bed and nestled her egg between the pillows. She heaved a heavy sigh. "I know a lot of other people were thinking it. But that doesn't make it okay to *say* it."

Nail nodded along. She got that it was a personal topic, but exactly why it had upset Muari so much was lost on her. "Right, okay."

Muari continued. "It's just… sighted people can be so wrapped up in their own experiences that they don't consider mine."

"Like I said, Vienna doesn't realize her helpful suggestions aren't helpful at all."

Muari huffed. "If Vienna suddenly lost her sight, I understand why she would want it back. That's *her* experience. But I've never had it. And saying that I should have it makes me feel like people don't think of me as a complete person without it."

Nail moved over to Muari's bed and put her arm around her. "I don't think of you like that. Vienna is just a complete… ass. I thought I was the ass. But, turns out, it's her."

Muari leaned her head onto Nail's shoulder. "I don't need to experience the world the same way she does. Because I don't think I'm experiencing it any less. I just experience it differently."

Nail hugged her. "I know. I like different."

Muari sighed. "Maybe you should tell her. Someone has to stop her endless stream of unwanted advice and stupid opinions."

Nail smiled. "We should think of a way to fix that."

"We could push her off a cliff," Muari said in a glum tone. A joking smile played at her lips.

"Maybe one of the fae dragons could help," Nail said. "Convince her she's actually a flying sack of sh—"

"You don't need a tricky fae for that," Muari said, fully enjoying the joke. "You need someone with the gift of illuminating the truth."

Nail snorted. "Or we could dress her up as a fish, and leave her in the river with the hydra."

Muari smiled wide. "Did the farm have a well? We could push her down a well."

"Vienna, I wish you well," Nail laughed. "Find one, fall in it, and stay there."

CHAPTER 4

Muari and Nail kept a wide berth from most of their classmates the next day. Steven still hadn't returned from the north side of the island, so individual counseling sessions were canceled yet again.

Jo spotted them under a mango tree and asked to join. She set her oblong, golden egg on the grass and sat next to them. She wore stretchy workout clothes, and sweat glistened over her dark skin. Wisps of naturally curly hair bobbed in the wind.

Jo smiled. "Hiking endorphins," she said.

"Are you guys supposed to be carrying them everywhere?" Nail pointed to her egg.

Jo shrugged. "Steven encouraged us to, after the pairing presentation. By the way, where have all the parents gone?"

"I saw a few yesterday," Nail said dryly.

"Mine weren't here," Muari said. "Neither of them are Lumen."

Jo nodded. "My mom was here, but dad wasn't." She chuckled. "He got a real big surprise when she explained it to him, the way she told the story. A gift of perfect balance." Jo laughed. "It explains why her cupcakes were always so magical."

"I think all the parents were getting together," Nail said. "My dad said he'd be gone for a few days."

"Makes sense, class reunion to Drasol," Jo said.

"To where?" Muari asked.

But before Jo could answer, Igo and Luca emerged from a pineapple grove and interrupted their conversation. Neither of them carried their eggs.

"Ladies," they said in unison.

"We're throwing a party tonight," Luca said.

"The Lumen superlative, class of Metal Dragons," Igo said. "Down at the beach. Can we count on you all to be there?"

Nail looked around the group. "I guess so."

"Excellent." Igo scribbled in his journal. "The festivities start at sundown."

"And remember," Luca said. "No babysitter needed, so leave the eggs at home tonight. Bathing suits optional, birthday suits preferred." He winked.

Jo rolled her eyes. "Get lost, creeps."

They left to go find more classmates, discussing who still needed to be crossed off their RSVP list.

Jo shook her head. "You know, when they get their magical gifts, I hope it makes them actually funny. Right now they're just our personal *Dumb and Dumber* clown show."

"I hope they end up learning some responsibility," Muari said. "They could both use a healthy dose of it."

Nail had always assumed that guys like Luca never grew up to amount to much of anything. They became the balding middle age man who lived in his mother's basement, played too many video games, and reeked of weed. She still held out hope that Igo could turn things around for himself.

She smiled. The thought of weed had brought back the memory of Finley. She hadn't even asked her father about Finley. Was he touting the same lie Steven had said, claiming that she was in an exchange program in Greece?

Nail doubted that Finley would believe that, but she would never guess the truth, either.

That evening, Nail helped Muari put together an outfit for the party. In turn, Muari convinced Nail to wear a dress.

There were only two to choose from in Nail's wardrobe. One was a sleek, bodycon cocktail dress that seemed far too formal for a beach party. Nail chose the other one, a maxi dress with mesh cutouts around the abdomen.

Nail admired herself in a mirror, describing the dress aloud.

"It looks nice on you," Muari said.

"The hell?" Nail replied. "It *looks* nice on me?"

"Well, it sounds like you think it looks nice on you. That's just as good of a compliment, isn't it?"

Muari wore a black skater dress and a new pair of sunglasses studded with fakes rubies. They walked down to the beach together. Deciding to take the long way, they crossed over the bridge north of Oracle's pond. Nail watched the water, hoping for a disturbance.

In the time since he'd dashed off to the north side of the island, she'd decided that if Steven was still gone the next day, she would throw rocks into that pond until Oracle gave her some answers. Boulders, if she had to.

They saw a couple of the guys before they reached the beach.

"Jace, Rorik, and Dax are in front of us," Nail said.

"Score!" Muari called, "Hey sexy boys, you looking for a good time?"

They turned. Jace and Rorik paused, assessing their dresses. Dax frowned.

"How's it going, ladies?" Rorik asked.

"Not too shabby," Muari said.

When the girls caught up, Jace leaned into Nail's ear. "You look very nice in that dress."

"I heard that," Muari said.

Jace smiled. "You look very nice too."

Nail looked up at him, blushing. "Thanks."

"Sweet necklace, Nail," Rorik commented.

She had never taken off the dragon scale pendant from her father.

Their small talk continued. Dax hung at the edges of their group, one arm folded across his chest. At some point, though Nail couldn't say when, Muari had put her hand on Rorik's arm like he was properly escorting her. She wished she had seen it. She was curious if Rorik had offered or if Muari had made the move.

She wondered if Jace would offer. Or if she should make the move.

But they made it to the horseshoe-shaped beach before she found the courage. Gentle waves rushed up along the white sand, and tall rocky cliffs corralled both the east and west sides of the beach. Out on the ocean, stronger waves thrashed against juts of volcanic black rocks, sending clouds of white mist into the air.

It seemed that Igo and Luca had received help from Vienna and Kerris in setting up the party. If Vienna would focus her efforts on helping those two mature, it would certainly leave her with too little time to pursue Jace. For Nail, it was a win-win.

Folding chairs and torches had been set up, as well as tables with refreshments. Between the chairs and the ocean stood a small stage. There was no microphone, but a handful of trophies were piled in one corner. Judging by their toppers, most of them had been for sports. Nail saw figurines representing bowling, baseball, volleyball, and chess.

Half a dozen humming bugs—which resembled oversized ladybugs—gathered around an older-looking stereo on one table. The stereo played a range of 90's pop music covers with the swear words altered. The humming bugs mimicked the melody and bass. Nail suspected the boombox had come from the supply closet. She didn't mind the tunes. A lot of her music was old-school.

The four of them sat together, taking up most of the second row. Dax wandered off, catching Elsie in conversation.

For whatever reason, Igo and Luca's wardrobes had included some tacky looking suits. Igo wore a leopard-print blazer with a matching tie, no shirt, and red swimming trunks.

Luca wore a similar ensemble, with neon polka dots covering his blazer and tie. But rather than wearing swimming trunks, he had opted for bright pink swim briefs which left mercilessly little to the imagination.

Luca rushed around, happily welcoming everyone to the party. He said hello to Nail and her group. She got an eyeful of pasty white cheeks poking out of the edges of his briefs as he skipped away down the beach.

"Dude," Nail said. "Why?"

Jace smiled. "You know that's what he's going for, right? Shock value."

"Sure," Nail said, "but do we all have to suffer for his art?"

Igo and Luca announced themselves as their MC's for the evening. They had prepared skits with bare-bones costumes, mocking many of the staff and a few of the dragons. Thankfully, none of them were present for the embarrassing display.

Whatever their magical gifts would be, it didn't seem like they had a natural knack for dramatic thespianism. But they knew how to perform crude sketch humor.

And although Nail had found it to be a little base at the start of the night, she was laughing with the rest of the group before long.

"Now we're proud to bring to you the Lumen Island superlatives," Igo announced.

Luca brought the baseball trophy to the center of the stage. "We're awarding this superlative to the person with the prettiest egg."

"That's right, everyone. The partner of this egg has made a *huge* splash in our community and has really left a mark on all of us," Igo said.

"Some of us more than others." Luca pointed to his left eye. "Get on up here, Dax."

Everyone clapped and laughed as Dax made his way to the stage. He accepted the trophy with a smile and bowed to the crowd.

"Got any words to say?" Igo asked.

Dax tucked the trophy under one of his massive arms. "No words, just one finger for both of you guys."

Everyone laughed even harder and Dax returned to his seat.

"Next up, the person most likely to have the funniest dragon," Luca announced.

Igo held the trophy. "Wait, we have a problem. That's both of us."

Igo held the trophy at opposite ends and snapped it in half over his knee. He handed the top piece to Luca.

Luca looked at it. "Eh, it was a piece of crap anyway."

They both tossed their broken halves over their shoulders and into the sand.

"Next up, we'd like to award the person with the dragon egg that's most likely to succeed in life. He's big. He's fun. He's everyone's favorite farm kid. Get on up here, Jace!"

Everyone clapped, and Jace slid out in front of Nail. He took the trophy, played to the crowd for a moment, and returned to his seat.

"Okay, just two more to go, folks."

The crowd groaned.

"Sorry, but all this took a lot longer to set up than we thought, so the writing suffered." Luca shrugged. "Deal with it."

Igo held the next trophy. "This one goes to someone we can all feel bad for. I mean really bad for. She didn't even get a dragon…"

Nail's stomach dropped. She caught Vienna looking back at her from the front row. Nail couldn't read her expression.

"All she got was a diseased ostrich egg, and no one has the heart to tell her any different!"

The crowd laughed again. "This award is more real than her dragon. Get on up here, Hazel!"

Hazel sat directly behind Nail. She rose from her seat and sheepishly accepted the award. Hazel got the baseball trophy, and she used it appropriately on Igo and Luca.

Igo grabbed the last trophy, hesitating for just a second before handing it to Luca.

"Now, last but not least," Luca said. "This award goes out to someone whose dreams have been crushed. Her hopes have been dashed. She's the loser queen of the whole group!"

Nail's stomach dropped out a second time.

Igo held up the chess trophy. "Congratulations, N—"

"Thank you!" Vienna jumped up and rushed the stage. She snatched the trophy and addressed the crowd.

Wait. What?

For a moment, Igo and Luca looked confused.

Igo recovered first, his gestures even more exaggerated. "Welcome to the stage, Vienna!"

"It's true, you all will still have the opportunity to someday watch your dragons grow large or ride one." She gestured to the tiny egg around her neck. "And I've had to say goodbye to those dreams. But, hey," she gestured to the two hosts. "At least I've got some fashion sense. Luca and Igo never paired with *that*."

Everyone applauded and whooped. Vienna shot a dirty look at Luca and Igo. And just before she took her seat, she winked at Nail.

Nail knew they weren't about to call Vienna's name. She might love attention, but that hadn't been her reason for rushing the stage. With all of the disappointment and frustration that had happened, the last thing Nail needed was to be publicly mocked.

And Vienna knew that. She'd done Nail a favor.

It made it harder to hate her.

And although she hated to admit it, even only to herself, she was grateful.

CHAPTER 5

Nail couldn't focus on the party. Everywhere she looked was another reminder that she didn't truly belong. There were excited conversations about whose egg would hatch first, or what magical gift people thought they were inclined to receive. As the night wore on, it only made her feel worse about herself.

Vienna showed off the trophy that had been meant for Nail. Igo and Luca had taken off their blazers and wore just their swimsuits and ties, splashing in the shallow waves and encouraging the girls to join them. Jace and Dax laughed with Muari and Rorik. Hazel and Maeve happily conversed, sorting through the old music CDs.

Nail looked around. No one would notice if she slipped away.

So she did.

On her walk toward the dorm, she let her feet do the work while her mind was elsewhere. She wondered when Steven would be back. She wondered why she was different from the rest of her class. She thought of her dad, and the things the other parents had said.

"Honey!" a familiar voice called.

Nail looked up. Her father was with a group of the other parents, all of them in hiking gear and carrying heavy backpacks, headed toward the eastern side of the valley. She stared at the ground again and picked up her pace.

But she wasn't fast enough. He caught up with her, a hand landing gently on her forearm.

"Please let me explain," he said.

She turned and looked at him. "There's nothing *to* explain."

"What you heard," he said, "it wasn't about you."

Nail rolled her eyes. "No? Then who was it about?"

He looked over his shoulder, back to where the rest of the group stood waiting for him. "It was... not you. It's complicated and... too big to explain right now."

Nail shrugged away from his hand.

"Please," he pleaded. "I'll be back in a few days. I'll explain everything then. I promise."

She searched his face. His eyes were watering. The concern folding the corners of his mouth seemed genuine.

Nail nodded her head once. "You'd better."

She didn't give him a goodbye or a hug. Instead, she did an about-face and continued on to the dorms.

It was well after midnight when everyone from the party began filtering back in. Nail had sat in the common room for hours, trying to decide what her next move should be, if anything.

Giggling girls flooded by her, most of them still wet from the ocean waves. Nail called out to Muari, who pleaded for her to come upstairs.

"It's not healthy to brood like this," she said. "Jace missed you at the party."

Nail made a non-committal noise, but she was secretly pleased. "I think I'm going to stay up a little while."

"Got a secret date tonight?" Muari asked.

"No," Nail said. "I'm just not tired yet."

Muari pushed her sunglasses higher on her nose. "Suit yourself."

Nail waited until everyone had gone to bed. Then she went back outside.

She was certain her plan was dumb. But she was impatient. It had been two whole days, and she still had no solid answers. Although the party had been fun, it had also been a constant reminder that she was different from the rest of her class. She was ready for those differences to end.

And the sooner the better.

After a few weeks on the island, even at night the path to Oracle's pond was familiar, and her mind began to wander.

Why did Vienna do that?

An uncomfortable hardness settled in Nail's stomach. The easiest reason also made the most sense. Vienna had wanted to spare her from being publicly humiliated because she cared. She cared about everyone.

Nail huffed and folded her arms as she walked. Even if Vienna did genuinely care, it didn't make dealing with her *I-know-better-than-everyone* attitude any easier.

She thought back to the night at the bonfire, how Vienna had lied to get her away from Jace. *She seems selfless, but she doesn't always act like it.*

Without warning, Nail crashed into something, tripped over tree roots, and fell. Her hips hit the ground hard.

"What in five hells?" said a female voice.

A lantern flicked on near the ground. Nail hadn't tripped over tree roots. She'd run right into Prioress Nora.

"What are you doing out here?" Prioress Nora asked. "It's nearly one in the morning."

Nail pushed herself into a sitting position—her hips were definitely going to bruise—and stood. "Just… taking a walk."

Prioress Nora stood. She wore normal clothes, jeans, a blouse, and ballet flats. Nail saw her raise one eyebrow in the light of the lantern. "Without a flashlight? Seems like you're sneaking around."

Nail shrugged. "Maybe."

"Can't sleep?" Prioress Nora asked.

Nail shook her head.

Prioress Nora pointed up toward the main building and picked up the lantern. "C'mon. I'll make you a cup of tea. And you can tell me all about where you weren't sneaking off to."

Nail glanced south, toward Oracle's pond. She'd wanted answers. But there was no easy way to get rid of a Prioress who could teleport.

Plus, she was Steven's sister. After Oracle, Prioress Nora might be the most likely person to give her answers.

Nail agreed, and they headed north.

"What are you doing out here?" Nail asked. If she could keep the conversation off herself, she might end up in less trouble.

"Serving the society," Nora said in a sarcastic tone. "Taking Dax's father home."

"He's a real piece of work," Nail said.

Prioress Nora frowned. "Dax isn't the first of his family to be invited to the society, but his father was. And he isn't happy about the egg Dax paired with."

Nail recalled the pairing. Dax had been lucky. His egg was easily the most enviable, covered in shimmering crystals.

"He didn't part with Dax on the best of terms," Prioress Nora said. "And his opinions are affecting Dax's ability to bond with the egg."

Nail reflected in silence. Her own father had been so supportive. It must have been awful for Dax, being torn between his family and the society.

"Anyway," the Prioress continued, "once all the parents go home, my life can go back to normal."

Nail looked over at her. The light of her lantern cast eerie shadows through the tropical landscape. "What does your normal life look like?"

They were ten yards shy of the main building. "A lot of traveling. Sometimes I check up on society members that aren't on the island. Sometimes I just like to go have lunch in Paris."

Prioress Nora led Nail into the main room. She flicked off the lantern as Nail studied the stained-glass window.

"Through here." Prioress Nora had opened a hidden door at the back of the room. Set into the rough stone, it would have been impossible to find unless you knew where it was.

The doorway led to an otherwise featureless corridor that ended in a flight of steps. The first flight led to a hallway with at least a dozen doors on each side. They went up the second flight. There were fewer doors in that hallway, each of them spaced farther apart.

Prioress Nora withdrew a key and unlocked the door marked #7. She held it open and gestured Nail inside.

The room didn't match the tropical location at all. The natural stone of the floor and ceiling had been painted white, and the walls were done in a light shade of blushing pink. Silhouette paintings done in thick black brushstrokes hung on the walls.

A retro, white-and-black kitchenette stood off to the left while a bed with a shimmering silver comforter stood in the far corner. The center of the apartment was set up as a living room with two poufy white sofas resting on opposite sides of a gray sheepskin rug. Between them sat a mirror coffee table with little cupboard doors beneath.

Altogether, it reminded Nail of a Chanel ad.

"Have a seat," Prioress Nora said.

Nail cautiously sat on the edge of one of the white sofas. "This isn't what I expected."

Prioress Nora busied herself around the small kitchenette, filling a white and black polka-dotted kettle with water. "Steven and I grew up in New York City. I've lived on this island for twelve years, but New York is the place is where I feel most at home."

She set down a silver tray of teabags, petite floral mugs, a sugar bowl, and crackers.

"Of course, we grew up surrounded by noisy neighbors in a tiny two-bedroom apartment that looked nothing like this." She smiled at Nail. "I don't miss the stink in the hallways, or neighbors shouting at all hours of the night." She sighed. "But there's no place in the world quite like NYC."

Prioress Nora relaxed on the sofa opposite Nail. "So tell me about where you definitely weren't sneaking off to."

Nail fidgeted. "Steven's gone away," she recounted. "I was going to see Oracle."

Prioress Nora made a small "ah" noise. "You want answers about why you didn't pair."

Nail nodded. "Everyone else is on their way to becoming 'who they are' or whatever. I just want what they have."

Prioress Nora sighed. Nail didn't think she looked much like a Prioress. The word had always reminded her of cloistered women, like nuns, with gray eyebrows and harsh frown lines. Sitting in the chic apartment, across from a woman not yet even thirty, the title just didn't suit her.

"You're not going to be like the others," she finally said.

"On the night of the pairing ceremony, Steven told me the same thing happened to him twenty-four years ago."

"It did," Nora said.

"How long did he have to wait to pair with Vigilus?" Nail asked.

"A few weeks," Nora answered. "But it took almost three years to hatch."

Nail's eyes widened. "That long?"

"I was four when he was brought to the society. We didn't grow up together very much. But I can still remember what he was like in those days. His egg wasn't hatching. He came home from 'school' for summer. And he was… unbearable.

"Headstrong, selfish. A different girlfriend every week. A terrible older brother and example for someone in first grade." Prioress Nora rolled her eyes. "He certainly wasn't a role model or a leader. He didn't want to accept that he would have to change, so his egg didn't hatch.

Without his egg hatching, his magical gift couldn't develop. And a good thing too."

Nail didn't need it explained, but Nora continued anyway.

"A selfish, womanizing teen with the ability to influence anyone into doing anything so long as some small part of them already wanted to do it? Certainly you've wanted to do something that your better judgment has stopped you from doing."

Nail thought of her hatred of Vienna. She nodded.

"If he had gained that power before developing a better moral compass the entire world could have collapsed under his spell. Luckily for them, he's content living most of his days on this island and bettering the relationship between humans and dragons." She scoffed. "Imagine the damage he could do if he got involved in politics."

"What about you? Your egg, and your gift? How long did it take?"

Prioress Nora smiled broadly. "Mine was the first of my class to hatch. Four days. Faes tend to be faster, but not always."

Nail groaned internally. If Nora was right, Vienna would be among the earliest ones to have a hatched dragon. Her status of barely tolerable would rise to totally insufferable.

The kettle whistled. Nora rose and removed it from the stove. She poured hot water into the little mugs as Nail picked out an herbal tea. No caffeine, something that would help her sleep.

"My gift manifested rather soon afterward. And that was messy," she said, laughing at the memory. "One moment I was napping under the shade of a palm tree on the beach, dreaming of New York City. And when I awoke, I was in the center of Times Square, still wearing my bikini. Certainly not the strangest sight for that place, but it was very alarming for me."

"What did you do?"

Prioress Nora spooned sugar into her tea. "It would be nice to say that I kept my cool, but I didn't. I thought I'd fallen into some nightmare dream world that I couldn't get out of. I ran around screaming my head off, and eventually got taken down to a police station. They thought I was as high as a kite, raving about dragons and magic and being trapped in a nightmare."

"You got out of it, didn't you?"

Prioress smiled. "I did. They threw me into an empty cell, the ones they usually use to hold people until they sober up. They called social services.

"I didn't have an ID on me, but they could tell I was underage. I curled up under a blanket one of the officers gave me, cried for a little while, wishing I was back on the island. I closed my eyes and poof. I was back here again. Well, sort of."

"Sort of?"

"I didn't stick the landing. I ended up about fifty feet offshore from the beach. It took a while, but I've learned to improve my aim." She winked.

Nail's tea sat untouched. The steam had stopped rising. "Well, do *you* have some answers for me?"

Prioress Nora frowned. "You were smart to seek out Oracle, but I don't think she would give you anything. It has to come from Steven. It's his responsibility now. All I can do is council patience, Nail. And I advise against roaming the island at night without an adult dragon."

Nail nodded, remembering the boar attack. "I think I'd better get back to my room, then. Thanks for the tea. And the story, Prioress."

"Please, just call me Nora." She smiled serenely. "Steven won't be gone forever. I promise."

But he sure is taking his sweet time.

As Nora showed Nail out, she gave her the lantern. "It would be a bad idea to go bothering Oracle at night anyway. She's old. She likes her sleep."

Nail made her way through the valley. The island was serene at night, the air warm but the breeze cool. She passed under a branch where a hummingbug murmured the tune of *Truly Madly Deeply*.

Nail felt tired. When she reached the large common room, she found Prioress Nora sitting on a chair in a corner.

She smiled up at Nail. "Had to make sure you'd make good on your word."

And with a tiny *pop*, she disappeared again.

The lights were still on in Nail's room when she went in, but Muari was fast asleep. Her carved white egg sat on her dresser, swaddled in a pile of blankets.

Nail yanked off her day clothes and slipped into sweatpants and a t-shirt. She took one last envious look at Muari's egg then flipped off the light.

But she lay awake, wondering how long it would take that egg to hatch. A small, bitter part of her hoped it never would. A slightly bigger part of her hoped none of them would.

The next morning, Nail and Muari were sitting in the valley after breakfast when Prioress Julia ran past them, her perfect bun askew, screaming her head off.

"Nora! Nora!" she cried, "You're needed on the grounds! The first hatching is happening!"

Nail and Muari went racing toward the spot Prioress Julia had come from. Muari kept one hand on Nail's arm, using her white cane in her other hand.

"Who do you think it is?" Muari asked.

"If you give me three guesses, I bet only need one," Nail said.

A crowd had begun to gather as Vienna and Kerris sat crossed legged with the tiny Fae egg between them. Prioress Nora *popped* into being at the edge of the group. She pushed and shoved her way to the center of the crowd and knelt.

The little egg shook. One by one, each of the overlapping layers began to peel away like flower petals. They revealed more colors than the egg had let on. Pinks and greens and blues changed to oranges and reds and purples. The egg opened and unfurled like a spring blossom.

Then the layers turned white. Then silver. Vienna had her hands cupped around the hatching egg, not interfering, but protecting the little dragon just in case. One silver petal remained. The dragon squirmed, and the final petal fell away.

The little fae dragon unfurled its wings. The whole crowd let out a hushed "aww," and Vienna cried a sobless tear. The dragon's wings were wisps of pink and yellow shades, and barely discernible.

"Ver coloration will darken with age," Nora whispered, an awe-struck smile spreading over her face.

The dragon's body was tiny, even compared to Aenu. Snout to tail-tip, it was smaller than Nail's pinky. Even its full wingspan was only the size of her hand.

"Hello, little friend," Vienna said. "My name is Vienna."

Like a chorus of high pitched bells, Nail heard a tiny voice answer. *"Lyva."*

CHAPTER 6

Finley had caught a lucky break. She'd made contact with two of the friends from Nail's *Vortex Beyond* group. One lived relatively close. All told, a five-hour drive one way wasn't that bad.

Two other members in her group had also disappeared from the game. But Finley hadn't managed to track down either of their offline names. Quitting a game they were globally ranked in was suspicious, but not outright illegal. Finley couldn't prove anything about them.

By the time she reached Dos Gatos Café her back was stiff and aching. Finley parked, went inside, and ordered at the register. She looked around the crowded coffee shop. Only one person fit the description of who she was supposed to meet with. The girl sat alone, hiding her face under curly brown hair, her gaze buried in her phone.

"Medium mocha latte and a lemon pound cake?"

The barista looked maybe early twenties, underweight, with patchy neck hair and a receding hairline. He slid Finley's order onto the counter and checked her out as much as the high-top would allow.

She rolled her eyes and claimed her cake and coffee.

Tally didn't look up until Finley had pulled out the metal chair, screeching it against the stone floor. Finley extended her hand.

Tally examined the extended hand but didn't return the gesture. She scrunched her face as though a handshake would rain every disease and contagion upon her.

Finley sat. "Okay, then. Well, thanks a lot for meeting me."

"Sorry you had to do all the driving." Tally finally set her phone aside. "I can give you money for gas."

That would be a start. "Sure, that would help a lot." She sipped her latte, but the drink was still too hot. "So what did you find?"

Tally began rummaging in her oversized purse. "You said your friend's in Greece? As an exchange student?"

"That's what her dad told me," Finley replied.

Tally produced half a dozen papers. "I found these in our basement."

Finley unfolded them and began to read. "You were going to Greece on exchange program too?"

Tally shook her head. "There's no way. And none of it makes sense. Look at the application acceptance date."

Finley scanned the paperwork. "That's the day before Nail and the others disappeared." She tried to put the pieces together, but they didn't fit. "That's an incredible coincidence. You didn't know about this 'exchange student' program?"

Tally began tapping the table nervously. "I never applied for one. I mean, I've been working on my anxiety, but it took years before I could leave the house for more than an hour, and I still need to plan for it. I can't handle traveling outside of town. Being trapped in a car for too long makes me anxious. Being on a plane would be my worst nightmare."

"So you never applied. But they accepted you. And… there's the lost time thing."

She nodded and looked into the distance, as if recalling a memory that wasn't there. "I remember playing the game, and then nothing. I woke up in my house, in my bed, and I have no memory of how I got there."

Tally started tearing up and hyperventilating. She opened her bag again and fished around in it—setting two bottles of pills on the table—before finding a third bottle. She took off the cap, slipped a blue pill into her hands, and swallowed it with a sip of water.

Tally sighed heavily. "I don't know what I did. I don't know if something happened to me. But something clearly *did* happen to me." She picked up one of the other bottles and took half a tablet.

Finley sipped her cooling latte and prepared herself for whatever came next. "Are you sure the memory lapse wasn't like… a medication side-effect or something?"

Tally nodded. "I know my meds. Whatever caused this, it wasn't that. And my parents are being so weird about it."

Finley cocked her head. Nail's father had always been nice enough, but he'd seemed annoyed when she'd gone to his house. "Weird how?"

Tally folded her arms. "Like, angry? Like it's my fault that I don't remember what happened. My mom's been really short-tempered with me. And my dad... he's started insisting that I 'have to get better' and I can't live at home forever. They've been fighting a lot too."

Finley folded the papers twice. "You mind if I keep these? There's contact information for this program and stuff. I'd like to look into it."

"That's fine. I just want it all to go away. I can't remember what happened to me." Tally's timidity gave way to a look of reserved determination. "I want to forget that this entire thing happened at all."

For a long moment, Tally looked dazed, lost in a daydream.

Finley waved a hand in front of her face. "You okay in there?"

Tally stared blankly.

Finley worried Tally had taken too many pills. What was she supposed to do if this girl was overdosing? She didn't know.

Tally snapped back to reality, blinking. She looked at her hands, at the table, and then at Finley.

Then she screamed. Loud, shrill, bloody-murder, *screamed*.

Tally stood, nearly falling over her chair. "Who the hell are you? Did you bring me here?"

The entire café was watching them. All the typing and chatter had died in an instant.

Finley looked from Tally to the confused patrons. Everyone stared at her. Heat flooded to her cheeks. "Y-you told me to meet you here. I drove five hours."

Tally shook her head, her curly hair bouncing itself into a mess. "No. No, I didn't. Did you kidnap me?"

Tally looked around, grabbed her purse, and bolted for the door.

"Wait—" Finley called. "Wait!"

But Tally was already out the door. A car alarm blared in the parking lot, and Tally rushed to it.

People kept staring at Finley, waiting for some sort of explanation.

She didn't have one. She stuffed the exchange papers deep into her purse and grabbed her coffee and cake.

Finley swore and muttered, "She didn't even give me gas money."

CHAPTER 7

Three days later, class was held in the mango grove of the valley. Rather than being led by Rankor or Prioress Nora, a woman Nail only vaguely recognized from the dining terrace stood around stacks and stacks of cages. She couldn't fully see inside them, but she caught flashes of feathers and fur. The woman wore grubby clothing with dark, sinister splotches. Her dishwater blonde hair was pulled into a practical braid.

Nail glanced around. Muari was captivating Rorik's attention. Nail liked the way he laughed at her jokes.

Nail kept looking to see how much of the class was there, but Dax stood at her side, blocking her vision. Thinking of what Nora had said about his father, Nail looked up at him.

Dax had dark rings under his eyes. He wasn't carrying his egg. He returned her gaze with a half smile.

"Not sleeping well?" Nail asked.

He scoffed. "That obvious?"

"I overheard your dad in Steven's office a few days ago," Nail confessed. "I'm sorry he's being pigheaded."

Dax shrugged, but his half-smile seemed a little more genuine. "He can get bent."

"Good morning, everyone," the woman said. "My name is Prioress Cameron. I'm in charge of the farm here on Lumen, and today you'll be receiving a brief lesson on caring for your newly hatched dragons."

Everyone seemed to perk up a little. The lessons on getting their dragons to hatch had grown stale. Something that prepared them for the next stage of their journey was a welcome relief.

Cameron tapped one of the cages beside her. Something inside rustled frantically against the straw. "Your dragons are natural hunters. There are several small bird species on the island, as well as a good range of insects for smaller dragons. However, a little encouragement goes a long way."

She opened the cage and reached inside. What she pulled out was one of the ugliest animals Nail had ever seen.

It had a patchy round tail and was covered in brown fur. Cameron held it aloft for everyone to see. The animal flailed its stubby legs fruitlessly in the air. It had short, pointed ears, and a smashed-in face. It looked like a cross between a deformed rabbit and a pug.

"Snub-nosed hares," Cameron said. "Bred especially for dragons, these little beasts give off a pheromone that attracts a dragon's hunger like a flame attracts a moth. They're fast breeders, clumsy runners, and easy prey for your young dragons. Most of your dragons will grow rapidly. Expect them to have two to four successful hunts every day."

Cameron set the snub-nosed hare down on the grass, and the critter scrambled away with an awkward gait through the crowd. Even for the flightless dragons, they would be easy prey.

She turned her attention to another cage. "After about a month or so, your dragons will enter a magpie phase of adolescence. To avoid stolen jewelry, broken windows, and missing spoons, we'll be populating the valley with royal golden pheasants."

She opened the cage, pulling out a gorgeous bird. Golden feathers crested its head and neck, and ruby feathers dressed its torso. A plume of cerulean blue feathers covered its back, and its tail fanned out in an impressive display of oranges, greens, and purples.

"Royal golden pheasants are also ideal prey for dragons learning to fly. They can't go far, and they can't go fast, but they're good for learning dive moves and stealth hunting."

The pheasant flapped its wings, revealing a ruby wingspan that shimmered in the sun.

"Your dragons will enjoy collecting their feathers and hunting in groups to take down this sprightly prey."

Elsie raised her hand. "Won't this upset the ecosystem of the island? Isn't it dangerous to introduce a non-native species?"

Cameron nodded. "Normally, yes. But your dragons are apex predators. By the time they're large enough to hunt for bigger prey, they will have wiped out all of the pheasants and hares."

Cameron gestured for everyone to come closer to the cages. The group unstacked them, opening the doors and freeing the inhabitants. Hares and pheasants scattered around them in a mad dash to reach safety.

A few wyverns had gathered for the release, snapping and chasing the prey to further spread them over the valley.

Cameron stood with her hands on her hips. "It may take some getting used to, but hunting is a natural behavior for dragons. You'll adjust to the blood and gore. Everyone does eventually."

Nail looked at Cameron more closely. The dark splotches on her clothing made more sense now.

Meals at the garden terrace frequently included beef and chicken. It wasn't Nora bringing in massive amounts of food every day, and Cameron wasn't just in charge of tending to the crops. She was their on-island butcher, too.

As the lesson ended, a few of the guys helped Cameron load the empty crates into a wagon pulled by two horses. Everyone spread out, either marveling at the pheasants, cooing over the ugly rabbits, or enraptured by the aerial diving moves of the adult dragons.

Ten yards away from Nail, Luca drew attention to himself again. His sunshine egg had begun to jump and crack.

"Knew mine was gonna happen before yours!" he shouted to Igo.

The class crowded around him, waiting to see what would emerge. Nail found Muari sitting nearby. They kept away from the main bulk of the crowd.

"How far along is it?" Muari asked her.

Nail peered over the shoulders of her classmates. "Maybe halfway? I hope that dragon has more intelligence than Luca."

Muari had earbuds and a voice recorder out. Her white egg remained unmoving. "Hopefully. They're going to be a real danger to each other if ve isn't."

"What have you been working on?" Nail asked.

"Studying. I've been looking into the correlation between a dragon and a human's magical gifts within a pairing."

"Find anything interesting?" Nail asked.

Muari shifted and resettled herself. "More specifically, I've been trying to find examples of a human or dragon's magic that alters medical conditions. What Steven said that night to Tally about people being healed has been on my mind."

The crowd gasped and awed. Nail looked. A small chip of the shell lay on the grass.

Nail squinted. "So, you're trying to figure out if there's a chance you're going to have sight forced upon you."

"Basically, yeah," Muari said. "But I haven't found anything definitive."

The crowd hushed. Nail looked over. Everyone took a collective inhale as a yellow lung dragon flew into the air and settled itself around Luca's shoulders.

"Steven should be here for this," Nail said. "I wonder what's taking him so long."

"It is odd," Muari replied.

"I wonder if someone should tell Oracle," Nail said.

"Prioress Nora has been doing a fine job in Steven's absence," Muari said.

Nail stood, wiping damp dirt off her jeans. Luca continued to show off the lung dragon like ve was a shiny new scarf. Nail wasn't close enough to hear the dragon's name.

"I want as little to do with Luca's personal brand of insanity as possible."

"It's not insanity," Muari said. "It's an impressively immature predisposition to avoiding responsibility. And unless he grows out of it, it'll be his downfall eventually."

Nail watched Luca. Everyone was enamored with the new dragon. Ve was lithe, already an adept flyer, and very sprightly. Ve was charming Vienna with aerial loops. Kerris looked on, arms crossed, and eyebrows furrowed.

How long until the little dragon caught sight of one of the golden pheasants or snub-nosed hares and instinct took over?

She also wondered how many other hatchings would happen before she finally got her own pairing.

Frustrated, Nail stamped a foot into the ground and set off to Oracle's pool, bidding Muari a hasty farewell.

No one from the group seemed to notice her coming or going anymore, except for Muari. Even Jace and Jo had grown distant. She wasn't a student like them. In some ways, she wasn't a student at all.

She took a left turn beyond a palm grove and was surprised to find Prior Adams already at the pool. Oracle was back to her dragon form and had her head and neck above the water. Nail approached, but Oracle didn't extend any conversation to her. When she got close, the dragon appraised her silently and slipped back beneath the waves.

"Sorry if I was interrupting something," Nail said.

Prior Adams stared at her. "Is there something you need?"

She told him of Luca's egg hatching, but his gaze remained far off and distant. She wanted him to leave. She knew Oracle was in the pond, and there were plenty of rocks on the shore to annoy the great dragon into giving her some answers.

The lines on his forehead deepened. He reminded her of an eagle, or a hawk, constantly searching his surroundings for prey.

"I just thought Oracle should know. Is something going on?" she asked. "Is it Steven?"

He scowled. "There's always something going on. Specifically, we have unexpected visitors on the island. And one of the older dragons is dying."

"Dying?" Nail asked. "Here? I haven't seen any of them sick or injured."

Prior Adams shook his head and began walking the way Nail had come. "It's not an island-based dragon. This one has resided in Scotland for quite some time."

Nail kept up his pace. Prior Adams walked like there was a watch in his head, ticking away the seconds.

"Scotland." She had assumed the dragons lived only the island. Her heart quickened. "Wait, does this dragon dwell in water?"

Prior Adams tried not to smirk, but he wasn't successful.

Nail's heart soared higher than when Steven had announced the pairing ceremony. "I knew it. I *knew* ve was real."

"Very real," Prior Adams said. "And you're bright to pick up on it."

The crowd was still gathered around Luca as they arrived.

"Go join your friends," Prior Adams told her.

Nail resumed her spot next to Muari.

"Did you talk to Oracle?" Muari asked.

"No, but I think the Loch Ness Monster is—"

"I need everyone's attention," Prioress Nora spoke before Nail could finish. "It has been brought to my concern that we have some unexpected visitors on the island. Two Drasol dragons have just arrived. I will be sending out a few of our own dragons to discover why they're here."

Prioress Nora looked at Prior Adams.

He stood tall, hands clasped behind his back. "These dragons are not bound to the Draconic and Anthro Treaty. Until we are certain they do not pose a threat, everyone will need to return to their dorms and stay there. Do not go exploring the island. If you see an unfamiliar dragon, do not approach it. Do not go out alone. Do not go out at all."

Vienna raised her hand. "Are we in danger?"

Nail rolled her eyes. The treaty made it impossible for dragons to harm them.

"Quite possibly, yes," he answered.

Nail furrowed her brow. About half the class looked confused, too.

Nail whispered to Muari, "How could a dragon not be bound to the treaty?"

"The treaty specifies Lumen dragons. I would assume these dragons are not Lumen," Muari replied.

The group broke apart with everyone heading back to their dorms. Nail and Muari hung to the back as Vienna put on a concerned face and led the way. Nail thought Vienna looked like a prairie dog, constantly scanning the area for any sign of an unfamiliar dragon.

Back in the common room, Vienna held a gathering.

"Rather than go back to our rooms, I think we should all stick together. There's safety in numbers." She stood in the center of the room with Lyva resting on her shoulder.

A few people muttered agreeably. A few people shrugged. Nail perused a bookshelf while everyone else sank into couches and armchairs. She selected a book on western dragon mythology and took a seat in an empty armchair within the circle of girls.

She flipped to a page on Norse mythology, skimming over a story of Thor killing a sea-serpent. Most of the old tales from western countries involved dragons that were tricksters, or poison-spewing monsters valiantly slain by gods and men. Nail glanced around the room. Elsie had her nose in a book as well.

"I'd like to know how these dragons are even a threat to us in the first place," Hazel said to no one particular. "I thought they were all magically bound by the treaty to not hurt us."

"Lumen dragons are bound by the treaty," Muari answered her. "The others aren't."

"What others?" asked Maeve.

Elsie answered without looking up from her book. "The ones born in Drasol, obviously."

Elsie's proclamation was met with silence from the group.

"What the hell is Drasol?" Hazel asked.

She snapped her book shut. "Honestly, all of this is totally available to you all. In addition to Earth, there are several other realities. Drasol is the dragons' original home world."

Maeve leaned forward. "There are other places besides Earth with life? Are some of them aliens?"

Nail smiled at Maeve.

Elsie rolled her eyes. "If you mean little green men that enjoy anal probing and cow abductions, no."

"How do they get here, then?" Nail asked. "Magic?"

"There's a portal room on the island, east of the valley. It's literally on your map," Elsie said.

Nail thought back to the image of the map hanging in her dorm room. "That spot is labeled in Latin."

Elsie stood, cradling her egg in one arm and her book under the other. Nail wasn't sure which she loved more.

"And apparently I'm the only one who's studied the subject." She huffed off toward the staircase and disappeared.

The noise disturbed Lyva, who rose from her perch on Vienna and fluttered over to Kerris.

Kerris allowed Lyva to settle on her shoulder. "I would think the treaty should still apply to them. I mean, we're on Earth."

"Magic doesn't work that way," Muari said.

Kerris raised an eyebrow at her. "These dragons are more likely to be a danger to the Lumen dragons then, not us."

Lyva shifted like ve was shaking off a chill, and a small cloud of silvery dust filled the air.

"We should organize a search party." Kerris looked to her fearless leader Vienna, searching her face for a sign of approval. "We're Lumen, too. Why can't we help?"

"I don't know," Vienna said. "Prior Adams told us to stay inside. That's probably the safer idea."

Kerris pouted, brushing the fae dust away. She folded her arms tightly around her body.

Nail returned to her book, happy to stay out of the conflict. The illustrations depicted a Viking called Segurt slaying the dragon Fafnir by lying in a pit and stabbing it through the belly.

"What do you think, Nail?" Vienna asked.

Nail looked up. "What do I think about what?"

Vienna smiled and flipped her hair back. "About a search party. Should we form one?"

Nail scanned the room. Everyone had their attention on her. "Why does my opinion matter?"

Vienna's bleached smile widened. "Well, you've got less to lose than the rest of us."

Heat rose in Nail's cheeks. Who did Vienna think she was, anyway? What was the point of saving Nail from humiliation on stage if she was just going to do it later?

Nail shut the book. She thought of what Vienna had said to Muari during their first circle.

And there weren't any wells nearby.

"You know what, Vienna?" Nail stood. "You're a self-righteous know-it-all who can't imagine a world that doesn't revolve around you," Nail blurted. "No one wants your advice on anything—ever—so stop passing it out like mono-infected Halloween candy."

Kerris started to interject when Nail rounded on her next.

"And you're a sniveling shadow. You *should* go out alone. It might get you some actual attention, instead of whatever toxic runoff happens to drip onto you from Vienna. No one would even notice you if you weren't attached at the hip with the Queen B."

Vienna folded her arms. "Queen bees are leaders." She said it like that settled the matter.

Nail smirked and remembered Vienna's lie the night of the bonfire. "I don't mean insects. You're the queen on the corner of Bullshit Avenue and Bitch Lane."

Nail followed Elsie's lead and stomped up the stairs.

She sat on her bed, fuming silently. She knew she'd just started an outright war with Vienna.

Consequences be damned, she deserved it.

Nail returned to reading, letting her anger sit on a low simmer, not really absorbing anything on the page.

It was late in the evening before Muari came up to the room. Nail had long finished the Norse myths and was thumbing through Greek mythology when the door opened.

"How's the world's most exclusive sorority?" Nail asked, her voice dripping with sarcasm.

Muari sighed, laying her egg gently on the bed then sitting. "Basically the cattiest club ever. That was epic, but you know you're not winning any popularity contests."

Nail turned a page and shrugged. "Never have. Why start now?"

"I went to the other side of the room after you left, hoping they would start gossiping about you."

Nail looked up. "And?"

Muari picked up her egg, turning it over in her hands and running her fingers over the designs. "Do you really want the truth? It's not kind."

"Yes," Nail said.

Muari sighed. "No one thinks Vienna deserved to be called out like that. Or at least, that's what they're saying to her face. Most of them are annoyed that you're here. They think it's unfair. Jo came to your defense a few times. But Kerris has really got it in for you."

Nail shut the book and laid it on the bed. "Why shouldn't I be here?"

"She seems to think that you're being given an unfair advantage by being the only one without an egg."

Nail eyed Muari's egg, selfishly grateful that she didn't have to disguise the envy on her face. "That's stupid. I don't have any advantage. And this isn't a competition."

Muari continued. "Kerris is dead-set on this search party idea. She really is the kind of girl who's used to being recognized, like she was the Vienna at her old school. Well, you're different, and Vienna's egg has hatched, but she can't take out her frustration on her BFF. So…"

Nail followed her logic. "So she thinks finding these intruders would earn her some real recognition."

"Precisely." Muari leaned to one side, resting her cane against her nightstand. She set the egg next to her and began unraveling the earbuds to her voice recorder.

"That's impressively stupid," Nail said. "I only said that to insult her."

"It worked," Muari replied.

A light outside the window caught Nail's attention. She left the book on the bed and went to the window. She scoffed. "And it gets stupider."

Muari had one earbud in. "What does?"

"Kerris is outside with a flashlight, hosting her own one-woman search party."

Muari *tsk*ed. "She's gonna get herself killed."

CHAPTER 8

Nail paced indecisively at the window.
"It's not my job to go chasing after her." But a ball of guilt stemming from her outburst grew heavier in her stomach.
Muari lay on her bed, completely unconcerned about Kerris' decision. "Well, it's not my job to do anything about it either. No one's gonna blame *me* for not chasing after her."
She looked outside again. The light of Kerris's flashlight grew more distant but was still visible. "I'm not responsible for this."
Muari rolled onto her back, her egg resting on her stomach. "Nope."
"We should tell Nora or Prior Adams, right?" She checked the window again.
Muari sighed. "Yeah, that'll go over well. Kerris already hates you. She's literally out there trying to prove that she's better than you. If you rat her out..."
Muari didn't have to finish her thought. Nail knew things would only get worse between her and the rest of the group. Vienna would double down on her efforts to humiliate Nail and pull Jace to her side.
Nail shook her head, trying to brush away thoughts of him.
"I'm going to go after her," Nail said. "If I bring her back myself, no one else will need to know. And maybe I can convince her that I'm not...." Nail wasn't sure how to finish that sentence. "Maybe I can convince her to see some sense in all of this."
"You could try apologizing. Like, tomorrow." Muari held her egg,

turning it over and over in her hands. "But suit yourself. I'm staying put."

Nail grabbed a jacket and a flashlight and headed for the door. She paused at the handle and looked over the map of the island.

There were fields and plains east of the valley. Set into a rock formation called Dragon's Spine was a place called *Et Portae Cubiculum*, the portal room. Nail assumed that this was where Kerris was headed. There was a tunnel set into the side of the valley, leading out toward Dragon's Spine.

Nail zipped up her jacket and headed out.

The night air was still warm. There was no moon, and the stars shone brighter than ever. Nail clicked on her flashlight and headed south toward the tunnel. The only noise came from the groan of several white wind turbines atop the valley's east range, turning steadily in the night's breeze. She picked up her pace.

The tunnel was easy to spot. Tall and wide enough for even the largest dragon she had seen, it was roughly cut and worn smooth in the center. She cast the beam of her flashlight along its walls. The tunnel curved slightly to the right, making the exit impossible to see.

Nail had delayed too long. So far there had been no sign of Kerris out in the valley. Nail hoped she'd find her first, before Prior Adams or another staff member did.

The legends of trickster dragons luring unsuspecting maidens to their deaths came back to her mind. She hoped they were simply fables, remnants of the symbolism between greed and innocence with a dash of old-world chauvinism thrown in for good measure.

But she now knew that wasn't likely. The treaty had been created for a reason. Even if all the stories weren't true, some of them had to be based on actual events.

Nail was halfway through the tunnel when she heard a noise that set her on edge. A scream, bloodcurdling and desperate. It sounded like a small child, a toddler, crying out in pain. The noise was distant, but it reverberated in the stone tunnel, bouncing off the walls and surrounding her from every angle.

She ran.

The horrible screaming continued, louder than her own footsteps hitting the rock and echoing down the walls.

The tunnel opened up into a field of tall yellow grass sparsely dotted with high, thin trees.

The screaming hit a higher note, peaking with desperation. Then it stopped.

Nail turned toward the sound and ran, the long grass whipping against her thighs.

It didn't make sense. The voice was too young to be Kerris. But Nail had never seen any children on the island, either.

In the distance ahead, Nail saw the light of another flashlight, flowing and moving between the thick grass.

There was already a pain growing in her stomach, but she picked up her pace, running recklessly toward the light. Her foot caught on a fallen branch, and Nail fell hard into the dirt. She could smell the wetness of the earth.

Then a pair of high-pitched laughs echoed in her mind.

"Come closer," said one.

"We can help," said the other.

She didn't recognize either of the voices. Her panic deepened.

Nail got to her feet. The other flashlight was even farther away. She ran hard toward it. The grass shortened, and the sound of waves crashing grew louder.

She kept her sight focused on the ground, determined not to trip again. It was the sight of blood that first caused Nail to stop.

It trailed through the grass, splattered and smeared over broken stalks of grass, gruesomely marking a crude path. In her pause, she followed the trail to the fresh carcass of a dead pig, bitten and shredded, nearly ripped in two.

For a moment, she felt relief. The screaming had been the dying squeals of a pig, not a girl.

She heard the pair of laughing voices again and a girl crying. There was a second and third trail meandering away from the dead pig.

Two English dragons, each as long as a pick-up truck, slithered and circled around Kerris. Her flashlight lay abandoned on the ground, pointing an eerie and ill-aimed spotlight on the taunting display.

But there was something wrong with them.

They lacked the bulk that Vigilus had. Instead, their legs were scrawny, and their wings were short, nearly flat against their too-thin bodies. They didn't look sturdy enough for flight. Even their snouts and tails looked emaciated.

Their scales were thin, more like the skin of a snake than the armored hide of a Lumen dragon. She could see the rise and fall of the ridges over their ribcages. These dragons looked sickly, starving, and crazed.

"W-what do you want with me?" Kerris said from between them. "I-I know you can't hurt me."

The dragons laughed again. They hissed and snapped at Kerris, like a game of monkey-in-the-middle, forcing her to repeatedly retreat from one and move closer to the other.

Nail crouched down into the long grass, hoping neither of the dragons had a gift for sight.

"*Of course we can hurt you,*" said one.

"*You're so vulnerable...*" said the other. Their voices were hollow and sharp, with all the strength of a twig of balsa wood.

Nail had no way of knowing which voice belonged to which dragon. But her cover worked and they hadn't noticed her yet.

She watched, frozen in horror. She didn't have a weapon on her. Even if she had Prior Adams's entire arsenal, she didn't know how to use a gun, let alone fire one accurately. She didn't know these dragons and didn't know how to persuade them.

Helpless.

"Kerris!" called a familiar male voice. Nail looked back. Steven came striding toward them from the north. His eyes landed on Nail for a moment but quickly darted away.

One of the dragons took vis attention off Kerris. "*Steven Parson,*" it said with a giggling lilt. "*You've lost a sheep.*"

"*And we found a meal,*" said the other dragon.

Nail saw the horror in Steven's face, the rage and fear. He stood a yard away from where she hid. "Stay down," he whispered.

"Leave her be," Steven called, trying to fill his voice with authority.

Both of the dragons laughed.

"*Your tricks won't work on us,*" said one dragon as the pair circled in closer and closer.

"*You can't* inspire *us to do anything we don't want to do,*" said the other.

Steven took two steps forward. "You don't want to do this."

The laughter reached a higher octave, almost squealing. It reminded Nail of hyenas at the end of a hunt, or the sound brake pads make when they need replacing. They spoke in unison. "*Yes, we do.*"

Nail whispered to Steven fervently. "What do we do?"

Steven's mouth was contorted with horror. He shook his head. "Help is coming."

From somewhere unseen, Vigilus's deep, booming voice filled Nail's mind. *"Xaos and Thovos, leave the girl!"*

"Help me!" Kerris screamed.

"Time to act," said one of the dragons.

The other dragon laughed.

"No!" Steven cried.

The dragons were moving in.

"Kerris," he called. "Kerris, look at me."

Her eyes were wide, mouth ajar. All of her hope rested on Steven.

He raised his head, daring the world to defy his order. "You don't want to feel any pain. Stop feeling pain."

Kerris had time to reply with one small nod.

There was a flash of scales, a terrible ripping sound, and satisfied groans. The noise was perverted and unbearable. The sound of liquid gushing to the ground, of a crumbled fall that crunched the grass blades below.

Nail had no way to block it out. A heavy iron smell intertwined with the salty air.

It took a second for the blood to come pouring through the grass in little streams.

But Kerris never screamed or cried. She hadn't felt any pain.

CHAPTER 9

Nail had blacked out for a moment. She was on the ground, on her hands and knees. She didn't remember getting sick, but the evidence was right in front of her. Trickles of blood flowed through the grass, swirling with dirt, heading right for her puddle of sick.

The air was filled with the sound of guttural growls and crunches. Bones in dragon maws.

She felt like throwing up again.

"Hold them there." Steven's voice was an angry command.

Nail stood and chanced looking back at the grisly scene. She wanted to avoid looking at what was left of Kerris, but it was unavoidable. She'd been ripped in half, and ropes of intestines lay strewn around the grass.

But the twin dragons weren't feasting on her. Instead, there were four dragons in front of Nail, not two.

Vigilus and Aurumis must have arrived when Nail blacked out. They dwarfed the Drasol invaders, each atop one of the murdering monsters.

Vigilus had vis jaw locked onto the base of one dragon's neck—Nail didn't know if it was Xaos or Thovos. Aurumis held the other one the same way. Their strong legs and fearsome claws tilled the earth as the foreigners struggled fruitlessly to escape.

Nail looked back to Steven. He had his eyes shut, and traces of tears rolled down his cheeks. A moment later, with a small *pop*, Nora and Oracle in her humanoid form appeared beside him.

Nora surveyed the scene and immediately crouched, her hands on her knees and back arched. She looked like she was going to be sick, too.

Oracle stood as tall as ever. She gazed unflinchingly at the murderers, at the rivers of blood, at Kerris's torn and destroyed body.

"Nora, compose yourself," Oracle said. "Get some wyverns back here to watch over the body. We don't want the boars making this worse. And bring Cameron. She can stomach what needs to be done."

Nora took a few deep breaths and steadied herself. She tried to look back at the grisly scene, but seemed to think better of it and shut her eyes. With another small *pop*, she was gone.

Oracle pointed at Nail. "What was this one doing here?"

"I don't know yet," Steven replied.

Oracle turned her head and stared down at Nail. The scale lines on her face seemed to have grown deeper. "Did you lure her out here?"

"No!" Nail replied. "No, I was following her."

"Was she alone?" Oracle asked.

"Yes," Nail said. "I came to bring her back to the dorm."

"Were you not instructed to stay inside? Do you realize we could have lost four tonight instead of two?"

Two? Who else was attacked? Her mind immediately went to Muari. She was sweating despite the temperate air.

Had Kerris brought Lyva? Or her egg?

Everything came spilling out of Nail's mouth in a rush. "We were all sitting around in the dorm, and Kerris thought we should form a search party, and then I got into a fight with Vienna. I went back to my room, and I saw Kerris leaving but I didn't want her to get in trouble so I followed her out here and, and…"

Tears welled up and spilled down Nail's cheeks without her blinking.

"That's enough," Steven said to her, his voice calm and reassuring.

The Drasol dragons still struggled under the weight and might of Vigilus and Aurumis but they made no progress.

Oracle redirected her attention to Steven. "Her actions were rash. There ought to be a consequence. Think of what she put on the line to go chasing after one human."

Steven nodded. "I understand, but she doesn't. She doesn't yet know the full… scope of her importance."

Oracle's expression turned stony. She commanded, "Repeat."

Steven swallowed hard. For the first time, it looked like it was his turn to be sick. "There was a quake on the north-eastern section of the island. I've been away, making sure everything—"

"Which is to be expected," Oracle interrupted. "Are you telling me that Nail has not yet been informed of her role?"

As terrible as the situation was, relief flooded Nail. It seemed like finally—*finally*—she might get some real answers. Nail stared at Steven.

He tried to compose himself, to look stoic. "No, she has not."

"You cowardly, incompetent fool," Oracle cursed.

The sound of rushing wings filled the air. Three wyverns, none quite as large as Aurumis, landed at the site. Growls echoed from their throats. They encircled Kerris's body. Nail could only imagine what threatening conversations the five Lumen dragons and the foreign Drasols shared.

With another small *pop*, Nora appeared with Aenu on her shoulder and Cameron at her side. Dressed in her normally grubby clothing, her hair was pulled into a loose braid. She carried a large, empty burlap sack.

Not exactly dignified.

Cameron frowned at the scene in front of her, but she didn't look sick. She certainly didn't black out and fall to the ground. Who better to handle a gruesome death than the butcher?

Cameron turned to Steven. "I'll get her cleaned up once those two beasts are out of the way. Equfid will meet me here."

Steven nodded. He looked relieved.

Xaos and Thovos had exhausted their energy trying to escape. They each lay limp beneath their captors.

"Vigilus, Aurumis," Steven said, "take these two to the docks. Oracle and I will meet you there to collar them until their trial."

A trial? Why? Surely there was no doubt of their guilt.

"No," Oracle said. "Nora, Aenu, and I can handle collaring them. You will stay behind and explain everything to Nail."

Steven looked pale again but only nodded.

Aenu fluttered toward the huffing Drasol dragons. Steven's gift hadn't worked on them, but Nail believed Aenu's would. Vigilus and Aurumis had overpowered them, but Aenu would render them immobile.

Everyone moved close to Nora. Steven and Oracle placed a hand on her, and Nail followed suit. With an almost instantaneous double pop, they all reappeared in what seemed to be a living room.

She felt dizzy, like she'd just stepped off a ride at a county fair, and her head hurt. She wondered if Nora suffered from constant headaches.

Nail and Steven removed their hands from Nora, and with a third pop, Nora and Oracle were gone. Nail and Steven were left alone.

His eyes were lined with heavy, dark bags. "You should sit down."

CHAPTER 10

Nail surveyed the room. The lights were already on. There was a quiet, Asian feel to the space. Most of the furniture was white, and canvas paintings of Japanese temples hung on the walls.

Windows overlooked the nighttime landscape of the valley, and the ocean was visible in the distance. A sliding rice paper door showed a bedroom in one direction and a kitchen in the other.

"Welcome to my home." Steven moved toward the kitchen, pulling two wide wine glasses down from a hanging rack. "Do you want a glass?"

"I'm sixteen," Nail said.

"And you've just witnessed a brutal murder. And your night isn't going to get any easier."

Nail realized she was shaking—shivering almost. "Okay. Sure."

Steven uncorked a bottle of red wine. He considered the label, frowning, and pushed the cork back in. He reached for a white wine instead.

"Your class will be informed of tonight's events tomorrow afternoon. Nora will inform all the other residents tonight. You're welcome to spend the night in her apartment. She won't be needing it tonight."

Nail nodded.

"Please, sit."

He placed the two glasses of wine on the coffee table in front of her and sat on the opposite couch. A geometrically patterned blanket rested over the back of the couch behind him. He pulled it down and handed it to her. Nail draped it over her legs.

Steven picked up his glass of wine and drained half of it. There was no clinking of glasses, no words of cheers. He rose again and returned to the kitchen. Nail took a small sip of her wine and appraised him.

His hair was a mess, and his clothes were dirty. The bottoms of his pant legs were ripped and fraying. He looked like he needed a hot shower and a week's-worth of sleep.

"Why am I here?" Nail asked.

Steven returned with the open bottle and placed it on the coffee table. "I can't send you back to the dorms after what—"

"No," Nail interrupted. "Why am I *here*, on Lumen Island, with no pairing and no answers?"

Steven looked away. He seemed to find it uncomfortable to make eye contact with her. "I was going to meet with you tomorrow morning. But then I suppose tonight would have derailed that as well."

"I've been waiting, jealously watching everyone else advance and pair with eggs. I've been bullied and rejected. I just watched another classmate get murdered by *dragons*, which I didn't even think was possible."

"They weren't Lumen," Steven reasoned.

Nail bristled. "Yes, from some other reality called Drasol. I gathered that."

Het foot tapped on the floor. It was about damn time for some answers.

"Why am I here?" Nail repeated a third time. "What did Oracle mean when she said my 'role?'"

Steven sighed and refilled his glass. "I'm sorry I've let you down. To be honest, I ran off to investigate the quakes because it bought me more time away from you. Away from this conversation."

Nail leaned forward, her insecurities rising. Had she offended him somehow? She hadn't meant to, but she was no stranger to unintentionally offending people. "What did I do?"

He shook his head. "It's nothing you did." He took a sip, much smaller than his first. "It's who you are."

"What does that even mean? 'Who I am?' Didn't you know who I was before you brought me here?"

Steven smirked into his glass. He still wouldn't make eye contact with her. "You were the daughter of two of our members. Intentionally born in the correct lunar year to hopefully become a member of the Lumen Society as well." He scoffed. "Well, it worked."

Nail put her glass down. "If you don't start giving me answers, I'm marching down to the girls' dorm and announcing Kerris's murder. And I'll blame you for it. I've been through enough. I've seen enough and you're just—"

"You're a Fated." He finally met her gaze. "That's what you are."

She appraised him. His eyes looked set. Honest. Searching for a reaction. "And what, exactly, is a 'Fated?' That means nothing to me."

He chuckled into his glass. "It's about to mean everything."

Steven sighed and looked up at the ceiling as though the smooth stone had all the answers carved into it.

Nail took a sip of her wine. It had a bitter bite, but she didn't hate it. She took another sip.

With another sigh, Steven heaved himself forward, placing his glass on the table and his forearms on his knees. "I didn't think I would have to do this. Not so soon, anyway. What happened to you in the incubation cave is... not common."

"Has my egg not been laid yet?"

Steven scooted the edge of the couch. "No, it has."

"Then it's... not on the island?"

"No, it is. There's a second incubation chamber—one that is rarely needed, and so, rarely visited. The last person to enter it was me, twenty-four years ago." He fidgeted with his sleeves and with the knees of his pants.

"Let me clarify," he continued. "Your other classmates will have partners. Meaning that they and their dragon will have different roles, but function together. They will build each other up. I'm sure you've realized by now that not all partnerships stay together forever."

Nail thought of her father. "Of course. I would've remembered growing up with a dragon in the house."

Steven nodded once. "Your father's partner wouldn't have fit in your house, but I take your meaning." He took a heavy sip, this time draining the glass. "Your mother and father fell in love. They wanted to continue on the familial line for Lumen.

"But the island is no place to raise children. And there's no guarantee that their child would be accepted, even if a child had been born in the correct lunar year."

"Although I was," Nail said, more to reassure herself than anything else.

He raised his empty glass in a mock toast. "You were. We all were."

He refilled his glass. The bottle was halfway gone.

"So, partners. Some of your classmates will eventually separate from their dragon partners to do what your mother and father did. Or to go into the world and use their magical gifts to help people. Or to game the stock market. Who knows? But you, like myself, will not have a partner."

Nail shifted her weight as she thought of Vigilus. "What do you mean? I won't have a dragon?"

He shook his head. "Oh, you'll have a dragon. And that dragon will have you. You're not entering into a partnership. You're entering into a permanent dyadic bond." He searched her face for a reaction.

Nail stared at him blankly. "I don't know that word."

"A partnership implies an alliance or arrangement between two separate entities. A dyadic bond is two incomplete pieces merging as one." He gestured to a painting on the wall. It showed a dragon that looked much like Oracle, circling the heavens in a halo of sunshine.

"Oracle?" Nail asked. "She's one of the… dyadic bonded?"

"*Fated* is the term. I am Fated. You are Fated. It's rare but," he pointed to a book on the table, "it's a well-documented event."

"I don't understand how that's different than being predestined for this society or having a dragon partner."

"You recall the stained-glass window from the first day? The one that shows a dragon and human merging into one? Those images show Oracle's transformation." He finished the glass and set it on the table.

Nail's stomach dropped and then jumped into her throat. "You're saying that Oracle was once a human and a dragon? That's what's going to happen to you… and to me?"

"Yes. Two separate entities. A human and a dragon with a partnership. But then…"

"They merged into one being." Her stomach settled with the weight of a giant stone. She finished the glass. Sweat from her fingers lingered on the stem.

"So that's it, then? I'm going to merge with my dragon someday? And I have no say in this?"

He nodded. "That's the basics of it. Once you merge… your human self is gone. And your mind changes, your personality. And the dragon you will know will be gone as well. It is a death and rebirth, in a way.

"You and your dragon become one single voice, one being, one mind, in one body. Forever. You'll retain the ability to have a humanoid form, but as you can see from Oracle… it's not quite normal."

Nail's heart began to hammer. "I… I don't think I want that."

She thought of losing her face, of it being replaced by one like Oracle's.

Her mind raced with thoughts. "I'll lose my face. My body. I'll never be able to walk among normal society again. I'll be an outcast. Forever."

Steven nodded grimly. "It's not all bad. Oracle has been around for two-and-half millennia now. And she's not slowing down anytime soon. When she merged, both her dragon's and her gifts amplified. She's invaluable to us. She's seen entire societies and worlds rise and fall and rise again. She's saved quite a few of those worlds, too."

"You mean civilizations." Nail kept picturing her own face covered in scale lines like Oracle's.

"No, I mean *worlds*. Worlds like Drasol. There are others."

Nail recalled the map in her dorm room, the hall of portals.

"Perhaps that's a discussion for another time." Steven cleared his throat. "Look, it won't happen immediately. It may not even happen for decades. You might live a long, happy life before…"

"Before it all ends?"

"Before it all changes. Oracle still has her human memories. She still remembers what it was like. And if she's lost some of her human demeanor, it's only because she's so… well, old."

Nail didn't know which possibility was worse: the idea that there would be no dragon at all for her, or the idea that one would eventually envelop her humanity. "What if there's no Fated egg for me?"

"There will be. There's always an egg."

"But what if there isn't?"

Steven's voice betrayed a hint of frustration. "What if the moon falls out of the sky? What if the oceans dry up? What if the sun turns cold? All those things are more likely than you not having an egg."

Nail rubbed her hands against her knees. "So when is my doom date?"

"You're looking at this the wrong way, and that's my fault. I could have explained it much better if… If tonight hadn't been what it's been. It's not your doom, Nail. It's your—"

"My fate," she spat bitterly. "I get that."

"You'll pair with an egg from the Fated chamber." Steven rubbed his temples. "But holding your ceremony will take some time to arrange. We don't call in any of the ancient dragons or the human Drasol clans for the typical pairing ceremony. And I expect the dragons won't like being called back to the island so soon after my own."

"Twenty-four years is soon?"

"In their minds, yes. It will take time. You'll need to be patient. In the meantime, we'll work to prepare as best as we can."

Nail shook her head. "I won't do it. I won't lose my humanity."

Steven frowned. "It's too late for that. You stood on the dais. You've been magically bound to the treaty. Besides, do you have any other plans for the next 5,000 years?"

Nail was about to retort when a small *pop* from the kitchen stole her attention. Nora stood there, holding a large, shimmering egg covered in red scales. Kerris's egg.

Steven turned toward his sister. "How did it go?"

"Vienna's light was on, but she wasn't in the room. I suspect she's down in the common room, waiting…"

"I know," said Steven. "Leave it on the counter. We can take it to the crypt after her funeral."

Nora nodded. She grabbed a wine glass from the kitchen and sat next to her brother.

"I need you to inform everyone else," he said.

Nora nodded. "I know. And I will."

She poured generously and offered to finish the bottle into Nail's glass. Nail accepted.

Steven sighed. "Tonight, Nora."

"I said *I will*."

Nail couldn't help but smile. But it quickly soured. She'd always wished she'd had a sibling, that her father had remarried. A part of her had always been angry with him for denying her a mother figure. Now she understood why.

"My father won't be staying in Maine," Nail said. "He'll want to rejoin his partner. That's where their 'class reunion' went. To visit their partners in Drasol."

"There's an entire community of Lumen members in Drasol," Nora said with a smirk. "It's almost like a retirement village."

Steven nodded. His gaze lingered on the doorknob for a moment. He rose and opened it.

Oracle was on the other side.

"They're collared," she said.

"Wine?" Nora offered.

Oracle shook her head. "But thank you. Nora, you will need to speak with everyone tonight."

Rolling her eyes, Nora took a long sip from her glass, swallowed and answered. "Yes, I know. I've already been ordered to do so."

"Good," Oracle replied. Steven offered for her to take his seat on the couch but again Oracle refused. "Has the young one been informed?"

Steven nodded as he sat. "Of the basics, yes."

Oracle pursed her lips. "We need to discuss the trial for the Drasols. It should happen just after sunrise."

Steven and Nora both looked at Nail. "I thought Nail could sleep in your home tonight, Nora. Shouldn't she get some rest before the three of us discuss a trial?"

Oracle shook her head. "Why delay the inevitable? She'll have to witness a trial eventually. And this was her classmate. She has a valid voice in this matter."

Nail looked to Nora. She was frowning, but her eyes said that she agreed with Oracle.

Steven took a moment to consider it. "It's grim business."

"Yes," said Oracle. "Ultimately, as kin to the condemned, I will have the final say. But she deserves to be there, to give her opinion, and to witness the judgment."

"Sorry," Nail interjected. "But what's the purpose of the trial? Steven and I both saw what… what Xaos and Thovos did."

A wicked grin spread across Oracle's face. "We are not going to determine their innocence or guilt. The penalty for their actions is undeniable. We're going to determine exactly how they die, and who should do it."

Nora looked to the floor.

"Who?" Steven asked, rebuking the question. "It's me, obviously. I'm the youngest…" His voice trailed off. He jumped to his feet. "You can't mean to… She hasn't even paired yet!"

"I do." Oracle turned to Nail. "Our laws state that when a dragon takes the life of a human, the youngest living Fated has the honor of delivering the penalty of death. And paired or not, that means you, Nail."

The memory of blood and gore and bones crunching in jaws came flooding back. Nail suddenly regretted the wine.

Even though Xaos and Thovos deserved it, Nail hated the idea of any dragon dying. Her stomach folded.

Oracle looked from Nail to Steven and back again. "Do they still teach swordsmanship on the mainland, or has that fallen out of fashion?"

EPISODE THREE

CHAPTER 1

It was the 12th of July as Elsie held her sister's hand walking back from the showers at the campgrounds. Spent fireworks shells were still scattered across the grass and gravel. The walk was a little over a mile, and while Elsie didn't mind it, her little sister complained the whole way.

"How come we can't shower at home?" Maggie asked.

Elsie looked down. The contrast of their skin tones was unmistakable —Elsie, pasty-bordering-on-unhealthy, and Maggie with a year-round beach tan. Maggie's deep hazel eyes stared up from behind her naturally curly light-brown hair, already drying in the hot summer air.

She was only four years old. She hadn't figured it out yet. Elsie had figured it out for herself when she was nine. Her mother's story about where her father was kept changing.

"He's a marine, on deployment," she would say when Elsie asked.

When there weren't any presents under the unlit Christmas tree in their trailer, her mother would explain that, "Daddy got laid off. He's looking for work in another state. We'll make it up to you next year."

But the next year would come, and mom would give a new excuse.

Elsie smiled down at her sister. "I told you, hun. If we turn on the shower at home, it'll open a portal to the shadow dimension, and the evil Night Witch will get through and destroy the entire Earth."

Maggie went wide-eyed and nodded solemnly. After a few more minutes of walking, she asked, "She can't though, right? We're safe?"

"We're very safe," Elsie said. "As long as you practice the alphabet every night, that keeps the magic strong, and she can't get through."

Maggie nodded and walked a little taller.

Before long, the lights of the trailer park glowed in the distance. Elsie quietly said a prayer that her mother would already be passed out for the night. They'd been gone for over an hour. That should've been plenty of time.

They turned left at the main road in the trailer park and passed a few homes. A couple chained-up dogs barked from a few lots over. Maggie didn't pay them any attention, but Elsie kept checking over her shoulder.

They turned right and walked past a few more lots. Weeds grew tall around cars on cinder blocks. Loud TVs and rock music blared from trailers. Shouting, swearing, the sounds of broken A/C units, and box fans on high split the night air.

At the lot next to theirs, an elderly woman sat on her stoop, clutching her 12-gauge shotgun and whistling an unrecognizable tune.

"Evening, Mrs. Humboldt," Elsie said.

She had wiry gray hair and she wore an old nightie dress that had frayed at the collar. The floral pattern was faded. A lit cigarette smoldered in an ashtray on the railing, and a paper plate with two bare hotdogs sat next to her.

"Evening girls. Y'all had dinner yet?" Mrs. Humboldt asked.

Maggie nodded her head. Elsie shook hers.

"Well, I made too many hotdogs tonight." Mrs. Humboldt handed them the paper plate. "They'll just go to waste. You girls want 'em?"

Maggie smiled and happily took a dog. Elsie took one, too, and thanked her. Mrs. Humboldt always made "too much" of something. Elsie was grateful.

"How's my Ma?" Elsie asked between bites. The hotdog was cold, but she didn't care.

Mrs. Humboldt frowned. "Y'all shoulda taken the long way."

A stone formed in Elsie's stomach. She'd finished her hotdog in four bites and now regretted it. Nausea swelled in her throat.

Maggie had finished her dinner in record time, too. Elsie wished she would've taken a bit longer.

Elsie took a deep breath. She took another. Neither helped; the stone in her stomach just grew heavier.

What she was about to walk into was normal—for her. But that didn't make it any easier. Her only hope was to insulate Maggie from as much of it as she could, for as long as she could.

But Maggie would start school soon—a good thing because it would be an escape from her home-life reality—but also a curse, because she didn't know what she didn't know until someone showed her differently.

Elsie said goodnight to Mrs. Humboldt. Maggie was still waving goodbye to her as they rounded the corner to their trailer.

Their mother, Tammy, stood out on the lowest step of their stoop, smoking a cigarette and leaning on the banister railing, talking to the man who owned the dogs on the other end of the park. Elsie didn't know his name. She tried very, very hard to never learn any of their names.

"There's my girls!" Tammy called. "Where've you been all night? I was gonna cook you dinner, but you ain't been here!"

Elsie walked up, keeping out of arm's reach of the man. Maggie hid behind her legs.

"We already ate," Elsie told her.

Her mother took another drag off her cigarette. The bruises at the crooks of her elbows her visible. She was wearing a low-cut tank top and no bra. Her sunspots were showing. "Why's your hair wet, then?"

A spark of anger roared in Elsie's chest. "When are you gonna get the shower fixed?"

Tammy flicked the cigarette, and ash trickled off the end. "When're you gonna get a job and help out around here, huh?"

Elsie didn't reply. She held her tongue when Maggie was around… or tried to, at least.

The man next to her mother looked Elsie up and down from head to toe. He took his time doing it.

"How old are you now, hun?" he asked.

"Fifteen," Elsie lied.

"Stupid," her mother said. "You're sixteen, girl, can't you remember even that?"

Elsie stood there for a moment, staring down her mother. She flicked the butt of the cigarette away and opened the pack. There were three left.

"I'm all outta cigarettes, Elsie. Why don't you run down to the store and get me another pack?" her mother said.

"I don't have any money," Elsie replied.

The man dug into one of his pockets and produced two crumbled five-dollar bills and a balled-up bit of plastic held shut with a bobby pin.

He gave the bobby-pinned plastic to Tammy and reached to give Elsie the money.

When Elsie took it, he grabbed her wrist with his free hand, forcing the bills into her palm and running his fingertips over the back of her hand.

Elsie's left fist balled up, ready to throw a punch, but he let her go just as quickly.

"Let me take Maggie with me," Elsie asked.

Her mother scoffed. "At this time of night? She wouldn't be safe! What kind of mother do you think I am?"

"Please," Elsie said.

"I already told you to go get me cigarettes, and you're just standing here with your fist up your ass! Now get goin'!" her mother yelled.

The man nodded and stared at Elsie expectantly.

Elsie's nausea rose up again. She turned away and crouched down to Maggie's level.

"Go inside," she told her sister. "Go sit on the top bunk. Close the curtains and put in earplugs like I showed you. Practice your letters until I come in, okay?"

Maggie nodded and scurried inside.

Elsie gave her mother one last scathing look and walked away. When she was at the corner of Mrs. Humboldt's trailer, she shouted back to Tammy, "I know exactly what kind of mother you are!"

Elsie broke into a run. She could hear slow footsteps on gravel. Whatever curses her mother was shouting were drowned out by Mrs. Humboldt's whooping. "You run, girl! You get yourself outta here for good and all!"

Elsie stopped running when she reached the main road beyond the trailer park. The gas station was only a half-mile walk. Her mother probably gave up chasing her after the first two or three trailers, but it felt good to give her anger something to do.

This was the worst part. Waiting, being away from Maggie. Hoping the earplugs were thick enough to drown out the noise. Hoping the curtains were closed enough and that Maggie was still too young to understand what the silhouettes at the table were doing.

At least the bedroom at the back had a folding door. Tammy usually closed it.

Elsie took angry, pounding footsteps all the way to the gas station. The bell above the door chimed a welcome. Elsie walked down the aisle and grabbed four cups of instant noodles—tomorrow's breakfast and lunch. She couldn't wait for school to start again.

She put the noodle cups on the counter and rang the bell. Jim came out of the back room, his hand in his salt-and-pepper hair, jeans stained, and his work shirt untucked.

"My favorite gal," he said. "How's them studies coming along?"

Elsie tried to smile. "Just fine."

"World geography next year, right?" he asked.

She nodded.

"What's the capital of Spain?" he asked.

"Madrid," she said.

"Japan?"

"Tokyo."

"South Africa?"

"Cape Town, Pretoria, and Bloemfontein."

"Shii-oot, I didn't know they had three," Jim said. "Your Ma need the usual?"

Elsie nodded again. Jim got a pack of cigarettes down and rang them up with the noodle cups. Elsie gave him the money and he gave her the change.

"You keep that up," he told her. "You'll get a scholarship. Go to college. Get yourself a good job." Jim nodded like he could see the future, like it was set in stone for Elsie. "You'll do real well someday."

Jim bagged up the purchase and handed it to her.

"I'll do my best," she said half-heartedly. But she couldn't imagine a future like that. Not quite like that, anyway.

She couldn't move out of the trailer park. Not without Maggie. And dorm rooms weren't friendly toward six-year-olds.

No, when school ended, Elsie would get a job. She'd get an apartment. And she'd take Maggie with her. Her mom might fuss for a week, but she wouldn't call the cops. After a week, Tammy would convince herself that it had been her idea.

When Maggie was old enough, maybe Elsie would go to night school and get an Associate's Degree. It was a lot of maybes.

Elsie said goodnight to Jim and started her walk home. Normally, it was a lonely one. Occasionally some of the other residents from the trailer park would cross paths with her, headed to the gas station for beer or cigarettes or whatever else.

This night was different.

A man she didn't recognize was walking straight for her. He had short, dark hair, nice jeans, and a clean shirt. He didn't look like he belonged at the trailer park.

She put her head down and pretended to not notice him. She gripped the bag tighter. He wore white tennis shoes.

"Elsie?" he said. "You're Elsie, right?"

She looked up. He had a warm smile and carried a brown leather shoulder bag, like a professor would. He looked nothing like the men that came around to see Tammy.

"Yeah," she said with hesitation. "That's me."

He continued to smile and gestured next to them, a bench under a streetlight that actually worked. "Will you sit with me a moment?"

She glanced over his shoulder, toward the trailer park. She wanted to get back home to Maggie, to make sure she was okay. Earplugs. Curtains. Letters.

"Just for a minute?" he asked again.

"Okay," Elsie agreed. "A minute."

She sat on the bench, placing the bag next to her and away from the man. He sunk down next to her.

"Rough night?" he asked.

Elsie shrugged. "Average night."

Why am I talking to him? But she felt oddly at ease around him, the warm summer air was more comforting than normal. She looked up and down the street, making sure there wasn't a windowless van parked anywhere. There wasn't.

He extended her a hand. "My name is Steven."

Her own hand froze an inch from his for a second, but she shook it.

"Look," he started, "hear me out. This is going to sound a bit odd, but I've been watching you. I represent a very prestigious school, and we think you'd be perfect for our next class."

"Like, a private school?" *Was this Jim's idea of a joke?* She blurted, "I can't afford tuition."

His smile was so easy and warm. Elsie felt herself relax.

"There's no tuition," he said. "We care about making sure our students achieve the most they can in life. All our funding comes from graduates who've gone on to be the very best in their fields."

"Okay, so, what? You want me to go to this private school in the fall?"

"Not quite," he said. "Our first term starts at the end of this week."

The end of this week? Maggie, alone, for six whole weeks of summer without her? *Impossible.*

"I can't do that," Elsie said. "I have to look after my sister."

"Because your mother can't. Or won't."

Elsie nodded.

"Our school has a lot of influence. *I* have a lot of influence. It's... unnatural, you might say."

"I'm not sure what you mean." Elsie scooted an inch away from him on the bench.

"Here's what I think will happen. On Friday morning, I think you're going to want to take Maggie down to campground again. Just taking a walk. And on your way back, you'll meet me and a female associate of mine right here at this bench.

"You'll tell Maggie to run back to Mrs. Humboldt and call the cops. You'll have left a note on your bed saying you've run away. The cops are going to come, and this time, Elsie, they're going to care. They're going to see the needles on the kitchen table. They're going to test the broken shower.

"They're going to take a hard, long look at your mother passed out on her mattress, and they're going to call Child Protective Services. Your sister is going to be placed in a new home until your mother finishes her jail time and her rehab."

"Rehab?" Elsie laughed, right from her core. "You must be smoking something. Tammy would never do rehab. And CPS doesn't care about some kids in a druggie's trailer. They've been called before. Our caseworker doesn't even visit anymore."

Steven's smile turned sad. "I know. The cops, CPS, even your mother, they all lack the proper motivation. I can change that."

"How?" Elsie demanded. "Prove it."

Steven seemed to think for a moment. "Did you get change at the gas station?"

Elsie nodded.

"What do you usually do with it?"

"I put it on the kitchen table with... with the other stuff you talked about."

He grinned. "Do you ever want to keep it? To have a little extra for your sister?"

Elsie nodded.

"Good." Steven turned himself to face her more directly. Their eyes locked. His voice turned commanding. "Tonight, don't put the money on the table. Keep it for yourself and your sister."

Something inside Elsie changed. The warm comfort within her doubled, and she felt confident. She knew she would do it. She'd been tempted before, but now she *knew* she would do this.

"How did you do that?" she asked. "Are you one of those new-age hypnotists or something?"

"I have a gift," Steven said. "Someday, you'll have one too. If you come to my school."

Elsie thought. "The foster care system is terrible. How do I know Maggie will be safe?"

Steven smiled. "I already talked to the agent that will be in charge of assigning her a home. I convinced her to bump up a couple that's on the waiting list. They can't have children, but they already have a room, clothes, and toys waiting for a child at just your sister's age. She'll be safe, loved, and looked after."

Elsie bit her lip. "What kind of school is this, anyway?"

Steven smiled and pulled his bag onto his lap. He undid the magnetic flaps keeping it closed and opened it wide. "I was hoping you'd ask."

Something crawled out of the bag. It was small, the size of a lizard, with jewel-like eyes. Even in the yellow light of the streetlight, its wings shone like pastel tissue paper. Tiny scales covered its hide, and it looked up at Elsie with a curious expression.

She heard a bell-like voice in her mind, cleaner and more delicate than wind chimes.

"Hello, Elsie. My name in Aenu."

Elsie jumped from the bench and onto her feet, unable to believe her own eyes.

Aenu disappeared back into the bag and Steven closed the flap again. "I run a school—a society—where humans and dragons partner together. Would you like to join?"

CHAPTER 2

There was an alarm clock ringing somewhere, but Nail couldn't find it. She groaned as she swung herself out of bed and her feet touched the fuzzy pink rug.

A clock with neon red numbers flashed 6:45 while the blaring buzz resounded throughout the apartment. Nail swatted at the clock indiscriminately until the noise stopped. Rubbing her eyes, she looked around the room in Nora's apartment.

A puffy white bench sat at the foot of the bed. A pile of black clothes rested on it, crowned with a note.

> Nail,
> Trial starts at 7:30. I'll be here by 7:15 to walk you down.
> Hope you got some rest.
> - Nora

She groaned. Her sleep had been sweaty and restless. It had been one long nightmare, dreams covered in blood and headless dragons. She felt sick again.

After a shower, Nail got dressed into the black pants and top that Nora had left for her. She made a cup of coffee, forced herself to eat a quick breakfast, and finished the last dregs as a knock on the door came at 7:15.

Nora stood in the hallway, dressed comparably to Nail. The black was

IGNITE

to mourn the one who had died, not the two that would be executed that day.

Nail's stomach twisted. Oracle had said Nail would be responsible for ending the lives of the two Drasols. She wasn't even close to ready for that kind of responsibility—or interested.

She loved dragons. She hated that these two had murdered Kerris, but still… the loss of even one dragon was a heavy burden. But two, and by her own hands? Morally, she couldn't bear it. On a practical level, she couldn't even imagine it.

"You've got a lot on your mind." Nora stepped into the apartment. "I hope you at least got some sleep."

"A little," Nail grumbled. "Not enough."

Nora fiddled with her hair in a mirror, her brunette locks slicked back into a tight bun. "More than me. Today will be hell."

Nail nodded and sat on the arm of a sofa.

Nora approached her, placing a reassuring hand on her arm. "You're going to get through this."

Another knock sounded at the door. Nora turned quickly at the noise, apparently as taken aback by the unexpected intrusion as she was. "Who…?"

The door swung open. Steven and Oracle stood in the hallway and quickly entered the apartment. He immediately directed his attention at Nail, who still sat on the sofa opposite Nora.

"I didn't know Vienna's dragon had hatched. Tell me exactly what happened last night before Kerris left."

Nail sighed. She was already tired and the day hadn't even begun.

"I'll make coffee," Nora offered.

Nail thought back. "It's like I said, we were all sitting around talking about the intruding dragons."

"What did Kerris think about it?" Steven asked.

Oracle stood off to the side, her mouth a straight line and scaly expression unreadable.

"She… she thought we should be doing more. That we should form a search party."

"And where was Lyva when Kerris voiced this opinion?" Steven's hands were on his knees.

Nail thought. So much had happened. "Ve was on Vienna's shoulder." She shut her eyes and tried to remember. "No, that's wrong. Lyva was on Kerris's shoulder."

Steven leaned in. "Did Lyva do anything? Was there any light or maybe…"

"Dust," Nail said. "Lyva shook, and a dust came off of ver. That's when Kerris said we should form a search party."

Steven leaned back, his eyes darting from one side to another, like he was reading invisible words on the ceiling.

"Is Lyva in trouble?" Nail asked. "I don't want to get ver in trouble."

"No," said Steven. "The dust may have nothing to do with Kerris's actions. Or it could be everything. The only way to find a human or a dragon's magical gift is with time. The dust could mean many things."

Steven rose from his spot on the sofa and looked to Oracle. She stood in the same spot, arms crossed, wearing a deep-set frown.

Oracle sighed. "No matter what Lyva's gift turns out to be, Kerris's murder wouldn't have happened without the actions of Xaos and Thovos. They bear the responsibility and the consequences."

Steven nodded in agreement. Nora brought over a platter of coffee, cream, and sugar.

"We need to go," Oracle said.

Nora frowned at her tray. She placed it on the coffee table.

"Then we'd better get going," Steven said.

"But this is Kona coffee," Nora complained.

Oracle was the first out the door, followed by Steven. Nail followed as Nora locked the apartment.

The walk down to the docks took Nail down hallways she didn't recognize. They passed the room where she'd first awoken, but they turned the opposite way of the valley. Down another short flight of steps, they were standing outside once more.

A bay sprawled in front of them, roughly just as wide as the valley's beach. There were three docks—two in disrepair, and one that looked new. A crowd had gathered in a semicircle facing the ocean. The door into the main building slammed shut, and heads turned to greet them.

Nail recognized many of the faces, but there were at least two-dozen gathered. They were all staff. Nail didn't see anyone from her class. The crowd parted at the middle and shuffled aside to make room for the four of them.

A few of the dragons had decided to attend as well. Nail saw Vigilus and Aurumis, as well as Rankor, the wyverns from the night before, and Ivisus, the hydra missing one head.

Standing dead-center of the human crowd, Nail finally saw what

IGNITE

everyone else had been staring at. The Drasols were chained up, but Nail especially noticed the collars around their necks.

They resembled something like a cross between a dog's choke collar and a medieval torture device. The collars were mounted to the ground, immovable, and lined with eight-inch spikes that faced inward, situated under the dragons' thin armor.

Trickles of blood ran down both their necks. The collars were so tight that any movement would dig the spikes into the dragons' soft flesh under their scales. The slightest movement would send the spikes into their vulnerable necks.

Oracle stepped out to the crowd. "Lumen, you are here to bear witness to the execution of Xaos and Thovos, citizens of Drasol, guilty of the murder of Kerris Herrington."

A murmur went through the crowd. A few heads turned toward Nail and Steven. Nail shifted her footing on the dewy grass. She swallowed. Her throat felt like gravel.

Oracle took confident strides toward the prisoners.

Nail found herself wondering if Drasol dragons had magical gifts. Was Oracle safe being so close to them?

"What was your purpose here? Were you hunting for sport?" Oracle asked the pair.

There was a pause.

Oracle paced in front of them. "Answer so that everyone can hear you."

Xaos and Thovos rolled their eyes. One loud, angry voice echoed in Nail's mind. *"It wasn't sport."*

The voice reminded Nail of a violin screeching its highest notes—a disconcerting sound.

"Then why come here?" Oracle asked.

The crowd murmured in agreement. Nail heard a chorus of whispers in her mind from the Lumen dragons.

One of the Drasols bared vis teeth and growled. Oracle didn't even flinch.

"Your theatrics don't intimidate me, Thovos," she said. "I've watched posturing hatchlings like you live and die by the hundreds. I existed long before you were an egg, and I'll be here long after your forgotten ashes have sunk to the bottom of the sea."

Thovos growled again. The same violin-voice entered Nail's mind. It must have come from Xaos.

"We serve the true Regent," Xaos spoke.

This stopped Oracle's pacing. She turned to Steven.

He took a few steps forward. "Who is this *Regent?*"

Xaos replied in a chorus of dissonant notes. *"You know her name. She was once one of you."*

"What does she want?" Steven asked.

Xaos and Thovos laughed. Thovos's laughter sounded like nails scraping down a tall chalkboard. Goosebumps rippled up Nail's arms.

"To take back what was stolen. To see the end," said Thovos.

"The end of what?" Steven asked.

The prisoners laughed and answered in unison. *"The end of you."*

Oracle scoffed. "Some Regent you have. She sent two bloodthirsty fools on a suicide mission. Now you're collared and cowering."

"She didn't send two. *She sent* three.*"*

Oracle and Steven shared a look of panic.

Nail glanced back to Vigilus. Ve looked ready to take to the skies.

"Who?" Steven demanded, striding up to one of the dragons. "Who else did this 'Regent' send to our island?"

"A fae," said Thovos. *"Too small to be seen."*

"We were the distraction," Xaos said. *"The fae came to see if you had what our Regent desires. And you do."*

Nail's mind went racing. What would someone who lives in Drasol want from Lumen Island? Was it the eggs? A specific dragon?

"Where is the fae now?" Steven asked. "Still on the island?"

"Gone," Xaos answered. *"Gone back home. We were nothing. Our Regent will send others."*

Steven approached Oracle. Their whispers were too quiet for Nail to hear over the crashing waves and murmurs in the crowd.

"What was stolen?" Steven asked. "What is she after?"

Oracle shifted her feet.

The dragons laughed, throaty and dry.

"What do you guard most? What would you protect above all else?" asked Thovos, vis voice a taunt. *"That is what our Regent will take."*

Xaos and Thovos stared pointedly at Nail, baring their fangs even as the collars dug an inch deeper into their necks. They were secure, but Nail couldn't help but take a faltering step backward.

Steven shot Nail a look of panic. Everyone was staring at her—she could feel their gazes.

Oracle seemed to have had enough. She turned her back to the condemned and addressed the crowd.

"I am sentencing Xaos and Thovos to die. How shall they be executed?"

The crowd shouted out suggestions. "Blade!" "Poison!" "Rip them apart! Justice!"

Oracle's attention fell on Nail. "What do you say? You must carry out their sentence. How will you kill them?"

"No," Steven interjected, stepping in front of Nail to block Oracle's path. "She's too young."

"It is tradition," Oracle replied. "She must."

Nail's hands were sweating. She couldn't kill dragons. Even though these two deserved it, she didn't have the skill. She didn't have the nerve.

"I... I can't," Nail said. "I can't"

"We won't be killed by some unpaired-Fated!" Thovos shouted.

"We won't be killed by any human!" Xaos echoed.

Steven's eyes lit up and he rounded on them. "You won't be killed by any human. Why? Because the thought disgusts you?"

Xaos and Thovos growled in reply, spittle flecking toward the Lumen leader.

"You came here on a suicide mission. You will die. And you will die by her hand!" He pointed an accusatory finger back at Nail.

Their anger flared again. They jostled in the dirt, digging the spikes of their collars in by another inch. Fresh blood flowed from both dragons, dripping onto the ground.

"No?" Steven taunted. "You don't want that? Fine. Then *kill yourselves.*" He spoke it with command and certainty.

Immediately, both dragons reared up, driving the spikes of their collars down into their spines. Guttural roars died into moans as they both collapsed and the bottom spikes pierced their throats, spilling terrible amounts of blood onto the ground. Shudders of life twitched through their bodies for a few seconds. Then the stillness of death.

Sickness and relief flooded through Nail. She watched their bodies go limp, tails lifeless on the grass.

"You puck of a man!" Oracle shouted. "You did that on purpose."

"You're damn right I did," Steven roared back at her. Again, he pointed at Nail. "She's too young. You wouldn't listen. Your old age has robbed you of compassion."

Oracle's hair whipped in the wind. "And your youth denies you of wisdom. She'll have to carry out a sentence one day. It should have been now. You've robbed her of her right."

"How?" Steven asked. "How would she have done it? She has no pairing, no gift! Would you have put a sword in her hand and let her butcher them?"

Oracle stared at Steven in silent fury.

"What's done is done," Steven said. "We have an entire class that needs to be informed of what happened last night. We have a funeral to plan. Kerris's egg needs to be entombed."

Oracle shook her head. "We're not finished with this conversation."

Steven strode away from her and toward Nail. "We are for now."

Steven grabbed Nail's arm a bit too roughly, nearly dragging her inside. When the door shut, he turned toward her. "Go into my office and wait there."

"Why? I want to be with everyone else when you break the news to them," she objected.

"You can't be. I'll explain later," he said. "We have to keep you safe."

Guilt welled up in Nail's throat. "What you did back there, using your gift on Xaos and Thovos… thank you."

Steven nodded, not really looking at her. "You're welcome. My office. Now."

"But why can't I be with everyone else?" Tears began to well up in Nail's eyes. "Muari must be worried sick."

"You heard what those dragons said. Someone is coming to end us, to end Lumen." He stared down at Nail. "They want to take away our future, which is now represented by you."

Nail faltered. "Then, I should be doing what you're doing. Helping everyone else process Kerris's death. I was there. I could—"

Steven waved her concerns away with a flick of his hand. "That's for me to handle. We need to get you off this island."

CHAPTER 3

After yet another rerouting menu, Finley slammed a fist against her headboard.

So far, the numbers on the exchange student paperwork Tally had given her had led to nothing but twisting dead-ends. Emails never yielded replies, and rarely did she get someone else on the other end of the phone. Most of the calls led to endless rerouting menus or full voicemail boxes.

"Please enter the extension you would like to reach or remain on the line to hear a full directory," said the robotic, female voice.

Finley sighed. She had resigned herself to seeing this thing through, no matter what it came to. Either she would run out of leads or—eventually—she'd get Nail on the phone and absolutely scream at her for ditching right before junior year.

Assuming, that is, that Nail hadn't been abducted into some sort of human-trafficking cult. Or worse, Scientology.

Finley fluffed up a few pillows on her bed and settled in. She kept a notebook on her lap, detailing all the numbers she had already called. Today, she would be trying the Medical Billing: Accidents and Crisis line.

It took some time to connect—a good sign, Finley figured—and eventually the line at the other end rang. Finley reached for her running sneakers, ready to get a workout in after another inevitably useless dead end.

Her parents had left that morning, gone for four days this time. Finley cringed at the memory of Nail's speculation on what her parents were really up to. She finished her laces.

The phone line continued to ring for at least a minute. Just when Finley thought she'd be cut off by another robotic rejection, a man's voice came over the speaker. She bolted upright.

His voice was warm, charming even. There was an accent to it, but she couldn't place where it was from. She couldn't explain why, but she felt her guard drop, like a blanket fresh from the dryer had been placed over her shoulders.

"Hello, you've reached the office of Mr. Parson. I am not able to take your call. *Leave a message detailing the exact nature of your concern* and I will return your call as soon as possible."

A beep.

Maybe it was the exhaustion or the betrayal. Maybe he just sounded like someone who would care. Maybe she just needed to say the words that were on her mind—out loud, even in a voicemail—so that she could admit, finally, to herself, exactly what she felt.

Finley started to talk.

NAIL WAITED IMPATIENTLY IN STEVEN'S OFFICE. SHE PACED THE floor and watched the valley from his office window.

When the sun had crested the eastern edge of the valley, she could spot a line of people coming from the girls' dorms. She was too far away to pick out anyone individually, but she imagined Vienna bravely leading the charge. Trees blocked her view of the boys' dorms, but they would surely be brought out soon too.

She paced and waited. The sound of a small pop startled her.

"I brought you brunch," Nora said, setting down a Styrofoam container that smelled like beef and soy. "It's from Tokyo. There's a great street vendor I love to visit."

Nail's stomach rumbled. She'd had breakfast, but the tumultuous events left her stomach unsettled. Nora laid a pair of disposable chopsticks atop the container.

"You had time to go all the way to Tokyo?" she asked.

Nora shrugged. "It doesn't take me long." Her foot tapped on the stone floor. "So how are you holding up?"

Nail opened the container. The aroma of beef, soy, and sesame had her salivating.

"Well enough, I guess," she said. "Steven really saved me back there."

Nora nodded, but a frown had formed on her face. "He did. And I think he did the right thing. But using his gift like that... It worries me. It's a slippery slope, that kind of power abuse."

Nail rolled her eyes and swallowed a mouthful of steaming noodles. "And popping over to Tokyo for lunch is a good use of your talents."

Nora shrugged. "Nobody died."

With another small pop, she disappeared again. Nail ate in peace for a while, until a phone rang—a clangy ring, from an old landline phone.

Nail put down her food and crossed to Steven's side of the desk. The phone had a handheld receiver that connected to the base with a cord.

It kept ringing. Nail half-heartedly considered answering it.

What would she even say? *Steven's office, this is Nail speaking. Steven is delivering the news of a teen's murder to all of her friends right now; can I take a message?*

A little screen on the phone, illuminated green with black text, displayed a number. For a moment, Nail's heart nearly stopped. The area code was the same as hers—as her father's. What if he was in trouble?

But, no. Wasn't he still in Drasol on his camping trip?

Her stomach dropped again. If he was in Drasol, was he safe? How would an attack from Drasol dragons affect him?

She leaned in closer and inspected the number. She sighed with relief, but it was short-lived. It didn't belong to her father.

It belonged to Finley.

Nail stared at the phone, frozen. How had she gotten Steven's number? Did she know about Lumen? About the dragons? Nail had figured her disappearance would hurt Finley, but to track her down?

She felt her first good feeling all day—love.

Nail smiled down at the screen. Sure, Finley might be angry, a bit hurt even, but she loved Nail like a sister. A sister would never give up so easily on such a flimsy excuse as "an exchange student in Greece."

Nail would've gone to end of the Earth for Finley. And Finley was doing the same.

Relief flooded her. No matter what happened with Lumen, or being Fated, or Jace's see-saw affection, Finley would always be there. For the first time since the failed pairing ceremony, Nail felt like she remembered who she was.

Nail picked up the receiver and answered, but there was no one on the other end. The little screen read, "RECORDING VOICEMAIL."

She panicked. She had missed her window. She began mashing buttons on the base. One of them changed the voicemail from being silently recorded to playing live.

"...and I'm calling about my friend, Naileen Sharp?"

Finley's voice. It had been so long since Nail had heard it. She felt happiness right down to her fingertips.

"I think she's in a foreign exchange student program, um, somewhere in Greece? But I can't get ahold of her, and no one has the phone number for her host family. I'm worried about her. She's my best friend. She wouldn't just leave me like this."

Nail stood a little straighter. Finley's voice was cracking.

"I'm worried she's been kidnapped by human traffickers. Are you guys Scientologists? Look, anyway, the *exact nature* of my concern is this, Mr. Parson. The Nail I knew wouldn't disappear on me. But..."

Finley's voice fully broke with one heavy sob. "But maybe I never knew her at all. So if you find her, tell her that Finley hates her. I hope she never comes home. Tell her... Tell her I hope she dies slow, and cold, and alone. Tell her she was never my friend."

The voicemail clicked. Finley had hung up.

Tears rolled down Nail's cheeks. Now Finley hated her too.

She choked back a sob, but it wouldn't work. She'd held it in for too long. It was too close to the surface. There was no way to hide it, ignore it, or stuff it back down.

Nail lowered herself to the floor, sobbing and gasping for air. Tears and snot rolled down her face. She crawled over to a couch in the corner and stole a pillow from the seat.

She curled into a ball and cried, hating herself for staying, hating herself for being unable to help Kerris, hating herself for leaving and for believing dragons would complete her.

She wished she'd never been invited to the Lumen Society. She wished she had gone home. Tally had the right idea. She wished she could be back in her own room, with her own bed.

And she slept.

Nail awoke to the sound of the office door closing. Her

hair clung to her face, and a small mountain of used tissues lay next to her, balled up and filled with snot. She looked out the window. The sun was almost at midday.

It was beautiful outside. For a flash of a second, Nail enjoyed that. And then she remembered Kerris. And being Fated. And the trial. And the voicemail from Finley.

She wanted to sink into a dark corner and disappear.

Steven gestured to the Styrofoam dish on his desk. "Did Nora go to Tokyo again? They have her favorite comfort food."

Nail sat up. She considered standing but decided that would require more effort than she had in her.

"You have to get up now," Steven said calmly. "We have to address your safety."

"Send me back h-home," Nail choked out. "Please. Make me not Lumen anymore. It'll be like none of this ever happened."

She sat crossed legged on the floor. Steven knelt down in front of her.

"I can't do that, Nail." He looked out the window. "You stood on the dais. You have a role now."

"This role is *shit*," she spat.

Steven nodded. "Yes, it can be." He handed her a fresh tissue. When she used that, he handed her the whole box.

He sighed. "For your safety, until we can be sure that no more unwanted visitors will be coming through the Drasol portal. I need to have Nora remove you from the island for a little while."

Nail held up an empty hand. "Do I have a choice?"

"Not really, no," he said. "But you'll be doing something useful. Something that will bring you closer to getting paired with an egg."

"Yeah, what's that?" Nail said.

"I'm sending you to Scotland with Nora and a reluctant Oracle. One of our dragons lives there. And ve has become… depressed, let's say."

"Nessie?" Nail perked up. "Nessie is secretly a depressed dragon?"

Steven frowned. "Ve wasn't always depressed. When the world was a simpler place, Nessie loved to come out at night and scare the local drunks leaving the taverns and pubs. But, with cameras and cell phones, ve can't do that anymore."

"What does that have to do with me?" Nail asked.

"You and Oracle will convince ver to come home to Lumen," he said.

"For what? A dragon-sized prescription of Zoloft?" Nail scoffed.

"No… You're going to convince Nessie to come home to die."

CHAPTER 4

Nail waited at the bank of Oracle's pond.

"I'll be back in half an hour. Don't worry about packing," Nora had told her before popping off to wherever she was headed.

The surface of the pond was calm and clear, and Nail was certain the pond was the last place Oracle would be. She sat on the riverbank trying—and failing—to skip stones across the surface.

"Hey," said a male voice from behind her.

Jace. He sat down next to her. He wore a sling that held his verdure egg.

"I didn't see you at the announcement," he said. "And Muari told me you didn't go back to the dorm last night."

Nail nodded and picked up another stone. "I was there when it happened. I stayed in Prioress Nora's apartment last night."

Jace sighed. He smelled like cedar, cloves, and mint. "I'm sorry. They told us she was murdered by Drasol dragons. Was it bad?"

Nail considered her words. Whatever she told Jace would probably get around to the entire class.

"It was quick," Nail said. "She didn't feel any pain."

Remembering that detail gave her a little comfort. Steven's gift could be truly just that—a gift.

Then images of Xaos and Thovos impaling themselves flooded her mind again. Nail shut her eyes, trying to push the images out of her head.

Jace put his arm around her, pulling her to himself. She leaned against him, her hair laying over his chest and forearm.

"It's going to be okay," he said.

"They're making me leave the island," she said.

"Leave?" He pulled away from her slightly and only for a second. "Why?"

Nail shook her head. "Some bullshit the condemned dragons said. Something about representing the future of Lumen." She thought back. "They didn't actually threaten me. It was just implied."

Jace nodded. "So it's for your safety?"

Nail shrugged. She should've felt excited. Visiting Loch Ness was one of her life goals. *Why don't I feel excited?* Nail tapped her fingers in the grass.

"Well," he said, "they have to bring you back eventually. You don't have your pairing yet."

Nail wiggled her way out of his hug and faced him. She wanted to tell him about being Fated and about the voicemail from Finley. He smiled at her, sad and small. Why shouldn't she tell him? No one said her Fated-ness-whatever was a secret.

"What is it?" he asked, his eyes wrinkled in their corners. He took her hand, squeezing four of her fingers with his thumb.

"I never apologized to you, for what I said about Vienna," she started. "It seems like a lifetime ago now, but…"

"That wasn't why I got upset." Jace looked downcast.

Nail could feel the stress of everything weighing down on her, making it hard to breathe and difficult to focus. "I think everything is about to change. Can you make me a promise?"

He cocked his head to one side. "Depends on the promise."

"Well, two promises. Promise one, if Rorik breaks Muari's heart, I want you to break his leg."

Jace laughed. "Promise. Done."

"Second promise…." She didn't know how to word this one. "Promise you won't hate me, no matter how long I'm gone."

He smiled, wide and warm. "I'll never hate you. I hate that you have to leave, but I want you to be safe. Honestly, the biggest thing I dislike about Lumen is that there's no *Vortex Beyond* here." He squeezed her hand.

She playfully pushed his arm. "You miss the game that much?"

"No," he said. "I miss the time I got to spend talking to you."

Heat started to rise to Nail's cheeks. Before she could reply, she heard a small pop. Nora and Oracle stood before her.

And Oracle was a sight.

She wore all black. Her clothes were painfully modern—black pants, a black hoodie, and a black handkerchief tied around her neck.

Nail looked her up and down. "Are you robbing a bank?"

Oracle rolled her eyes. "According to Nora, this is what you humans wear now. I don't mind the fabric, but these pants are uncomfortably tight. Apparently, modern fashion changes as often as the wind."

Nora held one duffle bag. She stood with her gait off-center, clearly weighed down by the bag. "It's just after 1am there," she said, looking at a watch on her wrist. "We should get going. Pubs will be closing soon."

"You gals hitting happy hour without me?" Jace joked.

Oracle stared down at him wordlessly. She looked like a snake in a glass enclosure at the zoo—bored but biding her time.

Nora looked at Nail. "We want to slip into town before the pubs let out en masse." Nora pointed a thumb at Oracle. "Hopefully no one gets a good look at her face."

Oracle scowled at her.

"Ready?" Nora asked Nail.

Nail and Jace stood.

"Just stay safe," he said. "I'll be here when you get back."

She desperately wanted to hug him, but the idea of doing that in front of Oracle felt mortifying. "We'll figure something out when I get back. We don't need *Vortex Beyond* anymore."

Nail put her hand on Nora's, and with one last glance at Jace, they were gone.

CHAPTER 5

It was the dead of night, and wherever they were, it smelled like sheep.

Oracle, Nora, and Nail stood in a field. A few distant lights shined between tree branches, and cool air chilled the back of Nail's neck. She wished she'd put on a hoodie before they left.

"There's an inn right up the road," Nora said in a quiet voice. "I'll get us a room and come back for you two."

Nail's eyes had begun to adjust to the dark. Oracle pulled the bandana over her face. Her dark clothing helped her to blend in, but it didn't hide the fact that she stood nearly seven feet tall.

"What are we supposed to do?" Nail asked. "Just stand in a field until you get back?"

Nora pulled up her hood to guard against the wind. "It's Scotland. Everyone stands in fields." She adjusted the strap on the bag so that it crossed over her torso. "I won't be long."

Then she took off at a light jog toward the town.

"She didn't think to get a room *before* hauling us to the opposite side of the globe?" Nail didn't really expect an answer.

Oracle leaned up against a fence post that Nail couldn't fully make out. She wondered if Oracle had better-than-human eyesight. "I doubt she thought that far ahead. She didn't sleep last night. And she took Steven to Kerris's parent's house to break the news."

"Oh," Nail said, hoping that Oracle's eyesight wasn't good enough to see her blush. Nail inspected the grass around her. It seemed safe enough.

"Don't sit," Oracle said. "There are cow chips by your feet."

"Perfect." Nail took a deep breath. The air was clean, save for the farm smell. "Where are we?"

"I believe we're in a town called Lewiston," Oracle said. "Urquhart Castle is nearby. It's will be our best place to contact Nessie."

"Why?" Nail asked. "Because dragons love castles?"

Oracle sighed. "Because it's located roughly at the center of the lake," she said. "But yes, we do tend to have an affection for well-constructed fortresses that withstand the strains of time, weather, and adversity. Personally, I find the intricate stonework to be very pleasing."

Nail nodded. Something had been nagging her. "Why does Nessie live so far away from the island?"

"Because of vis gift," Oracle said. "It's very unique, and quite lonely. Nessie has a passive magical gift, meaning ve can't control it."

Nail nodded, waiting for Oracle to continue.

"Nessie… cannot be remembered properly. I was present for vis hatching. I couldn't tell you if Nessie is blue or brown, has one head or ten. It's a lonely existence, when those around you constantly forget what you look like seconds after seeing you."

"That's sad," Nail said. "But why come to Loch Ness? Nessie must have had a name before ve became the Loch Ness Monster."

"Ve did," Oracle said. "But I can't remember that either. It's a very odd gift. Nessie left the island without permission. The secrecy of dragons is taken much more seriously now than it was back then.

"But eventually, Nessie discovered that while ve couldn't be remembered correctly, ve could be remembered *incorrectly*. Nessie used to show verself to sailors and drunken townspeople all the time. From what I hear, ve got a real kick out of it."

Nail nodded. "Because it was a way to be remembered."

"Exactly," Oracle said. "The legend of the Loch Ness Monster doesn't have any magic to it, so no one has trouble remembering that. And the conflicting descriptions just add to the mystique."

"That's clever," Nail said. "So what changed? Is ve just… old?"

"Humans," Oracle said simply. "Now everyone has a camera in their pocket everywhere they go. Humans have put cameras in the loch, they've used sonar to try to find ver. But it seems that Nessie's gift extends to technology as well."

"They can't find ver," Nail said.

"Correct," Oracle said. "The legend of the Loch Ness Monster will die because of the gift that allowed its creation. Nessie believes vis legacy is ending. And rather than let the legend die, Nessie has stopped eating."

"Why, though?" Nail asked. "What would that accomplish?"

Oracle smiled a macabre grin. "Magic lives and dies with the body. No more heartbeat, no more gift. Vis corpse will float to the surface, be discovered, and…"

"And the legend of Nessie lives on forever."

"Exactly," Oracle said. "Which risks the exposure of Lumen, dragons, and magic all at once."

Nail fidgeted. The idea of Nessie's corpse being discovered bothered her right down to her core, but she couldn't pinpoint why. Sure, the secrecy of Lumen was important, but it wasn't all that important to her. She tapped her foot and stopped, afraid of the nearby cow chips.

Why does this bother me so much?

A sudden *pop* startled Nail, though Oracle remained relaxed.

"We have a room," Nora said. "Shall we go?"

"I hope there's a tub," Oracle said as she reached for Nora.

Nail took hold of her, too, and the next instant, they landed in the middle of the living area. Nail looked around. The room could've been worse, but not by much.

A floral sofa faced an old TV, and a table doubled as a desk in the corner. To the left, a bedroom contained a large, uneven bed. The same dated floral fabric adorned both the comforter and the drapes.

To the right of the sofa, a claw-footed bathtub sat in the bathroom, separated from the rest of the facilities by a wall-mounted curtain.

Nora tossed the overstuffed duffel onto the bed.

Nail gave a low whistle. "Definitely not five stars."

Oracle harrumphed. "The sooner we leave, the better. I hope neither of you mind giving up the tub for my comfort." She strode toward the bathroom. "And if you do object, know that I don't care."

The door to the bathroom slammed shut. Nail heard the swish of the curtain and the sound of running water.

Nora rolled her eyes. "Drama queen."

Nora unpacked the top half of the duffel, handing Nail enough clothing and toiletries to last for a few days, or maybe a week.

"How long will we be here?" Nail asked.

"It depends," Nora said with a sigh, folding a shirt and placing it into an empty dresser drawer. "We can't go back until Steven is certain there's enough security at the portal. And we can't go back without Nessie."

"Which one will take longer?" Nail asked.

Nora shrugged. "Hard to say. Steven has to negotiate with the council in Drasol and bring them the bodies of Xaos and Thovos. That will either go well, or it will end in war." She looked up at Nail and smiled. "It's not going to come to war. The last war began and ended before Oracle was even a hundred."

Nora sighed again, placing another pair of pants into the dresser. "No, the real trick will be convincing Nessie to come home to Lumen. But at least having a suicidal dragon makes things more convenient."

Nail cocked her head to one side.

Nora searched Nail's face. She smiled and waved away Nail's unasked question. In that moment, she reminded Nail of Steven.

"A poor attempt at humor. Of course, it's not convenient at all."

But Nora's forced grin didn't sit well with Nail. She wasn't sure why Nora would lie, but Nail was certain she wasn't getting the full truth.

"When do we start?" Nail wanted to at least seem eager.

"We'll go down to Castle Urquhart tomorrow during the day. I've been all over, but I've never been *here*, exactly. We'll want to find a good spot, someplace with cover and close to the water."

"And then…? We just shout 'Nessie' at our reflection three times?"

The tub faucet shut off, rattling the old pipes.

Nora laughed. "Not quite." She sat down on the bed and removed her shoes. "Oracle will handle that part. We don't know if Nessie will welcome the presence of another dragon, so we'll play it by ear."

Nail nodded. "And what's my role in this, aside from getting me off the island and hiding me in Scotland for a while?"

"Just be there. Show Nessie that vis life has meaning. That the world keeps on turning." Nora smiled, and again Nail was reminded of Steven, specifically the smile he gave her right before he ran off to the north side of the island to avoid telling her about being Fated.

Nora was definitely hiding something.

"Steven said we need to convince Nessie to come home to Lumen. To come home to die," Nail questioned. "That doesn't seem like the same goal as showing ver that life still has meaning."

Nora made a small, agreeable sound. "Death can have meaning too."

She reached for a pair of pajamas, shooing Nail from the room, and she wouldn't say anything more.

CHAPTER 6

Nail and Nora slept head-to-foot that night. When Nail awoke with a backache from the lumpy old mattress, Nora was already up, ready for the day.

"Breakfast from Boston," she announced.

Nail stumbled out of the bedroom, still wearing her clothes from the day before. The breakfast spread was impressive—pancakes, French toast, eggs, bacon, and sausage. Curiously, a plastic tub of water lay on the floor, and inside it a panic-stricken and very much alive fifty-pound tuna fish.

Oracle left the bathroom, and Nail jumped at the opportunity. When she had finished brushing her hair and teeth, Oracle stood outside the door, holding the thrashing fish in her arms.

Nail's jaw hung open. "Are you going to...?"

"Eat this?" Oracle finished. "Yes, I am. And I'll do it privately so as to not offend your delicate and immature sensibilities about the food chain."

Nail pointed to the bathroom door as it shut. "Is she serious?"

Nora had a plate of pancakes, French toast, and bacon resting on the coffee table. "That's nothing. She requested pork. Honestly, she knows we need to be inconspicuous. Even a piglet running amok would raise a few questions just by the noise alone. After all, this is Scotland, not backwoods Wyoming."

Nail wondered if someday her appetite would be like Oracle's.

She set about getting her own breakfast as Nora informed her there was also coffee from New York. She joined Nora on the sofa.

She poked at her breakfast with a fork, eager to chase away thoughts of how her face would eventually change.

"What's the weirdest thing you've ever had to get? Or the weirdest place you've ever gone?" Nail asked.

"Hmm," Nora chewed as she thought. "That's tough. The most useless place I've ever gone was Antarctica. Nothing but ice, rocks, and researchers obsessed with ice and rocks."

"Do people give you weird looks when you buy things like an entire living tuna?"

"Not this time," Nora said. "I stole the fish."

Nail stared at her.

"What? I had to! The fish at markets are already dead, and Oracle was very specific that it needed to be—"

"I don't need the details." Nail put up a hand to stop her.

Nora shrugged, a limp pancake dangling from her fork. "I only steal the weird stuff. I always pay for things like food and clothes. With cash, of course, because banks tend to frown on making purchases on three different continents within an hour. Learned that one the hard way."

Nail bit into her French toast. It was still hot, and easily the best French toast she'd ever eaten.

"When I was getting the hang of my gift, I turned into a real prankster," Nora said. "Especially toward Steven. He'd been in charge for a couple years when I was brought to the island, and I was ready to make up for lost time as his annoying little sister."

She replaced her plate with a mug of coffee, raising fingers to count as she went.

"Let's see… there was the time I stole all the plastic flamingos from a Florida retirement community and stored them in his office. That was an avalanche of pink. Another time, I stole a long-haired cow and let it loose in the valley." She took a sip from the mug. "Cameron still cares for her on the farm. She named her Lois.

"And for fun, in 2010, I stole the nuclear football and hid it under the Vice President's pillow." Nora laughed to herself. "Poor Joe was baffled."

"Has anyone ever seen you using your gift? I mean, have you ever landed in a group of people or anything?"

"Oh, sure. Loads of times. One time, in a car, I thought I was landing us on a deserted back road." She shook her head. "Nope. Accidentally landed mid-turn on a busy street in Russia, almost caused a car accident. There are a couple 'landing' videos of me on the Internet, too. I try to wear a hood when I pop off somewhere that I'm not one hundred percent certain will be deserted."

Nail's brow furrowed. "If you've been spotted, how come this isn't all over the news? A disappearing woman who can steal *and* play scavenger hunt with the nuclear football seems like a big risk to national security."

Nora sipped her coffee. "Oh, there are theories out there. But they're all on crazy-lunatic sites. My activity ranks right up there with terrorism conspiracies and the existence of aliens and dinosaurs that live in the watery depths of Loch Ness."

Nora winked.

Nail sipped some coffee. The ache in her back hadn't gone away, but coffee helped her be less cranky about it.

"I suppose if someone went really crazy," Nora said, "they could possibly put most of the pieces together. Enough to make a semi-convincing claim of my existence.

"But even total nut-jobs don't fall that far down the rabbit hole. They get obsessed too easily; one day it's the magical disappearing woman, and the next it's lizard people or the Earth is flat." Nora shrugged. "You'd need to have a personal stake in it, I guess."

"Yeah." Nail tapped the cardboard rim of her coffee. "It'd have to be someone that you personally upset. Someone willing to believe insane theories or who thought you kidnapped someone they loved."

Nora nodded with a bright smile on her face. "Right. And we don't piss off the parents of the class. If they're in the society, they know what could be coming.

"If they're not, Steven makes a house call with Aenu a few days before the big move. And everyone gets some paperwork, an exchange student program, I think?" Nora shrugged again. "No missing teens, no story to track."

Nora said it simply, like a matter of fact. Who would go chasing after a missing teenager if their own parents didn't report them missing and had the proper paperwork to back up their disappearance?

"Right," Nail agreed half-heartedly, her mind on hatred, Scientologists, and an angry voicemail. What had her last words to Finley been? *If I go missing, you'll know where to look?*

"Right," Nail repeated. "The *parents* aren't going to go digging."

CHAPTER 7

Nail and Nora took a taxi over to Urquhart Castle. The old ruin sat on manicured grounds and right at the edge of the water. Time and strategic destruction had worn down many of the castle's towers and walls, but it was still safe to walk through.

As they toured the ruins, Nail imagined the people who built the castle walking its halls, climbing the uneven stairs, knights telling stories of slain dragons all while a real dragon lived in the loch.

"Did you know this castle was repeatedly won and lost by the English during the Wars of Scottish Independence?" Nail said absentmindedly. "It became a royal castle after it was taken back by Robert the Bruce."

Nora navigated a narrow stone staircase. "Like in Braveheart?"

Nail frowned. "Not quite."

They stood on an open balcony that overlooked the water.

"Down there." Nora pointed to an area a hundred yards away. "There's good coverage from the bushes and it's right against the water."

Nail nodded. "So, now what?"

"We wait 'til dark," Nora said.

Nail spent most of the day bored. The loch wasn't visible from the window of their room, which only added to her depressed mood. With Nora's apathetic permission, Nail decided to walk around the town.

It was exactly what Nail had expected—narrow streets, a few people out and about, but not much to see or do outside of signs and tourist shops packed with souvenirs.

She stopped to inspect a snow-globe of Nessie. It featured the Surgeon's Photograph, arguably one of the best Nessie hoaxes ever created. The blurry image was captioned with the name of the town, Lewiston on Loch Ness.

Nail frowned at the picture and put the snow globe back on the shelf. As the shop's bell dinged on her exit, it dawned on her why this trip hadn't felt right.

In all of the times she had imagined coming to Loch Ness, it had all been under the same, simple premise. She wanted to come to the loch to catch a glimpse of Nessie, holding out the secret hope that she would one day be the person to identify what exactly the creature was.

And now she knew. And the truth was more fascinating than a school of sturgeon fish, and possibly just as wonderful as surviving plesiosaur.

But it didn't matter how wonderful the truth was. The mystery had been solved.

She knew Nessie existed. She knew what Nessie was. The wonder, the raw draw of the unexplainable, was gone.

Nail arrived back in their room feeling a bit annoyed and sad. Lying on the couch, she covered her eyes with her forearm and napped.

At half past midnight, Nora said it was time to leave. Nail and Oracle placed a hand on her shoulder, and they all reappeared on the spot Nora had scouted.

Nail wore thick jeans and a heavy hoodie to fight against the chilly breeze blowing from the loch. The wind whipped her hair into her face, and she pulled up the hood.

Oracle had opted for a silk robe. Nora carried a bundle of towels under her arm.

Oracle curtly nodded to them both and approached the edge of the water. She abandoned her robe on the shore, and with one elegant motion, she swan-dove into the loch, disappearing beneath the waves. A moment later, a strong swell displaced the water as Oracle returned to her full dragon size.

"And now, we wait," Nora said.

Waiting grew dull quickly. Nail sat with her knees pulled to her chest, guarding herself against the night wind. She bit her lip.

Coming to Loch Ness had been one of her lifelong dreams. She lamented her dream of being one of the lucky few that glimpsed Nessie or managed to snap a picture. In Nail's fantasy, her picture of Nessie was always crystal clear, irrefutable proof of Nessie's existence.

Knowing that Nessie was real stole the joy from the hunt. Still, she kicked herself for not buying a disposable camera earlier that day.

Although, Nessie's gift would obscure the image anyway. She pouted. *Yet another joy robbed by Lumen.*

No, Nail reconsidered. *That's not it.*

The joy had been the mystery. But with the mystery solved, she didn't feel the rush or exhilaration she'd always imagined. Mostly, she just felt cold.

Aside from the odd flip of a fish's tail or the bobbing of driftwood—what she perceived as fish and driftwood, anyway—the lake remained calm and quiet.

After an hour, there was noise at the shoreline. Oracle climbed out of the water, dripping wet, and donned her robe.

"Nothing." Bitterness cut into the edges of her voice. "Nessie refuses to answer me. This entire endeavor is pointless. I should be back at Lumen, not running errands for Steven."

Nora sighed and handed Oracle a towel. "We'll try again tomorrow night."

She offered her hands to the other two.

Nail and Oracle took hold of Nora, and they popped back inside their room at the inn.

"This may not go according to plan," Oracle said, drying off her hair with the towel. "We may need to lure Nessie out of the lake and have you teleport ver onto the island."

"I don't think that would go well," Nora said. "We can't be sure how big Nessie is. Moving a large, uncooperative dragon could have disastrous results."

Nail interjected. "And what's to stop ver from returning even if Nora did? Ve has to come by vis own choice." She hated the idea of a Loch Ness without a Nessie.

Oracle sighed. "The bottom of that loch is disgusting. No wonder Nessie is depressed."

Oracle stalked off to the bathroom, shutting the door behind her.

The next three nights proved just as unsuccessful, and Oracle's temper grew shorter as the time dragged on. Nora popped back to Lumen once a day to catch up with Steven. On the fourth day—gone for hours longer than usual—she brought back some good news.

"Steven has gotten all the visiting Lumen members out of Drasol successfully and secured reliable sentries for the portal," she said, smiling at Nail. "We can go home as soon as we wrap up everything with Nessie."

Nail was anxious to return back to Lumen. She missed Muari. She'd been excluded from Kerris's funeral. The idea of someone hunting her down should have been more upsetting, but after everything else that had happened, Nail didn't have the emotional bandwidth to deal with it.

And waiting around in the Scottish hotel room had grown very dull very quickly. She didn't find the humor on TV to be entertaining, and the eternal news cycle was even more mind-numbing.

On the fifth night, Oracle was gone until nearly sunrise, then she rose from the loch looking pleased and wearing a predatory grin.

"I cornered Nessie. Ve had to speak with me. I explain the position ve is putting Lumen in," Oracle said, accepting a towel from Nora. "And ve wants to meet with you."

"Me?" Nora asked.

Oracle shook her head and pointed at Nail. "You."

Nail looked at them both. "Why me?"

Oracle rolled her eyes. "We need Nessie to open the Fated chamber. Did Steven not explain this to you?"

Nail shook her head.

Oracle scoffed. "If you're going to pair with an egg, you'd better convince Nessie to come back to Lumen. Otherwise we'll have to find another dragon for the job *and* clean up whatever mess Nessie makes here."

Excitement flooded through Nail. Waiting by the loch now seemed much more worthwhile since it was bringing her one step closer to her egg.

But dread also filled her stomach. The reality of being a Fated was conflicting. Until now, their errand to Scotland had helped to keep her mind off of everything waiting back on Lumen Island.

"I'll do it." Nail nodded. "I'll talk to Nessie."

Even with the sense of mystery gone, when push came to shove, there was no way she could give up an opportunity like that. At last, something on the trip felt right. It felt like destiny.

"Good," Oracle said. "Ve will meet us tomorrow at midnight at the shore of Urquhart Castle."

Nail anxiously paced around the living room all day, looking out the window and wishing for sunset. She binged on TV, watching cop dramas and sitcoms, but none of it helped to keep her mind off of Nessie.

Several times Nora popped in and out of the room, and Nail jumped each time. She found it impossible to sit still.

"Getting to meet Nessie is a huge deal for me," she explained to Nora over lunch. "Ve's *the* Loch Ness Monster."

"Nessie is a dragon," Nora said, exasperated with Nail's day-long twitching. "You've met other dragons. There's one in our bathroom."

Nail shook her head. "Nessie isn't just another dragon. She's a myth. A *legend*. Probably the greatest unexplained mystery in the world."

"Ve," Nora corrected her. "Ve is a myth."

Nail waved away her correction. "You know there's a guy—Steve Hamfelt—living in a van who has dedicated the last twenty-five years of his life to searching for Nessie?"

Nora shrugged. "So he's crazy?"

Nail smacked her hand onto the coffee table. "No. He *believes* in something. He's chasing a dream."

"He's chasing a dragon that, by vis very nature, cannot be found, recorded, or accurately remembered. That's not inspirational. It's moronic. And moreover, you've met a dozen dragons that defy the laws of nature and logic just as much as Nessie."

Nail sighed and sank deeper into the couch. "The beauty of Nessie's legend is that no one really wants to learn what Nessie is. No one wants to find out ve's a driftwood log or a school of salmon or even a long-necked dinosaur that survived extinction. People want proof that Nessie is real, without any evidence of what Nessie is."

Nora folded her arms, raising one eyebrow. "You're telling me that Hamfelt guy, who has spent twenty-five years in pursuit of one mystery, doesn't really want to solve it?"

"Of course not," Nail said. "People want just enough evidence to say that *something* is out there, but not enough to determine what it *is*."

Oracle emerged from the bathroom. "Your theory is ridiculous. Why would anyone search for something they don't want to find?"

Nail looked at her. Oracle wore heavy clothing for once, rather than a flowing silk robe. A thick dress with a hood. She wouldn't be getting in the water. Nail glanced at the time on the VCR under the TV. 11:47. It was nearly time.

"Cryptid hunters aren't doing it to find an answer," Nail said. "They do it because they're in love with the question."

No wonder Nessie won't open up to you. You don't understand this at all.

"Get changed," Nora said. "We can leave soon. If nothing else, Nessie will appreciate talking to one crazy fan."

Five minutes later, Nail was ready to leave, bouncing on the balls of her feet.

"Let's go," she said. "Nessie is waiting."

Nora and Oracle exchanged a look of doubt. But together, they popped off to the edge of Urquhart castle.

Nail sat at the edge of Loch Ness, her feet dangling over a rocky ledge above the gentle waves.

Castle Urquhart was well placed. She could see up and down the loch, lights from the surrounding towns reflecting on its surface. The sounds of a rowdy party carried over the water.

Nail watched the rippling waves, looking for any sign of disturbance.

She heard a voice before the water moved. It sounded old and rusted, squeaking like a neglected rocking chair.

"You came," said Nessie. *"Thank you."*

Two eyes broke the surface and peered at Nail. She was pretty certain there were only two eyes… or maybe four. Each time she blinked, she couldn't remember what they looked like… Were they green? Or black?

"Of course," Nail said. "It's an *honor* to meet you."

Bubbles drifted up from where Nail imagined the dragon's maw would be.

"Is it okay if I just call you Nessie?" Nail asked.

"Please. I prefer it."

"So what can I do for you?"

A gurgling noise came from the water.

"I am old," Nessie said. *"I have lived in this loch nearly all my life."* Nessie gurgled again. *"I want to be found."*

"Why?" Nail asked. "The legend of the Loch Ness monster is known around the world."

Nessie made a humming noise. *"I am hunted but unseen. I am seen but not remembered. I exist and I do not."*

Nail frowned. Lake monster riddles were not her specialty. "You can't be recorded or photographed, but your legend remains epic," she reasoned. "Isn't the legend what you've wanted to create all this time?"

"Yes," Nessie agreed. *"But it will soon die. Humans send their noisy machines. They keep looking. There's nothing to be found. Eventually..."*

"Eventually there will be enough proof to disprove your existence," Nail said, genuine sadness in her own voice.

Nessie heaved a heavy sigh, raising vis head out of the water. Nail couldn't recall its shape or if there was only one, or if Nessie resembled an English dragon or a wyrm or a plesiosaur.

"Yes," Nessie said. *"The only way to exist is to not exist."*

"You know you can't do that," Nail said. "You risk exposing Lumen. A dragon—a real dragon—floating to the surface of Loch Ness? The entire world would be enthralled."

"Yes," Nessie agreed, vis voice turning jubilant. *"Yes, they would."*

"And then they wouldn't," Nail said. "They'd drag you out, dissect you, and call you a previously unknown species. They'd look at your DNA. They'd theorize over how you survived so long. They'd dredge up the whole loch looking for more of you."

Nessie chuckled. *"They wouldn't find anything."*

"Exactly!" Nail shouted, her voice carrying over the water. She had to make Nessie understand. "Your legend would end. You'd become explainable. No one really wants the mystery to be solved.

"You give people hope that there are still questions that cannot be answered, that there are things we can see but not explain. People don't write legends about the explainable. They write about the mysteries."

Nessie went quiet. *"I had not considered it that way before."*

"I—that is, we—want you to come home to Lumen. You don't want your legend to end," Nail said. "You want it to continue."

"I do."

"Then what we have to do is simple." Nail had concocted this plan earlier that day. "We have to create enough evidence to prove you exist without proving what you are."

"How can I do that?" Nessie asked. *"It is against my very nature to be remembered."*

"I have an idea," Nail said. "If I can make sure that the world sees the Loch Ness Monster and knows ve isn't a fish, driftwood, or anything else explainable, will you return to Lumen with us?"

Nessie blinked. *"Yes, little Fated. If you can make me remembered, I will do as you ask."*

Nail and Oracle argued for half an hour after returning to the room.

"It meets all of the goals," Nail said. "Nessie returns to Lumen, dragons will remain a secret, and Nessie's legend will be stronger than ever. I don't see the problem here."

Oracle stood with her hands on her hips. "You're flirting with a very fine line between secrecy and suspicion."

"Only if you mess it up," Nail said. "My plan is so obvious that no one could possibly figure it out."

Nora laughed. She sat on the couch, sipping tea. "Your plan is so dumb, it might actually work. How can you be certain Oracle will be filmed? I agree that it's likely, but it's not a guarantee."

Nail waved away her concern. "That will be easy. I'm worried Oracle won't pull it off."

Nail thought of Oracle's grand entrance when she had first arrived on Lumen. She knew the ancient dragon had a flair for the dramatic. And she was certain that Oracle *would* pull it off. Goading Oracle into it was just the icing on the cake.

"I will not be known as some murky, freshwater beast that delights in scaring tavern drunks!" Oracle shouted, her arms crossed, nose in the air. "It's debasing."

"You won't. Nessie will."

Nora sighed. "I hate to say it, but I think this is our best option. I'm not going to go popping off with a possibly giant dragon who doesn't want to go where I'm leading. The size difference alone...."

Nora shook her head, shuddering.

"Exactly," Nail said. "We can't have Nessie appearing in the middle of New York City or a busy Russian street." She shrugged, giving Oracle an unimpressed look. "But if you think you can't handle it...."

"Fine," Oracle said. "I'll do it. But you should know, I will pull this off *spectacularly*."

Nail smiled. "Then let's finalize our timing. We need to have Nessie out of that loch before the media goes insane."

She couldn't help but be excited. She was going to pull off the greatest Nessie hoax in history, and the entire world was going to buy it, hook, line, and sinker.

The next morning, at exactly 11:15am, Nora and Nail popped into a small grove of trees in Dores. The loch was a two-minute walk away.

"I need some money," Nail said.

"For what?" Nora asked. Bags rimmed her eyes. Their planning had run late into the night.

"If you think I'm going to come all this way and meet Steve Hamfelt without buying a handmade Nessie figurine then you're absolutely *insane*," Nail said.

"Fine." Nora dug into her jacket pocket and produced a plain black wallet. She opened it, revealing an impressive array of international currency. She handed Nail a £50 note.

"I'll meet you back here." Nail started to walk through the trees toward the beach. A familiar pop told her that Nora had left.

Excitement flooded through Nail. Was this how Steven felt when he and Nora were collecting the class of Metal Dragons? She was about to change a man's life forever. He would probably remember it as the best day of his life, and she would get to help him have it.

As she walked down the beach, Nail found a pair of binoculars permanently mounted to the ground, attended to by a thin man with wispy, wild, white hair. His truck sat farther up the beach. It reminded Nail of an ice cream truck, but the paneling was wood.

And she knew better—it had once been a food delivery truck that he'd converted into a home. Outside the parked truck was a gray table and benches. Several brightly painted Nessie figurines sat on top. A defiant piece of driftwood rested nearby.

"Morning," Nail called to the man.

He turned away from his binoculars to greet her. "Morning."

Nail strode forward, her hand extended.

"My name is Muari," she said as they shook hands. "I was hoping you wouldn't mind if I hung out with you for a bit."

"Steve." He released her hand. "You're a Nessie hunter too, eh?"

"Not as much as you, but then, who is?" Nail said.

He gave her an appraising look.

"I think it's inspiring," Nail continued, unable to stop her inner fangirl from gushing. "Dedicating your life to solving this mystery. I want to buy a figurine, too."

Steve's face brightened at that idea.

"Are you filming today?" she asked.

He shrugged and pointed to the overcast sky. "I had planned to, but the weather isn't promising."

Nail smiled at him and pulled out the £50 note. "Just for a bit?"

Steve raised an eyebrow. "No need for bribery," he said, taking the note anyway. He returned with his camera and a tripod and began setting it up. "Pick out any figurine you like," he said, meddling with the settings.

She stood at the table and chose a pink one sitting on a rock from the loch. It had googly eyes and lolling tongue. By the time she returned to him, he had finished setting up.

"What brings you to Scotland, Muari? You're an American?" he said.

"Family holiday," Nail said. "Some older relatives live around here."

Steven swapped lenses on the camera and Nail stepped up to have a look. The view was perfect.

"And now we wait," he said with a smile. "Over twenty years I've waited for a second sighting. And I'll be here 'til I get it."

Nail nodded. "Maybe your luck is about to change."

She stood off to the side of the camera's view, skipping rocks into the water. One. Two-three. Four-five-six. A coded message.

She moved back to stand with him, angling herself to watch his face.

She heard the movement in the water.

His eyes lit up. The smile that spread across his face was made of the purest joy she'd ever seen. Slack-jawed, he pulled off his hat, staring at the water in awestruck wonder.

She swelled with pride. Normally she had mixed feelings about Nessie hoaxes. But this was the greatest of all. It was a masterpiece. And she'd orchestrated it.

Nail heard the final splash.

Steve began to whoop and dance and scream.

"Can you believe it! That was unreal! That was incredible!" He looked at her, tears in his eyes. "That was Nessie!"

He hastily checked the camera, making sure he'd gotten the Loch Ness Monster on video for the world to see.

Nail smiled.

CHAPTER 8

It was the middle of the night when Nora and Nail arrived back at Lumen Island. They had popped down right where they left, at the edge of Oracle's pond.

"The real Nessie is safe and sound on the north shore," Nora said. "Now I've got to pop back and grab Oracle before the search parties have time to organize."

"Thanks for letting me be a part of this." Nail clutched the Nessie figurine in her hand. "That was one of the coolest things I've ever done."

Nora winked, and with a wrinkle of her nose, she was gone again.

Nail sighed. The air on Lumen felt different than anywhere else. She looked up at the night sky. Unencumbered by city lights, it glimmered with more stars than Nail thought could ever be seen. Helping Nessie had taken her mind off of Kerris, but now she would have to face everyone in the morning and their inevitable questions.

"One step at a time," she told herself, heading toward the girls' dorms.

Nail was relieved to find the common room empty aside from Elsie. She sat with her legs folded in an oversized plush armchair, her nautical-looking egg resting between her legs, and her nose deep in a thick book. She glanced up momentarily at Nail and then returned to her reading.

"Welcome back," she said to the page.

"Thanks," Nail said.

Elsie's pallor had improved, and she looked healthier, too. Her once stick-thin arms were showing a little muscle. Nail considered complimenting her but stopped short. Her last attempt at befriending Elsie hadn't gone well.

She headed up the stairs and reached the door at the end of the hall. Without knocking, she pushed it open.

The first surprise was that the lights were still on, despite the late hour. The second surprise was the tangle of legs on Muari's bed. All three of them shouted in surprise. Nail raised her hands to her eyes.

"I didn't see anything!" she shouted, turning toward the wall. "Also, what the *hell?*"

"You didn't even knock!" Muari shouted back.

"It's my room, too!" Nail said.

"You can look, we're fully clothed," said a male voice.

Nail hesitantly lowered her hands and turned toward them.

Rorik and Muari were both wearing shorts, hence the shock of legs. They were spooning on Muari's bed with a couple of notebooks near them and Muari's voice recorder.

"We were studying," Rorik said.

"Uh-huh," Nail said.

Muari sat up, and Rorik followed her lead.

"We're also dating," she said with a squeal in her voice.

"Congrats." Nail genuinely meant it. "That's excellent news."

"So tell us everything," Muari said. "All we've gotten since that night is rumor and half-truths."

Nail heaved a heavy sigh and sat on her bed, across the room from the new couple.

She explained what had happened when she'd followed Kerris. She breezed over the details of her death, sticking to her line that it was fast and painless. She told them about her Fated conversation with Steven, about the trial, and about her plan to solidify Nessie's legend.

She wanted to tell Muari about the voicemail from Finley but decided to hold off on that until Rorik was gone.

"So one day you'll look like Oracle?" Rorik asked.

Nail swallowed. "Something like that."

"Wicked," he said, awe in his voice.

"And you saved the day." Muari clapped her hands. "Nessie will remain a legend, and dragons won't be exposed."

Nail nodded. "Pretty much. What's new here, aside from your budding romance?"

Muari sighed. "You missed a lot. There was a funeral for Kerris the day after they broke the news to us. They had a funeral for her egg, too. Apparently, it will never hatch."

"That's awful." Nail remembered what Oracle had said that terrible night. With Kerris's death, Lumen had lost two members, not just one.

"Steven has been running around like a chicken without a head," Rorik said. "Really short-tempered, too."

"There's a lot on his plate," Nail said.

"You missed a couple hatchings," Muari said. "Quinn, Jagdesh, and Maeve have all hatched their eggs."

"Jagdesh hatched a drake," Rorik said. "Quinn got a wyvern, and Maeve has a lung dragon."

"Nice," Nail said, but a wave of jealousy started to swell in her.

"Everyone has been pretty bummed out. Vienna's been out of her mind," Muari said.

"Crying a lot?" Nail asked.

Rorik groaned in a frustrated tone. "No, that would be understandable."

"She's been organizing vigils. Not just one for Kerris and one for her egg. She's been trying to get us all to attend a friendship vigil for Kerris and everyone else. Individually. Kerris and Jace, Kerris and Luca, you get the idea. Even with the people who weren't really friends with her. She insists the island needs some sort of memorial, and that there should be some sort of scholarship or something in Kerris's name."

"Scholarship?" Nail asked. "Lumen doesn't charge tuition."

"I know," Rorik said. "No one else seems to know how that would work either."

Muari agreed. "She's ignoring her own grief and trying to smother it with events and organization."

"That's sad," Nail said. "Has anyone tried talking to her?"

"Steven," Rorik answered. "A couple times. He's been preoccupied though."

Nail glanced at the clock. It was nearly 3am.

"I'd better get back." Rorik stood and kissed Muari, following it with a good night to Nail.

Nail watched the door shut and turned toward Muari. "There's one more thing I didn't tell you about."

She unloaded everything she could remember Finley saying. Fresh tears threatened to well up, but Nail fought them off.

"She's definitely looking for you," Muari said. "And she's gotten pretty far."

Nail nodded. "I don't know how to get her off of this. Ghosting her certainly didn't work."

Muari cocked her head to one side in thought. "Maybe you could write her a letter? And have Prioress Nora mail it from Greece?"

"That's an excellent idea!" Nail said.

"Except that everything you tell her will have to be a lie, and given your Fated status, you probably won't ever see her again, and the friendship is likely doomed, anyway," Muari said.

"Wow," Nail said. "You're a real ray of sunshine."

THE NEXT MORNING REVEALED THE FULL DEPTHS OF VIENNA'S madness. She sat on the ground outside the dining hall with handmade signs that read, "HUNGER STRIKE FOR KERRIS SCHOLARSHIP" and "JOIN THE REVOLUTION" and "#RESIST". A snub-nosed hare chewed on the corner of the hunger strike sign.

Nail described it to Muari.

"Told you," Muari said. "She's become completely unhinged."

"How does she expect anyone to use hashtags here, anyway?" Nail asked. "No one has phones."

Nail felt bad for her, but a bigger part of her was relieved. Vienna's inability to handle grief meant she couldn't have had enough time to poach Jace while she was gone.

"What's up with Jace?" Nail asked, looking around the terrace. Several fae dragons flitted through the air. "I don't see him."

"Camping trip with Dax," Muari replied. "Steven suggested they go into the woods and bond. Aurumis agreed to accompany them."

"Awesome," Nail said, dejected.

A few of the staff members filtered in and out of the back section of the terrace.

"Good morning, ladies." Nora approached and smiled down at their table. "Nail, Steven would like to see you in his office."

Nail stared down at her untouched breakfast sandwich and coffee.

"Take 'em with," Nora said. "He's running a tight schedule."

Nail apologized to Muari and grabbed her breakfast, following behind Nora. As she looked back, Rorik had already taken up residence at her table.

She ate as they walked. Sipping coffee from an open mug while moving proved quite difficult.

"I have a question for you," Nail said. "If I wrote a letter to someone back home, could you mail it to her from Greece?"

Nora frowned as they approached the main building. "Sadly, no. Contact with anyone in your old life—unless it's an extreme emergency—is strictly off limits."

"Well, so is stealing but that doesn't stop you," Nail said.

Nora laughed. "Stealing actually isn't off limits. What if your gift was to be an uncatchable thief? How would you ever learn?"

Nail looked at her. "Has that happened?"

They climbed the stairs leading to Steven's office. "I can't say either way. But we encourage outside-the-box creativity and expression."

"That explains why no one is saving Vienna from herself," Nail said.

Nora knocked on Steven's door. "She's processing in her own way. It won't last forever."

Nail wasn't so sure.

Steven's voice sounded from the other side of the door. "Come in."

Nora swung the door open and gestured Nail inside.

"Duty calls." Nora waved then swept back down the staircase.

Nail sat on a chair opposite Steven, finally able to sip her coffee safely.

"I hear you were the one who convinced Nessie to come home," he said. "Congratulations."

Nail nodded. "Thanks."

"I need to catch you up on what's happened while you were gone." He had bags under his eyes, and his skin looked paler than usual.

"Sure." Nail took another sip.

Steven drummed his fingers on the desk. "First, this so-called Regent. Her identity is still unknown, but we have reason to believe she was once a member of Lumen. I have visited with the Drasol Council, and they have agreed to post guards at the portal for now."

"That's good," said Nail.

Steven frowned. "It's a temporary solution to a larger problem. With the portal under tight patrol, we can't rely on open communication from Drasol. Many of our previous Lumen members live there. Some still have family on this side of reality. They won't be happy about the security."

"Oh," Nail said.

"It will reopen once everyone is confident that this 'Regent' has been dealt with," Steven turned in his chair and moved to a bookshelf. He rummaged around a few items, eventually pulling down an old scroll.

"In other news, a date has been set for your pairing. It will happen in a little more than two weeks." He sat again, placing the scroll on his desk.

"Ah…" Nail tried to sound more excited than anxious. "That's great."

Steven nodded. "As I expected, many of the older dragons from Drasol are displeased that they're being called back to Lumen so soon. A few have agreed to attend your pairing, and with the portal situation being what it is, I'm afraid that's as well as we can do."

"I have to admit, I don't really care who is or isn't there," Nail said.

"Well, no. But years from now, when you're 700 and trying to negotiate with the Council and many of the ancient members do not recognize you…" He raised his palms. "What's done is done. We've solved the problem as best we can for now. It's not your fault a Fated pairing happened so soon."

Nail cocked her head. Surely dragons had a different idea about what amount of time qualified as short or long, but twenty-four years seemed like a good long while.

"For comparison's sake, the last Fated to happen before me was in the 1800s," he said. "I expected to be fully transitioned into my Fated status when the next one happened. I thought I'd have more wisdom, more experience…"

He trailed off, looking somewhere over Nail's shoulder. Concern pinched at the corners of his eyes.

He's scared.

Steven shook his head as if to shoo a fly and gave a false smile. "What's done is done."

He pushed the scroll on his desk closer to Nail. She took it.

"I was so rushed when we spoke that I don't think I gave you a very complete picture of what makes someone Fated or not," he said.

"That's true," Nail said. "You didn't."

Steven bobbed his head and took a deep breath. "The mechanics are this: any member of Lumen can become like Oracle. The magic for a dyadic bond is in every member. It almost always happens when both the human and dragon are dying. They both must choose to join together, to become one entity, for the process to begin. Neither can force the other."

Nail nodded along.

Steven pointed to the scroll. "Throughout history, there are countless tales of people, of humans, who turned *into* dragons. That's not quite how it works. All of the eggs in the chamber your class entered are from paired dragons who were born on Earth and had human pairings. Two separate entities.

"All of the eggs in the *Fated* chamber are from dragons who laid *after* they joined with a human, post dyadic bond. We—you and I—are known as Fated because everyone who has ever paired with one of those eggs goes on to join with their dragon. It is inescapable."

"It's fate," Nail said.

"Precisely," Steven said with a sigh. "That scroll is a list of all the Fated eggs, their lineage, and their legends."

Nail turned it over in her hands. "Will I be choosing an egg? Like... based on merit?"

"No," Steven said. "It's already done. One of those eggs is the pairing you were meant to have, and you'll be drawn to it the same way the rest of your class was drawn to theirs. I want you to read that scroll because..."

His words stalled. He looked conflicted.

"Vigilus has a good lineage. Dragons who lived in the east were benefactors, forces of good. They were worshipped and loved. Dragons in the west, however... They were murderous blights on society. They breathed fire, and their blood was poison. They were symbols of greed and violence. Not all the tales are true or unbiased of course, but...."

Nail stared down at the scroll. "In every rumor there's a grain of truth."

Steven nodded. "Some of that is exaggeration, some of it is completely false. And some of it is entirely true. The power of a dragon combined with the selfishness of the human spirit can create—for lack of a better word—evil."

"My dragon could come from a lineage that's done evil," Nail said.

"It's entirely possible," Steven said. "I regret Kerris's death, but there has never been a Lumen class that's seen all of its new members—human or dragon—survive. Dragons are predators. They rely on death to survive. Humans are the dominating species of Earth. This type of union lends itself toward violence. And death is natural."

Nail looked out the window. *Everyone is the hero of their own story.*

Apparently, that wasn't the only option on the table.

"A fae is often a trickster," Steven said. "Hydras are infuriating to be around, and unnervingly hypnotic. Wyverns are often drawn to some mechanic of flight. These are common averages, not set-in-stone rules. You deserve to know that a Fated dragon is going to be more difficult to handle and to bond with. It took me years to hatch Vigilus."

Nail frowned. "Nora told me some stories about that."

Steven rolled his eyes. "I'm not surprised." He cleared his throat and leaned forward. "I want you to be prepared for whatever comes. When I was in your shoes, I had Oracle as a guide. That was… challenging."

Nail recalled their trip to Scotland and the fifty-pound tuna. "I can imagine."

"I want to do better by you," he said. "Unlike her, I haven't lost my humanity. Perhaps I can help to make your process easier. I want to be a better leader."

Nail tightened her hold on the scroll. "I'm sure you will."

Steven released his breath and leaned back into his chair. "Let's hope so. I don't want all of your time in Scotland to be for nothing."

Nail laughed, though she wasn't sure why. "What do you mean?"

"Didn't I explain Nessie's significance to your pairing?"

Nail shook her head. Had this been what Nora was secretive about?

"Oh." Steven shifted in his chair. "I didn't?"

"Only that Nessie needed to come home to Lumen to die."

Steven's gaze went all around the room—everywhere else but meeting Nail's eyes. "The Fated chamber requires a sacrifice."

"Like what?" Nail asked. "A perfect lamb? Three doves?"

Steven's skin had turned a light shade of green. "The death of one dragon."

CHAPTER 9

Nail half-stumbled, half-stormed out of Steven's office and onto the grounds of the valley. Her breath came in short bursts.

That was why they needed Nessie to return.

She regretted eating breakfast.

"Hey," called a familiar voice.

Nail straightened up to see Jo jogging toward her. She wore athletic gear, her egg secured to her with a front-facing backpack.

"Hey," Nail said.

Jo nodded toward Nail's hand. "Sweet scroll. That's real cloak-and-dagger stuff."

"Yeah," Nail said. "I was just gonna…" she trailed off. Ahead of them was a group of at least ten students, several of them pointing at Nail. A few of them called her over.

"Not ready to face the firing squad?" Jo asked.

Nail shook her head. "I just got more bad news."

Jo motioned for Nail to follow her. "I know where you can hide. But I run a five-minute mile, so keep up."

Jo led them away from the gossiping group and through a grove of large bushes. Nail struggled to keep pace. On the western side of the valley, Jo stopped them at the base of an unusual tree.

Its trunk was thick and massive. Heavy branches bowed under their own weight and touched the ground. Vines dangled from the thinner branches. It looked alien, like hundreds of saplings had been planted on the same spot and grew into one massive tree.

"Cool, huh?" Jo said. "It's a banyan tree."

Nail nodded. "Yeah, I guess."

Jo leaned closer to the trunk and pointed. "If you're standing at just the right angle…"

Nail leaned and saw it. Tiny steps—footholds, really—had been carved into the trunk.

"There's a sweet little hideout up there. Pretty sure no one else knows about it yet. I've never been disturbed, anyway." Jo smiled.

Nail grinned and thanked her, and Jo took off jogging again.

Nail slipped the scroll into the back pocket of her jeans and started her climb. It was awkward at first, but the main section of the trunk was only thirty feet tall.

By the time she reached the top, her clothes were dusted with dirt and her hands smelled like bark, but the climb was worth it. Nail didn't know what the top of a banyan tree normally looked like, but she assumed someone had carved the sight in front of her.

Shaped a bit like a bowl, the hideout was about the size of a small car's interior. It had two wooden chairs, a footstool, and a table, weather-worn but still in passable condition.

Nail pulled the scroll from her pocket and sat in the chair with the footstool. She couldn't see over the top of the hideout's carved walls. Branches swayed overhead, letting in plenty of light while still giving her shade.

Nail nodded to herself. "Not bad, Jo. Not bad at all."

She took in a deep breath and exhaled, unrolling the scroll.

It was much longer than she expected. The text scrawled from left to right, with the lineages and legends separated by lines. Nail looked all the way to the left, to the beginning of the tales. The legends noted how many eggs each Fated dragon had lain and if they had been paired.

Nail took a deep breath and steeled her will.

The first listed tale was of a woman in Japan from a year too long ago to be remembered. She had just given birth, but her bleeding wouldn't stop. Her dragon, who had been unusually small, could not bear to part with her and they merged, making them Fated. That dyadic joining had lain three eggs.

Another story told of a woman who was forced to marry an old king. She agreed but only if the king would promise to never watch her bathe.

For years, her husband bitterly followed her request but became drunk one night at a feast. Before the feast ended, the wife retired to bed.

One of her guards, a man who was half her husband's age and twice as strong, was tasked with watching over her, as the king had invited enemies to their feast and the king still lacked an heir. The king, being a jealous man, became suspicious of his wife and her guard. He followed them, and when she went into the bathhouse, the king stabbed the guard.

Still drunk and bloodthirsty, the kind spied on his wife in the bath through a hole in the wall. But when she entered the water, she transformed into a dragon.

The king yelled out in shock, and the dragon-queen roared with anger. With claws like swords, she killed the king. That Fated had lain two eggs.

Nail read on and on. Sometimes the stories were kinder, and they spoke of men and women who'd turned into dragons to save their people from invaders, or to bring rain for crops, or to save the sun from dying out. Steven's pairing with Vigilus came from a Fated that had restored fertility to the crops of an entire village.

As the stories progressed through time, the tales became less hyperbolic but no more hopeful.

There was the dragon Fafnir, who had once been a man who slew his own brother. His tale was one of the most depressing. She'd read the tale before, on the same night Kerris had died.

Fafnir guarded a cursed treasure of gold and spewed poison when he breathed. One of his relatives—Nail had a hard time keeping all the Norse names and relations straight—named Sigurd decided to dig a pit and wait for Fafnir to walk over it, exposing the dragon's vulnerable belly.

The deception was a success, and Fafnir died having laid only one egg. While roasting Fafnir's heart, Sigurd was forced to kill his own brother. But the gold brought only ruin to Sigurd's life and eventually caused his own death.

Oracle was listed about two-thirds of the way through. She had lain only two eggs in her time, and one of them had been paired already.

The last entry was for Vigilus and Steven. Most of his page was blank.

Her own entry hadn't been created yet. Nail wasn't sure how she felt about that. Maybe a Fated wasn't recorded until their pairing. But the thought resurrected her old anxiety that there was no egg for her.

Nail stayed in the tree for most of the day, skipping lunch. She wanted to know everything she could about the Fated dragons. As she read and reread, her dread and concern solidified.

Aside from a handful of happy tales, the life of a Fated dragon almost always ended in violent death. And most of the Fated dragons were—by her standards—evil.

They spat fire or poison. They demanded virgin sacrifices. They terrorized towns and kidnapped children.

Nail finished the scroll for a third time. She guessed that there would be roughly forty eggs in the Fated chamber. Fewer than ten of them had a happy lineage.

She laid the scroll on the table next to her. Her odds weren't good.

Hunger eventually drove Nail out of the tree. She stopped at her dorm room—which was thankfully empty—and dropped off the scroll. It was only five o'clock, but her stomach rumbled from missing lunch.

If she went to dinner early, there was a good chance she could duck out before the crowds arrived with their questions.

Vienna still sat outside the dining hall, her hunger strike in full effect. Lyva lay contentedly on her knee, napping in the waning sun. Nail slipped by them as quickly as she could and was greeted with a surprise.

Dax and Jace sat at a four-person table, their eggs in tow. Nail approached their table.

"She's back," Jace said with a wide smile.

Dax greeted her with a grin and a nod. They both smelled like they could use a hot shower and fresh clothes.

As usual, dinner was served family-style. Nail sat between them.

"How was the camping trip?" she asked.

Jace caught her up on the highlights of the trip. They had first gone to the caves on the southwestern corner of the island. Dax said that was his second favorite part.

"I might go back," he said. "There's a lot of unexplored tunnels we didn't get to. I'm thinking of setting up shop there for a while, actually."

"The first rule of caving is 'never go alone,'" Jace admonished him.

Dax shrugged, his huge shoulder muscles rippling.

"The best part was today," Jace said. "We found a hidden crevice on the north side of the island. We had trouble fitting through it, but it led to this bay absolutely teeming with sea turtles."

"Turtle Bay," Nail said. "I've seen it on the island map."

"Yeah, but you'll never guess the coolest part," Jace said.

Dax shook his head. "Here we go again. I'm telling you, it was just a pile of driftwood."

Jace pointed an accusatory finger at Dax. "No, it wasn't. I know what I saw." He leaned closer to Nail. "I saw a sea monster."

Dax rolled his eyes, head shaking. "It was driftwood."

"And it wasn't just a dragon." Jace looked at Nail. "I know what a dragon looks like. I think ve was Nessie, or maybe one of vis cousins."

Nail smiled, lost in Jace's excitement, the joy on his face. For Nail, it confirmed her theory. People didn't want to solve the mystery; they just wanted to have one.

Then she remembered what Steven had said about the Fated chamber needing a sacrifice. Her appetite dampened.

"Not possible, dude," Dax said. "No way Nessie could swim all the way from Scotland. She lives in a loch. Loch means lake. It's landlocked."

"Actually," Nail said almost automatically, "it's been theorized that there could be underwater streams that lead into the ocean. So it's not impossible that Nessie could reach the sea. It's one of the top theories for how she could survive even though the ecosystem of the loch can't contain enough food to sustain her."

Jace lifted a hand toward Nail as though her opinion settled it.

"Also, you *did* see Nessie." Nail caught them both up on her trip to Scotland and the hoax video she had helped create.

At the end of her story, heat flushed her cheeks. She'd intentionally left out the detail of a sacrifice being needed to open the Fated chamber.

Jace shook his head when she was done. "Knowing that Nessie is just a dragon takes some magic out of the legend. Now she's—"

"Explainable?" Nail said.

"Exactly," Jace agreed.

"That's what I said, too."

Jace looked down at his egg in his lap. "I guess, given enough time, everything becomes explainable."

"Maybe," Nail said.

"I don't know." Dax's fork casually dangled in his hand. "I still think it was just driftwood."

"Stop," Jace said, his eyes wide.

"Sorry, but it just didn't look like a monster or a dragon," Dax said.

"No, stop!" Jace shouted. He stared wide-eyed at his flora-covered egg, a huge smile on his face. It had begun to quake. "It's hatching!"

CHAPTER 10

"My egg can't hatch in a *dining hall*," Jace said.

A crowd of classmates quickly approached, gathering for a later dinner. A few of them waved to Jace and Dax. Nail felt panicked.

"I don't want a huge crowd," he said. "This moment is personal."

"I know where to go," Nail said. "Follow me."

For the second time that day, she ran through the lush vegetation of the valley. It didn't take long before they arrived at the banyan tree.

Nail stood where Jo had shown her. "Stand at the right spot and…"

Jace stood behind her. "I see it!"

He navigated the footholds faster than she had. Nail reached the hideout next, and Dax was right behind her. The space was cramped with the three of them, especially given Dax and Jace's large frames.

Jace set the egg in the middle of the floor. It continued to rock back and forth. A crack had developed near the top, perfectly aligned with the twisting branches adorning its shell.

Dax and Nail sat off to the side, watching. Jace knelt on all fours, whispering encouragement to his new partner.

The egg continued to shake. A piece of shell along the crack broke away. They could see the dragon moving inside.

"I wonder what triggered it." Dax leaned toward Nail.

"Probably the camping trip," Nail said. "Bonding or something?"

She had missed a week's worth of classes, but in the little time since she had returned from Scotland, it seemed like class structure was becoming less and less formal.

Dax made an affirmative grumble. "Yeah, guess so..."

He held his egg, but something was off about his posture—like he didn't want the egg to get too close, or he was afraid it would harm him.

Nail remembered what Nora had said about Dax and the fight he'd had with his father.

The crack in the egg widened. Nail saw a green eye inside the shell.

"You've got this, lil' buddy," Jace said. "You can do it."

Nail looked up at Dax. There was something in his eyes. Nail thought it looked like jealousy.

That makes sense. He's having trouble bonding with his egg, and Jace is hatching his already.

Leathery green wings moved within the egg.

"C'mon," Jace said, beaming from ear to ear. "Wyvern? English?"

The dragon inside gave a big heave, and the egg toppled over. The crack split the top of the egg off, and the dragon came crawling out.

Blinking, ve looked up to Nail and Dax with huge eyes like two emeralds. Little buds of horns already protruded from vis head.

Vis scales were small, and the dragon was the size of a housecat. Green wings folded gracefully over vis ribs, and four powerful feet ended in kitten-like claws.

The English dragon turned and looked at Jace.

"Hey," he said, extending a hand. "I'm Jace. We're gonna be partners. What's your name?"

The dragon looked back to Dax and Nail again before considering Jace. Ve flapped vis wings twice, flicking vis tail into the air.

Nail heard a flute-like voice in her mind. The dragon's voice was high-pitched and lovely.

"Shyren," the little dragon spoke.

Shyren reared up onto vis hind legs like an excited puppy. Ve rushed toward Jace and darted up his arm. Ve curled around Jace's neck, green tail dangling over his chest.

Shyren winked.

Jace stood, nothing but smiles. He pointed to Dax's egg. "Now we gotta get yours to hatch."

Jace was busy teasing Shyren. But Nail watched Dax's face. His deepening frown confirmed the worst for Nail.

Dax was nowhere close to hatching his egg.

CHAPTER 11

With the help of Igo and Luca's party-planning expertise, Jace officially introduced Shyren to the rest of the class after lunch the next day.

Everyone had gathered around the fire pit. Some came with their eggs, some came with their hatched dragons.

Wearing stained shorts and a stretched-out tank top, even Vienna abandoned her hunger strike to join the fun. Lyva sat perched on her shoulder. Ve was still small, but it seemed to Nail that the dragon had done a little bit of growing. She wondered how long it took faes to reach adulthood.

A few of the staff members had been invited, too. Igo and Luca kept begging Nora to pop off to random places and bring them things. She kept declining, but as her smile widened, Nail wondered if her old prankster ways might yet make a reappearance.

Luca's dragon did loops and figure-8s in the air above him, vis golden scales shimmering in the sun.

Rankor stood as far off to the side as possible with Prior Adams, who clutched a plastic red cup, looking terrified of conversation.

Jace approached with Shyren still draped like a love-sick kitten around his shoulders. He wore a colorful party hat complete with a glittery pom-pom. He offered one to Nail.

"Go ahead," he said. "Igo and Luca got them from Hank."

Nail accepted the hat tentatively. "I still haven't met Hank."

Jace's jaw hung loose. "How is that possible? I'll take you to meet him tomorrow. It's a real mixed bag with Hank."

"What do you mean?" Nail asked.

Jace shrugged, disturbing Shyren. The dragon nipped playfully at his ear. "Sometimes Hank is chipper. Sometimes he's cowering under his desk from grenades that only he can see. Sometimes he's just stoned to all oblivion."

Nail made a mental note of Hank's stoner status. "So what are we celebrating?"

"Almost half of the eggs have hatched." Jace lowered his voice. "This is just the 'official' party. Igo and Luca have something else planned for tonight."

"Ah, I see," Nail said. She thought she had hidden her disappointment well, but Jace frowned. He touched her arm.

His eyes went soft, and his mouth curled into a sad half-smile. "When you get your egg, they're going to throw the biggest party."

Nail rolled her eyes. "As if."

But her heart filled with a little bit of hope.

Jace shook his head. "I mean it. They've already got plans and contingency plans and working ideas. To be fair, I think it's more because it's going to be an epic excuse to party more than anything."

Nail shrugged. "I'll take it."

She took a party hat from Jace and fixed the thin string under her chin.

Jace pointed a thumb over his shoulder toward a two-person couch on the outskirts of the group. "Can we actually talk for a minute?"

Nail suddenly became acutely aware of her heartbeat. Sweat had already formed on her palms.

"Sure," she squeaked.

Jace led the way and she sat next to him.

"I wanted to give you a heads up," he said. "Rorik has a bit of a mouth."

"Mouth is for eating," Shyren said.

Nail looked over her shoulder. Rorik, Muari, Quinn, and Elsie stood conversing in a happy group. Vienna stood off to the side, alone for once. She stared at Nail. Hard.

"In what way?" Nail looked over again.

Vienna's upper lip was curled up slightly higher on one side. Nail remembered her first fireside conversation with Jace that Vienna had so rudely interrupted.

Nail made a show of putting a concerned hand onto Jace's knee. "Should Muari be worried?"

Jace shook his head, eyes glancing down to her hand and back up again. "He's tight-lipped about her. But...."

The crowd as a whole broke into cheers and objections at once. Nail looked over. Luca's dragon, the golden lung dragon, was swishing vis tail vigorously and flying high into the sky.

"Oh." Nail snapped back to the conversation. "But he's loose-lipped about... the trial?"

"Yep."

"And being Fated?"

"Yep."

"Nessie?"

"Yes." Jace nodded. "In his defense, he didn't immediately offer it. But he's been leaking bits and pieces when group conversation turns, you know, toward those topics."

"Which is often, I'm sure," she said.

Jace nodded again.

Nail rolled her eyes. She was grateful she'd had the discretion to not talk about Finley in front of Rorik. "So he's spreading rumors."

Nail glanced around. Vienna whispered something to Lyva. The fae dragon shuddered, and silvery dust rolled off vis body.

"He has," Jace said. "But it's been in your favor. I think he's said enough to quell the mob that wanted to pin you down for details. I just wanted you to know what—"

The crowd had gasped again. But it wasn't for Luca's lung dragon.

Vienna had reached a new level of insanity. She had been wearing shorts and a sporty tank top. The tank top was gone.

Everyone else, including Nail, froze.

She sauntered over to Jace and Nail, all hips and cleavage and lacy bra. Everyone behind her was dumbstruck, jaws open. Someone wolf-whistled.

Vienna stood in front of Jace and Nail, thumbs through the belt loops of her shorts.

"So why aren't we happening yet?" she posed to Jace.

His eyes wide, he glanced from Nail to Vienna and back again and stammered for words.

Vienna didn't waste the opportunity. She pushed Nail to the ground and swung one leg over Jace's lap, facing him. She settled into a straddle and wiggled her hips against him, deftly removing his silly party hat. Shyren snapped at her fingers before gliding to the ground.

"Jace is for Shyren," the little dragon said, assuming an aggressive crouch that was no more threatening than an angry terrier.

"Well?" Vienna asked. "Am I not hot enough for you?"

Nail's anger reached a new high. There was no insult, no barbed word strong enough to make Vienna suffer the way she was going to. She'd never been a fight, but this seemed like the perfect time.

Jace's face had gone blank.

Nail looked over. The crowd gaped at Vienna's display. Prior Adams still stood there, stone-faced. Rankor looked uninterested. There were plenty of witnesses. But Luca had gotten off scot-free from punching Dax. Her situation made much more sense.

Nail turned back toward Vienna, deciding which part of her pretty face she was going to bruise first. She ripped off her own hat and the string snapped.

Lyva winked down at her from Vienna's shoulder.

It was just enough. Nail froze and considered. She had a hunch.

She stood and moved to the arm of the couch, staring down at Jace. Vienna shot her one scathing glance over her shoulder and returned to Jace with doe-eyes.

Nail shut her own eyes. *What would Steven do?*

Nail knelt, making herself lower than Jace's head, putting herself at the same level as Vienna's ample cleavage. She silently, slowly, and painfully swallowed her pride, pushed her anger away, and chose her words very carefully.

Nail reached out and removed one of Vienna's hands from Jace's shoulder.

"Vienna, honey," she said softly. "I just want to offer my condolences on Kerris's passing. It's a terrible thing to lose a friend like that. It can make a person want to do all sorts of wild things."

Vienna looked at her, eyes still wide like a doe. Not as a seducer, but as a friend struck with overwhelming grief. Her voice came out as a whisper. "It's been awful. And everyone thinks I'm crazy."

Nail shook her head. Lyva still wore a sickening grin.

"You're not crazy. If I were you, I wouldn't have done all those vigils. I wouldn't go on a hunger strike," Nail said. "You know what I'd do?"

"What?" Vienna asked. She looked so full of hope, full of desperation. "Please, what would you do?"

"I'd want to sleep," Nail said. "*Alone*, undisturbed. For at least eighteen hours."

Vienna appraised Nail and then her gaze went to the ground. Her eyes darted back and forth, deciding. She raised her head again. "I think I should do that, too."

Lyva shivered. More silvery dust fell through the air. Nail saw Vienna inhale some of it.

Suddenly, like the last few moments had never happened, Vienna swung herself off of Jace. "I'm going to bed," she announced. Vienna looked to Lyva on her shoulder and brushed the dragon away. "I don't want you to come with me."

Lyva took to the air as Vienna strode away from the group and toward the girl's dorm. Nail, like she had done with lightning bugs as a child, cupped Lyva midair into her hands.

"Rankor said you're all tricksters," Nail muttered.

The crowd, now disinterested since a shirtless Vienna had her back to them, returned their attention to the sky. A few people pointed.

Rankor was the first to cry out. *"Fool! You fool!"*

Something was approaching rapidly, falling quickly toward them.

Luca's dragon.

Pandemonium ensued. The dragon fell spine first, curled like a halfmoon, golden tail flailing helplessly in the wind. Ve was in freefall. There were cries and shouts of catching it. People immediately ran toward the beach. The dragon was falling toward the ocean.

People shouted and ran. Nail stood rooted to the spot, Lyva still clutched in her hands.

"It's not my fault!" Luca shouted. "It was just a dare!"

But the unmoving dragon came crashing down just the same. Nail stood horrified as a fountain of spray splashed from where the dragon had landed at sea. There was no other movement.

"Seize him." Prior Adams pointed at Luca.

Rankor's voice thundered. *"Save the dragon!"*

Dax dove into the ocean. Luca didn't need to be seized. He knelt in the grass close to the sandy beach.

His dragon was dead.

CHAPTER 12

Nail sat on the couch in Steven's office. Luca sat in front of her, in a chair facing Steven's desk. Lyva fluttered in the empty fish tank in Steven's office, muttering mild-mannered curses at them both. Nail paid the fae no attention.

There were worse matters at hand.

Luca wrung his hands. Tears stained his cheeks and shirt. He asked Nail, "How bad is this going to be?"

Nail didn't want to answer that.

Luca looked over at her. He had eyes like a puppy.

"C'mon," he pleaded. "How bad will this be?"

Nail shook her head. "I don't know."

"Am I going to get a second egg?"

Nail's mouth tightened. "I don't know what's going to become of you, but you only get one pairing."

It had been a dismal scene. Dax, swimming back to the shore with a limp dragon. The desperate attempts to revive the poor thing. Luca crying. Everyone crying. Rankor screaming in their heads. Nora popping onto the beach with Steven and Oracle close behind.

"You killed your dragon," Nail said.

"I didn't mean to!" Desperation dripped from Luca's voice. "It was just a dare!"

"Just a dare," Nail repeated.

There was no easy way to tell what had killed the dragon. Frost from the altitude? A lack of atmospheric pressure? Lung dragons were good fliers, but the winds at that elevation... The baby had been tiny. Maybe it just couldn't maintain control.

It could have been lack of oxygen, making ver black out high in the sky and die on impact. Nail had heard that was how the astronauts of the Challenger had died—alive and helpless the whole way down.

"You dared a juvenile dragon to swallow the sun," Nail said, trying to unclench her teeth.

Luca responded with sobbing.

Nail folded her arms and leaned back, waiting for someone—anyone—else to arrive in the room.

She hated Luca and she didn't care if he knew it. He'd been given the greatest opportunity in the world: to be a part of Lumen, with no drawbacks of being Fated, no extra complications.

And he'd ruined it all.

Xaos and Thovos had paid for Kerris with their own lives. Did Luca deserve any less?

The door flung open unceremoniously. Steven strode in first, followed by Oracle and Nora who shut—and locked—the door.

Steven stood behind his desk, seething. He stared down wordlessly at Luca who continued to sob.

It was Oracle who broke the silence. She demanded, "Speak!"

Steven held up a hand. "I, Steven Parson, do commence this trial into hearing. Luca Costa, as a fellow citizen of Earth, member of the human race, and inductee of the Lumen Society, I accuse you of negligence and gross indifference leading to the death of the dragon known as Kaeylo."

Steven motioned toward Oracle.

"You did this!" Oracle shouted. "You caused the death of a Lumen dragon!"

Luca continued to cry. He nodded his head.

Oracle pointed at him. "You see? He doesn't deny the murder."

Nora stepped forward. "I was there. He didn't murder Kaeylo."

Oracle rounded on Nora. "A dragon is dead on his orders. What else would you call it?"

Nora pointed back to Steven. "Exactly what my brother said. Negligence and gross indifference, not murder."

Luca collected himself enough to speak. "I dared Kaeylo to swallow the sun," he choked out. "I never meant for him to get hurt."

"*Ver*," Oracle corrected with a snarl.

Luca just nodded.

"The laws of Lumen are black and white," Steven said. "Yet this is clearly an area of gray."

"It is *not*." Oracle shot back. "Life pays for life and death for death. We just saw it with Kerris."

Luca cried harder.

"That's not justice," Nora said.

Nail didn't feel brave, but her nerve came from somewhere within her, somewhere she knew to be true. She looked up at Nora, nodding in agreement. "That was different."

Oracle's temper rounded on her. "What would *you* know? You were a coward with Xaos and Thovos. You didn't—"

Steven held up a hand to stop her. "I changed that situation, remember? It was my gift that ended them, much to your displeasure, Oracle. You wanted Nail to have a say in their trial. Why shouldn't she have a say here as well?"

Oracle looked back and forth between Steven and Nail.

Steven gestured for Nail to continue.

It was harder to find the words this time.

"Kerris was murdered," Nail said. "Xaos and Thovos intended to kill her. Luca…"

Luca looked at her. Tears continued to stream down his face.

Nail continued, "Luca is a child. Naïve and without self-control. He didn't intend harm, but he didn't take active measures to prevent it either."

Nora nodded approvingly.

Oracle shook her head. "He still caused a death."

Nail nodded. "He did. But he didn't intend for that to be the result."

Steven folded his arms. "Oracle clearly wants to put Luca to death for this crime. But he's a human, and so final judgment rests with us. What do you propose, Nail?"

She thought for a long moment. What would be fair? The loss of a dragon couldn't be taken lightly.

Finally, Nail spoke. "The loss of one life paid for by the loss of another."

Oracle raised her hands. "Finally, the girl makes sense."

Nail shook her head. "I don't mean the loss of his physical life. I mean the loss of his life on Lumen."

Luca was sixteen too, but he wasn't as old as her. Not in spirit, anyway.

"Banish him," she finished. "You banished Tally. Why not Luca?"

Steven considered it for a long moment, his fingers stroking his chin. "It's possible. But Luca has had good memories here. He won't want to forget like Tally did. I can't make him."

Nail kept a straight face. Her solution was elegant and simple. "Then don't. Let him keep his memory. Let him remember what was offered and what he lost. He'll either learn from it and rise to the challenge or he'll crumble beneath it. If he ever tells anyone about Lumen, they won't believe him. He can't prove he was here."

Luca looked at her, but his expression was too mottled for Nail to read.

"Send him back home." Steven nodded as he worked through the concept. "Let him live with regret for the rest of his life."

Nail sighed. *Just let Luca live.*

Steven looked resigned. "Oracle?"

She wore a snarl. Nail wondered, even if they banished Luca, would it satisfy her desire for revenge? And if she wanted to take an eye for an eye, was there anything anyone could do to stop her?

CHAPTER 13

Three days after Finley left the most embarrassing voicemail of her life, she still hadn't heard from Mr. Parson, whoever he was.

A week after that voicemail, shocking footage bombarded every headline in the world. The Loch Ness Monster was real and alive.

Two weeks after the voicemail, Finley had the TV in her bedroom set to mute. Camera crews flooded Loch Ness, every news outlet in the world wanting to get another glimpse of Nessie. If Nail had an internet connection or a TV signal, she'd seen the footage.

Finley had redoubled her efforts on the cryptozoology forums, hunting for Nail. No matter where she was in the world, there was no way she would miss this opportunity to theorize about Nessie.

But her searches didn't yield results. She never saw a single username that could have been Nail.

Finley looked up from the empty space on her wall, the space she'd cleared out within an hour of seeing the shocking footage.

The video started off uneventful. A large ripple moved the water, seemingly caused by a fish or a seal. Then it grew, and scales poked just an inch or two above the surface. Then nothing.

Then came a great storm of bubbles and thrashing, the water in turbulence. Three distinct and complete humps rose from the water, one at a time. Shimmering blue scales danced in the overcast light. Yellow tendrils floated and snaked at the surface like ribbons. Two nostrils appeared and disappeared underwater again. The humps faded away.

And after the waves were still and calm again for a moment, a serpentine tail, blue and brilliant yellow, flicked out of the water then plummeted back into the depths.

Finley turned back to her board. There was nothing new to add. She had posted the facts up there like a detective would. Nail's date of disappearance, Tally's memory loss, their odd connection in Greece, screenshots of the Nessie footage.

More likely than not, Nessie had nothing to do with Nail. But the footage broke Finley's heart. The discovery would have been the greatest moment of Nail's life. But she was nowhere to be found.

Her laptop dinged. Finley leaned over to read it.

8Ecraskrell: hey, you know that Nessie footage?
WinnaFin: yeah
8Ecraskrell: I met someone. says he knows Nail
8Ecraskrell: And that she's in the original vid, right at the end.

Finley sat dumbfounded. She sprang into a flurry of action, grabbing her headphones and searching for the original video.

She watched the creature splash in the water. All told, Nessie was on camera for less than thirty seconds.

A man with wiry white hair yelled and celebrated. The camera kept rolling, but nothing happened on the water.

All the news outlets cut out the ending. Nessie was the star of the show. No one wanted to watch still water or listen to people shouting.

People. There were two voices.

Finley turned up her volume. The video continued to play.

A young woman stepped into the frame, laughing and celebrating.

Finley knew that silhouette. She knew that laugh.

She paused the video and took a screenshot of the still frame. The first shred of real proof.

She knew for sure Nail wasn't in Greece.

WinnaFin: Who is this guy? How does he know Nail?
WinnaFin: Is he willing to talk to me?

8Ecraskrell's chat bubble showed him typing.
He stopped. He started again.
Finley held her breath.

EPISODE FOUR

CHAPTER 1

Elsie sat on her dorm bed, surrounded by her favorite friends—books. The Lumen library, while not particularly large, still contained a vast amount of knowledge. Dragons were featured in many of the books but not all.

Soon, the class would begin figuring out their magical gifts. There was no telling what those gifts would be like, or what resources they would need.

Elsie shut a book on astrophysics and replaced it with one that focused on the marine biology of the Pacific Ocean. She mused to herself, "What is magic if not science inspired by imagination?"

Everyone else was likely outside or milling about in the common room, discussing the latest gossip—Luca's banishment—but Elsie preferred the solitude. She'd never liked Luca very much. She imagined he'd had a spoiled upbringing complete with a lack of discipline or responsibility.

She had a hard time relating to people like that.

She looked over at her egg. It was a beautiful thing, covered in swirls of blue above a sandy and rocky base. She examined the titles spread out on her bed. The subjects ranged from philosophy to modern art to theoretical science.

"Perhaps I should focus more on physics," she said.

A knock at the door caught her by surprise.

Elsie reached for her favorite bookmark—a slender sheet of instant film showing Elsie and her little sister, Maggie. They sat smiling in the cramped photo booth, laughing and making faces at each other. She slipped the bookmark in front of page 143 and shut the marine biology book.

"Come in," she called.

Prioress Nora peeked inside. "Can I join you?"

Elsie nodded. If the Prioress had wanted, she could have simply teleported directly into the room. Elsie appreciated her thoughtfulness regarding privacy.

Prioress Nora sat on the bed. Her hair was pulled into a French braid that kissed the base of her neck. She wore street clothes—ankle boots, jeans, a grungy tee, and a leather cross-body bag. She looked like she'd blend right into a crowd in Chicago. Perhaps that's where she was heading.

"I wanted to check in on you," Prioress Nora said. "See how you're adjusting."

Elsie sat up straighter. "It's going great. I'm really glad to be here."

Prioress Nora nodded. "I've noticed you haven't made a lot of friends."

Elsie shrugged. "I didn't have a lot of friends back home, either."

Prioress Nora tilted her head, clearly wanting more of an answer.

"I don't need many friends," Elsie pushed. "Plus, Maeve and I are friendly."

"She's your roommate." Prioress Nora raised an eyebrow.

"Her dragon just hatched a week ago," Elsie said. "I see less and less of her every day. Which is just fine, it gives me more of a chance to read in quiet."

Prioress Nora nodded. "Reading for learning or reading for pleasure?"

"All reading is pleasure," Elsie quipped. "I'm trying to prepare myself for whatever my dragon may be and whatever gifts we may develop. I'm making the most of my time."

Prioress Nora smiled. "I appreciate that you don't want to waste this opportunity."

"I don't."

"But you are. You're not making friends with the only people in the world who will be able to relate to what you're going through. You were pulled out of a dingy trailer park and brought to a tropical paradise… and you're inside. *Reading.*"

Elsie looked down. The first photo of her and Maggie poked out of the top of the marine biology book.

"You miss your sister," Prioress Nora said.

Elsie nodded, her mouth a hard line.

"Which is why I checked up on her today," Prioress Nora said.

Elsie's head snapped upright. "You did?"

"I did." Prioress Nora flipped open the bag. She handed Elsie a stack of 3x5 photos.

They showed Maggie on a carousel with a woman Elsie didn't know. Maggie on a slide at a park. Maggie riding an elephant at a zoo with a man Elsie didn't know.

She looked happy. She'd gained some much-needed weight.

Elsie stopped. She couldn't see clearly through her welling tears.

"Dan and Carol are excellent foster parents," Prioress Nora said. "They love her like she was their own. She's in preschool, too. And making lots of friends. Her teacher says she has a gifted imagination."

"What does she think happened to me?" Elsie asked. Steven and Nora had taken Elsie away from the trailer park and onto Lumen Island. But to the rest of the world, she was probably just another sad runaway.

"Dan was in my Lumen class," Nora explained. "He understands. And Carol knows, too. They've told her that you've been accepted at an elite school. Maggie is happy, safe, and thriving. But she misses you."

Tears fell down Elsie's face. She was filled with gratitude for what Lumen had done for Maggie and for herself. "She does?"

Nora nodded. "Dearly." She pulled out another item from her purse, a notebook and pen. "Technically, I'm not allowed to do this. But I'm invaluable to Lumen, so how much trouble can I get in?"

Nora winked and handed the pen and paper to Elsie.

"Write her a letter," Nora said. "Don't hold back. Speak from your heart. It may be years until you're ready to return to the mainland and society. Give her something to hold onto."

Elsie nodded. Her next question stumbled over the lump in her throat. "And my mother?"

Prioress Nora smiled, but her mouth turned sad at the corners. "She's been sentenced to ten years, with parole eligibility in five. Steven spoke with her, too."

"He did?" Elsie said. She remembered the promise he'd made that night on the bench outside the gas station. But she was never sure if she really believed he'd follow through on it.

"Normally, he's against this sort of thing, but I think he felt like it was his humanitarian duty to do something. He used his gift on her. She's been clean since they spoke. And as long as some tiny part of her wants to stay clean, she will."

"Maggie could be nine when she gets out. Even if she's clean…"

Prioress Nora smiled. "Adoption has been talked about. We'll see how it goes. I know Steven won't interfere there, one way or another."

Elsie nodded. Her decision to come to Lumen had led the police to their home, to see Maggie's neglect and her mother's heroin addiction. She shut her eyes and fought off the flood of negative thoughts that threatened to overwhelm her.

She's in jail because of her actions, not mine. She repeated the mantra over and over until she could feel her heart rate returning to normal.

Nora stood and headed for the door. "I'll come get the letter from you tomorrow." She paused with her fingers on the handle. "Don't squander this experience because of guilt. Everyone is exactly where they should be, and they're all getting better because of the decisions you made. You should be proud of that."

Then Prioress Nora left.

Elsie looked back at the books on her bed, at the bookmark peeking up at her. She pushed her way free from the pile and stood.

Carrying her egg with more pride than ever, she turned her back on the books and headed outside.

CHAPTER 2

Nail had been in the room when Nora seized Luca and they both disappeared. Luca had cried and pleaded to stay, but eventually he saw sense. His life had been spared, even though his carelessness had cost Kaeylo vis life.

Oracle had left Steven's office shortly after Nora and Luca had popped off to wherever Luca came from. Nail hadn't known him well aside from his pranking and partying antics.

"We need to talk," Nail said to Steven.

Steven sat in his chair, sinking deep into the leather cushioning. "Clearly. There's a fae in my fish tank."

Nail looked over at Lyva. The little fae dragon, no bigger than a gecko, fluttered vis pastel, butterfly-like wings in agitation.

"I think I can explain Vienna's odd behavior." Nail recapped everything she'd heard and seen: Vienna's insistence on multiple vigils for Kerris, her idea of a scholarship for a school that had no tuition, her hunger strike, and finally her outburst earlier that day and public indecency.

"And I think it relates to Kerris's murder, too," Nail continued. "Kerris wanted to search for the intruding dragons. Lyva was on her shoulder and produced some sort of dust after Kerris said as much. At the party earlier, I saw Lyva make the same kind of dust right before Vienna went… loco."

Steven nodded along.

"I think Lyva's gift has something to do with convincing a person to take action," Nail said.

"Or it removes inhibitions, or it convinces them to make bad choices, or it convinces a person that they're infallible." Steven rubbed his chin.

"I gave Vienna the idea that if I were her, I would want to sleep for about eighteen hours straight," Nail said.

Steven smiled. "Smart. Let me guess: she repeated the idea, and more dust?"

Nail nodded.

"Impressive. Quick thinking, especially given the… circumstances."

Nail shuddered. Vienna hadn't simply removed her shirt in front of everyone. She'd done that and then straddled Jace's lap.

"I didn't kick anyone. That's a victory in my book."

"It is indeed." Steven turned toward Lyva. "What do you have to say for yourself?"

A sound echoed in Nail's mind, like tiny Christmas bells ringing. Laughter. Fae laughter.

"It was a funny joke," Lyva's dragon voice rang melodically.

Steven shook his head. "No, it wasn't." He turned back to Nail. "Even a mature fae has difficulty restraining vis desire for trickery."

Nail glanced nervously to the fish tank. "Will there be consequences for Lyva?"

Steven shook his head. "Magical gifts always have growing pains, some worse than others."

Nail nodded. She wasn't sure what else to say.

He sighed heavily. "I have yet another funeral to arrange."

Nail nodded. "When will that be?"

"Tomorrow afternoon. I need to speak with Vienna in the morning." He turned toward Lyva. "Sorry, little one. Until Vienna is better, we're going to have to keep you cooped up."

Lyva growled, which sounded like a dampened bell.

"There's other news," Steven said to Nail. "Your pairing date has changed."

"Oh." Nail sat up a little straighter. She didn't want to wait longer, but she didn't want it to come sooner, either. She wasn't sure if she really wanted it at all anymore. "To when?"

"Three days from now," Steven said. "Get ready."

CHAPTER 3

Nail and Steven stood outside of Vienna's dorm. He exhaled. Hands trembling, he knocked. Nail shifted her weight and pulled on her shirtsleeves.

A groggy voice behind the door answered. "Come in."

Steven opened the door and ushered Nail in first.

She stumbled in shock. Nail had expected Vienna's room to look like it came out of a catalogue—crystal chandelier, fur rug, glitz and sparkle.

Instead, it looked just like hers. A living area, two desks, two beds, and the same doors. The view out the window was almost identical, too.

Kerris's bed was immaculately made. A mountain of her personal items were laid across the comforter. A large photo of Kerris leaned against the pillows surrounded by pictures from home, band posters, sea shells, handmade cards from some of her Lumen classmates, her sneakers, and freshly cut flowers.

No wonder Vienna is struggling. She's sleeping next to a shrine.

The door clicked shut.

"Vienna," Steven's voice had a warm tone. It reminded Nail of old wood. "How are you?"

Vienna sat up in her bed. Her pajamas looked like they belonged in the Hamptons. She pulled a lilac-colored eye mask off her face.

"I feel better," she said with a sigh. "I slept quite a lot."

Steven chuckled. "Eighteen hours, I think."

Vienna nodded, glancing between the two of them.

Steven motioned toward Nail. "Nail is doing some training with me. Is it okay if she's here too?"

Vienna smiled sweetly. "Of course."

Nail cringed internally. She'd hoped Vienna would send her out of the room. Kerris's shrine was deeply unsettling.

Steven pointed to the bed. Vienna nodded and he sat. "We need to talk about Lyva."

Vienna's eyes widened. "Oh, no. Is ve okay?"

"Lyva is fine," Steven said. "But we need to talk about Lyva's gift."

"No," Vienna said. "Lyva's gift hasn't revealed itself yet."

Nail took a step closer to the bed. "Actually, we think it has."

"We think Lyva has some sort inhibition-removing gift," Steven said. "Something that activates when someone around ver expresses a desire."

"Oh." Vienna looked down, her eyes darting. "*Oh.* I see."

Steven gave her a moment to process.

"You think my... my behavior has been altered by Lyva."

"Ve gives off a dust," Steven said. "Once inhaled... it does seem to affect a person's mind."

Vienna looked from Steven to Nail. "Lyva has affected others?"

Steven raised a hand to stop her conjecture. "Minimally."

"It seems to happen when someone verbalizes a desire," Nail said.

Steven nodded. "But that could change. Lyva shows great potential. It will be exciting to see your gift develop alongside Lyva's."

Vienna adjusted the covers, her fingers mindlessly tugging the fabric.

"Because of that, it's too risky to have you so vulnerable with your dragon. Your bond is important. We need to talk about Kerris."

Vienna's eyes filled with tears at Kerris's name. She glanced over at the shrine-bed and stammered, "O-okay."

"Grief is natural. It's normal. And it's something you *should* feel. But the level to which you've expressed it is not," Steven said. "I'm not making a judgment. My class had its fair share of losses too. Every class does. It's part of the risk."

"There was no way to interfere with or anticipate Lyva's influence. There was no way to prevent..." Steven trailed off.

"He means to say," Nail clenched her fists, "that no one blames you."

"No one," Steven echoed. "And I think we can help you get better. Nora has contacted a grief counselor. She's Lumen, and retired, but still quite competent. Is that something you'd be open to?"

Vienna nodded.

"Excellent," Steven said. "So how can I help right now?"

It took a moment for Vienna to respond. After she had finished drying her cheeks and blowing her nose, her voice came out as a crackled plea. "Can you make me not sad anymore?"

"I can," Steven said, "but I won't."

Vienna started to cry again.

"Do you want to heal?" Steven asked gently. "To get better?"

Her tears were too heavy to speak. She nodded.

"Okay, then I think I can help," Steven said.

Vienna looked up at him. "Please," she begged. "I need...."

"Hope," Nail said. "You need hope."

Vienna looked at her brightly, blonde hair clumped and greasy. Nail felt guilty. Caked-on eyeliner and mascara streamed down her face.

Steven reached out, and Vienna put her hands in his.

"Vienna," his voice went deeper. It was a tone of command and compassion. "Recognize Kerris's life and death. Grieve, but don't be pulled under by the grief. Recognize that you still have meaning and purpose even though she is gone. Believe that life can still be good even when things seem hopeless."

Nail could see it. Vienna's breathing steadied. Already, she looked stronger. Tears still fell openly, but there was a slight curl to her lips. Not quite a smile, but almost.

"I can do that." She turned toward Nail with an outstretched hand.

Nail begrudgingly shuffled closer and accepted the gesture.

"I remember last night," Vienna said. "You had every reason to hate me. But you helped me instead."

Nail wanted to run from the room. She hated this emotional crap. "You helped me, too. When Luca and Igo threw that awards ceremony? They were going to call my name. You took my place."

Vienna grinned and squeezed Nail's hand. Nail was ready to ask her for a truce when Vienna took it to another level.

"Friends?" she asked. Her blue eyes were full of hope, grief, optimism, and loneliness.

Nail exhaled. She cursed herself for being naïve enough to go into the room in the first place. She'd only wanted Vienna to recognize that Nail had saved her. She didn't want Vienna to see that she had been *helpful*.

Saving Vienna gave Nail the upper hand.

But helping her meant that they might actually end up becoming....

Fake smile. "Friends."

CHAPTER 4

Later that day, Nail stood with the rest of the class on the far western tip of the island. She had never explored the area, but her classmates seemed to know where they were going.

Everyone wore black—funeral attire. A few of them had opted to bring their eggs along. The other hatched dragons—aside from Lyva—attended with their partners.

Steven led the way with Oracle at his side and in her humanoid form. She carried the body of Kaeylo.

West of the farm were old lava tubes and caves. The terrain suddenly changed from lush fields to crumbling black rock. The hummingbugs watched their march, singing out Beethoven's Symphony No. 7 in A Major from Opera 92.

Muari had decided not to attend. As Nail had gotten ready, she relayed the nightmare of trying to traverse the rocky terrain when the class had interned Kerris's egg.

"Without Nora there," she had said, "it's not worth the effort or risk."

Nail looked around. Jace and Dax walked together. Vienna was nowhere to be seen.

Steven led them toward a cave. A two-door iron gate, decorated in an elaborate, gothic style, stood open and ready to receive them.

Nail wondered if some long-gone Lumen member had been gifted with metalwork. Motifs of all kinds of dragons—too detailed to seem possible—decorated the door.

The group passed under the archway of the cave and paused in the entryway. Steven silently passed out black candles with little paper collars to collect the wax. He lit his candle with a lighter and they passed the flame from person to person.

The light of the candles danced on Kaeylo's scales, making them dance again with golden radiance.

Beyond the initial vestibule, a wide set of stairs led down into the darkness.

As they moved deeper into the catacomb, Nail noticed odd rock formations at the outside edges of the steps. They were jagged with many points, like a lopsided star.

From the bottom landing, she glanced back up the steps. They weren't rock formations, but dragon vertebrae bones. She shuddered.

At the base of the stairs, dark tunnels branched in many maze-like directions, each wide enough for even a large dragon to pass through. Their candles cast only a few feet of light ahead. The rest, whatever lay beyond, remained shrouded in darkness.

Steven approached the usually exuberant Igo and put a hand on his shoulder. Nail hadn't noticed earlier, but Igo had been crying. Nail wondered if he was mourning the loss of a dragon or the banishment of his best friend. Maybe it was both.

Oracle didn't share Steven's sympathy. She chose the tunnel farthest to the right, and the group was forced to carry on or be left behind.

Smooth, black rock that echoed their footfalls formed the mouth and neck of the tunnel, but at the end they encountered a terrifying sight. A dragon skull, maw opened wide, served as the archway to the next room.

It was far larger than any dragon Nail had ever seen. Its eye sockets were as wide as she was tall. Several teeth were missing from the dragon's bottom jaw, allowing just enough space for them to pass through single-file.

The circular room beyond the dragon's skull was a horrific sight.

The walls reached three stories high, with carved steps reaching to different levels. Hundreds of alcoves gaped open in the walls, some smaller than shoeboxes, others the size of a child's bed. Some of the alcoves were empty, but many more were filled with the dusty bones of dragons long dead.

A massive dead tree stood in the center of the room. Eggs rested on its stone branches, never to hatch. Kerris's red egg sat front and center.

Nail shivered. The air was dusty and dry. She scanned all the dragon bones. She'd expected to see the remains of larger dragons. She hadn't predicted there would be so many small dragons.

She sniffed, fighting back the urge to tear up. This wasn't a normal mausoleum. The giant skull archway had been a reminder of what should have been but wasn't. This was a shared sarcophagus for babies—infant dragons whose lives were cut short.

Nail began to doubt her suggestion to only have Luca banished. He had stood in that very room not long ago, when Kerris's egg was laid to rest. He should've known better.

Oracle took a flight of steps to the second level. Steven and the class remained below, huddled far enough back to still see her clearly. Oracle took her time, each footstep placed deliberately and silently.

She reached an empty alcove on the right side of the room. It was about waist-high off the ground and roughly the size of a nightstand. Oracle laid Kaeylo's corpse inside. She began to hum.

It was one long, drawn-out note. Steven joined her. Everyone stood either clasping their eggs or with their dragons at their sides. Soon, little one-note voices filled Nail's mind—the other dragons singing.

Her class began to hum as well. It seemed random, that everyone had simply picked a note. She felt silly and unsure, but she joined in.

The sound filled the chamber, echoing back at them. It bounced from wall to wall, folding in on itself and jumping out again. It swelled to a buzz. It wasn't a song, and it wasn't simply a noise. Somehow, the humming felt like a heartbeat thronging through the crowd. Everyone kept their gazes on Oracle.

Oracle raised an open hand, clenched it into a fist, and everyone stopped. Their hums echoed for a moment, eventually dying out.

Oracle descended and led them back through the dragon's maw. There was no eulogy, no cautionary words. As Nail filed out with her class, she was certain it had been the strangest funeral she'd ever attended.

Out of nowhere, she remembered her mother. She couldn't remember anything about that day—she'd been only three—and no one had taken pictures. But she and her father would visit the gravesite every Mother's Day to lay flowers. Her father would tell her stories, her mother's favorite songs, favorite breakfast, the way she could light up a room.

Nail realized she didn't know what magical gift her mother had had. Her fingers touched the scale necklace.

Outside the cave, everyone blew out their candles. It felt unnatural that the sun would be shining so bright. The catacombs had been dark, full of despair. It was a fitting resting place for those poor dragons.

As Steven began collecting the candles, a cry sounded from the crowd. Nail whirled around.

Hazel knelt on the ground, her ugly gray egg trembling in front of her. Everyone gathered around her, speaking in hushed tones. The reverence of the catacombs still lingered among them.

Nail hung to the back of the crowd. Steven stood next to her.

"That's odd, isn't it?" Nail asked.

Steven nodded.

"Did she have her egg with her for Kerris's egg's…" Nail trailed off. She wasn't sure what to call it. If a dragon would never hatch, did it still die? If not, was it truly a funeral?

"Yes," Steven said. "Which makes this very odd."

"Good odd? Or bad odd?"

Steven glanced back to the cave's entrance. His voice came out foreboding. Worried. "Only time will tell."

The egg gave a final shudder, and the top piece of its shell fell away.

Two stone-gray eyes peeked out.

The small dragon had the beginnings of spikey scales over vis head and running down vis spine. Vis scales were a mottled ombré of gray, black, and charcoal. Ve flicked vis tongue and slithered out of the egg.

Ve was a wyrm dragon—no legs, no wings. Nail thought the dragon looked like an oddly proportioned snake. Vis head was thicker than the rest of vis body, but not by much. For being such a normal-sized egg, the dragon seemed impossibly long, at least four feet.

The dragon looked up at Hazel. Ve blinked.

Hazel looked around. The group had gone from grief to elation to revulsion.

Something about the dragon just seemed weird to Nail. Judging by the class's glances and frowns, it appeared that everyone else felt it too.

The dragon didn't regard Hazel or the group again. It began to slither away, making almost no noise. It blended in with the rocky terrain and quickly disappeared into the tall grass, heading toward the farm.

"Well," Maeve asked. Her magenta and lavender lung dragon sniffed at the empty shell. "What is vis name?"

Hazel stared off in the direction of her disappeared dragon. "I don't know. Ve was silent."

CHAPTER 5

Everyone gathered in the valley the next day. Dozens of wooden crates had been placed in a clearing surrounded by palm trees. Students broke off into groups, their dragons in tow. Prior Adams distributed the crates to them seemingly at random.

Nail sat with Muari, Rorik, Dax, Jace, and Shyren. The little dragon had grown exponentially—largely thanks to ver skill at hunting the island pheasants.

"There's an array of items in your crates," Prior Adam said. "Finding your gifts is largely done by trial and error. Best of luck."

He stalked off and went to sit at the edge of the group with Steven and Rankor under a cherry blossom tree.

Jace was the only one of their small group to have hatched a dragon. He reached into the crate and pulled out an array of random items—an alarm clock, potted plants, metal chains, a set of juggling balls, and—curiously—handcuffs.

Jace held up the cuffs. "I don't want to know why Hank has these in that storage room."

Dax flashed him a smile. "Maybe you do."

"I still haven't seen him." Nail glanced around.

Jace dropped the cuffs on the grass. Shyren nuzzled at the potted plants curiously.

"*Odd.*" The little dragon's voice sounded like wind whispering through the trees. "*Why are they caged?*"

Jace chucked.

Shyren jumped into the crate. Ve was larger than a housecat, roughly the size of a large terrier.

Nail glanced around at the other groups. Hazel and Maeve sat together, but only Maeve's lung dragon had joined them. Nail hadn't seen Hazel's wyrm since it hatched.

Maeve's lung dragon was longer than Shyren, with vibrant, shimmering scales. A rainbow pheasant streaked by them, and the little dragon crouched into predator mode, stalking the bird over the short grass.

"Mind if we borrow those?" a feminine voice asked.

Nail looked up.

Vienna stood above them with Lyva on her shoulder. She'd washed her hair and flawlessly applied her makeup. She looked like herself again.

Jace handed her the handcuffs. "Sure."

Vienna smiled brightly at him. "Let me know if you want them back."

Then she winked and flounced back toward Igo and Jagdesh.

Nail caught Dax rolling his eyes. He said, "I don't think I've ever met anyone so full of herself."

Nail nodded.

"She's not full of herself," Jace said. "She's just… confident."

Muari scoffed. "Maybe her gift will bring her down a peg or two."

Jace scowled but didn't object further.

Nail smirked. The other groups were busy with their assortment of items, but it didn't seem like anyone was making much progress.

Quinn's black wyvern had joined Maeve's lung dragon on the pheasant hunt. They chased the regal bird in circles around the tree, with neither dragon sure how cooperative hunting worked.

A great rush of wings thundered overhead, and Vigilus landed on the grass next to Steven. He seemed to converse with the dragon for a moment. Then Vigilus took off again, heading back toward the eastern part of the island.

Steven waved at Nail, motioning her over.

"Here we go," Nail said.

"What's up?" Muari asked.

Nail explained what she'd seen. "I'm supposed to have my pairing soon. Any day now."

The group smiled as she stood, though Jace still looked sour from Dax's comment about Vienna.

"Best of luck," Dax said, waving her off.

Nail swallowed. Her stomach was in knots.

As she neared him, he walked away from the group. She followed, and they stood together outside the palm tree clearing, halfway between the treeline and the rocky edge of the eastern ridge.

Nail crossed her arms and gave Steven an expectant look, eyebrows raised.

"Emissaries from Drasol are arriving today," he said. "Leaders of some of the human clans and a few of the dragons, too. But not as many as I'd hoped."

"So what does that mean?" Nail asked.

Steven glanced up the way Vigilus had flown. "Doing the ceremony without a full audience is… unheard of." He looked at her, pity folding the corners of his eyes. "But there's no point in delaying. They've made their choices. We'll continue on with the ceremony."

"When?" Nail asked.

"Tonight."

Nail's knees went weak and wobbly. "Tonight?"

He nodded. "There's a trail that starts by the waterfall. It will be marked. Be there at sunset. You'll be hiking, so dress appropriately."

Nail swallowed hard.

"You'll need to bring one classmate with you, to bear witness that you didn't pair in the first chamber. Others will meet you on the way."

Nail nodded and glanced back to her group. Muari and Rorik had coupled off with their eggs. Dax played with Shyren as Jace looked toward the sky.

"Does it matter who I pick?" she asked.

Steven kept his gaze on the eastern tunnel. "Only to you. This is a night you'll always remember. Pick someone who supports you."

Nail thought back to her conversation with Jace at the pond's edge. They hadn't spent time together the way he'd promised. But life had gotten busy. Maybe this hike was exactly what they needed to get them back on course.

"Eat an early dinner," Steven said. "Ah, good. They're arriving."

Nail looked toward the tunnel. A group of men and women in modern but tattered clothes strode up the valley, heading for where she stood with Steven. Judging by their average age, Nail guessed most of them were from the Drasol Lumen retirement community. Nail recognized some of the faces from the first ceremony. They passed the new class, whispering to each other. A few of them waved or stopped to hug their children. As the crowd shuffled, Nail spotted her father.

He shook hands with Steven and then pulled Nail into a hug. His brown eyes wrinkled from his wide smile. "The big night. It's finally here."

Relief flooded into Nail. If her dad was at the ceremony, she could get through anything.

"Are you nervous?" he asked.

She hesitated. "Only a little."

"You'd be crazy not to be. I've never seen a Fated ceremony, but I hear you're in for a real treat." He looked at Steven. "The other tribes aren't far behind."

Steven nodded. "There's food in the hall."

Her father clapped Steven on the arm and hugged Nail one last time. "You'll do great. I'm sure of it."

Nail watched as her father walked away, eventually turning back toward the clearing and the Metal Dragons.

Her class had started to disperse. Some of the guys were already heading back to their dorms.

Nail gestured toward the departing groups. "I'd better catch up."

Steven called out after her, "Someone who supports you *unconditionally*."

Jace and Dax were still milling about. Nail was pretty sure Steven wouldn't approve of her asking Jace to walk her. But who would be better? He knew her more than anyone else did. And this hike could bond them together. Nail hoped so, anyway.

She waited until most of the class started drifting away in small groups. Some of them headed toward the waterfall, curious about the new people arriving on the island. Muari and Rorik walked hand-in-hand toward the beach.

Nail interrupted a conversation between Dax and Jace. Dax had been laughing, running his hand in his hair which only highlighted his abnormally large biceps. Shyren had caught the scent of a snub-nosed hare and kept vis snout low to the ground, looking more like a prowling lynx than a fierce dragon. Nail apologized and pulled Jace aside.

"Tonight is my pairing," she told him.

Jace's face lit up. "That's amazing! Congratulations!"

Nail nodded. "I need to bring a witness to the ceremony. Someone who can vouch that I didn't pair the first time. And you were the last to pair, so I thought…"

"Oh." Jace glanced over his shoulder. "Yeah, that makes sense."

Nail saw a hint of a frown in the corner of his eyes. "What's wrong?"

Jace shook it off. "I'll tell you about it later. Are you sure you want me to be your witness?"

"Of course," Nail nodded. "We'll be doing some hiking, so dress accordingly."

Jace chuckled. "I'll save the three-piece suit for another time, then." He glanced over his shoulder again.

This time, Nail leaned past him to look. Vienna stood a couple yards away, eyeing them.

"Is she waiting for you?" Nail asked.

Jace scratched the back of his neck. "Yeah. We're going down to the beach in a bit. You're welcome to join if…"

Nail vigorously waved away his offer, but it didn't help ease the queasiness in her stomach. Her heart felt like a pincushion. "I need to go prepare."

Jace nodded. He pointed over her shoulder. "It looks like more guests are arriving."

A tribe of people strode up the valley—at least a dozen of them, men and women. They wore rough clothing that looked hand-sewn. Fur capes draped over many of their shoulders.

Every member of the group wore an ornate and realistic animal mask—a bear, several mountain lions, stags, owls, and deer.

One woman in particular caught Nail's eye.

She was thin and tall. Even in her baggy clothing, the strength of her stride looked effortless and lean. The hypnotic movement of her hips transfixed Nail. She wore a mask from an albino doe.

I wonder if she's single.

The woman looked at her. The doe's muzzle rose, dipped, and rose again as the woman behind the mask made a show of checking Nail out, head to toe and back again.

Nail felt her cheeks burn.

"What time tonight?" Jace asked.

Nail started to raise a hand to greet the woman but stopped herself halfway through. She felt the awkward jerkiness of the motion. Her cheeks grew hotter.

"Hello?" Jace said.

The woman gave a full nod. Then, with a graceful turn of her head, she refocused herself to the march of her tribe.

"What the hell was that?" Jace said, the cadence of his voice rising in pitch.

"What?" Nail said, pulling herself out of a daze. "What was what?"

Jace gestured with an open palm toward the disappearing group. "That."

Nail shifted her weight. "Just someone saying hello, I guess."

"That looked like a lot more than a hello."

Who does he think he is?

"Maybe it was," she raised an eyebrow. "Aren't you going to meet up with your beach date?"

Jace scowled. "What time tonight? For the pairing?"

"Sunset," Nail said. "By the waterfall."

"I'll see you then." A frown played at the corners of Jace's mouth, then he turned and met with Vienna. Together, they walked toward the shore.

Nail watched them walk away, but only for a moment. Not caring if he looked back, she searched for the woman in the albino doe mask.

But there was no sign of their group, so she trekked back toward her dorm room, keeping her head on a swivel for the woman. Back in her room, Nail opened the drawers of her wardrobe, searching for flattering hiking clothes.

Half an hour later, she realized she'd never been this picky about her wardrobe before. She sunk to her bed, glancing toward the beach, but the trees in the valley made it almost impossible to see anyone at the shore.

She could see the valley just fine, though, and it was alive with action. Men and women lingered in groups, and dragons filled the sky.

At the sight of a Drasol dragon walking the grounds, Nail's heart stuttered. The dragon was thin and reptilian like Xaos and Thovos, more like an ancient predecessor to dinosaurs than a legendary creature of fire and magic. She relaxed again when she saw Vigilus walking by vis side.

She looked for the woman in the albino deer mask but saw no sign of her, either. She couldn't put her finger on what exactly had intrigued her. But she desperately wanted to know more.

With a resigned sigh, Nail changed into her outfit for the evening. Glancing in the mirror, she was certain she was trying to catch someone's eye. She just wasn't sure whose.

CHAPTER 6

Nail spent the afternoon and early evening in her room. Too nervous to eat, she had skipped dinner. Now restless and unable to wait any longer, she checked the horizon. Sunset was at least half an hour away.

Screw it. She tugged on her hiking boots and headed out for the waterfall trail.

Most of the class was still at dinner. The din of their conversation carried softly across the valley.

Anxiety had needlessly controlled her thoughts. She'd bitten half her nails down in a fit of nerves over finding the waterfall trail.

But her concerns had been for nothing. A group of four burning torches stood at the path, and firelight danced against the rocky walls higher up the trail.

Nail waited, listening to the waterfall and trying to take deep, calming breaths. Her heart pounded in her chest. Everyone had been so certain that there would be a Fated egg for her. And she wanted to continue living on the island. She wanted a dragon of her own.

But she wasn't ready for the loss of her humanity or for her personality to change. Steven said those things wouldn't happen immediately. But once she received her egg, an invisible timer would start ticking down, counting away her last days and hours as human.

The only thing more unbearable than losing her humanity would be losing a world with dragons.

Nail was ready to be done waiting for whatever came next.

She stared into the pool of water, watching little fish swim and nip around.

"Have you seen Jace anywhere?"

She looked up. Dax stood with Shyren napping on his shoulder.

Nail shook her head.

Dax frowned. "I needed to talk to him about something."

"He should be here soon." Nail explained to him about her ceremony and needing a witness. She looked toward the horizon again.

Dax nodded and half-mumbled, "Maybe tonight isn't the best night to talk to him then."

Nail heard laughter in the distance, a little louder than the normal din of voices. She looked west.

Jace and Vienna stood paused in a clearing halfway between the waterfall and the dining terrace. *Did he spend the whole day with her?*

Nail tried to remind herself that Vienna had just needed a friend. She needed support. And she'd promised her friendship to Nail as well.

Plus, she didn't want to react like Jace had, jealous and possessive at the first sign of distress.

Then Vienna faced him. They stood close together. Nail's uneasiness grew.

Jace reached out and tucked a lock of hair behind Vienna's ear. His hands settled on her hips.

"Oh, God," Dax groaned.

Nail felt her stomach drop out before it happened. Vienna was looking at Jace. Then she was on her tiptoes. Her face was dangerously close to Jace's.

Jace leaned in and kissed her.

Nail's stomach lurched, and she turned away.

"Well, that settles it." Dax cursed.

Nail steadied herself, hands on her hips. She fought an urge to dry heave right into the pond.

"He's coming this way," Dax said, anger rising in his voice. "I don't want to be here for this."

Nail want to run, too. She wanted to scream at Jace, or become invisible, or fall off the edge of the world. Possibly all of them, together, at once. She needed to disappear immediately.

"Be my witness," she blurted to Dax, finally looking at him.

His face was flushed. His fists were clenched and his eyes shone with barely contained tears.

His distress had woken Shyren, who wordlessly took flight in Jace's direction but quickly got distracted by the scent of a snub-nosed hare scampering through the underbrush.

"I don't care if I stand him up. I hope he waits here all night," she added bitterly. "I *cannot* walk this trail with him, on this night of all nights, after seeing *that*."

Dax looked at her quizzically. "Are you sure you want me?"

True, they didn't have the strongest friendship. But Jace was getting closer. He kept his eyes on the grass, a stupidly broad grin plastered his face.

"Let's be better friends." Nail grabbed Dax's hand and yanked him toward the trail. "No time like the present."

Dax abandoned his hesitation, and Nail dropped his hand. Her heart thundered as she nearly ran to reach the trail, wanting to be well-hidden before Jace reached the pond. After a few minutes of racing, she paused. Involuntary tears welled up in her eyes.

"God, I am so stupid," she said.

Dax paused too. He kept taking big, deep breaths, releasing them slowly. It reminded Nail of an anger management technique.

Dax shook his head. "You weren't being stupid. I thought he had a thing for you too. *I* was being stupid."

Nail shook her head and more tears fell. "It's just so... typical! Going for a girl like Vienna. I thought more of him than that."

Dax scoffed. "You and me both."

"I'm sorry," Nail said. "I'm insulting her, and you're crushed that she went for him. I'm... not great at being sensitive."

Dax smiled, but it was small and sad. "Insult her all you like. Her romantic life doesn't bother me."

Nail cocked her head.

Dax scratched at his forearm, his gaze falling to the dirt at their feet. He opened his mouth several times, but the words he searched for didn't come out.

"Let's keep walking," he finally said. "It might be easier to talk if we're moving."

Nail agreed. They kept their pace light, almost meandering, following the torch-lined path. This was her night, after all. No such thing as being late to your own party.

"I love my family," Dax said. "But some of them can be… pig-headed. Stubborn. And backward-thinking."

Nail nodded along, careful of her footing.

"My dad was really upset about the egg I paired with." Dax sighed heavily. "I've had a couple girlfriends, but last summer I started dating someone he didn't approve of. And it was pretty serious. I thought so, anyway."

"Parents can be that way," Nail said.

"We broke up because my dad kept harassing him."

"That sucks," Nail said. And then it hit her. "Oh." Harassing *him*. "*Oh*."

"Yeah," Dax said. "I'm bisexual. And he doesn't approve."

It hit her. The slurs his father had used, the reluctance to bond with an egg his father didn't approve of, the time he had spent with Jace. Suddenly, Nail had a much clearer picture of what Dax had been going through.

"Oh my God… that's amazing," Nail said.

Dax stared at her.

She shook her head. "Not that he doesn't approve or that he's acting so…. I'm sorry. I meant that it's amazing that you're bi. I thought I was the only one on the island."

Dax laughed. "I play it pretty close to the chest. I've had a lot more experience flirting with girls than I have with guys. And sometimes… it's just harder to read the signals."

Nail nodded emphatically. "I never know if I'm being hit on or if she's just friendly." *Unless she makes a show of checking me out.* "And if I'm trying to flirt, girls just take it as a hetero compliment."

Dax shook his head. "It's maddening."

Nail replayed the scene of Jace and Vienna in her mind. "So tonight…"

"I decided I'd pull Jace aside for a few minutes and just get the measure of him. Ask him directly. Was it flirting or friendship? Either way was fine. I just wanted to know for sure."

"What a love triangle," Nail said. "Or maybe it's a love rectangle?"

Dax smirked. "Parallel sides with irregular corners? It's a love trapezoid."

"Definitely." Nail smiled broadly. "I'm sorry that we both had to find out like that. I would have enjoyed competing for Jace's affections with you."

Dax grinned back. "That would've been a great challenge."

"Let's start over. We part-timers gotta stick together." Nail stuck out her hand. "My name is Nail. I'm bisexual. I like men that laugh easily and lithe, athletic women."

Dax shook her hand. "I'm Dax. I like curvy brunettes of both genders."

They stood awkwardly smiling at each other for a moment. A lock of Nail's red hair brushed against her face in wind. She raised one eyebrow at Dax. "Just brunettes, huh?"

They both broke into laughter.

"Too soon!" he said. "Don't twist the trapezoid!"

The trail continued uphill, winding through rocks and patches of dense greenery. She and Dax passed the time with stories of their home lives—both of them avoiding tales of the island. Neither of them had had smooth transitions so far.

As they crested the top of the range, they paused to look down at the valley below. Nail saw the sunset casting a fiery glow over the distant horizon.

After a long, silent moment, Dax said, "It's all going to work out."

She turned her head further up the trail. Steven stood waiting for her a few yards ahead, illuminated by a burning torch.

"Sure," Nail said. "What's the worst that could happen?"

CHAPTER 7

Nail and Steven continued up the trail which now curved east toward the active volcanic side of the island. Dax followed behind.

"I like your choice of witness," Steven pointed back at Dax.

Nail nodded and decided to keep the full story to herself. "We have more in common than you might think."

Steven said, "This will be good for him. I think he needs a stronger connection to Lumen. It will help with his egg."

"If you say so."

They crossed over a natural bridge. Fields of long grass stretched out to the south. Nail thought of Kerris.

"Something's been bothering me," Nail said. "Oracle can see our futures, right? Couldn't she have seen was going to happen to Kerris?"

Steven didn't miss a beat. "Oracle's gift isn't exactly seeing futures. It's more about who we are and where we're headed. Sometimes she can get a general idea of what a person's life will be like. She foresaw your whole class being on the island, but…" He searched the darkening horizon. "It's difficult to explain. You should ask her sometime."

Nail nodded.

"There's something I should warn you about," he said. "It's about Nessie."

Nail's footing slipped on a loose rock for just a second.

Steven came to a stop and turned so Dax could fully join them.

"Oracle's presence was the only safeguard needed to open the main incubation chamber. But this chamber... it contains all of our future leaders. The magic that was placed on it is a bit more medieval."

She and Dax looked at each other. Nail already knew what fate awaited Nessie, and she hated it. She hated that it was being done in her name.

"It requires a sacrifice," Steven said. "A death."

All the color drained from Dax's face. He looked frantically to Nail. "Hey, I'm just a witness, not a—"

"No." Steven waved his hand. "A dragon sacrifice. Specifically, a fully-grown Lumen dragon willing to die to open the chamber."

Dax's face contorted in horror, but some of the color came back. "That's barbaric."

"Agreed," Steven said. "I don't like it any more than you do. But it's kept the chamber safe for a millennium." He turned to Nail again. "Once it opens, you'll have only a few seconds to enter before it closes again. I suggest you do it at a run."

A new thought occurred to Nail. "How will it open again, once I'm finished?"

Steven answered that. "The magic responds to the death of one and the new beginning of another. Once you've paired, the door will know. Place your hand on it, and it will open again."

Nail nodded.

Dax looked unconvinced. "What if she doesn't pair?"

Nail tried to not be agitated, but the old anxiety had long taken root deep under her skin.

"She will," Steven said. "I'm certain that she wasn't lying about not pairing before. And Oracle has never been wrong about a Lumen member, not in all her years."

"I don't think she's lying either." Dax cast a hesitant glance to Nail. "But what's to stop someone from lying about pairing to begin with, just to get into the second chamber?"

Steven smirked. "Someone did try that, a couple hundred years ago. Some power-hungry lord's son. The door won't open without a death or a rebirth. He went in. But the door didn't reopen for two and a half days."

Dax looked at Nail, eyebrows furrowed. "He died?"

Steven nodded.

With more confidence than what she felt, she said, "It'll reopen for me."

"This won't be like putting down your pet at the vet's office," Steven warned, a hard look in his eyes. "There will be blood. And sounds. But the sacrifice that's being made is among the noblest. You would dishonor the dragon and Lumen to look away or object when the moment comes."

Nail nodded. Dax's face still seemed sour, but he nodded too.

Steven started walking again.

Lost in thought, Nail wondered if her obsession with Nessie had some connection to this night. If, perhaps, something about being Fated meant she was more connected to the strings woven into her life.

Or maybe it had nothing to do with her pairing at all. Maybe it was just part of who she was, a fan of the strange and unbelievable. Maybe *that* was part of why she was invited to Lumen in the first place.

She kept pace with Steven as her thoughts went around in circles, spiraling down with no solid conclusions.

"This is as far as I take you," Steven said. "Dax can walk ahead with me."

Nail hadn't been paying conscious attention, but their surroundings had changed. The grass fields were far behind them, and they drew ever closer to the volcano. High up at its peak, a small ribbon of smoke lingered in the air.

"Am I going the rest of the way alone?" Nail asked.

It would be fitting. As a Fated, she would be separate from her class in a sense. She'd finally have what they all had, but none of them were inherently destined to share her fate.

Steven shook his head. "Dax represents your class. I represent the society. Another, from Drasol, will see you to the end of your journey." He shuffled aside and pointed up the hill.

Nail expected to see a Drasolian dragon behind Steven, or perhaps a grizzled leader with crow's feet etched into the corners of his eyes. But the face just up the trail wasn't familiar to Nail. It was a woman, maybe two years older than Nail.

She had a slender chin, high cheekbones, and a pixie-like face. Her blonde hair fell just past her shoulder on one side and was cut down to her scalp on the other.

Nail swallowed hard. Her nervousness tripled in intensity.

Dangling from the woman's belt was the mask of a white doe.

CHAPTER 8

Nail stood frozen in place as Steven and Dax continued up the path. The woman came down to meet Nail. As soon as she passed the two guys, Dax turned around and gave Nail a cheeky smile and two thumbs up.

Nail swallowed again.

The woman carried a long, slender stick, at least seven feet long. She walked with confident grace and smiled at Nail.

Nail realized she wasn't smiling back. She tried to grin, but only one side of her mouth cooperated.

The woman stood an arm's length from Nail. "Hello," she said, an accent to her voice.

Of course she has an accent, too.

Nail eked out a timid, "Hi."

The woman extended her hand. "My name is Rhin. I am an Apex of one of the clans from Drasol."

"Cool," Nail said, hating herself. "What the heck is that?"

Rhin smirked. "A leader, essentially. Shall we continue up the trail?"

Nail nodded. The first few minutes passed in silence, save for the noise of their feet on the slope. Nail wracked her brain for something—anything—to say.

She looked at Rhin. "You're young to be an Apex." It was a bullshit line. She didn't really know.

Rhin smirked. "Our calendar differs from yours. But by your age-counting, I am almost nineteen. I became an Apex when I was seventeen."

"Is that normal, at such a young age?"

Rhin shrugged. "It's not unheard of. We count a person's merit by their skills, not years."

Nail couldn't help but continually steal glances of Rhin's face. Her jawline was sharper than glass. Nail's mind tripped and fumbled for conversation.

"So what gave you merit?" Nail asked.

Rhin gestured to her mask as a partial answer and smiled. "It's a good story. But a bit long." She made eye contact with Nail. "Perhaps it should be told over a shared meal or a beachside campfire."

Nail gulped. *Is she asking me out?* "With me?"

Rhin laughed. "Of course, with you. It's good ambassadorship. You'll be a Lumen leader for much longer than I'll be an Apex. If I can endear you to my people, and a day comes when the clans need your help, won't you run to them first?"

It didn't take much for Nail to be endeared to whatever Rhin wanted. "I suppose so."

"You'll visit Drasol sometime. When you come to my clan, you're welcome to stay in my home."

Nail felt like she had all the grace of someone falling down a flight of stairs. "That's very generous of you."

Rhin stopped and examined Nail. "Are you always this slow?"

Nail looked back. She thought they'd been covering ground fast enough.

Rhin tapped her on the temple. "Up here. Are you always this slow?"

"I…" Heat flushed Nail's cheeks. "I'm nervous. It's a big night. Actually, I'm usually more quick-witted than this."

Rhin nodded and pointed again to the doe mask on her hip. "I know the feeling. All clan Apexes must kill their chosen animal. I grew up seeing this deer all my childhood. Many other hunters tried to kill it, wanting to wear its likeness. But the deer was too quick and too clever."

"How did you manage it?" Nail wanted her to keep talking. The more Rhin talked, the more Nail's nerves began to settle.

"I started tracking the doe when I was eleven," Rhin said. "I found where she liked to drink water. We have a special flower that grows high up in the trees. Its leaves taste like honey. Deer love them. But they can only eat them in autumn when the flowers fall to the ground.

"I would climb a tree and pick the flowers, and leave them for the doe. Eventually, she let me watch her eat them. Then, she let me approach. And after a long time, she would follow me through the forest, nudging me for more."

"And that's how you got close enough to kill her?" The idea repulsed Nail—earning an animal's trust just to kill it.

"Yes and no." Rhin made a noncommittal gesture. "We had a friendship for a long time. But one day, she didn't come to the stream. I looked for her. She had broken a leg. She was old then, and even before the break, she didn't move like she used to.

"She looked at me, and I knew. I could either let my friend die slowly, painfully, and alone. Or I could end her suffering. And so I did.

"Now I wear her likeness with pride. It reminds me of what it takes to be a leader. Compassion, patience, strength, and an ability to outsmart everyone else who wants what you want." Rhin winked.

Nail nodded. "That's a good ending to the story."

"It was a good ending for the doe, too," Rhin said. "How do you feel? A little more at ease?"

"I think so, yes." Nail's heart wasn't threatening to beat out of her chest anymore. They continued up the trail. The scenery turned to barren, black rock with sharp edges and wavy flows. "Any advice to offer?"

Rhin seemed to consider that for a long moment. "Be the kind of leader your people need. I suppose it is odd for you because Steven is so young." She thought for another long moment. "You will both share the leadership. Does this mean you are—what's the word—betrothed?"

Nail laughed hard and loud. "No way! He's far too old. That's not even legal, or something I'm interested in, or something he's interested in."

Nail shuddered at the thought. But the more she considered it, the more it made sense—from an outsider's perspective anyway.

"I didn't mean to offend," Rhin said.

"You didn't," Nail replied. "It's just... not something I would ever consider."

"We do not consider marriage, either," Rhin said approvingly. "At least, not the way I have been told your societies do."

Nail cocked her head. "What does that mean?"

As they continued to walk, Rhin regaled her with cultural tales. The clans, she explained, were very communal. Many of them gathered together in the winter months and lived in one giant community. Most people did not have a single partner. Some did, but they were rare. Some had partners for certain seasons.

"Perhaps in autumn you live with a skilled hunter and winter with a woman who has many children. We care about the survival of everyone, not the grand betterment of a few," Rhin said.

"So," Nail said, trying to keep her voice casual, "do you have a partner for your current season? Or is that sort of thing forbidden for an Apex?"

"It is not forbidden," Rhin said. "Our Prime Apex has two partners and many children. But I do not have a partner."

"Why not?" Nail asked. "You must be a desirable partner, to be so beautiful and an Apex at such a young age. That can't be common."

A wry smile danced on Rhin's face. "You think I am beautiful?"

Nail stammered over her words. "You have a symmetrical face, clear skin, a… healthy build."

Rhin waved away Nail's justifications. "Do you think I am beautiful?"

She raised an eyebrow, a singularly alluring expression. Rhin was baiting an already attractive hook and making it irresistible.

"Attractive, romantically?" Rhin clarified.

Nail's breath caught in her lungs. How had she put herself into this position?

There was a slender chance she would never come out of the Fated chamber.

What have I got to lose?

"Yes," she exhaled.

Rhin looked her up and down, her smile still dancing on her pink lips. "Do you know the stories of your stars?"

"What?" Nail said.

Rhin pointed to the darkening night sky. "Your stars have names and stories, do they not? Like ours?"

Nail nodded and lied, "Sure, I know a bunch of them."

Rhin tucked a lock of hair behind Nail's ear. "Tomorrow night, I would like to meet you on the beach. I'll build the fire. You bring the stories of your stars. Agreeable?"

Jace had his beach date. Now I'll have mine.

Nail couldn't stop the ear-to-ear grin smeared across her face. "That sounds delightful."

I'm going to have to learn some constellations. And how to find them.

The torches occurred in five-foot intervals and led to the crest of a hill. Rhin grabbed Nail's forearm, turning her to face her.

"Don't be intimidated," Rhin said. "Don't flinch."

"Flinch at what?" Nail asked.

Rhin winked and leaned in. She kissed Nail's cheek softly. "They'll laugh at me if I'm infatuated with a coward."

Nail stood there, stunned. Rhin continued up the hill, crested the peak, and continued out of sight.

Nail looked around. No one else was coming to continue her path.

"This is it," Nail whispered to herself. "Over that hill, and there's no going back."

She turned around. Below her, she could see almost all of the island. The valley felt like a world away.

The sun had set, casting a fiery glow on the horizon. Wispy clouds were painted in shades of pink, purple, and blue. In the east, the sky shone with glittering stars. The Milky Way hung like a banner across the sky.

Nail took a deep breath and turned back to the hill. She could hear a faint rumble of chatter. There would be a crowd.

No turning back now.

CHAPTER 9

The crowd was larger than she'd expected. From the crest of the hill, Nail recognized many faces from the Lumen Society. Steven stood below her and alongside Oracle and Dax. Nail's father had a hand on Dax's shoulder, eyes beaming.

The clan wearing animal masks stood grouped together. Nail spotted Rhin's white doe mask near the front of their lines. But there were other groups, too.

A clan of unusually tall people stood together. One man wore a tunic of brown, black, and white feathers. A massive bird of prey with black eyes perched on his shoulder.

Another group, muscular and covered in rings of black tattoos, stood with their arms crossed.

A group of all women, adorned in bright clothing and complicated beaded necklaces and headdresses, smiled at Nail.

At the back of the human group, five dragons and two Fated, in humanoid form, watched silently. Nail tensed. Three of the dragons had the same thin, sickly look of the dragons that had killed Kerris.

The other two were distinctly Lumen—one, a five-headed hydra, and the other, an English dragon, tall as a house, with iridescent scales that reflected the sunset's dying rays and the torches' firelight.

Behind the dragons, a wall of black lava rock soared up toward the peak of the volcano, high above their heads.

Steven motioned for her to approach.

Nail stood at the base of the small hill, and Steven joined her.

"Friends," he called out, a slight tremor in his voice. "Here comes one called Naileen to claim the title of Fated. How do you answer?"

A chorus of human and dragon voices resounded, "Witness!"

Steven turned toward Dax. "Darien Alexander. You stood with Naileen in the incubation chamber. Did her feet falter? Did her hand hesitate? Has she concealed a pairing?"

Dax looked around the crowd. "No."

"Do you swear witness to this?" Steven asked.

Dax shuffled. Nail couldn't suppress her smile. There was something ridiculous about the way Steven spoke to him.

"I do," Dax answered.

Steven addressed the crowd again. "A witness has given testimony. How do you find Naileen?"

Again, the crowd answered in unison. "Received!"

"Heard," Steven replied. "Have you gifts, welcomes, or warnings?"

A woman from the brightly dressed clan stepped forward. She had tan skin and brilliant gray eyes. "The women of the southern shores bring a gift."

Steven nodded and the woman approached.

She stood at arm's-length and removed the complex beaded necklace from around her neck. "Naileen, the newest Fated. We welcome you. We pledge eternal support, loyalty, and hospitality on the southern shores."

The woman placed the wide necklace on Nail, and it rested on her shoulders more than it hung around her neck. Then the woman returned to her clan.

Two of the tattooed men stepped forward. The taller of the two was in his forties, Nail guessed. The shorter man looked closer to seventy. His face was lined with wrinkles, and thick black bands of tattoos striped his face.

He carried three items—a little pot, a stick the length of his forearm, and a tool finished with a sharp edge like a miniature garden hoe.

The younger man appraised Nail and said something to the older man in a tongue Nail didn't recognize.

The older man wordlessly pointed to Nail's left hand.

Steven nodded.

"We offer a marking," said the younger man to the crowd. He, too, had face tattoos, but not as many as his elder companion. He looked directly at Nail. "Not even half of the clans and only a few of the eldest dragons have come to your ceremony, Naileen. The people of Minwae find their disrespect shameful.

"We will have it known that Minwae recognized you on this night, to bring you honor, and to humiliate the doubters. With this mark, you will be forever known to us, and to them."

The people of Minwae cried out in support of their leader.

He held out his right arm and tapped it with his fingertips. Nail placed her left hand on his forearm. The man pinched the skin of her middle finger, drawing it tight.

She wasn't opposed to getting a tattoo, and although it hadn't been part of her plans for the night, it didn't seem like the kind of gesture she could refuse.

The older man set to his work. He hummed—again in the language Nail didn't know—and dipped the sharpened tool into the little pot. It dripped with black ink.

The little hoe hovered over her finger, and with the third tool, he struck it. The blade came down, and Nail jumped from the sudden pain. The younger man held her finger more tightly, as though to say, "remain still".

Nail tried to cooperate. The older man kept tapping the inked blade into her flesh, over and over. It felt like needles were drilling into her bones, chipping away and fragmenting them.

Nail reminded herself of Rhin's warning. She summoned up every stoic thought she could and set her mouth into a hard, straight line. She refused to flinch again.

It took only a few minutes. Nail was relieved they wouldn't be marking a ring on her finger—or her face, for that matter. Her hand cramped from the pain. It felt like it had been slammed in a car door a dozen times and set on fire.

When she looked down, she was amazed how small the tattoo was. Roughly the size of her fingernail was a letter F, done in bold, blocky fashion.

The man stopped humming. Nail gave them both a sturdy, short nod. The pain was searing, and she couldn't find it in herself to smile. The men returned to their clan, who looked at Nail with approval. Aside from her initial flinch, she'd done something right.

"Feeling okay?" Steven asked in a whisper.

Nail nodded. "A little dizzy."

"They tried to humiliate me," Steven said. "I got the F on my—"

A war cry interrupted Steven's words, and a man wearing a bear mask stepped forward.

"The flatlands clans offer a warning," his voice was deep and booming.

Everyone wearing an animal mask stepped forward. The rest of the crowd moved back, apparently expecting whatever they were about to do. Rhin gave the slightest nod to Nail.

Steven quickly squeezed Nail's arm. She braced herself.

The man in the bear mask widened his stance. With his chin raised to the heavens, he shouted a phrase in a tongue Nail didn't understand.

The crowd of clans behind him answered with a guttural cry.

He lowered his mask from his face, allowing it to settle atop his clavicle. The people behind him did the same.

The leader cried out again, stomping the earth, kicking up swirls of dirt and dust. The clans echoed him.

He continued, stamping the ground, and the clans mimicked his movements and cries, thrumming the night air with percussion. They moved to a complicated beat, part war cry, part warning. Wide eyes and shouting tongues barked at Nail, daring her to back down, to flee, to cower.

She held her ground. As they slapped and smacked their chests with fists like hammers, Nail felt a chill run down her spine.

Strong heels struck and dragged, open palms slapped thighs and biceps, creating a wave of noise like the ocean crashing upon rocks. Goosebumps flowed down her arms, a chill rippled through the wind, and still the clans continued.

They advanced slowly, inching closer and closer. Nail bunched her fingers into fists, willing her spine to remain tall and firm.

The leader crouched, stalking her with a plodding step. His eyes were wild, staring deep at her. He chanted and howled so close to her face she could feel his hot breath on her cheeks. Nail kept her eyes open, forcing herself to remain perfectly still, fixing her gaze upon a spot on the man's forehead. She was a statue under assault.

With one final wail, the leader thrust his fist into the sky, his foot crashing to the ground. All the clans followed his example as their passion, rage, and battle cries rolled over the hills of the island.

When silence returned, the leader looked at Nail. There was a smile in his eyes that didn't extend to his mouth. He nodded once to her, clasped hands with Steven, and the group retreated.

With the bear-masked Apex's back turned, Nail heaved a sigh.

Steven turned his attention to the tall man with the bird on his shoulder. Nail had never seen one quite like it.

Although it had the lithe build of a falcon, the bird was massive, nearly the size of an eagle. Its white underbelly was speckled with brown, and dark feathers covered its back and wings. It watched everything with a precise gaze, constantly narrowing its focus.

Combined with the man's already impressive stature, the bird loomed over everyone, even Oracle. Nail thought it looked like an omen of death, assessing the weaknesses of everyone below.

Steven smirked. "Kornoc, Vic of the Deadlem Mountain peoples. What do you offer?"

Kornoc stepped forward, regarding Nail with little more than a cursory glance. He stood proudly, and the bird perched upon him flapped its wings, revealing its massive wingspan.

Kornoc spat to the ground, barely missing the toes of Nail's shoes. "We offer nothing. From chick to expert hunter, the Deadlem Falcon takes three years to mature. Before that time, they cannot be trusted to hunt with the rest of the tower."

The falcon flapped its wings again, crying out with a piercing screech.

"What skills of value does this girl have? I see none. And I do not trust what I cannot see. I say to you, until this nestling has been raised and trained for three years, we do not recognize her authority." Kornoc nodded as though that settled the matter and returned to his people.

In confusion, Nail turned to Steven, hoping for clarity.

He rolled his eyes. "They said the same thing to me. Of all the Drasol clans, the Deadlem are the most prideful."

Nail nodded. But the falcon's piercing gaze prickled the skin on the back of her neck.

Steven sighed heavily. "Last one."

Nail's knees began to wobble.

The two Fated approached Nail. Oracle moved forward to join them.

The Fated on her right was female, silvery, and slightly shorter than Oracle. Her hair was cut to her shoulders, and even in the waning light, it still bore shade of pink. She wore a white robe with long bell sleeves.

The Fated on Oracle's left was as black as obsidian, with emerald eyes that filled Nail with a calm feeling the same as after a spring rain shower.

He wore a long, black cloak, and green braids flowed long past his shoulders.

"We offer the final gift," Oracle said. "Never has our island played host to two non-dyadic Fated at once. The gift we have chosen is one that has not been given for a thousand years. It is the tale of creation—the creation of all of us."

Murmurs rippled through the crowd. Steven let out a long, low exhale.

Dax shuffled uncomfortably.

Her father took a step closer.

The obsidian Fated waved his claw-like hands through the air, which shimmered and stirred. Dust and mist gathered above the dirt beneath his open palms, glowing and forming shapes. To Nail, it looked like an entire galaxy, miniaturized like a puppet show.

Oracle began the tale. "In the dark beginning, the creator hung over the abyss for eternity. Perfect in power and knowing, the creator was complete, but in its perfection, lonely. And in its loneliness, arrogant. The creator sought to end its loneliness. And with a great clap of thunder, the creator split its heart into untold creatures and worlds."

The misty scene flashed and split itself into five galaxies.

"Five of these creatures contained shards of the heart of the creator—the Leviathan, the Dragon, the Chimera, the Phoenix, and the Storm."

The scene narrowed onto one world, one landscape, laid out flat like a chess board. Five foggy figures encircled the land. There was a dragon, a thundercloud, a beast that looked like a lion, a goat, and a bat combined, a great looming mountain, and a human with fiery wings.

"Together, they ruled over all the worlds. The Leviathans, the largest of them all, watched in guarded silence. The Chimeras encouraged growth in every land they touched, sparking new species in all sorts of life.

"The Dragons sought knowledge and truth. The Storm brought destruction and devastation. And the Phoenixes balanced everything, preventing hell and utopia the same."

The creatures moved through the world, sometimes cooperatively, sometimes combatively.

"But four of the five creatures fought among themselves. They sought to rule each other, each believing themselves the strongest. They fought endless battles, ravaged the worlds, and forgot their duty to the creator.

"The Phoenixes sought to bring balance. In their endless wisdom, the

Phoenixes knew the creatures would never end their fighting. They stole a fractal from every heart shard. And from that seed, they created humankind."

A tree grew rapidly in the center of the five creatures. Leaves blossomed to flowers, growing fruits that looked like children and then fell to the ground as adults. Soon humans dotted the land, vastly outnumbering the creatures.

"The Phoenixes vowed to keep mankind balanced—never allowing extinction nor ending all strife. The Storm sought to end them, and the Chimera battled to improve them. The dragons watched, and they gave mankind knowledge and truth.

"The Leviathans, being the largest of all the creatures, found mankind too small for their concern, and settled as mountains or as the chasms of the oceans, to slumber until mankind's demise.

"With a new creation to focus upon, the great creatures fostered a new coexistence, ensuring that mankind would never be extinguished or untroubled. At last, the creator was no longer lonely. Until one creature betrayed their purpose."

The dragon struck out at the men and women, spewing fire, poison, and filling the people with greed. The people warred among each other, forming tribes and armies.

"The dragons had forgotten their purpose and grown jealous of mankind. They sought to end mankind, envying the tiny seed from which they had come. But their hearts could not contain their corruption, and it spread to the heart shard of the creator. Their magic became weaker, and soon the heart shard died."

The scene changed to one dragon and one human, encircling in each other.

"Many dragons perished from their anger and diseased purpose, but not all. Those who were uncorrupted, seeking the survival of their ancient species, formed a treaty with the humans.

"No longer would the dragons harm humans. Instead, they entered into a partnership with mankind, allowing their magic to be shared. Thus, the treaty was born, and any dragon who accepted the terms of the treaty could attain magic once more."

The dragon and human became entwined, forming a Fated humanoid like Oracle.

"This was the birth of the Lumen Society, destined and determined to ensure the survival of both species."

The scene slowly dissolved into the night air, carried away on the wind.

The crowd watched in silence, awed.

Steven had tears in his eyes. He managed to say, "Thank you."

Nail nodded in agreement.

Oracle turned, surveying the entire crowd. "The preparation is complete. Let us continue on."

"Ready?" Steven asked Nail.

She took a few deep breaths, in through her nose and out through her mouth. Another nod.

Steven grimaced. The wrinkles at the corners of his eyes deepened. "It's time for the sacrifice."

CHAPTER 10

The crowd parted. Nail followed Steven and Oracle closer to the mountainside. She could feel their eyes on her and was certain everyone could hear her heart pounding. It felt ready to crack through her ribs and break out of her chest.

Steven hung back and leaned into her ear. "This will be graphic. It was made in a different time. The magic is—"

"Old," Nail said. "Yeah, I get it. Is Nessie…?"

"There and waiting."

Nail's heart ached. It was a nightmare. She'd spent so much of her adolescence poring over the evidence for Nessie. Finding out the beast was real was almost as exciting as learning that dragons were real. But now… now she wished the ancient dragon had stayed in Scotland.

A few dragons loomed at the corners of the crowd. Some of them were clearly Lumen, but the Drasolians had eyes that bulged too far from their sockets.

Nail refocused her gaze onto the ground. Her knees wobbled, making even the smallest steps difficult. When Steven came to an abrupt stop, she bumped into him. Recovering, she stepped around to his side.

Carved into the cliff side was a large, stone door. Ancient writing encircled the round opening, their chiseled letters worn and softened from centuries of rain and winds.

Two troughs, cut into the stone, led away from the door and toward where Nail stood. Just a few feet from her toes, they connected at a dais.

Nessie rested upon it and the carved hand symbol beneath ver swirled in and out of focus.

Nail couldn't hold it in anymore. Tears leaked down her cheeks. With the crowd behind her, she let them flow freely as she looked upon the dais.

Even outside the loch, Nail couldn't clearly make out Nessie's form. She didn't know if Nessie was a hydra or a lung dragon or wyvern. She couldn't hold her gaze on the great creature. Her sight kept slipping off, like rain down an umbrella. Her sorrow would abate as she looked away, and it cut anew when she dragged her gaze back again.

Nail felt like Nessie was looking at her, even though she couldn't truly discern the dragon's eyes.

"Do not cry, young one," the dragon said. *"I am so very tired."*

"I'm sorry," Nail choked.

"Do not be sorry. You have kept my legacy alive. And now, with such a crowd, I will finally be remembered."

"Is there a... dragon afterlife?"

Nessie chuckled, deep and rippling. *"Haven't you seen the stars?"*

Another movement caught Nail's attention. Oracle stood to the side of the dais. She reached toward the ground, withdrawing a long, dark blade. It looked like black glass, thick, with a jagged edge.

"Oh, god," Nail said. "Is this it?"

Steven nodded. He reached out. His hand grasped her forearm.

Oracle began to mutter an incantation, running her free hand through the air around the blade. Cracks began to show across the blade, illuminated with an eerie red light.

"I can't watch this again," Nail said, turning her head away.

Steven squeezed her forearm. "You must."

The blade seemed to be more cracked than whole. Part of Nail hoped it shattered against Nessie's hide.

Oracle held it under what seemed like Nessie's throat, sharp edge to the sky. With a deep breath and piercing scream, she pulled up and drew it back to herself. Red blood poured out immediately, flowing into the carved channels.

For a moment longer, Nessie was still hard to see. And then, in an instant, the dragon's body materialized, as clear as could be.

Nail was entranced. Nessie was certainly no plesiosaur, nor a hydra. Ve was similar to a wyvern, but clearly made for the water. Nessie's wings resembled oversized fins. Instead of a barbed tail, Nessie's tail forked and fanned, like that of a mermaid.

And ver scales... Nail had never seen another dragon like ver. Nessie was gone, but light from ver scales still glowed dimly.

They were bold, beautiful colors, grander than a peacock, brighter than a rainbow after a summer shower. Ve put the plumage of the royal pheasants to shame, with shades of fuchsia, scarlet, lime, ocean blue, sunshine, strawberries, fresh snow, and rippled with flecks of silver.

Nail had expected to see a muddy, almost dinosaur-like dragon. She was breathless for a moment—until her grief doubled at the sight.

Steven squeezed her arm again. "Get ready."

Nail looked beyond Nessie. The blood in the dais oozed through the channels and began to disappear into the cliff side. The carved words began to glow red like the dark blade, each side of the door slowly illuminating.

"Better make a run for it," he said.

Nail moved forward and rested a hand on Nessie's motionless head. She whispered, "Thank you."

She took several hesitant steps around the dragon's fading corpse, gaze lingering on the sacrifice that was made for her.

"Go, Nail!" Steven yelled.

She looked back at him. He pointed to the door.

All of the lettering glowed red. The round door cracked down the middle and retracted into the cliff side.

Nail made a run for it. By the time she cleared the dais, the doors were fully open. Her toes hit the graveled ground, threatening to send her flying into the rocks.

At half the distance, the door shuddered and began to close again.

She pushed through the ache in her legs, cursing herself for getting distracted.

With a jump, she crossed the threshold, rolling across the smooth floor as the stone behind her slammed shut. Something in Nail's chest felt heavy.

For a moment, the cave was completely dark.

She was alone. She breathed heavily.

There was no one to help her, and no way out except to pair. And if she didn't... a dragon life for a Fated pairing was already a high cost. But two dragon lives for someone that wasn't truly Lumen?

Nail knew the truth. They'd let her suffocate or starve first, just like what had happened the lordling's son that Steven had warned her about.

The light of a bonfire flame roared to life in the center of the room, blue and white. Sconces on the walls around her lit on their own. The walls were carved with alcoves, each containing a different dragon egg. The scroll had been accurate. There seemed to be about forty eggs.

Nail's breathing evened out, but her heartbeat remained erratic.

She steadied herself on the floor, but her heart wouldn't calm down. Nail raised her fingers to her neck, searching for her pulse. It was fast, but not erratic as she'd expected. She felt twice the number of beats in her chest as she did beneath her fingertips.

She stood, puzzled, and glanced around the room. Her gaze fell on one egg, drawn to it like it was under a spotlight.

"Oh," Nail whispered. "It's *you*."

CHAPTER 11

All of Nail's hesitation melted away. Her fears puddled on the floor, and she walked away from them with secured purpose, taking steadfast steps toward her egg.

Its base resembled black lava rock, and the colors cascaded upward into orange and yellow hues, flecked with black. The egg was crowned in gold. It looked to be made of half-cooled lava. The colors danced in the firelight of the chamber, daring Nail to come closer.

She'd never felt anything like it. An invisible force seemed to pull her forward, yanking on the heaviness in her chest, like chains attached to her ribs. She was a penny tossed from a skyscraper, a kite hurtling through a cyclone. She was in free fall and loving it.

Even in her mesmerized movements, she recognized the egg from the scroll's description. Hundreds of years earlier, the dragon Fafnir had laid it.

She reached out. A magnetic force tingled in her palm, radiating through her fingertips and vibrating her bones. This was the one.

Her hand touched the egg, and the free fall stopped.

She felt herself become grounded, solid, heavy—as if gravity had all at once tripled in strength. Iron links strong enough to reel in an anchor pulled her in, cuffing her to the dragon inside. She stumbled under the weight of sudden connection, fighting to pull air into her lungs.

She was paired.

"It *is* you," she managed.

IGNITE

The egg heard her. The dragon inside rumbled, shaking the egg under her grip, as if to say, *What took you so long?*

Nail smiled wide, elated. "I got here as soon as I could."

The egg went still, but Nail thought she could feel the little dragon inside roll vis eyes.

With a half-step forward, she placed her other hand on the egg and lifted it up.

She appraised its surface, admiring the intricate beauty of the shell. The dragon seemed to purr, happy to have left the alcove.

"Right, then," Nail said. "Back out we go."

With the egg in her right arm, Nail placed her left hand on the stone door. Whatever old magic it contained recognized their pairing and fired awake. The flames inside the chamber extinguished on their own, and the door retracted again.

The crowd waited on bended knees for Nail's emergence. Congratulatory shouts mixed with war cries. A baritone chorus of dragon bellows rounded out the celebration. Dax cheered and clapped. Steven and Oracle stood together, proud and tall.

But Nail's father smiled the widest and proudest. A tear rolled down his cheek.

Nail held up her egg proudly for the crowd to see. Their cries doubled.

But a voice clattered over her mind.

"She knew you could do it," said a hypnotic dragon tone. It was almost synthetic, like the plastic ring of a cheap piano keyboard.

Nail looked around for the source.

The Lumen dragon she'd seen earlier with shimmering scales had moved to the back of the crowd. Ve flapped vis wings to grab Nail's attention and stared down at her.

Nail was caught in the dragon's gaze. Ve winked.

Who? Nail mouthed across the crowd.

The dragon lowered vis head, arching vis powerful neck. A woman sat astride the dragon, her red hair flowing like a flooded river.

Nail nearly fell to the ground.

She was older than the pictures that had frozen her memory in time, and there were wrinkles on her face, but Nail was certain. She'd gone her whole life wishing to see that face again, to make one true memory with her.

Amid the thundering celebration, Nail said, "Mom?"

CHAPTER 12

Nail clutched the fiery egg in her arms, and it seemed to purr with approval. The warmth radiating from the little dragon inside felt like the only thing still anchoring her to the ground.

Steven and her father pulled her back down the mountain trail, both joyously vying for her attention. Behind them, the crowd swelled and chattered, an avalanche of noise that drowned out specific words.

Nail couldn't believe what she had seen. She couldn't believe it to be true. She desperately wanted it to have been her.

She'd shut her eyes, certain that the image of her mother astride the back of a dragon had been her imagination. When she'd reopened them, the dragon had stood there all the same, but her mother had disappeared.

It couldn't have been her. But Nail was certain her mind hadn't played tricks on her. Thirteen years after her supposed death, riding a dragon whose scales matched the one on the necklace Nail still wore, her mother had come to Nail's pairing.

And why this one? Why now?

What had her father said the dragon's name was?

Nail stumbled over a rock, and her father caught her before she could hit the ground.

"Careful," he said, helping her back up to her feet. "I know it's an exciting time, but mind your footing while—"

"What was the name of Mom's dragon?" Nail stared into his eyes.

"Liliganth," he replied. And then the color began to drain from his face. "W-Why?"

"Ve was there." Nail looked back up the hill, searching the skies, her heart racing.

If her mother was alive, did Nail even want to see her? After thirteen years of lies, of abandonment? Physical pain stabbed her heart. It ached in a way Nail thought was reserved for love-struck songwriters.

"W-who was there?" her father asked, pale and beginning to tremble.

Nail couldn't get the word out. She held her egg tighter, clinging to its warmth, and looked at her father, pleading for an answer, for honesty.

"Liliganth was there?" he asked. "Or…"

That dangling question was all the confirmation Nail needed. An involuntary tear ran down her cheek, and everything around her stilled. The pounding in her ears drowned out the noise.

Her father's conversation with his friends flooded back to Nail's memory. His friends had said it wasn't his fault. He'd admitted how he thought he knew her. Raw heartbreak had lined his voice.

"You weren't talking about me," Nail said. "That day. You weren't talking about *me*."

She wished he had been. That would've been forgivable. But this…?

"Gillian," he exhaled, suddenly looking around.

"Mom," Nail said.

She waited only a second. She needed him to immediately apologize, to fall to his knees, to beg forgiveness. He simply stood there, rooted to the spot, staring at her, mouth opening and shutting, not making a damned sound.

She wouldn't wait any longer.

Nail sprinted down the path. Cheers from the crowd, mistaking her horror for excitement, roared out from behind her. She ran past torches, hurtled over rocks, and slid down the path with reckless abandon. She had to get away from him, away from everyone.

Hiding Lumen from her had been a shock. But with time, she'd understood why. But hiding her mother? Her mother, who had been where, exactly?

Drasol, most likely.

She couldn't remember navigating the rest of the trail down or reaching the pool at the waterfall. And she hated the face she soon found in front of her.

Jace.

She put up a hand to brush past him. "Not now."

Jace grabbed her arm, and they both slid on the small stones of the pool's shore. "You paired! Look at that egg!" He beamed down at her, smiling wildly. "Congratulations!"

Nail shook herself free of his grip. "Not now. Something's happened."

His face darkened. "I can explain. Lyva was with Vienna and—"

She wanted to scream and hit him. "No, not *you*."

She couldn't find the willpower to make herself say the words.

My mother is alive.

Tears leaked out again. "I don't want to be around anyone right now. I *can't*."

"What happened?" Jace reached out for her, but she backed away. "Are you okay?"

She could only shake her head.

"What about your party?" Jace motioned over his shoulder.

Nail looked. The entire class stood behind the tree line, most of them trying to appear as though they hadn't just been gaping at her theatrics.

Perfect.

"No."

The hurt and confusion on Jace's face was plain. But Nail couldn't handle it. She couldn't comfort someone else. In the span of half an hour, her entire world had changed.

Your path will be alone.

Nail took off running again.

She ran through trees and zigzagged between bushes. She ran until she couldn't tell what was sweat and what was tears.

Her egg seemed to coo within her arms. *It'll be okay. I'm here*, it said.

At the base of the banyan tree, she finally stopped.

Nail looked around. Without a flashlight, it was hard to see the camouflaged steps. While she searched, a dragon flew overhead. Shining, iridescent.

Liliganth.

Nail watched the dragon's flight, entranced.

Liliganth glided effortlessly, landing on the ridge near the dais, the compass stone that Nail had stood on that first day.

Nail felt her breath catch in her chest. *I can't.*

Her heart hammered. *I have to.*

Her egg clicked in approval. She took off for the staircase that would bring her to her mother.

CHAPTER 13

Heart pounding, Nail arrived at the top of the ridge. Wind whipped through her hair, and the light of the moon reflected off the sea waves. She could hear a party raging in the valley below, but she focused on the sight in front of her.

Her mother, Gillian, stood at the dais. Liliganth raised vis thick tail and then slammed it onto the stone surface of the dais. A piece of the stone chipped off, and Liliganth raised vis tail again for another strike, barbed scales cracking the stone.

Nail wanted to shout at them to stop. But it was only ceremonial rock, and miraculously her mother stood in front of her.

Gillian looked over her shoulder. Her eyes met with Nail's.

A chill ran down Nail's spine. It was like looking at a photograph that had come to life.

Gillian smiled.

With trepidation pulling at her heels, Nail stepped forward. Her mother ran to her, arms outstretched.

Unsure if she wanted it, and still holding her egg, Nail braced herself. Her heart ached and swelled. Her mother's embrace was warm, soft, and close. Nail could smell the wildflowers in her hair, and felt her mother's heart beat against her own chest.

"My darling girl," she said, still not pulling away. "I'm so proud of you."

"You're alive." Nail broke the embrace. "How?"

Gillian's brow furrowed. "Alive? Of course I'm alive." She looked Nail up and down. "Why would you think otherwise?"

Nail gaped. "Dad..." was all she managed to get out.

That traitor. She felt the knots in her shoulders tighten. *My mother is alive. He made it all up.*

Gillian smiled, sweet and sad. She had green eyes and more freckles than Nail.

"I see." She wrapped an arm around Nail's back and pulled her to her side. "There's a lot to explain and not much time, I'm afraid."

Together they walked to the dais. Liliganth's tail had carved a crater into the stone, now about three feet deep.

"I have to be quick. But you must know the truth. Your father lied to you," her mother said. "And Lumen has lied to you, too."

"Lied?" Nail knew of her father's deception, but Lumen? Had Steven known her mother was alive, too?

"That banner, in Steven's office," her mother said. "The one with the hand and all the symbols?"

Nail nodded, recalling all the odd symbols on the fingertips.

"Smart girl," her mother said. She spoke at a fast, breathless pace. "All the magical races. Dragons, chimeras, phoenixes, Leviathans, the Storm. They all possessed a heart shard. It's what gave them their magical powers."

The story Oracle told.

"No," Nail corrected her. "Lumen's magic comes from the treaty. And the dragons' heart shard died thousands of years ago."

"Burn it," her mother scoffed. "I thought that, too, when I was your age. But as I got older, I did some investigation of my own. All the magical races tell a similar origin story, Nail. But a piece of parchment being the source of all this magic? It just doesn't make sense. I had to find out the truth for myself."

"So... you left me?"

Gillian's eyes watered. "I hated to leave you. But I wanted what was best for you and for all dragons. There was no other way." Her voice turned quiet. "I thought your father would have explained that to you, or parts of it at least."

She looked down to Nail's collarbone. "I'm glad he gave you my necklace."

Nail touched it reflexively.

Liliganth continued to pound away at the dais, occasionally clawing at the stone to remove chunks of obliterated rock.

Nail bit her lip. She desperately wanted to believe her mother.

"I traveled, and I researched. I heard the way the other races remember the beginning. But no one else remembers the dragons' heart shard becoming corrupted. Because it didn't happen."

"But Oracle..." Nail's head was in a hypnotist's spiral. "Then what happened?"

"The dragons' shard was stolen from Drasol, whole and intact. Without it, the dragons there lost their magic. They became weak and sickly. The Drasol council believes the shard died, but that's a lie. It was brought to Earth, giving dragons on *this side* of reality magic.

"It was constrained, twisting its magic to affect humans as well. Every class to ever walk this island has first stood on that dais and received its magic."

"Mother..." Liliganth said.

Nail looked. She'd never heard a dragon refer to a human as their mother before. The crater in the stone was now four feet deep. Something glowed red at the bottom.

"Who stole it?" Nail asked. "Why would anyone want to—"

"Gillian," said a familiar voice from behind them.

They turned. Oracle, in her humanoid form, stood watching the scene in front of her.

Gillian's mouth twisted into a cruel smile.

"Her," she answered Nail. "Long, long ago. And she's been covering up her lies ever since."

Oracle took a measured step closer. "You don't want to do this, *Regent.*"

That word struck Nail faster and sharper than lightning. Xaos and Thovos had killed Kerris, claiming to be following their Regent's orders.

Was her mother responsible for what they did?

Gillian laughed. "Age hasn't dulled your wits. *You* don't want *me* to do this, but I most certainly do. Do the Lumen dragons know what you've stolen from their siblings? Does Steven?"

Oracle's mouth twitched. Liliganth stood behind Gillian, towering over her.

"Could you ever count the cost?" Gillian taunted. "How high would that mountain be?"

"Mother..." Liliganth urged. *"It is there."*

"Go!" Gillian cried.

Liliganth launched verself at Oracle while Gillian ducked and rolled back toward the dais. Nail stood frozen in the middle, unable to help Oracle, unwilling to stop her mother.

Faster than lightning, Oracle's whole body trembled. She rippled like the surface of a pond and transformed into her full and terrifying dragon form, hovering in the air.

But Liliganth was already atop her, a rain of claws and teeth, intense fury, and feral growling.

The ridge barely had enough room to accommodate them both as they fought. Oracle was larger, but Liliganth's speed was unbelievable. With every snap of Oracle's jaws, she found only empty air where vis shimmering form had been split seconds before.

Then a dragon cried out in pain, and blood splattered onto the rocks.

"Finish it, Liliganth!" Gillian cried.

She held a shard of crystal in her hand. It glowed red, lighting up the veins in her arm.

The heart shard.

Proof. Proof that they lied.

Liliganth had Oracle pinned to the ground. The dragons thrashed at each other with claws and teeth. Liliganth's barbed tail repeatedly slammed and jabbed into Oracle.

With a roar, Liliganth anchored Oracle's head beneath vis sharp claws. Then ve lunged, sinking teeth into Oracle's neck. With a sickening rip, Liliganth tore at Oracle's flesh.

"Time to go." Gillian grabbed Nail's arm with her free hand, the same arm that held Nail's fiery egg. The egg rocked under her protective grip, trying to pull Nail away from Gillian. "Come with me. Build a new Drasol at my side."

Nail stared at her mother, the woman she had longed for all her life. She thought of every empty moment, the extra chair at the dining table, the dust-covered pictures in the living room.

She thought of her father's lies.

She thought of Oracle's deception and the unknowable number of dragons that had suffered for it.

Her egg quaked again.

Then she thought of Xaos and Thovos. Of Kerris ripped in half. Of Nessie's sacrifice.

"I can't," Nail said.

Her mother's eyes filled with sadness. "You have to walk your own path. I know ours will cross again." She touched the necklace around Nail's neck, her fingertips lingering on Liliganth's scale. "Come find me when you're ready."

She climbed over Oracle's body, onto Liliganth's back.

"Sweet daughter," she said. "I love you."

Nail never got the chance to say it back. With a rush of wings and wind, Liliganth took off, flying east for the portal.

Nail stared, but only for a moment. Oracle lay on the ground unmoving. Nail set down her egg.

With a shiver, Oracle returned to human form. Nail crouched over her, pressing her fingers into the gaping wound at Oracle's neck, trying to stop the bleeding.

Her face was cut, her clothing ripped and bloodstained. One of her arms hung at an odd angle. Even without the wound on her neck, Oracle was in dire need of help. There was fear in Oracle's eyes, but no pain.

"She took it?" Oracle choked out.

Nail nodded.

Oracle sighed and went limp in Nail's hands.

The rush of wings in the air made Nail think her mother had returned. Instead, it was Vigilus with Steven and Nora on vis back.

Vigilus's claws had barely touched the blood-soaked ground when Nora slid from vis back. She rushed to Oracle's side. Then, gripping Oracle's hand, they both disappeared.

"Where has she gone?" Panic spiked Nail's voice.

But Steven wasn't listening. He ran to inspect the dais. "What happened here?" he demanded of her. "Why would someone do this?"

"The shard…" Nail said.

Steven's brow furrowed. "The shard? What shard?"

Nail stared back at him. He didn't know. And she barely understood it herself.

The only person aside from Gillian who might have known all the pieces was Oracle. Without her, the truth could be lost forever.

CHAPTER 14

Steven and Nail stood in the treaty room. Under its protective glass casing and concentrated lights, the treaty looked impressive.

But Nail knew the truth. It was just a useless piece of parchment. There wasn't an ounce of power to it at all.

They waited in silence. Nail held her egg, rocking back and forth on her feet. Soon Prior Adams, Prioress Julia, and Rankor entered the room. The archway, and the room itself, wasn't large enough for Vigilus.

Members of the Drasol Council gathered there was well. The tattooed leader of the Minwae clan entered first, followed by the woman in bright clothes with beaded jewelry. Kornoc came without his imposing Deadlem Falcon.

Three of the flatlands clans' Apexes entered together, including the man with the bear mask who had led the dance, a woman with an owl mask, and—Nail's heart involuntarily danced—Rhin.

Rhin's mouth was a hard line. At the sight of Nail, one side curled up slightly, and she winked again.

A drab Drasol dragon—the smallest of those Nail had seen—entered after them. Like the others, it was difficult to discern vis color. Nail thought it most closely resembled mud or decaying leaves.

The two Fated dragons in humanoid form, who had helped Oracle recount the tale of the shard, joined their group last.

Nail wished there were chairs. She was exhausted. All she wanted was some sleep. Catching Steven up on everything had drained every last bit of energy out of her.

"Council," Steven said. "Thank you for coming. I'm afraid we have terrible business to discuss."

The Minwae leader snorted. "Some council. Barely a third of us are here. The absent Drasol leaders heap shame upon themselves."

Steven's gaze darted to floor. Nail knew he'd realized something she hadn't put together yet.

He took a deep breath. With as little emotion as he could, he relayed the events at the dais to the group. Largely, they listened quietly. But when he told them of the hidden shard, whispers went throughout the room.

The only one who didn't look surprised was the Drasol dragon.

"The shard can't be intact."

"If the shard returns to Drasol, will magic follow?"

"Our people are not equipped to deal with this."

Steven held up his hands to silence the room. "We don't know precisely what effect the shard will have on Drasol, but we have to assume it will take place soon."

"We are all facing winter soon," said the bear Apex. "She will use the time to gather strength and attack during spring."

"Or worse," suggested the Minwae leader. "She may attack during winter, when our food supplies are low, and many of our fighters are weak."

"Either way is disaster," said the woman leading the group from the southern shores. "We cannot hope to win a fight against dragons with magic."

The clans fell into bickering, some of them bartering shelter for food, some of them insulting the others, and a few of them insisting that their fighters were the strongest and most likely to win in a war.

"Enough!" Steven shouted. He paced back and forth in front of the treaty. Nail realized this would be her role someday—not just the leader of Lumen island and the society, but holding together the peace of many different and argumentative clans. "To complicate the issue, this Regent, Gillian, is not just Lumen. She is Nail's mother."

Suspicious glares rounded on Nail.

Kornoc said what the others were thinking. "Then she cannot be trusted. Nothing she has said can be trusted. The bond between a mother and child—"

"Is nonexistent," Steven interrupted. "In this case, at least."

But Nail knew that wasn't fully true. She didn't know her mother like most daughters did, but she wanted to. Even before dragons, it was the first thing she ever wanted.

Steven continued. "With today being what it was, Gillian made it past the guards," he gestured to Nail, "security wasn't as vigilant as it might have been. Now that Gillian has returned to Drasol, there's no telling where she and Liliganth might be, or exactly what they intend to do with the shard."

"Hide it," said the dark Fated. "She will hide it and return Drasol to its once formidable power."

The silvery Fated countered him. "It was once twisted to affect humans. If she discovered that truth, then she may well know how to warp it again."

The human leaders all exchanged concerned glances.

"I don't think that's her plan," Nail said. She could feel everyone's gaze on her. She looked to the floor, embarrassed to have spoken.

"You have no authority here," Kornoc said with a dismissive grunt.

Steven's lip curled at the Deadlem leader. "I say she does." He gestured for Nail to continue.

She took a deep breath. "Just think about her self-given title, Regent. She didn't style herself a queen or an empress or a dictator."

Rankor hummed in agreement. *A Regent holds a position of power until the rightful ruler can assume the role."*

"Exactly," Nail said. "I heard her own dragon refer to her as 'mother.' I think it's more likely that she intends to restore the Drasol dragons to what they once were. Back when..."

She recalled the scroll, the innumerable ancient tales she'd read about the old dragons. If her mother followed through with this plan, the cost of human life on both sides of reality would be catastrophic.

Silence filled the room.

Rhin spoke next. "We must agree on this: if those dragons regain magic, every human in Drasol will die. We struggle to survive now. With magic on their side, we'll be little more than ants under their bellies."

The other human members agreed.

Steven nodded. "Which raises several questions. Half of my new Lumen class has hatched their dragons. None of them have discovered their gifts yet. Can their magic develop if the shard is no longer on this side of reality?"

IGNITE

He looked to the Fated dragons, who exchanged a glance.

"We don't know," said the silvery one said. "The shard was said to have died hundreds of years before either of us were born."

Steven nodded. "And Nail," he said. She looked at him. "Can her egg hatch without the shard here? Will her dragon even survive without its magic to sustain its incubation?"

Nail reflexively clutched her egg tighter. As her dragon tittered inside the egg, fear gripped her stomach.

"Oracle would know," Rankor said. *"Will she make it?"*

Steven shook his head. "My sister, Nora, took her to our best surgeon—a Lumen member from her class. He has a gift with healing. She hasn't returned. Had Oracle died, Nora would've returned straight away. But I saw her wounds. It will test his abilities, to be certain."

The entire room seemed to sway with this news. Oracle was older than any of them—older than most of the combined. Without her knowledge, they were flying blind.

"We *must* get the shard back," Steven said. "But make no mistake, I do not believe Gillian is acting alone."

He stared hard at the lone Drasol dragon in the group.

"The dragons of the Drasol Council were dismissive when I offered my invitation," he said. "Almost all of them refused. Now I see why. You knew, Minjak. You knew she was coming, what she would take, and what she would do to obtain it."

Everyone stared at Minjak. The mud-colored dragon nodded vis head. *"The other Drasol dragons have already fled Lumen Island. I stayed out of pride and loyalty to our Regent."*

Steven swore.

"I bear you, Steven, no ill will. I believe you were ignorant of what Oracle has done. But even in your ignorance, you helped her deception. And you stole from Drasol."

"Muck of Drasol," Prior Adams spat. "We should kill you here and now."

Minjak looked at him, no emotion reading on vis face. *"And so you might."* Ve turned back to Steven. *"But consider Oracle's choice. Countless generations of our children have lived and died short, fruitless lives. We've been reduced to laboring beasts. Most of us cannot even fly anymore. The heart shard belonged to dragons and to Drasol, not to Lumen or humanity."*

Rankor took a half-step forward. Minjak was larger than ver, but not by much. The gray dragon growled. *"When the dragons of Drasol had* magic, they were a blight upon the Earth. They killed, maimed, corrupted. They were full of greed.

"Without humanity at a dragon's side, they would have engaged in an bloody, terrible war that could only end with genocide. Whatever Oracle did, I am certain she did it for the greater good."

Minjak growled. "And who was she to make that decision for two species and two realities? By what right was she given it?"

"I'm detaining you, Minjak," Steven said. "You will have a trial. I appreciate your bravery, to face me yourself. Do you swear on your honor not to leave Lumen Island until after your trial?"

"I knew the risks when I chose to stay," Minjak said, looking at Nail. "I will remain for your judgment."

"Then you are dismissed from this council," Steven said.

Minjak turned and left the room, head held high.

Nail had to admit, though only to herself, that she didn't fully disagree with Minjak. She didn't disagree with her mother.

But the attack on Oracle, the death of Kerris... She couldn't excuse those. Minjak spoke as though a war was unavoidable. Perhaps it was.

"Is that wise?" Prior Adams asked. "How can you trust Minjak will remain?"

Steven frowned. "Because we still have Nail—not only her daughter, but a Lumen Fated. Gillian did not come during the first ceremony, when the rest of the new Lumen members paired. She waited, biding her time, wanting to know exactly what our island hid."

Nail's heart sank. Steven's words rang true, but they cut deeper than the blade Oracle had plunged into Nessie.

"One way or another, I am certain she will never let Nail out of her sights again. For whatever else Gillian has become, she is still a mother."

"You're wise to understand this, Steven," said the woman from the southern shores. "These blustering men cannot know that protective bond. And it seems Gillian has made herself a mother to many. But no child is more precious than the first."

Nail felt dizzy. The early loss of her mother—her guarded wound—was on full display for everyone to discuss and dissect as they saw fit. She wanted to run from the room.

Steven looked around the group. "The days ahead may be the darkest yet for Lumen and Drasol, humans and dragons alike. I still have a fledgling class to look after and a Fated student who has been torn away from the source of magic.

"Drasol may be the most dangerous place for Nail, but it also may be the only place that her egg can survive and hatch. It may be best if she travels to Drasol for a time. But anywhere she would stay would almost certainly be a target for Gillian.

"Almost all you offered hospitality and safety to Nail tonight. Given the events of this evening, I won't hold it against you if you must rescind your invitation. But if that is true, I ask you to speak now."

Nail looked around the room. No one spoke. No one moved. No one even blinked.

Rhin gave her another wry smirk.

For all their arguing, the people of Drasol were either very brave or very prideful. Nail didn't know any of them well enough to discern the difference.

"Good," Steven said. "There is much planning to be done. Lumen will become a haven for any and all humans on Drasol that no longer wish to live there. When you return home, spread this word to your peoples far and wide. If they are unsafe, they are welcome here."

"Steven," Prioress Julia said. "There are thousands on Drasol. Tens of thousands, possibly. We cannot host so many—"

Steven held up his hand. "And there are billions on Earth. Drasol dragons with magic threaten us all. Lumen will find a way. Sacrifices will be made. This Regent seeks to tear us apart. We must stand together."

A few of the Drasol leaders cheered in agreement.

"We must strike first before the dragons of Drasol become too strong to overwhelm," Steven said.

Nail held onto her egg, horrified. No one, no voice of compromise suggested peace or any other option that didn't lead to fighting.

Either her mother would destroy Lumen or they would destroy her. Dragons might die in their eggs or be born without magic. Yet others would find new, terrifying powers, laying waste to both sides of reality.

She tried to remain as stoic as she could, to not betray how her heart was ripping into two symmetrical pieces. She fought back tears and held her mouth in a straight line even as an internal war ignited within her.

Steven stood taller than ever. "We will answer Gillian's challenge with one of our own!"

"With steel!" cried the bear-masked Apex.

"And blood!" called the owl.

"And fire!" yelled Rhin.

With the strength of an earthquake, Nail's egg jumped.

EPILOGUE

Finley stared at the e-mail, rereading it for the fourth time. It had come from a guy in California, the one Skrell had connected with. He'd been right about Nail being in the Nessie video. He claimed to know Nail, and where she was.

But he also claimed that he'd met her on a secret tropical island inhabited by dragons.

He said his name was Luca.

She drummed her fingers on the desk. The dragons weren't the part that unnerved her. It was his description of her best friend that set her on edge.

In all of her searching, she'd been careful what details to include. Physical descriptions? Full name? Those, obviously, were crucial to finding her.

But she hadn't said anything about Nail's tendency to brood in silence or her insulting wit. She'd never mentioned how Nail was quick with an insult, or introverted, or obsessed with Nessie.

Yet Luca knew all that. He poured the unprompted details into the email.

Still, that could have pieced together by someone crafty enough. Someone trying to humiliate Finley, maybe? Someone who went to their high school and who'd found her posts about Nail's disappearance?

It could have been just an online troll with too much time on his hands—which was all of them, really.

Luca claimed they'd been taken by this society, this group of people called Lumen. And not just a few of them, but over a dozen. He claimed they lived with dragons and could do magic.

He also said he couldn't prove it. He'd been kicked out before he got any magic. His dragon had died in an accident. He didn't have any pictures because cell phones were forbidden.

It was ludicrous.

Yet he knew Nail.

But it wasn't his descriptions of Nail that made Finley feel like she was standing six feet deep in a rabbit hole with no end.

It was his inclusion of Tally.

Never, anywhere, had Finley ever written a word about the girl. She'd been content to write Tally off as a crazy person, a total dead-end of a lead. She hadn't recovered any of her memory, and after their meeting, she'd never answered any more emails or messages.

Luca had described her accurately, too. Her hair, her nervousness. "She didn't stay," he'd said. "She chose to leave. You should look for her too."

That was the proof Finley had never wanted to find. As crazy and impossible as Luca's explanation was—and she didn't fully buy the dragon thing (who could?)—he had, most certainly, met Nail.

And in her certainty, Finley was lost in sorrow.

She read over his last words again.

"She'll never come back," Luca wrote. "Everyone in Lumen is special, but she's next-level. 'Fated,' they're calling her. She didn't get her dragon egg at the same time the rest of us did. They have something else for her.

"She's in love with the place. I guess Lumens can leave eventually, but it seemed like that would take years. And her... she's supposed to be leadership or something. She might never leave that island again.

"That group is nothing but trouble and heartbreak. I wish I'd never met them. Forget about your friend and run far away."

Finley slapped her desk and slammed her laptop shut.

"Hey, songbird," said her mother from her doorway. "No need to be hotheaded."

Finley faced her mother and grimaced, remembering her conversation with Nail about her parents' alleged extracurricular activities.

Her mother was the picture of a hippie. Long, unruly brown hair, paint stains on most of her wardrobe, a crooked smile that only made her more endearing.

"She's never coming back," Finley choked out.

Her mother crouched down, pulling Finley into a hug and sighed. "That must feel horrible. I hope it's not true, but that doesn't make it any easier to deal with right now."

"There's this hole in my heart without her, mom." Finley wiped her tears on her sleeve. "How could she do this?"

Then she broke down fully, explaining the email to her mother, the details she'd never included anywhere in her search. She even told her about the dragons.

At that, her mother broke their embrace.

"A society for dragons?"

Finley expected her to smile, to laugh it off. It was ridiculous. But instead, her expression changed with concern and confusion.

"And this boy, he called her Fated?"

"Yeah." Finley glanced back at her closed computer. "I think so."

Her mother nodded and cracked a little smile.

"What?" Finley asked.

Her mother reached into the back pocket of her jeans. "Nail didn't have a choice."

Finley's brow furrowed. "What are you talking about?"

Her mother pulled a piece of paper from her back pocket. But, no... it wasn't paper at all.

It was thinly pressed leather, worn rough on its edges. There was a hand drawn on it, with symbols on each of the fingers.

Her mother pointed to the ring finger, which bore a snowflake marking.

"You have a choice," she said, placing the leather into Finley's palm. "You can reverse everything."

Finley stared at the leather, not understanding.

Her mother wiped Finley's tears with her thumb. "The Storm consumes all."

The story continues in ***Sunder***, Episodes 5-8 of the Lumen Fates Saga!

Want updates on Charis Crowe's new projects and appearances?

Join her newsletter at **www.subscribepage.com/chariscrowe**.

Acknowledgments

Behind every book is the story of how that book came to be. This story's story began with Mushu, Charizard, The Hungarian Horntail, Nessie, Saphira, Drogon, *Reign of Fire*, and the desire we all feel to explain the unexplainable. Thanks to anyone and everyone who attempts to turn fantasy into reality and to bridge the gaps therein.

Unending thanks to my husband, Ben Wolf, for his support, encouragement, superior editing, dedicated hard work, and overall positive outlook on life. You're always there to help me laugh when I need it, and I've needed it often. Thanks for being the firm foundation under my feet and for coming down to the cave when I couldn't crawl out of it alone.

Thanks to Bri and Ari, for your kindness, love, and unending questions. A questioning mind is a growing mind, so keep them coming. You're both always true to exactly who you are, and there's nothing more a mama dragon could ask for.

Thanks to Amanda, for being a friend who bore my complaints about late hours, that garlic smell, Season 8, and much, much more.

To Mike Murafka for reminding me of my inner zenith when I had forgotten it most. And for making it this far into the book. We can't all be Hawthorne, but that's no excuse to not follow a dream.

To Arpit Mehta for bringing it all together with your magical gifts with photoshop and photography.

To Teddi Deppner for swooping in at the 11th hour and helping get the print version ready for publication—THANK YOU!

To Paige Guido for being quite simply the best beta reader anyone could ever ask for—you are amazing.

To the island of Kauai, for all of its beauty and chickens. (So, so many chickens.)

To everyone who has ever shared their experiences of being marginalized, minimized, or dismissed, your bravery is seen and loved.

Minimal thanks to Marco Man the cat. Your snuggles were appreciated. Your bites were not.

Last and certainly not least, absolutely no thanks, acknowledgments, gratitude, or any other synonym given to anxiety, depression, and insomnia. You guys are the worst roommates ever. Get bent.

About Charis Crowe

Charis Crowe is not a *New York Times* best-selling author, nor is she Instagram-famous or Twitter-infamous. She did not graduate from an Ivy League university, and that's quite all right with her.

She is, however, a fan of gratitude, sunny afternoons, dark chocolate, a smooth cigar, and stand-up comedy. She enjoys spending time with her children, husband, friends, and her cats, so long as the latter aren't walking across the keyboard.

Charis hopes to someday compete on the reality TV show *Survivor*, to live in a place without snow, and to have a dragon of her own.

Two out of three wouldn't be bad.

Want updates on Charis Crowe's new projects and appearances?

Join her newsletter at **WWW.SUBSCRIBEPAGE.COM/CHARISCROWE**.

instagram.com/chariscrowe
facebook.com/chariscrowe